WELCOME TO

The Abyss line of cutting-edge psychological horror is committed to publishing the best, most innovative works of dark fiction available. Abyss is horror unlike anything you've ever read before. It's not about haunted houses or evil children or ancient Indian burial grounds. We've all read those books, and we all know their plots by heart.

Abyss is for the seeker of truth, no matter how disturbing or twisted it may be. It's about people, and the darkness we all carry within us. Abyss is the new horror from the dark frontier. And in that place, where we come face-to-face with terror, what we find is ourselves.

"THANK YOU FOR INTRODUCING ME TO THE REMARKABLE LINE OF NOVELS CURRENTLY BEING ISSUED UNDER DELL'S ABYSS IMPRINT. I HAVE GIVEN A GREAT MANY BLURBS OVER THE LAST TWELVE YEARS OR SO, BUT THIS ONE MARKS TWO FIRSTS: FIRST *UNSOLICITED* BLURB (*I* CALLED *YOU*) AND THE FIRST TIME I HAVE BLURBED A WHOLE *LINE* OF BOOKS. IN TERMS OF QUALITY, PRODUCTION, AND PLAIN OLD STORYTELLING RELIABILITY (THAT'S THE BOTTOM LINE, ISN'T IT?), DELL'S NEW LINE IS AMAZINGLY SATISFYING . . . A RARE AND WONDERFUL BARGAIN FOR READERS. I HOPE TO BE LOOKING INTO THE ABYSS FOR A LONG TIME TO COME."
—Stephen King

Please turn the page for more extraordinary
acclaim . . .

CRITICAL RAVES FOR

NANCY HOLDER
best-selling author of Making Love
and winner of the Bram Stoker Award
for Best Short Story
from the Horror Writers of America

"A nasty tale well told, infused with the eerily surreal quality of fevered nightmares. Discovering Nancy Holder is like finding a vein of true horror gold."
—Cheri Scotch, author of *The Werewolf's Touch*

"Man the lifeboats. Don your life jacket. Nancy Holder takes you on a cruise you won't soon forget. Scary stuff."
—Maxine O'Callaghan, author of *Dark Time*

"*Dead in the Water* is saturated with brooding, claustrophobic, hallucinatory menace. Nancy Holder's vivid voice and sharp characterization make it all real. I'm never going on a boat again!"
—Poppy Z. Brite, author of *Lost Souls* and *Drawing Blood*

"I couldn't put it down! A whale of a tale. A page-turner— the first sentence will hook you and what follows will reel you in. *Dead in the Water* is fast-paced and exciting, mysterious and spooky! Nancy Holder is a writer who's going places. I can hardly wait to read her next novel!"
—Chris Curry, author of *Panic*

"Nancy Holder enshrouds fascinating characters within a chilling atmosphere and creates a relentless tale of terror at sea. Holder is one of my favorite writers."
—Elizabeth Massie, author of *Sineater*

Also by Nancy Holder

MAKING LOVE (with Melanie Tem)

ROUGH CUT

DEAD IN THE WATER

NANCY HOLDER

A Dell Book

Published by
Dell Publishing
a division of
Bantam Doubleday Dell Publishing Group, Inc.
1540 Broadway
New York, New York 10036

ISBN:978-0-440-61407-4

Printed in the United States of America

Published simultaneously in Canada

146614399

For:

Kathy Ptacek and Charlie Grant,
who manned the lighthouse;

Joe Elder,
who held the compass;

Leslie Jones, Elise Jones, Joan Mohr,
and Ashley McConnell,
who packed the supplies;

and most of all, for my husband, Wayne,
who yelled, "Row, damn it, row!"

ACKNOWLEDGMENTS

I would like to thank those who helped, encouraged, and inspired me during the writing of this book: Joseph Elder, Jeanne Cavelos, Danielle Clemens, Kathy Ptacek, Charlie Grant, Russ Boelhauf, Ashley McConnell, Wayne Holder, Leslie Jones, Elise Jones, Rick Anderson, Matt Pallamary, Doug Clegg, Kathe Koja, Rick Lieder, Cheryl Sayre, Eric and Stinne Lighthart, Debi and Scott Nelson, Steve and Melanie Tem, and Jeff Saar. Thank you, S.K. and P.S.

And for great writing music: John Carpenter, for *The Fog;* and Goblin (thank you, Doug Winter and Craig Shaw Gardner); Aerosmith, Led Zeppelin, and Oingo Boingo. And a special thanks to Michael "Misha" Newton for the "Strange Brew" tape.

AUTHOR'S NOTE

As of this writing, the *Queen Mary,* while still docked at Long Beach, remains a tourist attraction but is no longer a hotel.
   It is, reportedly, still haunted.

He went to hell in his own boat,
having no need of the ferry of the dead.

Epitaph by Prefect Juliannus

PROLOGUE:

Message Found in a Bottle, II; or, An Invitation from Your Captain

This is how it will be when you drown:

You'll start out, of course, in water. The particulars really don't matter, but for the sake of argument, let's say you're swimming. Of course, your boat might sink, or your plane may go down, and then there are ponds and lakes and rivers. And bathtubs. Or hot tubs. Dreadful things can happen in Jacuzzis. Have happened.

But imagine that it's a dazzling, warm day at the beach. You've arrived not half an hour before with friends, and you decide to take a dip while the others lie in the sun, play cards, and roast the weenies.

You shuffle through the velvet sand, watching the water roll ever closer to your toes. The rippled flow is frosted with bubbles that remind you of champagne; beneath the crystal-clear curtain, seashells glisten in the sun. You look up and down the deserted coastline at patches of grass and lavender boulders, planted by Nature in a thoughtful breakwater pattern, and you're grateful no one else bothers with the five-mile trek on the unpaved road that leads to this secret spot.

A breeze ruffles your hair, tickles the hair on your arms. The water laps at the end of your toes; you jump playfully back, daring it to touch you. While it recedes into the ocean, you write your initials in the wet sand with your big toe, blot them out, jump back as the water rolls back in. It catches you this time, and licks your foot like a puppy; to your delight it is cool and refreshing, not cold at all. And quite clear: you can see your toenails as you wade deeper, up to your ankles, your shins, just below your knees.

You call to your friends—they're missing out! But they're hungry, and busy preparing lunch, and they tell you to go ahead and enjoy yourself. You, after all, are the one who loves the water most.

Knowing you're amusing them, you move faster, going deeper and making little noises because now the water's a tiny bit chillier. You prance up to your thighs and then you rise up on your toes as the swell gooses you. Then one, two, three big steps farther out, you dive into the rolling wave as it curls chest-high.

Cowabunga! It wakes you up! It's salty and clean, and washes the sweat and sand off your chest and arms. The sun dances on the droplets that cling to your hair and eyelashes as you pop up, shaking your head and wiping your eyes. You turn and wave, let out a whoop; your friends wave back. At this distance, you can hear the radio, see the smoke rising from the fire ring; and in the otherwise deserted parking lot your car sits, waiting to be refilled with damp bodies and sand, and the leftover firewood.

You swim a little farther out, waiting for the moment when the bottom dips and you lose contact. Whoops! You duck under for a second, bob back up, tread water while you get your bearings. The water is a deep azure-blue, like a picture in a resort brochure or a travelogue about the South Pacific. You cannot believe the perfection of this moment, as buoyed by the salt, you dip your head back so the water can slick your hair. You squint into the golden, gauzy sun. You wave again to your friends with a rush of shy tenderness, because they seem so happy to see you enjoying yourself.

Adventurous now, you flop onto your stomach and swim away from shore. You watch the waves; one swells beneath you, carrying you toward the beach as you ride it backward. It was just a small one, so you cut the trip short by standing up. Eagerly, you swim back out. Jump headfirst into the next one and swim through it before it crests.

The sky is a reflection of the water—or is it the other way around? There's not a single cloud up there, just the warm, gentle ball, a Goldilocks orb, not too hot, just right.

And then a wavelet smacks you. Your mouth is open and you swallow some sandy saltwater. Your throat and eyes sting a bit. A piece of seaweed brushes against you, lazes away. You wonder if there are any fish in the water. One of your friends brought a fishing pole, and has high hopes for later.

You give yourself a thrill by searching for jellyfish. But how could there be any, in this paradise? As if to confirm your opinion, a thirty-second scan of the area yields nothing.

You swim farther out. You watch the waves, travel over and up, waiting for just the one to ride in, anticipating the rough-and-tumble exit you'll make as you hit the shore. Your stomach rumbles and you imagine the tastes of potato chips and potato salad and remember you'll need to reapply your sunscreen after you dry off.

You turn around to see your friends again.

And they're farther away than you thought they'd be.

A lot farther.

For a moment you're puzzled, and then slightly panicked, as you understand you've been caught in an undertow. The current has dragged you out to sea. Yes, and why didn't you notice before that you're cold? In fact, you're shivering. You have another uncertain moment, but then you recall that now you must swim parallel to shore. Eventually you'll make your way out of the current—which is, by the way, growing still colder. It's practically frigid, and your muscles are cramping. Gooseflesh coats you like a wetsuit.

Swim parallel. You say it to yourself three or four times as you swim. Hand over hand, steady, legs kicking easily. You move right along; after all, everyone says you're part fish. You have it aced, you think; you're in no danger.

The undertow grabs hold of your ankles and drags you. You feel it this time, feel the process; have a frightening half-formed vision of someone actually wrapping their hands—

—their bony fingers—

around your ankles and swimming off with you, depositing you in deeper waters. You forget you must not fight directly against the force. Legs kicking, arms flailing like windmills, you lose the rhythm of your breathing and stop, gasping. Your lungs hurt.

The waves are surging around you; they're big enough to surf on. The water has deepened to a dark blue-gray like the skin of a humpback whale. You think you see things moving below the surface. Before you can be sure, a succession of waves crash right over you, and you go under, gagging. You try repeatedly to catch one and bodysurf in. Each time, you fail. They roar and crash, pummeling you. You stop, because all you're doing is exhausting yourself.

You go back to treading water. The water is thick and cold. The sun, once so benevolent, beats down on your head and makes you squint hard at the coastline. Perhaps due to the harshness of the shadows it makes, the lavender boulders jut like hard, sharp rocks into the breakers, and you wonder, for the first time since you found the beach, if you could seriously hurt yourself riding the surf back to shore.

Something knocks into you, moves away. You don't bother with it now, because you see your friends on shore: tiny dots. Your heart clutches. The something bobs against you again, and you look around. In a different direction, you see five huge Portuguese men-of-war, stinging tentacles streaming behind them. They drift in front of you, another obstacle between you and the beach.

You wave at your friends. "Hey!" you call, but your voice is raw from the salt and it comes out scratchy and thin. Yet it must have done the trick: they're looking around, looking for you, so you relax a little. They're going to come for you and help you back. They'll razz you, but you won't mind, because you were pretty stupid to let this happen. You, after all, are an expert swimmer. But it'll feel so good to be back on land, nothing can bother you. You'll let them tease you all they want.

All you need to do is wait. To conserve your strength, you flip over on your back and lay your head in the water, spread-eagle yourself. Your buddies are probably already on their way.

But how? They don't have a boat, or a raft, or even a life ring. And none of them can swim as well as you. Well, then, they'll get in the car and drive for help.

Except that you drove, and the keys are in your waterproof wallet, safety-pinned to the cutoffs you're wearing.

They'll flag someone down, someone else in a car.

But no one ever comes down that unpaved road. It's your secret spot. You read about it when you first moved to the area, in a book of local legends. Some ghostly nonsense you've forgotten now, evidently scary enough to keep everyone else away.

The undertow gives you another yank. You gasp, flip upright, and tread water again. You're pulled past the breakers, into an ice-cube sea that rolls and dips but has no waves. Then even those highs and lows flatten out, and you're floating on the liquid equivalent of a desert. The beating sun above, the cold depths below; the dark waters, where you can no longer see the lower half of your body. The ocean has swallowed it up and it's pulling the rest of you down, sucking at your tired back and arms like quicksand.

You scan the horizon for your friends.

They're gone.

The coastline itself is gone. You see nothing but endless, heartless gray. You turn in all directions, but there is nothing to see but more jellyfish and the painful reflections of the sun. No sailboats miraculously passing by, no other swimmers, no land. A line behind you where both the sea and sky bleach to gray and become the same horizon, where you might simply float away into oblivion.

You shout again for help. You realize you should have tried to shout louder when you were closer.

The shore, the world, is still gone.

You tread faster, comprehend that you're doing the wrong thing, and rest back into the water so you'll float again, while you consider your options.

But what you don't understand is that you have no options.

And then something bobs against you again, against your calf, then your hip, then your side, and you think, Oh, my God, it's a shark. Your heart skips a couplet, you hold your breath, and touch the thing.

Not a shark. You exhale. Only a dark green flask you mistake at first for a 7-Up bottle. But there are antique brown lines running through it, and dazzling red and blue stones circling the neck like a coronet. No, the brown is actually golden, and the bottle's corked; and there's something yellow and gooey half covering the cork.

You pick it up. It's quite heavy, for something that's floating. As are you.

There's a piece of paper inside. A message in a bottle.

And because your hands are shaking, and you're already getting tired and trying to keep floating; and you're becoming giddy because you can't believe this is actually happening—that you've drifted out to sea and no one's come yet—*no one's come yet!*—because it makes for something to focus on, a diversion from the fact that you've just realized you can't swim or float or tread water too much longer—

—because you have nothing else to do but be so afraid you want to vomit, you pry off the coating, which is wax, pull out the cork, and tip the bottle upside down.

A piece of thick, yellowed paper slides into your hand. Decorated with an anchor—or is it a skull and crossbones?—the elaborately scrolled letterhead reads:

The Captain, H.M.S. Pandora.

Beneath it are engraved the following words:

The Captain respectfully requests your presence at the Captain's Table for dinner this evening.

And something rings a bell. Something in the local legends concerning messages in bottles.

And death warrants.

Because no one can swim for very long, and you certainly can't hold your breath forever.

And when the drowning itself begins? Your actual last few minutes?

You have some final throes, of course. You do not go gentle into that deep ocean. You tire, and so you struggle harder, which tires you more. You tell yourself to float, but you can no longer manage it. You're hyperventilating. You're crying. You wet yourself, and the warm stream reminds you how cold you are.

You sink, fight back to the surface, sink, surface, and so on, until you find yourself mindlessly reaching for a gasping, terrified gulp of air. It hurts when you inhale, feels better when you exhale. This seems to go on for an eternity, but ten, perhaps fifteen minutes elapse at most.

Your body is heavy and numb, and clumsy. You can no longer see because you're blind with fear. You can think of nothing but the next breath.

And you can no longer make your way to the surface. Down, down, you go, and then you struggle against your fate again, but to no purpose. Your eyes bulging, you stare up into the dazzling glare of the sun as it strikes the surface above you; and it looks unbelievably far away, that surface, that sunshine. Conversely, you can see nothing past your feet as they helplessly dangle.

Unbearable pressure pushes against your lungs, so you let the air out a bit at a time—a puff at a time, a slow leak, until your body aches. It feels thin and flaccid, like an empty balloon. Your throat tightens and aches. Your muscles tense and strain.

The surface above you dances and glitters.

Your lungs are almost drained, and you are hovering in the water, and that damn bottle knocks into your head once, twice, and you shut your eyes tight and hope it does the job. But it drifts a few feet away, suspended and unmoving as if it's waiting—and it is waiting. For your RSVP.

And you oblige. Because you are completely out of air, and now there is only one thing left for you to do.

Inhale.

And just as you do, and your eyes begin to roll back in your head, the shadow of a ship's hull casts a large, gray net over you and you think, Thank God, thank God, you're saved.

But you're wrong. More wrong than you can imagine.

And that is what it will be like. And, more or less, how it will happen.

And it *will* happen. Sooner. Or later.

So nice you can join us.

I
UNDERTOW

1

UNDERTOW

1

Spinning the Bottle

Glenn Boelhauf slipped his snow-white 1965 Mustang into the parking lot across the street from the Long Beach freight docks. The white sidewalls crunched over gravel, the shatters of a Bud Light bottle, the remains of a dark blue sneaker crusted with dried blood. Across the quay, a long line of semis snaked along, engines rumbling. Air brakes hissed beneath a blast of Willie Nelson on a radio. At the front of the parade, a bright yellow cab airbrushed with a mural of a sunset drove between the towering trestle supports of an immense gantry crane. On his deck, a white boxcar container stenciled "Mazda/Santa Fe 2203022" rode like a fat woman on a parade float.

The crab, a box that slid back and forth across the crane's bridge several stories in the air, positioned itself over the white boxcar. Rigging whirred down from it like silk webbing from a spider, and men hurried to fasten the hoists to the container.

Glenn let the engine hum for a few more seconds before he turned it off. He caressed the gearshift, gave it a couple suggestive jerks, and grinned at his partner. "New carb's cherry, wouldn't you say?"

Donna shook her head and sighed. "You know, for what you've blown on this thing in the last six months, you could've taken Barb and the kids on the cruise with me."

He made a face. He was blond, brown, angular; his hobbies were his car and his Top Gun fighter-pilot image, which he'd honed to perfection. Ray–Bans, bronze muscles, straight-arrow khaki authority. *Viva* Officer Hunk: he and Donna were partners on the San Diego police force. He was senior to her, and the most conceited man she'd ever met.

"Sorry, Donny-O. Hopping rust buckets is not my idea of an alternative to humping my Ford. And anyway, there's no way on earth I'd take my kids on anything longer than a harbor cruise. You know I can't stand the little bastards."

Donna nodded sagely. The only reason he'd driven her up the coast was because he was meeting his wife and kids for a weekend at Disneyland. He'd put in a couple of extra shifts so the little bastards could have all the junk food and souvenirs their greedy hearts desired. Tough guy. Like all the other tough guys on the force. Slammed any show of tenderness, then fell apart when a puppy died en route to the vet's. Hooted and whistled during the confiscated kiddie porn movies at the keggers and then went home and cried all night because they just couldn't take it anymore.

"And I sure as hell wouldn't want to spend my vacation around *you*," he added.

Tough guy. She kept her face blank. She'd told him ten months ago the only reason he was having trouble was the way her gunbelt nipped her waist. Tried to be cool, tried to be flip when she laughed off his fumbled confession. That night she put Lady Day, Miss Billie Holiday, on the stereo and sang herself to exhaustion; because they both knew it was her problem, too, and something more than raging hormones; and they both knew it would be deadly to do something about it.

And they both were still working on that. But it was getting worse, not better, and last night, he had been thinking hard about kissing her again; and she knew all about it because she was his partner and she could read his tiny cop pea-brain like a fucking book. Yes, he was conceited, and yes, he was unbearable, and yes, she had been thinking hard about kissing him again, too.

She studied her nails, red and slick, not her usual set of hands. She'd gone to a manicurist yesterday for the first time since she'd become a cop, four years before. Her vacation was a relief, and a reprieve. But it wasn't a solution. Their mutual attraction would still beckon with its own set of siren fingers when she returned. Donna was going to think a lot while she was out of his sphere of influence. She wondered if he was going to, too, and that frightened her. Because she really did love him, and not just in the girl-boy way. She'd take a bullet for him without hesitation, stand up for him, stand by him no matter what. She loved him like she'd never loved anybody before, a kind of transcendent, spiritual emotion that was subverbal: she couldn't describe it, she could only feel it. And she sure as hell didn't want to ruin it just to get her itch scratched.

"Donna, Donna," he said in a soft tone. She saw herself mirrored in his sunglasses and thought tartly, Not bad for thirty-four, you sultry raven-haired babe. But it wasn't really very funny. She knew when he looked at her, he saw someone special. Mocking herself didn't take the edge off that knowledge.

And now he was reading her pea-brain, because he looked away and stared out the window. She joined him. A man in a dark brown jumpsuit had lifted himself up the steps of the truck and was talking animatedly with the driver, who had on a blue baseball cap. It was nine-thirty in the morning; there was a sound in the rhythm of the cranes, the tinniness of the boom-boxes that twanged about a long night of hoisting and loading to get the truckers ready to go back out.

A sea gull wheeled above them, hovered, skittered away. On her side of the car, a flock of pigeons descended on the remains of a cardboard plate of rolled tacos. The freight side of the harbor was very different from the side where the

Queen Mary was berthed. Cousin to the *Titanic,* the venerable old ocean liner had been transformed some years before into a floating hotel. It was popular with honeymooners, anniversary veterans, the romance crowd. When Glenn and Donna swung off the freeway, the sight of it had raised the tension level in the Mustang, particularly when Glenn mentioned offhandedly that he had another two hours before his rendezvous with Barb and the kids. That was the closest they'd come to getting close to it, ever.

Maybe it was being alone in civilian clothes. Together and alone meant work and uniforms. But now there was a hooky-holiday feeling, rules relaxed, like kids ditching school. And yards of bare skin—he had on shorts and a rugby shirt—perfectly pressed, of course, right in style; damn, he was conceited—and she had on a sleeveless sundress that ended midthigh. Miles of skin, and lots of thoughts, and she concentrated hard on the crane and the way it whirred and zizzed, and the two guys jawing, and pondered how much dope came in and out of Long Beach, and who were the dockhands who helped pass it. There was a part of a cop's brain that never switched off; at least, hers never did. She wondered what Glenn thought about when he made love with Barbara.

Not really.

"Hey, we got you something. I almost forgot." With a flourish he reached into the back seat and grabbed a dark green champagne bottle banded with a silver bow.

"Oh, baby!" Donna said, holding out her palms. "Come to Mama!"

He snickered, and when she grabbed it from him, she realized it was made of plastic, and too light to have much of anything in it. She held it up to the light through the windshield; it was empty except for something that looked like a wadded piece of cloth. She looked at him quizzically and he snickered again. She hated it when he snickered. It sounded as if his nose was full of goobers. Some of the guys said "bon appetite" whenever he did it. With the American pronunciation. There was this anti-intellectual thing on the force. Nineteen forever, the way the song went. Be cool, hang loose, duh, let's go beach. No worries about wives and kids and

homewrecking, or losing that boy in Tahoe because that idiot
Daniel had gotten in her way.

Kiddie-porn movies, just to be contrary. Just to be assholes
and to prove they weren't men and women who bore terrible
pressures.

"Open it." He took off his sunglasses and grinned at her.
Big blue aviator eyes. He constantly cracked jokes about
modeling for *Playgirl.*

The plastic cork made a plastic pop as she eased it off. She
turned the bottle upside down and shook it. A jot of leopard-
pattern fabric and a foil condom package fell into her hand.

He snickered hard. "Read the label."

"Oh, brother." She shook the fabric and it unfolded into a
jockstrap kind of thing. Holding it like a dead rat between
her thumb and forefinger, she turned the bottle with her free
hand so she could scan the bright pink sticker on the front.
" 'Chateau Monsieur Bubble,' " she read. " 'Spin Me for Lots
of Les Kicks and Le Bouf! Fun.' "

She laughed and fluttered her lashes. "Jesus, Glenn, just
what I always wanted. A leopard-skin jock. Who got this,
Martinez?" Carlos was their friend in Vice.

"No way. I bought it myself. And it's called a sling, cuddle-
cakes." Glenn chortled. "Had to turn down the cashier when
he asked me for a date." He batted her shoulder as she examined the jockstrap doubtfully. "Oh, come on, Donald! It
might come in useful. And besides"—he reached into the
back seat again—"we got you some of the real stuff, too."

"What's Le Bouf! Fun?" she asked, then saw the second
bottle cradled in the crook of his arm. Moët & Chandon.
Spiffy stuff. "Oh, Glenn, thanks."

"Oh, hell, the guys chipped in. A little." He gestured at the
sling. "I figure one'll lead to the other, yes?"

They looked at each other. Yeah, that would solve a few
things, if she fell in love with someone else. Maybe. Or
maybe it would just make it worse.

She hadn't told him everything about that scene in Tahoe.
He knew about the boy she'd lost, and the interference, but
not that she'd been sleeping with the guy she knocked out.
With a wobbly grin, she slid two fingers into the socklike

pouch and waved at him, hand-puppet style. "Did you buy one of these for yourself?"

"Naw. Tried that one on. It was too small."

She rolled her eyes. "Why'd I even ask."

He leaned over then, brushed her lips with his. His eyes widened—he'd obviously surprised himself; he recovered, winked.

"I'd better get rid of you now, Donny-O. I've got a date with a mouse."

"And a duck." She stuffed the jockstrap and the condom back into the bottle and popped the plastic stopper back in. "Thanks for the goodies, partner. You're too keen for words."

"Millions can't be wrong." He posed, raising his chin to the light. "Donna," he said gently. "Donna, I know you're going to . . . I . . ."

She put up a hand to stop him. "Gotta go. Clean exit, okay?"

Clean break.

No. Never.

No. She was not a homewrecker. She would never do anything, *anything* that would hurt him or the ones he loved.

"I can walk you over there," he ventured.

"No way, bro. Don't want you cramping my style." She jiggled the plastic bottle at him, opened her door, and slung her leg out. "Grab my stuff, won't you?"

He got out and went around to the trunk. By the time she reached him, he was leaning into it, pretending to struggle with her suitcase. The round of his ass, the way his muscles moved . . . she stared at him.

With a theatrical groan, he hefted the bag out and set it by her feet. "Christ, what've you got in there?"

"Coors," she retorted. "Somebody told me they don't sell it in Hawaii. I'm going to make a mint."

"That's bullshit. They've got everything we've got."

She grinned at him. "That's for sure, Monsieur Bubble."

"Hey, fuck you," he said amiably. Then he grew serious. His hand reached toward her cheek, lowered. "Come back."

Donna raised her brows. "Well, of course I will, dumbo. Where else would I go?"

Another gull cried. The semis crept forward. The men inside them must be very patient souls. Oh, brave new world. Oh, world . . .

The boy she'd lost in Tahoe, the one who had drowned. She had run down the trail from the cabin with her bathrobe hanging open, Daniel racing after in the chill air. Slushy snow stung her feet. It was really too late for spring skiing, but serious skiers never believed the season was over until the rocks gouged their boards.

She had run down there, lungs pumping steam, and seen the kid facedown, spinning, oddly, in a circle; very, very slowly, he was a little satellite circling a sun. Donna's mind raced at fever pitch as she neared the shoreline. C'mon, baby, c'mon, c'mon. Godalmighty, where were his folks?

C'mon, baby. Spinning in a lazy, deadly circle. Something glinted near him, a piece of glass, a toy, maybe. Her mind burst ahead to a door, and her ringing the bell, and telling two strangers their kid was—

No!

She'd pumped hard. Her robe flapped behind her, exposing her naked body. Her cheeks stretched tautly as she hissed through her teeth, damning herself for not running faster. The results of a bad spill the day before seized up her ankle and tried to make her limp. She ignored her pain. He was a dot on the vast, ice-cold lake. Tahoe never froze; it was too deep. And things that went beneath its surface were said to remain preserved in the frigid freshwater. Another mental flash of a thoroughly upsetting nature, which she forced away.

Then she was dragging him out, half her body submerged in the icy water as she yanked on his wrists and hauled him onto the frosty earth. Hard, cold pebbles cut the soles of her feet. He was practically a baby, with fine brown hair that flared around his head like the fur lining of his hood; yellow reindeer on his red snow mittens. Even shrouded in sopping layers of snow gear, he was vulnerably lightweight.

His lips were blue, his face washed with purple and ivory. Christ.

She leaned over the boy with her ear to his mouth and two fingers on his neck. Thank God, thank the dear Lord, there was a pulse.

Then she slipped on the ice—to this day, she couldn't figure it—but she tumbled into the water and for a second, just a flash, she thought someone was *pulling* her—

Then Daniel, the man she'd met in Caesar's two nights before, flung himself down beside the boy and shouted, "I know CPR!" and smashed down hard on the kid's chest.

"No, he's got a pulse." Donna scrabbled, searching with her feet for purchase. She was freezing; she couldn't make her legs work. "Don't do that!"

Daniel rammed down again. A sharp crack split the air: the boy's ribs. "Stop it, goddamn it! Stop!" she yelled, but he pumped away. "Turn him over! Get the water out!"

The boy started to gag. Daniel brought his hands down on the boy's chest. The fur on the boy's hood rippled as he heaved.

"Turn him on his side, goddamn you!"

And then he was vomiting, spewing water and food and bile, and Daniel reared back, startled; and she tried to climb, tried to climb; goddamn it, her ankle just wouldn't work right; and the boy was spewing it out and she cried, "C'mon, baby! C'mon!"

And she got up the bank, and staggered behind Daniel, who, incredibly, repositioned his hands over the boy's chest. She caught him around the neck, straining to pull him off, and when that didn't work, she pulled up and back very hard, and threw him backward to the ground. His eyes rolled back and his head fell to the right.

Shit. Maybe she'd broken Daniel's neck. She leaned over the boy and threw him on his side, dug with her fingers, get that shit out of him, get it out! Draped him over, fought to a standing position, hefted him upside down, as best she could, and—

He was dead.

She screamed, "911! Emergency, somebody!" But she

knew that wouldn't help. She did everything she could, laid him down and tried to jumpstart his heart, and Daniel came around and started swearing at her.

Dead from drowning in his own vomit.

She had watched the kid die, stiffen and struggle and go; but before that, she had watched him spin in a slow, lazy circle, like the wheel of fortune at Caesar's Palace as it spun around to zero.

Like the bottle at a teenage party, and you had to kiss the one it pointed to; and it was always the guy you really, really liked, and to your utter shame he groaned when you puckered up, your own small heart hammering wildly out of control.

And if Donna could have cried—God, if she could have, maybe she'd have been able to let him go.

That night, in the bathtub, with a hot washcloth over her eyes, listening to Billie Holiday singing the blues in a drunken whiskey voice. Slugging back Scotch with her eyes covered, pretending to daydream about her singing career (what career, Donna?). Replaying last month's gig at a joint in Santa Monica, where none of the guys on the force would see her. Smoke and a tight dress, black and low, and a rose in her hair; holding back, because there was so much inside, too much . . .

No, there wasn't. She was a big girl, a big, regular girl with a regular girl's problems. A cop, which was a bit unusual maybe, but not given the way she grew up, Marine Corps pop and four brothers. Tomboy. And maybe a torch singer, when she grew up. A cop who happened to lose somebody. Hell, they all lost people now and then. Glenn had lost a little old lady once, smoke inhalation. Arson.

The hot rag on her eyes, and that was sweat trickling down her temples and into the tub, because tears weren't in her vocabulary. Drinking and singing, and feeling so very sorry for Miss Billie Holiday, who'd had a hell of a life and had suffered through it, really suffered. The woman had had no idea how to shut out the pain.

The pain that people like Donna didn't have.

Back at the station house, the guys had made sure she was

all right, some ski trip, eh, Osmond? (Her name was Donna Almond; in the time-honored tradition of cops and nicknames, they called her Donny Osmond.) As soon as she had assured them her rock-solid cop *cojones* were still hard as golf balls, they started in with the Natalie Wood jokes and ghoulish stories about other "floaters" and general CPR horror shows. Topped each other unmercifully. Told her the story of the Tahoe school bus, just in case she hadn't heard it up there in Squaw Valley.

Red mittens. The boy's mother hadn't made a sound, simply collapsed into her husband's arms. The child had been deaf. It was likely he hadn't made a sound, either, when he had fallen in while reaching for something, God knew what. His dog, a beagle named Dottie, was never found. Donna had searched for hours, joined by the paramedics when they got off duty. Perhaps she had fallen in, and he'd been trying to save her.

Donna didn't remember the glinting object until much later—saw it when she fell in, some bottle or something—but it seemed unnecessary to amend her report over it.

While packing, Daniel had called her a cunt and a dyke.

"Jesus, where would I go?" Donna said again, standing beside Glenn's white-as-a-charger Mustang. She held her real champagne bottle in her right hand and her suitcase with the left. The plastic bottle was stashed in her oversize purse. Glenn frowned at her and she quickly added, "Say hi to Barb and the little shitheads."

"Will do. Over and." He took a step toward her. She lifted her chin, just enough.

As he sped away, her throat tightened. She watched him go, and she knew she should let him go. Really. She stood alone, as he took the corners too tight and heated up the rubber. Off to his Disney life, his Disney kids and wife, tra la, and she stood there.

Alone.

She swallowed. Well, girl, she thought, here was some grist for the mill. A lady wanted to sing the blues, she had to suffer, feel it way down in her gut, that sorrow, that pain, that . . .

No. As his car disappeared, she could sense the walls rising inside her. Thick armored plates closing over, making her mouth twist into a half smile as she murmured, "Blowjob, you drive like an asshole."

Cutting it off. Tamping it down.

Alone. And helpless to do anything . . .

No. Never helpless.

She turned on her heel and started looking for her ship.

Dr. John Fielder wasn't sure about this whole deal. He leaned against a dirty, rusted railing of the *Robert X. Morris,* absently pushing his glasses up his nose as he watched his son, Matt, scrabble along the pitted deck. The *Morris* was, to put it mildly, a bucket of bolts. Rusty bolts. Bolts he wasn't sure were riveted together very well. If at all. Would it hold together long enough to get them to Honolulu?

A tall, muscular man hailed Matt. It was Ramón Diaz, the suave first mate. Matt leaped and bounded over pieces of chain and boxes and joined Diaz. They began to talk, Matt gesticulating wildly.

Sighing, John looked down at the glossy brochure in his hands. An elderly couple in nautical attire touched champagne glasses as they leaned against a pristine white railing. A Hawaiian sea spread behind them. He looked up at reality: a sailor in filthy dungarees hung over the side, which was spotted with mint-green paint, Rust-Oleum, and rust proper, a Mountain Dew in his fist, and hocked a loogie. Another sailor joined him, pulled out a cigarette, flicked the match into the filthy waters of Long Beach.

John cocked his head. The superstructure, all seven uncertain stories of it, loomed above him. More mint, more rust, splattered with guano. Radar and masts bristled from it at all angles, so that it looked like an upside-down centipede.

Another sailor loped past him, calling to the other two. He sported a spectacular handlebar mustache.

"You seen Chiefy? We gotta check the starboard bilge pump."

Chiefy. Bilge. Would they talk like that on the *Island Princess*? John doubted it. Heck, if it was just him, he'd probably stay on the *Morris* if only for the sake of adventure. But he had the Mattman to think of.

As if on cue, Matty whirled around and waved at him. The pale little face was glowing. Christ, he was all mouth and eyes these days. John had hoped he'd fatten up in remission. He ate a lot; damn, he was a bottomless pit. But somehow, his metabolism . . .

The cancer . . .

John waved back. Smiled brightly as tears sprang to his eyes. How, in all the unfair unfairnesses of life, had his son contracted the very disease for which John was paid inordinate amounts of money to discover a cure? His psychologist had tried to make him understand it was just a rotten coincidence, but John still had the hand-washing compulsion; still worried about touching his boy, breathing on him. Somewhere, in the back of his mind (to be honest, not so far back at all), he thought he'd infected Matty by something he'd brought home from the lab.

Deeper back, he thought he was being punished, through his son, for giving up his practice with AIDS patients and moving into pure research.

Couldn't take it anymore.

Dear God, couldn't take this, either. He was terrified that in these five short days, somehow Matty would sicken and die. Waves of guilt washed over him at the thought of taking him away from the safe harbor of the hospital. *You've got to let him live while he's alive,* Dr. Eling had told him, over and over and over. *If you spend every moment afraid that he's going to die, he may as well be dead.* Harsh words, but very true. He had counseled the families and lovers of his former patients with a litany very like it.

He watched the boy jogging along, hopping over an open can of something, skirting a jumble of large, crumbling chain.

"Everything all right, Dr. Fielder?" Mr. Saar, the second mate, paused beside him. He was carrying a clipboard and he looked harried. Fine-trimmed red beard, sunglasses, a snappy white uniform. More brochurelike than the sailors. That was something. "Are you settled in your cabin?"

John deliberated a moment. Should they bail out? Or was

he overreacting? He needed to talk this over with Matty. After all, this trip was for him.

Because it might be his last . . .

Christ, stop it! "I . . . I'm fine," John blurted out. He turned his attention to Matt and the first mate. "If he gets in the way, you let me know."

Saar nodded, glanced at his watch, and made a notation on his clipboard.

"Well, we'll resume loading in about five minutes, sir. It would be fun for him to watch for a while. They're serving tea for the passengers in the dining room."

John raised an eyebrow. The *Morris* couldn't be all that bad if it served afternoon tea, could it?

"Thank you," he told the second mate, who nodded and ambled toward the trio of sailors. They all rolled from one foot to the other, these seafaring men. As if the boat perpetually rocked. Must be hell on the inner ear.

"Matt!" he called. "Hey, Mattman! C'mere!"

Matt didn't hear him. The boy sauntered along with the first mate, making broad motions with his hands. Looked so cute, in his baggy black shorts and black running shoes and military green T-shirt. His hair was too long for his flat-top; it folded over on the right side like an Elvis pompadour. Should have had it cut. That was another hangup of John's: hating to trim Matty's hair, because finally (thank you, God, again, and please, again) Matty *had* some hair. Chemotherapy was rough on everybody, but roughest on dark-haired nine-year-old boys who liked baseball and heavy metal and paging through their fathers' gross surgery textbooks.

Another man joined Matt and the first mate, stepping over the grimy metal lip of a heavy, round door painted the same mint-green. He was an old hippie, with gray hair down to the middle of his back, a braided leather headband, a tie-dyed T-shirt, and a stained white apron. He cradled a metal bowl against his chest and stirred the contents with a wooden spoon as he talked. Then he bent down and offered a taste to Matt. Ye gods, he must be the cook.

Matt tipped back his head: the turned-up nose, the freckles, the long lashes that were Gretchen's.

"Matt!" The name came out too frantic. John flushed and tempered his outburst with a smile.

The trio turned toward him. He motioned Matt to him, feeling his stomach clench as the boy parted from the men and scampered toward him. Dennis the Menace, the Beaver, Matty the Mattman.

"Hiya," John said as Matt approached, and held out his arms for a hug. His stomach burned. Matt had (*had* had) cancer, and his old man had (still had) an ulcer.

"Oh, Dad." Matt held back. "C'mon. I'm too old. There's dudes here."

John grabbed his wrists and pulled him against his body. Matt's T-shirt was damp; the body inside it so damn skinny.

"Listen, buckwheat, when you're *twenty*-nine, you still won't be too old for hugging."

"I'll never be that old," Matty shot back, and it took John a second to understand that he wasn't being serious. That he wasn't talking about *that*.

"Listen," John said, crouching down so he was at Matt's level. He made a face. "This boat. It's kind of older than I thought it would be."

"It was in Viet Nam!" Matty announced. His eyes widened. All eyes. No flesh. He looked like a commercial for one of those save-the-starving children funds they advertised on TV. "It was loaded with ammunition so they could blast the gooks!"

John blinked. "Oh? Did Mr. Diaz tell you that?"

Matt shook his head. "Cha-cha did." He frowned impatiently. "You know, the old guy. He's the cook. He was on it when it was in Viet Nam. Isn't that on fire?"

On fire. John was keenly aware of the crow's-feet around his eyes when he grinned faintly at his little boy. The Haight and the Summer of Love had never seemed so long ago. Isla Vista, too—burn down that Bank of Amerika—if you wanted to talk about fires. Never trust anyone over thirty, hell; and now his kid used the sacred and arcane vocabulary of the newest new generation, and he was stuck in his own time zone like some old geezer, trying to translate, if not keep up.

"Well, you shouldn't say gooks. You know about that. But

listen, do you like this boat?" He grew serious. "If you want to do something else, we can. We could take another boat to Hawaii. Or we could—"

"No way! This is neat!" Matt turned to race off.

John caught the neck of his T-shirt. "Cool your jets, Jack. They're going to load the deck and they want us out of the way. We can watch from the dining room."

"All right! Cha-cha's making a cake. It's Mr. Diaz's birthday."

John started to hold Matty's hand, brushed his shoulder instead. Tea and cakes. Okay, maybe. It wasn't the brochure, but maybe it was okay.

In the dining room of her temporary home, the *Robert X. Morris,* Ruth Hamilton sat on an overstuffed chair and sipped her tea, eavesdropping on the argument two of the other passengers were having on the opposite side of the room, not ten feet away.

"It's my vacation, too. And I'll be damned if I'll spend it on this wreck." That was Ms. Elise van Buren-*Hadley,* as the lady had said it. *Hadley,* as in, forget to say that and I'll turn you to stone with a mere gaze.

Quite possible, Ruth thought, and went on placidly stirring her tea.

"I mean, *really.*" The woman wrinkled her nose and moved her shoulders in a gesture of complete and utter distaste. She practically raised her lizard-skin flats off the ground.

Ruth could understand her disappointment. The *Morris* was not as advertised, and the dining room was a particular disaster. Small and gloomy, despite two sets of large square windows that framed the profiles of sleek, blond Ms. van Buren-Hadley and her husband, Phil, whose sandy brown hair and short, trimmed beard reminded Ruth of Stephen. The windows were covered with yellowed venetian blinds that muffled the sepia sunbeams of Long Beach, a long-polluted suburb of Los Angeles, and cast the combatants in a drab olive light.

The furniture felt dirty, and the carpet was an ugly dark green that curled up near the walls, and the three coffee tables had cigarette burns in them. One was an old kidney shape that Ruth thought might have fetched a good price at an auction, if only it had been taken better care of. The other two were standard oak veneer rectangles; motel issue.

But the best part was the walls. They were papered with blue and green in a sea-kelp pattern, and over this were draped dusty dark blue fishing nets. And in these nets—Ruth had held back a peal of laughter when the sexy first mate had grandly escorted her into the room—dozens of stuffed fish bounded the waves among bright orange starfish and blown-glass bubbles of aquamarine. The taxidermist had not done a very good job: the fish looked furry and moth-eaten, and it seemed their glass eyes cried with humiliation.

And in an apocalypse of good taste, a culmination of all that seemed to be this ship, the *Morris,* the entire weepy school swam toward the room's pièce de résistance: a three-dimensional model of the *Morris* itself, created out of matchsticks. Under glass, as it were, captured inside an oversize cutout of a bottle that rode plaster waves of Day-Glo turquoise.

"I kinda like it, honey," Mr. van Buren said in a slow Southern drawl. He reached for his wife's hand. With an angry jerk of her head, Ms. van Buren-Hadley crossed her arms. Yuppies. Their clothes must have cost them a fortune. They dripped good living. Ruth's stomach growled and she eyed the cookie plate wistfully, but didn't want to spoil the mood. She had a suspicion they'd forgotten she was there, and she didn't want to remind them in case they got embarrassed and stopped fighting.

Her hazel eyes twinkled and she took another sip of tea. Wondered if that crazy old cook had washed the pot out within the last decade. That was likely, since the tea tasted like soap.

She looked down at her gnarled, arthritic fingers, and beyond to her bony feet in her nautical-themed espadrilles with anchors appliquéd on the tops. She had on a pair of navy slacks and a white sailor middy blouse piped in blue trim. Her grand-nephew, Richard, said she was a "hot old dame," and she did her best, but she *was* old, damn it. Seventy-one (though she had managed to lie her way onto the freighter by claiming she was sixty-eight; they had an age limit). There were wrinkles all over her face and her lipstick bled into the skin around her mouth; her chin was a turkey wattle, and though she was in love with her frosted blond hair, she was sure she looked ridiculous in it. Still, people were forever telling her how attractive she was, for her age.

For her age, and that selfish girl across the room had no idea how lucky she was.

Now, now, she mustn't get into a dander. Growing old was preferable to the alternative, as she well knew. And as for that, well, fate had handed her a bad hand, but she had to stay upbeat, at least until she talked to Marion Chang.

She took a breath. Marion could be another charlatan, too. Ever since Ruth's *Oprah* appearance, all kinds of people had been contacting her. So to speak. All kinds, with outrageous claims and convincing stories. Marion's had been the most convincing yet.

Ruth's hand shook beneath the saucer. She pressed her lips together and made herself calm down. The tea was the color of brine. It needed more sugar to cut the soapy taste.

She needed to know about Stephen. She would give anything, do anything, just to know. Even if he was . . . if it didn't come out as she hoped.

"We'll just cancel the AmEx," Ms. van Buren-Hadley was saying, clipped, harsh, a foil to her husband's honey accent.

Ruth got up noisily and took three steps to the long table laid out with tea and coffee urns, white china plates, and plastic serving trays lined with homemade chocolate chip and sugar cookies. The old guy had made these, too. They probably tasted like scouring powder.

"Wow, cool!" someone piped in a shrill little voice behind her. She turned around. Phil van Buren was rising from his chair, and his wife was fishing in her Gucci bag for something.

A small, thin boy raced past them and stopped inches from the tableau of the *Morris*. Nose pressed to the oversize bottle, he gestured eagerly to a man who was at that moment stepping across the threshold. His father, probably, and there was something very appealing about him. Very tall, just a little bit out of shape in white pleated pants and a light blue cotton shirt. He had straight dark hair that thinned on top, but at least he'd gotten some gray before he went bald. There was a help-me, puppy-dog air about him, and his tortoiseshell glasses added to it. Clark Kentish. The child was his miniature, with darker hair, and even more fragile. He looked seriously ill.

"Good God," the man said slowly, surveying the room.

"Precisely my reaction," Ms. van Buren-Hadley announced.

The boy bobbed from side to side, examining the bottle picture, and flashed a bright grin at Ruth. To the man, he cried, "This is cool! How'd they do it?"

The man turned to Ruth and shook his head bemusedly. She smiled back at him and picked up a cookie.

"Hello," Mr. van Buren said, holding out his hand. "I'm Phil van Buren. This is my wife, Elise."

Ruth waited to see if she would add the "Hadley." She didn't, only lowered her invisible tiara once as she pulled out a pack of cigarettes with a silver lighter stuffed into the cellophane.

"John Fielder," the chestnut-haired man said as he shook with Phil van Buren. "That's my son, Matty."

"Da-ad." The boy glared at him.

The man cleared his throat. "I beg your pardon. Matt."

The boy—Matt—turned back to the bottle. "How'd they do this?"

"It's not a real bottle," Ms. van Buren-Hadley said sharply as she put a cigarette in her mouth and flicked her lighter. She inhaled slowly, tipped back her head, and blew smoke at the ceiling. The sharp phosphorous odor, the pungent odor of tobacco, traveled on a slender thread toward Ruth.

"Oh." Matt was clearly disappointed. Ruth picked up another cookie and walked over to him. She held it out. He took it after checking with his father. "Thanks, ma'am."

She beamed. "You're welcome." Then she pointed at the picture. "They do make real ships in bottles. I mean, they're models, but they go into real bottles. Have you ever seen one?"

He shook his head and took a large bite out of the cookie. Crumbs dotted his face and she almost brushed them off. She had never had any children, though she had wanted them desperately.

John Fielder came up beside her. She introduced herself and told him to call her Ruth.

"Can you make those? The ships in the real bottles?" Matt asked her as he stuffed the rest of the cookie into his mouth. His gaze darted toward the table and the cookie trays.

"No," she said. "But I bet you could learn how. Maybe somebody on the ship makes them."

"Like Cha-cha!" the boy said eagerly. Good heavens, his wrists were like sticks. His chin must have been a couple of inches wide.

"Somehow, I don't think so," his father drawled. But the child wasn't listening.

"He'll show me. Cool! Can I have another cookie, Dad?"

John laughed. "Sure."

"Mr. Fielder—" Ms. van Buren-Hadley began.

"My dad's a doctor," Matt said. He dove into the cookie plate, gathering two, three, four large ones like a cormorant.

"Hey, don't be piggy," his father admonished.

"*Dr.* Fielder, then," Ms. van Buren-Hadley amended. "Is this"—she held out her arms and pivoted in a semicircle, taking in the room—"what you expected when you paid for this cruise? I mean, really, this thing can barely float!"

Elise van Buren-Hadley, master mariner, Ruth thought. Her husband looked pleadingly at John Fielder.

The man shrugged. "Well, I'm not so sure about that. Not floating."

"Well, I don't think I'd bring a child of mine on a boat like this." She took a drag on her cigarette.

"It's probably safer than smoking around one," he teased. Oh, bravo, Ruth thought. Good for you.

"My dad hates smoking," Matt whispered to Ruth, speaking through clumps of half-chewed cookie. "He says people who sell cigarettes should be shot."

"Does he," Ruth replied, amused.

"Well." Elise van Buren-Hadley stretched her mouth into a tight, angry line. "Well."

Two more people appeared in the doorway: the sexy first officer, Mr. Diaz, and a short woman, an Italian, with a soft, round face, a rather hooked nose, and a black perm Ruth thought was a year or two out-of-date. Her sunglasses were pushed on top of her head and her big brown eyes were heavily made-up. She wore a revealing sundress that showed off a marvelous tan and a hint of cleavage.

With a hoot, the woman stopped in her tracks and cried, "Holy shit! What the hell is that?" To Mr. Diaz's obvious discomfort, she burst into laughter and pointed to the bottle picture. Then she caught herself and said, "Oh, Ramón, you didn't make that, did you?"

Then she saw Matt and murmured, "Oops." Matt giggled and glanced up at his father, who was trying not to smile as well. Mr. van Buren looked startled, and Ms. van Buren-Hadley inhaled long and hard, her eyes glittering with dislike.

"You must be the other passengers," the woman said, flouncing into the room. New dress, and she felt good in it. Women could always tell about other women and their fashion habits.

Elise van Buren-Hadley's eyes narrowed, snakelike. Hiding a smile, Ruth started pouring the newcomer a cup of tea.

Mr. Diaz cleared his throat. "The guy who made that is dead," he said. "He was the captain's son."

"Double oops," the woman said, not very contritely.

"So you can see," the man went on, as a smile stretched across his handsome Latin face, "why we're stuck with it."

He winked at Ruth and left the room.

"I wonder if his son decorated this room, too," the woman said, surveying it. She shuddered theatrically, opened her mouth to say something to the van Burens, and swung her head toward Dr. Fielder.

"Donna Almond," she said. "Hi."

Introductions were made all around. She took the tea from Ruth with a cheery thank you and made herself at home on a green sofa, crossing her legs high on the thigh. She looked around again and laughed.

"I wonder if the captain's son was shot for all this."

"No, baby." A rear door to the left-hand side of the long table cracked open and what looked to Ruth like an aged street person hung around the edge. The smell of baking wafted out with him. It was the cook.

"No, baby, he wasn't shot, he was drowned," the man told Donna Almond. "I was there. I seen it happen. Bad trip, way down. Worst trip for a human being. Worst trip there is."

Something happened to the woman's face and she set her tea down on the coffee table.

"Hi, Cha-cha!" Matt chirped.

"Love, brother. Peace. Cake's gonna be psychedelically dee-lish." The shabby man flashed a peace sign and disappeared around the door.

There was a pause. Elise van Buren-Hadley tamped out her cigarette.

"I'm going to see the captain," she said, and rose. Her husband followed her out. Everyone watched them go.

"Lovely woman," John Fielder said ironically.

"Yeah, she's pretty good-looking," Matt concurred, and the three adults chuckled. Ruth carried her tea to a chair at right angles with the sofa and sat carefully. Old bones, old lower back problem.

"It's a little less than I expected, too," she said.

"Mmm." Donna made a face. "This tea tastes like dishwashing liquid."

"I can't wait to try the cake." John Fielder joined them, stretching his long legs under the coffee table. Matt dribbled cookie crumbs in a trail as he walked back to the bottle picture.

"Me, either," he said.

"Well, it's just us, now," Ruth said, and a strange feeling ghosted through her, a sense that she had just said something very true. Just the four of them—the doctor, his son, the girl, and she herself—the ship's fools.

Beyond the door, the loading continued. Ramón Diaz had explained that the crane jennies were controlled by computer; the operator was there mostly to make sure nothing happened. He told her this as if naturally she was apprehensive about it; and naturally, he, the dashing maritime officer, could put her fears to rest.

Now, as the cars were bolted onto the runway of the deck, and she sat with her new shipmates, she was surprised to realize she *was* apprehensive. Not much, maybe just a jot to the right of uneasy. Her fingertips tingled and she jerked like a puppet when something slammed onto the deck and something else creaked. Anticipation, she told herself. Waiting for whatever lay ahead in Hawaii.

But there was something else. Something that was creeping up the fear barometer, past uneasy, raising the hairs on her neck. Could this be a psychic experience, a real one at long last?

Listening to her heartbeat, Ruth searched the room for a clue to what had caused this sudden, intense feeling. Scrutinized the people—the man, the woman, the child. No, no bogeymen here. As for the room itself, it was a cross between a fifties' theme restaurant and a garage sale. And that ship in the bottle—

That bottle—

As she looked at it, a tight, clutching sensation worked at her throat. It didn't make sense that as she sat there in an open room, with open windows and open doors, she should feel so claustrophobic. But that was exactly what the sensation was.

Her breathing was shallow, her hands numb and cold. She gazed at the bottle since it had seemed to trigger her reaction. It was truly ugly, but not bad enough to give anybody the jig-jags. And those fish, weeping as they swam toward it, glassy eyeballs grouted onto rotted bodies, a most unhappy group.

A chill at the base of her spine indented her skin. She rose away from the back of her chair, her heart lurching thickly. The air in the room seemed muddy, as if something rippled through it. Ruth shook her head, squinted hard to see if she could detect anything. No one else seemed to notice. Matt had gotten up for more cookies. Donna held her teacup close to her face and frowned at it. The young doctor was doing something to his watch, raising it to his ear.

Thunder shuddered the floor; another container had been deposited onto the deck.

"Ms. Hamilton?" Donna said. Ruth blinked. "Are you all right?"

"Yes," Ruth murmured, and took a gulp from her cup. She felt woozy, out of kilter. Maybe she needed to lie down.

A momentary flash of another, larger bottle swallowing up the real *Morris* shot through her mind. They were imprisoned inside, blithely drinking dishwater, totally unaware . . .

She took a deep breath. The image vanished. Swallowing, she let the soapy tea dribble down her throat.

And thought of her husband.

And wished—oh, how she wished!—that he were there.

2
The Rime

April 7, 1797,
in the shipping lanes of the Owhyhee route

A shroud lay in a launch; blood—both caked and fresh—
splattered on the canvas that whipped with the wind and the
waves. Sodden and weighted from the hail of rain, the slaps
of whitewater, green. Like echoes in a tube, thunder and
curses hounded the bier as it clung to the tops of the ocean
mountains, hovering there, poised for the deluge, the capsize.

Within the shroud, Thomas Reade, captain of the *Royal
Grace,* thrashed with fury. His blood-soaked hands clenched
into claws that kneaded the canvas, searching for the seams.
Blackness, blackness and the filthy wet of an old, worn sheet.
His nails ripped from their roots as he struggled to find the
opening, frenzied, raging, shouting. The very raindrops sizzled with his rage, and he cursed his treacherous shipmates
and promised them:

I'll not die, you weaklings, you fish! I'll have you for my belly timber. I'll have you for slaves.

You think you've murdered me. But I've prayed, prayed to the sea, and she'll not desert me. I've sacrificed to her—given her our little brother, our best—ah, me boyo!

And she loves me.

Ay, and she'll save me.

And I'll be back, a thousand times a thousand, to pay you back for this. For them that sails the seas, I'll come. And they'll wish they'd never even thought of living, because I'll drag them down to the bottom of the sea.

I'll drag them down, this I swear.

A thousand times a thousand.

Six hundred miles from the Owhyee Islands, on the rough Pacific sea.

3
The Sea
According
to Cha-cha

" 'Alone, alone, all, all alone,
Alone on a wide, wide sea!' "

John Fielder leaned over the taffrail with his arms spread, the rosy wind blowing his hair. Droplets of water clung to his glasses. Donna didn't know what the hell he was reciting, but the *Morris* was alone, alone-alone-alone, a lot, lot alone, on the water. It was almost sundown, and there was just the ocean, the boat, and the darkening sky. Nothing else, for miles and miles and miles. It was very unnerving.

John turned around and smiled at Donna, Ruth, and Ramón. "That's from 'The Rime of the Ancient Mariner.' "

"Cheerful," Donna drawled. Her sundress whipped around her thighs and she smoothed it down; noticed that he noticed, didn't mind.

He looked at her. "Do you know it?"

She shook her head, a bit embarrassed. He was a doctor,

for God's sake, probably went to school until he was thirty, and her claim to higher education was a couple of business classes (typing and dictation) at Mesa Junior College. She still couldn't type; she'd been in a panic then, completely freaked out and unable to learn anything. Well, it had been a shock, sailing into the Country Cafe, their restaurant, for the twelve thousandth time, only to discover that her mother was putting it up for sale and moving to Albuquerque to be with Aunt Leslie. *Yeah, Mom, and thanks a shitpile; I stick around and sling hash for you while the boys go off to have lives, and now I'm thirty and you're splitting on me?*

Didn't even give her part of the proceeds. Loaded up a U-Haul, gave her a kiss, and now she sent Christmas cards and cheap turquoise jewelry. Typing courses, fuck.

Thank God for the silver-haired police officer—Marcellis, still walked a beat in El Cajon—who suggested the police academy. Well, they sure as hell didn't teach poetry there. If the Rhyme of the Whatever even was a poem.

"It's great," John said, and Donna realized she'd been drifting out to sea again. Ha ha. "It's about a man on a sailing ship who shoots an albatross. He's doomed to sail with a ghost crew and—"

"Oh," she cut in, brightening, "I do know it. He's the Flying Dutchman, right?"

He paused and cocked his head, as if he were running through the rest of the story. Finally he smiled. "Why yes, I guess it is. I guess it's the same thing."

Triumphant, she gave her shoulders a modest shrug. Not so ignorant after all.

Below them, the *Morris*'s propeller geysered up balloons of water, great packets of bubbles that burst apart and sprayed their faces. Gray octopus shapes pulsed below the surface, surprises the sea was keeping to itself.

"It's his crew that dies," Ruth supplied. "The Ancient Mariner is the captain. And there's a Spirit that propels his ship toward a ghost ship."

Donna shifted. "A spirit like a ghost?"

John nodded. "Yes."

"Or a force of nature. Some kind of motivation," Ruth cut in.

John's brows rose above, his glasses frames. "I never thought of it that way. But you're right. It could be simply a force. But didn't the ship come to him? It found him? And there was a beautiful woman aboard. Death in Life? Life in Death? She was the thing that cursed him."

"Behind every great man," Donna said, and drew a chuckle from John. She warmed a bit, though she was growing uneasier by the moment as the sun sank down, down, down toward the rabbit hole of water, water everywhere. The vastness made her feel insignificant.

And a bit helpless. If there was one thing in the world she hated more than feeling uneducated, it was feeling helpless. Helpless got you squat.

"And his crew is filled with dead men?" Ramón asked.

"Yes, he's the only living person," Ruth replied. "And he has such a terrible thirst; it's all he can think of, and—"

Donna lost track of the conversation as she focused on the drowning sun. Ghost ships, and ghosts. Kids' stories.

And ghosts. Before she realized it she was thinking about the little boy. Death spasms, right in front of her. Her stupid ankle. Hell.

She shook herself and flashed a fake, generalized smile at the others. People who dealt in violence—and death was the ultimate violence—had to learn how to compartmentalize their minds. It had been nearly two years since her first corpse, an old man who died of a heart attack, and she still hadn't developed the knack. Glenn had quizzed her about her choice of a freighter to Hawaii, if it was too soon to go back into the water, so to speak. Maybe she'd figured she had something to prove. Or to get over. She told him it was none of his business what she did.

"Yes, it is," he'd answered breathlessly. "It most certainly is."

"And there's the symbolism of the woman of course," John was saying.

Ah, the symbolism of the woman. There always was one, wasn't there? The woman behind the man, push-push, pull-

pull; and so he runs off, leaves his old lady to mind things—
Country Cafes, for instance—doesn't come back. What the
Marines needed was a newer, younger wife. So Dad took off
way before Mom did. Waited until the kids were grown up, at
least. Almost grown up, anyway: Baby Donna had been fifteen. That was pretty good of him, ha.

Good men didn't leave in the first place. And Glenn was
the best, the very best there was.

"Ah, the woman," Ramón said huskily. He brushed his
fingertips against Donna's forearm. "*Señorita?* Are you
watching?" Though she kept her face impassive, she wanted
to chuckle at his pseudo-intensity. Far be it from her to
wound his male ego, but with this action, he'd now hit on
every woman aboard. Ruth had been first, flattered but taking him no more seriously than Donna did now. She'd treated
him kindly, like a wayward child. But Elise van Buren-Al-
phabitch had practically taken his head off. Dumb-dumb
should've known he was circling a shark when he'd moved in
on her.

So now it was Donna's turn, and she waited for the rest of
his routine to purr forth, as if she were watching a stand-up
comedian.

"Are you? Watching?" he murmured into her ear. His hot
breath made her lobe tingle. What the hell. She was single.

Alone.

"Yes, yes, I'm waiting for your flash." Big guy; how he
puffed up at that. Christ, sometimes men were awful simple.

There was some commotion on Donna's right, closer amid-
ships, where Phil and Elise had been sitting on deck chairs,
reading their books and not speaking. Donna had no idea
how Phil had finessed the situation, but the couple had stayed
aboard the *Morris.* During the hour Donna and the others
had chatted and watched the ocean, she'd also watched Phil.
Now and then he leaned toward his wife, as if watching for a
chance to engage her. Steadfastly she kept her gaze on the
pages. The love on his face, and the yearning, struck a chord;
Donna prayed she'd never looked at Glenn that way, especially not in public.

"I'm going inside," Elise announced, slamming shut her

book. She swung her legs onto the deck and rose in a graceful motion. She was tall and lithe; as Carlos in vice would say, "*Bien preservada.*"

Phil opened his mouth—probably to ask permission to come with her; c'mon, man, don't be such a weenie—but shut it at the last minute and stayed where he was. Looking sad. Donna thought about inviting him to join them but shit, he was a big boy, and if he wanted to come over, he would.

"So you were saying?" she said abruptly. Everyone stopped talking and looked at her.

She shrugged. "Sorry. I was drifting there."

"Easy to do," Ramón offered gallantly. Please, dude, maintain, she thought. As far as she was concerned, a little Latin lovejive went a long way.

No one spoke, and Donna never did find out what topic they'd shifted to after the poem. Now they stood in a line, studying the horizon. Mr. Saar had sent everyone out to see the fabled green flash, when the ocean lit up with phosphorescence at the precise moment of twilight.

After a time, the ocean punctured the sun and syrupy crimson oozed onto the water. Triangles sloshed in prisms of acid-green, turquoise, orange, deep purple—tropical cocktails garnished with slices of crystal whitewater. Donna thought about having a beer.

The group stood at the stern, gazes obediently trained on the horizon, while beneath them the wake luffed and gurgled and a fine spray misted their faces. A distance away, Kevin, a young, hairy surfer who was working in the galley in exchange for a lower fare, muttered at a crew member and glanced nervously at Donna. Drug deal, maybe, but probably for something benign like a lid of marijuana; Kevin wasn't the type for hard stuff. Everyone aboard knew she was a cop, and the guilty were prancing around like ballerinas.

The sun melted into a semicircle.

"Okay, it should happen any second," Ramón announced. The onlookers held their breath. Donna sighted down his outstretched finger and squinted.

"There!" he shouted, jabbing the air. "There! Do you see it?"

"Oh!" Ruth cried. She laid her forefingers on either side of her chin. "Yes! It's beautiful!" She smiled at Donna and John.

The doctor cocked his head. "I think I did." He laughed. "What was it supposed to look like?"

"A thin green line," Ramón told him, gesturing with his hands. "Glowing, like."

"Mmm." John lifted his chin and considered.

"Yeah!" Kevin called from his place. He waved at Ramón.

Ramón touched the back of Donna's hand. "You saw it?"

"No." Donna lifted her shoulders, shook her head, dropped her arms to her sides. "I guess I missed the magic moment."

Ramón's brows knitted as he pointed out to sea. "But it was there."

"I saw it," Ruth repeated. John was still craning his neck. One for sure, one uncertain.

Donna made a peace sign and pointed it at her eyes. "Not for these. Sorry."

Without missing a beat, he took her hand and held it. "There is always tomorrow, as you say. Three more nights."

Smoothly, she snaked herself out of his grip. "Now that's something to look forward to."

"Where's Matt?" John asked abruptly, looking toward the van Burens' abandoned chairs. "I thought he was over there."

"I saw him go off with Cha-cha a while ago," Donna said.

He pursed his lips. "Damn it," he said, and took off.

As he brushed past her, she wanted to give him a pat, tell him not to be so smothering, that his son was fine. Hell, he was nine years old. But she had a feeling he knew better than she that Matt wasn't fine, and wasn't likely to ever be.

He jogged away, unsteady on the deck. Watching him, Ruth clicked her teeth and shook her head in sympathy. Donna knew what she was thinking: Though it was Matt who was ill, it was his father who seemed more needy. It must be terrible to contemplate losing your child.

To lose one . . .

. . . spinning in a slow circle . . .

"Hey, Matt!" John cried in the distance. "Matty! Where are you?"

"I think I'll go get my sweater," Ruth said to Donna. She seemed jumpy. "It's a bit breezy, don't you think?"

Donna nodded absently. Kevin and the crewman were scattering like ducks on a pond. "I think I'll stay here."

Ramón remained beside her. She and Ruth passed a glance and the old lady covered her smile as she turned.

Kevin ambled over, moving on tanned, scarred legs with knobby knees. Ah ha, the innocent expression of the naughty boy. She waited while he approached her.

"Hiya," he said. He nodded in Ramón's direction. "Hi, dude."

"*Buenas noches,*" Ramón replied. "Did you see the flash?"

Kevin pulled a happy face. "Yeah. It was cool."

"*Sí.*" The first officer paused, glanced at Donna, cleared his throat. "Well, I have to get back to work. I have the watch tonight," he told her. "Would you like to come up and see the bridge?"

Ho ho, said the spider to the fly. "If I'm still awake," she replied. "Sea air always knocks me out."

"Take the companionway on the other side of the ship's office," he told her. Then he grinned and pointed. "Or you can use the catwalk." He pointed to a ribbon of metal that switchbacked all the way to the top of the superstructure. It reminded Donna of a roller-coaster track.

She made a face. "No elevator?"

He laughed. "Not on the *Morris.* On newer ships, yes." He touched his hat. "*Hasta luego.*"

"Okay." She waved at him in parting, giving her attention to Kevin.

"What's up?"

Furtively, he looked back over his shoulder as if to satisfy himself that Ramón was out of earshot. "It's that Cha-cha dude," he said under his breath. "Man, I'm really worried about him."

She rested her back against the rail. "Oh?"

He raked his sun-streaked hair with both hands. It fell long and unruly over shoulders riddled with freckles. His bare

chest was muscular, his pants low-riding his hips the way surf-
ers' pants did. A pang jabbed her; must be nice, the endless
summer of youth; riding the curls and smoking some weed.
Worst problem you have is that the rent's due.

"That dude is certifiable, man. I mean, no shit. He's been
in a VA hospital. You know what? He talks to King Neptune.
He says the king is going to tell him to sink the *Morris* someday."

Startled, Donna pulled in her chin and raised her eyebrows. "Say again?"

Kevin stuffed his hands into his pockets. He slouched into
a classic S-curve and shuffled his feet. He wore thongs; his
toenails were dirty. "That's what he told me today. I was
peeling potatoes when you guys were in the dining room—
the galley's on the other side of that door he opened, and I
could hear you talking about the bottle on the wall. When he
came back in, he told me King Neptune had loved the captain's son so much he took him. Then he said that the king
loved everybody on board the *Morris,* except he hated the
Morris itself 'cuz it was in Viet Nam, like, ferrying ammo up
the Delta, and he couldn't bring himself to let it—I mean her,
he calls the boat a her—to let her down into his kingdom."
He pulled out a cigarette and said, "Got a match?"

"Sorry." Donna frowned. "Does the captain know about
this?"

Kevin was distracted, searching through his pocket for a
match. Donna noted the tip of a hand-rolled joint in the
wadding of the pocket lining. Sensing her eyes on him, he
peered through his lashes and said, "Huh? Oh, oh, yeah. I
freaked. I went and told Mr. Saar. He just laughed. He says
Cha-cha's been going on like that for years. No one listens to
him anymore."

"Mmm."

"Cha-cha also said the *Morris* might sink all by itself someday, because it's got too many souls on board. Like, war
dead." Kevin rocked back on his heels. "That old dude is *way*
scary, Officer Almond."

"Okay," she said authoritatively, since that was what he
seemed to want from her. She could also tell he'd a nodding

acquaintance with cops before: his deferential posture, the careful way he called her "Officer Almond." Drugs, probably. Ditching school. He seemed pretty harmless. Surfing and worrying about the rent. Shit. "I'll check into it."

He relaxed visibly. "Thanks."

She crossed her arms and gazed up at him with a steely cop gaze. "But just in case something strange *does* go down, don't you think it might be a good idea to be straight when it happens?"

More feigned innocence. He opened his eyes very wide. She pointed to his pocket.

"I don't really care if you do it," she said, "but frankly, I'm not real thrilled about the crew doing it. Tell them I have a nose like a bloodhound. And tell them I already know there's lots of drugs going down on this boat, but I'll be reasonable if they stop right now."

Kevin had the good sense to blush. He flashed a guilty grin at her and dangled the cigarette between his lips. "No prob."

"And if I catch anyone doing anything around that little kid, I'll personally throw them overboard."

The cigarette clung to his lower lip as his mouth dropped open. She left him at the rail, satisfied that she'd gotten through to him, and looked out at the sea.

Water, water everywhere. And she was sailing with the Ancient Maniac.

Great.

Below, on the main deck, the containers made eerie sounds in the wind, low moans, crescendos of scraping metal and vibrations that seemed to alternate in an elusive rhythm as John searched among them for Matt. As if they were talking to each other: *Let's make the break tonight.*

"Matt!" John shouted, but the cacophony drowned him out.

Goddamn it, he thought. His heart beat hard and his ulcer stung him. He ran a hand through his hair and took a step forward, slamming painfully into the corner of a container.

He kept going, threading his way toward the bow. And then he heard voices, and relief flooded over him with the satisfying sensation of a good jolt of coffee in the morning, or a nice long pee after you've been holding it through surgery.

"And then there's your starfish," the old guy was saying.

John came around the corner as Cha-cha took a bite of a candy bar and held it out to the boy with his grimy fingers.

"Matt!" John stumbled into the corner of one of the containers and grabbed his shin.

"Hi, Dad," Matt said happily, calmly. Not a clue that his old man had been burning with fear over him.

He and Cha-cha were sitting on oil barrels stenciled with the words "DANGER. CORROSIVE. KEEP DRY AND COOL." Salt spray misted them; alarmed, John took his wrist and said, "Get off of that, honey."

Cha-cha waved his hand. "It's okay, doctor man. Every trip, these barrels come out and sit here. At the end of the voyage, they disappear. Been going on that way for five, six years."

"Nevertheless," John said. Christ, Cha-cha looked the way he used to, bandanna, embroidery, peace and love. He felt stuffy in his Dockers and sneakers. He and Gretchen used to laugh about becoming bourgeois. Now here he was.

Was that why she'd left him and Matt?

"Listen, Dad." Matt sighed and slid off the barrel as John gestured for him to do so. "The starfish have this stomach that sticks out of their faces and it digests its prey with stomach acid because its stomach is inside out! Isn't that cool?"

"Butterfinger, doctor man?" Cha-cha asked, indicating that Matt should share with his father.

"No, thank you." Stuffy, stuffy. "On second thought, thanks." He took a bite and handed it to Cha-cha. He had a brief flash of the two of them passing a joint.

"And there's these, what do you call them?" Matt's eyes shone as he spoke to the old man. "Lumps?"

"Limpets." Cha-cha cleaned the chocolate off his jagged front teeth—practically the only ones he had—with sucking noises.

"Yeah, they shi—poop—all over oyster beds and the oysters suffocate in it."

"That's right," Cha-cha said. He cleaned under his

thumbnail with his front teeth, sucked in. "Kee-rect, love baby."

"Really." John took off his glasses and cleaned them on his shirt, pausing because he didn't know what else to say. This was the kind of thing little boys loved to hear about, but why did it sound like something he should forbid Matt to discuss? Hell, he was getting to be a pompous ass, wasn't he.

Behind them, the boxcar containers rose like patchwork castle walls, yellow, red, metallic, Rust-Oleum. The superstructure loomed above them. The running lights blinked on, Christmas red, Christmas green, sparkling against the dark sky. John thought of the blinking light atop the hospital back in San Francisco. He'd made the mistake of telling Matt it was to warn any low-flying aircraft; that night, the nurse had found Matt cowering underneath his covers, certain a 727 would come crashing through the window at any moment. What to tell a child? What not to?

You were dying, but now you're not, but you might get sick again?

That your mother really loves you even though she split on you?

"The sea is not a nice place, love baby," Cha-cha observed, breaking John's mental tape. He spit a wad of tobacco into an empty Coke can. "Captain don't allow the crew no alcohol," he said. "Everyone drinks anyway, just not in public. Why, they pitch their cans in the sea, too. I wouldn't desecrate the sea in any way, no way, José. King would have my hide." He whipped his head to the right. "Wouldn't you, Your Highness?"

John started. Matty jerked on his fingers and muttered, "He talks to King Neptune." Stifled a giggle.

"Ah. Nope." Cha-cha looked at John and said, "The king wanted to know if Matt's the cabin boy." He pivoted back to face the bow. "No, sir, this here's my love brother. He's going to Hawaiah with his old man."

"Um, Matt, I think we'd better go in now. It's getting dark." Firmly he took Matt's hand and stepped away from the withered old cook. The withered old crazy cook.

"Okay." Matt started walking without a word. Then he

stopped at the end of the leash that was his father's reach and said, "Thanks for the Butterfinger."

"Hey, be cool, baby. Peace and love." Cha-cha flashed a peace sign.

Father and son entered the maze of containers. Matt bobbed along as if there were springs on the bottoms of his shoes.

"The sea sounds really great," he said.

"Mmm."

"I think Cha-cha's totally cool. I want to learn how to spit tobacco."

"No way." John rattled Matt's hand.

Matt tittered like a girl, obviously pleased to have him on. "He looks like Willie Nelson, huh. He knows so much cool stuff."

"I'm not sure you should bother him," John said slowly, navigating through tricky water. Jesus H. Christ, the guy was nuts. A sweat of chill heat shook John. Nuts, and he'd left Matty alone with him. God, that bastard could've done anything to him. Anything. What kind of shitty father was he, anyway?

The kind that let his baby get sick.

"Do you know about lampreys?" Matty queried.

"I love you." John bent down. "You know that, don't you?"

Matt screwed up his face. "Don't go weird on me."

John sighed. He wanted to tell his kid he loved him, and that made him weird. Cha-cha talked to the king of the sea, and he was totally cool.

A long time, buckwheat, since the Summer of Love.

They walked along. John read the shipping labels as they went: Kavco, Alawai, Smith & Barnett. Matson. Matson. Matson. What was in them? He made a fist and rapped one gently. Solid and thick. You would be history if one of these things fell on you.

The ship tilted. Matt stumbled against a container, then into him. The ship rolled the opposite way, and John slammed into the container behind him.

"Whoa." He held Matt's shoulders and waited for the ship to stop rocking. A metallic cold seeped into his clothes as the night came on. It was getting dark; a breeze off the water ruffled his hair and added a layer of sheen to his cold sweat. He smelled the ocean and the ship, redolent of the odors of a gas station.

John rubbed his arm with his right hand and shivered hard. The breeze strengthened, whistling among the posts and towers that blinked above them. Wires thrummed; a gust of spray billowed above the rectangular landscape. The sky directly above them grew darker, as if a shadow had crossed it—he found himself thinking of a massive spiderweb, stretched from one side of the vessel to the other—and an unsettling sense of pressure bore down on the crown of his head.

Like being brushed with a web, or a net.

A net. And the *Morris* was a big grouper, lumbering straight into it—

"C'mon," he said to Matt. He pushed himself away from the container and hurried down the passage between the mountains of boxcars; and hurried faster, because for some reason he couldn't explain, he had to get out of there immediately.

Back on his barrel, Cha-cha dangled his feet over the side of the ship and crossed his legs. He wiped his fingers with the chocolate-coated Butterfinger wrapper and stuffed it into his back pocket.

His Oceanic Highness retired for the evening, sinking majestically into the sea. Cha-cha waved, and sat, and watched the stars come out. The water sluiced beneath the bow like the rush of freeway traffic outside an opened window. This was the most peaceful time of day: meals behind him, the king attended to, nothing to do but sit and watch. Behind him, on the bridge, Mr. Saar said something into the public address system, and someone answered him. Cha-cha couldn't make it out.

He should go astern and check his fishing lines and his nets. He smiled. Tomorrow there'd be good eating. Dorado, probably. Wished he could make blackened Cajun style again, but last time they'd thought there was a fire in the galley. Whoo-ee! What a trip! All that fire extinguisher stuff all over everything.

He'd have to tell the little love baby about that one. He'd like that story.

And the one about the loggerhead sponges. Now that was the worst tale of the sea:

Baby shrimps, too young to know what's going to happen, swim into the cavities of loggerhead sponges, maybe because they think it's groovy, or they're curious, who knows? And they start eating and growing and pretty soon, they're too big to get back out. And they can't see where they're going because it's too dang dark, so they spend their lives stumblin' around these corridors in the sponge, scraping the sides with their claws for food, which is mostly rotten garbage.

And if that wasn't heavy enough, love baby, creeping through black halls for the rest of your life, they have to defend themselves against thousands of other shrimp, and worms, and all kinds of other enemies that have gotten stuck coming in from the opposite direction. Somebody has to get out of the way, but nobody can, so there's lots of bad stuff coming down, all the time.

That's their life, scraping food, fighting enemies, in a chamber of horrors God made on bad acid.

Then they have babies, and those babies swim off, and if they're lucky, they get imprisoned inside another sponge. If they're not, they float out to sea, and drown.

And which ones make it, and which ones don't?

Karma, man.

And that's the life of a ship, love baby, and everybody aboard her, just a bunch of nineteen-year-olds, ferrying ammo up the Delta.

4
The Fog

Ruth, perhaps,
dear Ruth, perhaps,
oh, Ruth, perhaps,
you are the first to get the word:

Messages come in small packages.
Messages come in dead men's voices.
And here is a message for you, Ruth:

I have heard your siren call;
I have heard you wish your wish.
I come to you in waves, on waves;
Now come to me, oh, Ruth, dear Ruth.

Come dine with me,
Come wine with me,

Come down to the sea,
Come down, dear Ruth.

Come
down,
down,
down, and

Jump
overboard
now.

Ruth sat up fast, panicking as her gaze darted around the close, unfamiliar cabin. "Where . . . ?" she asked groggily, and it came back to her: she was on a ship called the *Morris,* in a cabin near the end of a long corridor.

With a shudder, she closed her eyes and blew out a breath. Her heart stuttered against her silky pink nightgown, which was damp with sweat. As she rested her weight on her wrists, they shook as though she were having some kind of seizure.

"Heavens." She took a deep breath. She was safe; she was all right. She was in a cabin, and the van Burens were next door, and the young policewoman's cabin was on the other side of the bathroom.

All right. Everything was all right.

Her wrists wobbled as she sucked in a few more deep breaths. She had had a dream. Yes, that was it. That was all. Something about a man. An invitation. Or was it about struggling, and not inhaling . . . The vague outlines of an image floated behind her eyes. A ship. This ship? Too late; too hazy. It floated onward.

"Heavens," she said again.

Her wedding ring caught in her hair as she pushed a stray tendril out of her eyes. She stared into the dark, rolled onto her side to check the clock. The luminous dial was a beacon in the pitch-dark cabin. Ten-fifty. Normally that was too early for her—she was an old night owl, always had been—but the movements of the ship had made her drowsy. She'd caught herself dosing in the dining room while watching *Far and*

Away with John Fielder. Matt and Donna Almond had been sequestered in a corner, playing checkers by the light of a crook-necked lamp. Donna let Matt win most of the games, and he whooped whenever he triumphed, only to giggle and clamp his hands over his mouth when his father told him to be quiet.

The van Burens (and Hadley) had marched straight to their cabin after dinner. Hers shared a common wall with theirs, and she had come into the cabin after refusing an offer of escort from John, to find her empty room reverberating with the gasps and groans of her neighbors' lovemaking. A very strange couple. But then, so much was different between men and women these days. Donna was sweet, but rather hard—or acted hard, Ruth wasn't sure which. In Ruth's day, she might've been considered "fast." The young men were flocking around her. Like that sexy but very silly Spanish man, Ramón, and John, who needed a woman's strength just now. Poor man.

Ruth yawned, stretched, decided to use the toilet. The head, she reminded herself. On a ship, it was called the head. For a few moments she groped around the nightstand, then found the light and flicked it on. The sheets were twisted around her—she must have had a busy night, though certainly not like the van Burens—and she pushed them down and swung her legs over the bed. Her knees brushed the wall and her bare feet touched the linoleum floor. It was damp. The ship was sinking!

She planted her left foot, pressed down. Not soggy, just damp. The night air was humid; ocean air was full of ocean. With a click of her teeth she dismissed her panicky thought. Foolish old woman. Falling asleep watching a movie. And now imagining the ship was in trouble—

The dream. Something like that in her dream. Herself falling into the water, having to jump in, and there was something there. She squinted, concentrating. Something in the water.

No, it had been some*one* in the water. Waiting for her.

Well, dreams like that were natural. People on planes dreamed about crashing. And people on boats . . .

No, not just people on boats. People whose husbands were missing at sea, they had dreams like that.

She rubbed her arms and pushed herself off the bed and stood practically cheek by jowl to the wall. Such a tiny cabin. Not at all like the brochure, and not even that much cheaper than flying. Well, that was all right; she wasn't a very big woman, and she was on the sea where Stephen had sailed; traveling over the very same droplets of water, maybe even the exact location where he had—

Her throat closed up. He had not gone down. He had *not*.

She edged along the side of the bed and felt with her hand for the sliding partition to the bathroom. Her heart was finally slowing down. As she groped for the handle, she thought about the afternoon, and the way she had prickled inside, as if she'd been electrified. That awful claustrophobic pressure. She'd had a foolish thought, one she'd barely acknowledged: Perhaps Stephen had tried to contact her. To warn her that the ship wasn't safe, that she should jum . . . that she should leave it. That she should have left it. And now, the dream.

"Oh, come now, come now," she muttered in a tight voice through a film of tears. She was being silly. Stephen had not communicated with her. Her belief in the possibility of another world had grown only slightly stronger in the eleven months since his disappearance, though it was strong enough to pursue avenues that once she and he would have scoffed at.

For the belief, the *certainty*, that he was still alive, would not leave her alone. On *Oprah* she'd likened it to knowing your spouse is in the next room, although you can't see or hear him. You just know he's home.

You just know it.

The flimsy partition slid open beneath her hand. To her left, the sink gleamed in the lamplight; beyond it, the toilet. Oh, gleaming throne of Psyche, she thought wryly. With a flourish, she lifted up nightgown and sat down. The floor was damp in there, too.

Around her, the ship creaked and groaned. That vessels were so noisy had been a surprise. The engines rattled and men stomped constantly down the halls and outside on the deck, thumping in their work boots, the masses of keys fastened to their jeans with huge turnbuckles jangling like Marley's ghost. Up and down, back and forth, and everything squeaked and squealed and shuddered. It was a miracle she'd fallen asleep with all the racket going on. The van Burens had been but one grace note in the symphony.

She sat forward on her elbows and waited, realizing she didn't have to go after all. With an embarrassed humph, she rose and walked the few feet back into her cabin.

The sheets on the twin bed heaped into a long cocoon like a body. She saw the head, the shoulder, the hip, the foot, and the resemblance was unnerving. She studied it for a moment, trying to recall the last time Stephen had slept with her. Blue pajamas. The ones with the navy piping. His eyes were bluer than Paul Newman's, she always liked to say.

Weak yellow light cast shadows on the white sheets and the dingy walls, and the thin brown curtain that covered the porthole above her bed.

The ship creaked. The form on the bed became nothing to her but a pile of bedclothes. Those pajamas were in the cherrywood bureau back home. All his things were in their proper places, awaiting his return. The only missing items were the clothes he'd had on—white Windbreaker, the shirt with the boat blueprints on it, the white duck trousers. His dazzling white sneakers. His wallet and keys. She doubled her fists. He was substantial, somewhere out there in the world, not an old widow's dream made of blankets. Damn it, she knew he was alive.

She burst into tears, missing him so badly, so terribly. Doubling her fists, she pressed them into her midsection and bent over, weeping. He was alive.

The boat rocked. It creaked. The shadows shifted.

Something was awry. Out of kilter. She felt it. She stood perfectly still, moving only her eyes, as a thick dread crawled over her feet, up her legs, touched her fingertips.

Suddenly a chill rippled up her spine. She straightened. A finger of ice on each vertebra, pressing in hard, someone testing how thick her body was. Goose bumps plucked at her scalp. Her heart started racing again. Unwillingly, she slid her glance to the bed. There was nothing there that shouldn't be.

Nothing there that should be.

The dread covered her chest and shoulders, closed around her neck. She held her breath.

There. On the lamp side of her bed, the closet door was open. It gaped like an unhappy, hungry mouth. Back home in Pomona, it was part of her bedtime ritual. Here, she'd forgotten to close it, and that had startled her when she'd come back into the room.

That's what it was, and—

A chill fanned her shoulders like a shawl. She shivered once, violently. This was silly, worrying about a closet door. Not even she, the quintessential creature of habit, would be so jolted by a triviality like that. It was the dream that was frightening her. She had probably heard a noise and that had awakened her from her dream, and she was still a bit disoriented.

Pursing her lips, she shook her head. Not disoriented, not a jot. She was frightened, as she had been in the dining room that afternoon.

The ship rolled to the right. The closet door slid shut with a crack and Ruth jumped. It slid back open, cracked again. Roll, crack. Roll, crack.

"Is someone there?" she asked in a firm voice, though not very loud. She didn't want the van Burens to think she was a senile old woman, given to talking to herself. Then she realized that wasn't the question she really wanted to ask.

"Is someone *here*?" She licked her lips.

A sense. A presence. A shadow in the corner, a dark spot on the ceiling. The dampness of the floor.

A sense. A presence.

Oh, God. Oh, could it be?

Her heart hammered. She didn't dare move again, or speak. It couldn't be; she'd never believed any of it, the table-rapping and the automatic writing. Now she saw all that for what it had been, and how she'd been going through the paces because there was nothing left to do. The Coast Guard was no longer looking for him, and no one else seemed to care.

She hadn't believed. Ever.

But something was wrong.

Yet if it were wrong, how could *he* be the source of it?

A looming presence. Something that was walking closer; she could almost hear the footsteps on the clammy floor. Almost feel someone touch her hand with a finger like a frozen bone.

"Stephen?" she rasped. "Are you . . . are you trying to reach me, darling?"

Listening to herself, she flushed to her roots and stepped boldly to the foot of the bed.

No presence. Nothing.

Sat down hard on top of the cocoon. It deflated beneath her weight.

Heavens, maybe she *was* a senile old lady. How unbelievably depressing.

And yet, she had felt . . . something. She had been frightened for some reason.

Was still frightened.

On the other side of the wall, someone mumbled, stirred. Oh, no, she'd awakened the van Burens. She sat, poised, listening. It was stuffy in the cabin. The air hung in layers that were hard to draw in.

She looked around the room. Nothing. And the feeling of fear was dissipating like a tide pulling itself back into the ocean.

The van Burens made no more sounds. She sat quietly, collecting herself. The mantle of unbelief cloaked her once more, and she told herself that when she met Marion Chang, she would tell her she'd decided not to pursue—

It was so damn hard to breathe! No wonder she was upset. She laid a hand over her chest and climbed onto the bed. Lifting her nightgown, she walked on her knees to the head and pushed the curtain away from the porthole. Some fresh air would clear her head. If the van Burens came to her door to see how she was, she'd say she'd been cursing at the porthole, trying to get it open. That it had been stuck . . .

It swung open at her light touch.

The closet door rolled and cracked, rolled and cracked. Outside, the sailors tromped and cursed and jangled their ghostly chains.

A Spirit propelled the ship, she found herself thinking, with no idea why. It sailed the Ancient Mariner straight for perdition. He had wanted to round the Horn, and boasted to God and the devil that he could do it. His pride had lured him to his doom.

The dream, the person in the water. Could that have been Stephen? Had she dreamed that her love was luring her to *her* doom?

"Good grief," she murmured, and thrust her head out the porthole.

Surrounded by the night, Donna and John stood beside Ramón Diaz on the bridge. Clad in a dark blue jumpsuit, he pointed to various instruments and droned on about what they were, a very dry textbook visit for tourists. When he'd invited her up, Donna guessed, he hadn't expected her to bring someone else along, especially not another man.

As Kevin would say, Bummer, dude.

She checked her watch. It was eleven-fifteen, but it felt like o-dark-thirty. Well, she'd told Ramón that sea air made her sleepy, hadn't she? Not realizing, of course, that it was true.

"Okay, now, this is our LORAN system. We navigate using this device," Ramón instructed them, as if there would be a quiz at the end of the visit.

Donna shifted her weight and surveyed the bridge, idly wishing she'd worn a sweater over her shorts and white Fruit of the Loom T-shirt. It was dark, save for a muted overhead light fixture that basically gave you a fix on things, but not a very good look. In the aft section of the room stood a large light table, now turned off, where they could lay the charts and study them, triangulate, all that jazz. A dozen charts rolled like house plans hung out of pigeonholes beneath the table, and thick books, of more charts, she assumed, leaned against each other drunkenly on a shelf above the pigeonholes. The colors of their covers had bled into the darkness; they all looked a sickening shade of mustard-yellow.

Donna noted the wheel, small and made of gray plastic, like the kind of thing you used to find on an infant's car seat, beep-beep, baby driver. At least it was a wheel. Ramón told them some ships were operated with joysticks.

Glenn would have said something crude and dumb about that.

She rubbed her nose. The circular windscreen on the upper left quadrant of the panorama window whirled around and around, a windshield wiper gone amuck. Talk about your symbols; that was how her mind was, too, trying to make a decision about Glenn. Maybe she could get it taken care of early so she could enjoy her vacation, goddamn it.

So. The smartest and best thing to do was also the most obvious: transfer. Get another partner. There were plenty of good officers on the force who wouldn't have a spasm over working with a woman. Not, frankly, that *she* wouldn't. *Cagney and Lacey* had been a TV show, hon, not a rational life-style for a female person trying to survive in Macholand. How'd *you* like to put your life on the line for some stupid bitch mooning over a guy?

Her throat hurt. Surreptitiously she touched her face—no tears—and wandered toward the back of the bridge. An out-of-date calendar advertised Mei Nin Chinese Foods with a large-breasted Chinese broad seated beside a waterfall. Glenn would say something stupid about that, too, like Nice melons, or I've got a nice big banana for her. Idiot.

". . . and if we have any trouble, the Coast Guard will pick up this frequency," Ramón was saying. You had to give the guy credit for sensitivity: he was promoting the safety features heavily. It was clear to everyone John was concerned about the voyage vis-à-vis his son—

—floating like a little planet, a precious lifespark comet—

Donna furiously rubbed her eyes. Damn, she must be getting PMS or something. Overtired. It wasn't like her to whine and sniffle.

Hey, maybe she should go get her presents and play spin the bottle with these guys. Le Bouf! It would cheer John up

and get Ramón off Ruth's back, ho-ho. And it might shut off
the Poor-Me's, 'cuz that's all this was, nothing wing-ding-ding
cosmic—you could make a career out of singing about Mr.
Wrong, but that was about the only instance where brooding
about it made any sense; and there weren't going to be any
good decisions made tonight, officer ma'am, sorry gee.

So. What about humping one of these guys? Sorry there,
too, girl, because the old bump and grind was not much more
than that without the love factor, witness Daniel.

Yeah, witness him for involuntary manslaughter, but the
parents weren't interested and she was out of her territory;
and his parting shot was that she should see a shrink about
her hostility toward men.

She took a deep breath and slid her hands under her arms.
Maybe she shouldn't have come on this cruise. Damn straight
she should've; she was in no condition to work. Maybe Randolph, her big boss, had known that. Hadn't he told her she'd
logged too much vacation time? Sometimes the subtleties
were lost on her. Sometimes not.

"Hey, what's that?" John asked. He was hovering over a
gray box with a screen in the middle. Donna recognized it as
the radar, chocked up a point on the quiz for herself and a
demerit for John.

"*Hijo*," Ramón murmured, standing beside him. The green
on his olive face made him look ghastly. The hollows beneath
his eyes lengthened into diamonds as he glanced up, at the
window. "Big fog bank, dead ahead."

"Wow." John left the box and walked to the front of the
bridge. "You see, Donna?"

"Excuse me," Ramón said. "I'm going to make sure they
know about this."

He left. John said, "Don't they have some kind of commu-
nications in here?"

She shrugged. "Yeah, a couple of cans and some string."
She traced a circle on the unlit light table. "Listen, have you
heard anything about this Cha-cha character?"

"Look." John pointed at the windows.

Donna looked. Blinked. One moment there'd been nothing but black, rocky water; now, a swirling line of fog rose like

steam. It floated in the air, spotlighted by the moon, rolling and churning like a whirlpool. It glowed bone-white in the moonbeams as it thickened and expanded. Curls fanned outward, grasping upward, east, west, looping back into the water. Like a long, huge log on the water, or the white curl of a monster surf wave. For ghosts.

"Weird," Donna said.

"It just came up on us. Ten seconds ago, there was nothing there. I was watching the radar screen."

Donna heard the tension in his voice. His eyes were wide, uneasy.

The lights on the *Morris*'s king posts cast glowing spheres like disembodied heads along the waves of mist.

"There sure is a lot of it," he said.

Hey, I saw this one, she wanted to tease him. John Carpenter directed it and Adrienne Boobeau (as Glenn called her) starred in it. There's this evil fog, see, and it takes over a town. But everything ends okay. Trust me on this one.

'Course, a whole lotta shakin' goes on first, heh heh . . .

But she wasn't sure he could take a joke. He was worn out, too, didn't look so hot; and people in that condition sometimes forgot to laugh. So she put a hand on his shoulder and said, "We'll probably go right through it. You've got to expect fog on the ocean, John."

"It looks dirty," he said, not listening to her.

Donna peered out the window. Streaks of moisture ran down the glass. The windscreen caught some of them and flung them in strips back into the night.

And when they went, they were tinged with a gray cast, like some kind of sea-smog pollution. The moon must have shifted behind some clouds, she reasoned; and the fog that hung a few miles from the bow was colored the same unwholesome mustard as the charts.

Beyond it, the inky ocean lay untouched.

Blackness.

Donna distinctly heard the word and turned her head expectantly toward John. He stared at the fog with his hands in his pockets.

"Did you say something?" she asked. He shook his head. "Well, then, did you hear something?"

The door opened and Ramón strode back into the room, looking unhappy. He slammed it behind him and muttered something in Spanish.

"Something the matter?" Donna asked.

He waved his hand. "No. It's okay." His face belied his words.

"It's coming toward us." John crossed his arms and held his body stiffly as if bracing himself for impact.

The fog unfurled and began to travel at a fast pace toward the ship. It moved faster, running at them, lengthening on either side until it exceeded Donna's line of vision. Unconsciously, John took a step backward. Donna leaned forward, putting her hands on the base of the window.

"It's all right," she said. "It's just a fog bank. It can't hurt us."

"Absolutely," Ramón agreed. "Air and water. That's all it is." He crossed to a small desk in the left aft corner and picked up a phone receiver, punched a button.

"Sir, thick fog conditions. I, ah, had some trouble with Ruffino. Need a replacement. Recommend we do a search of his fo'c'sle ASAP."

Donna looked over her shoulder. He reddened and shifted his shoulder as if to shield the phone from her.

"Aye, sir."

The fog rushed faster, faster, as if it actually would collide with them. John said, "I've got to get back to my son."

As he turned to go, an earsplitting bellow pierced the air. John cried out and Donna grabbed his wrist.

"Sorry." Ramón pressed another button. A few seconds later, the bellowing repeated, less loudly. A foghorn. Donna nodded to herself.

"We put the horn on for other ships," Ramón explained, lapsing back into his teacher voice. "No one's around for hundreds and hundreds of miles. You saw that on the radar, Doctor. But just in case, we start it up. We have our own signal." He cocked his head, listening, counting like an orchestra conductor. "Three short blasts, one long."

Who, who, who, whooooo?

"That's good," Donna supplied, straight man to his safety lecture.

He cracked a smile, showing off his dazzling teeth. He seemed pleasant enough, but it was hard to tell if that was his real self or just his bait. But if he didn't grow out of his superficial gotta-have-you routine, he'd either end up lonely or with some chick (in the worst sense of the word) who married him because she liked his ass or his clothes.

"That *señora* won't think it's comforting. The rich one."

"Oh, you mean the divine Ms. VB?" Donna said, trading a grin with him.

"That's Ms. VBH. H, you peasant." John chuckled, seeming a little more relaxed as he resumed his walk to the door.

"You know," he said, "in the olden days, ships used to sacrifice one of the crew to the gods if there was a crisis aboard. Think we got us a candidate?"

"Unfortunately, a little fog doesn't qualify." Ramón put his hands on his hips and cocked his head, watching the thick, white blankets. The foghorn blared as the mists covered the bow and spread over the containers, waves on a giant's beach spilling over fragile seashells.

"Maybe it'll get worse," Donna said, making a show of crossing her fingers. "We can always hope."

"I've got to go back to Matt," John said. "This might frighten him."

Donna said, "I'll go with you." Ramón opened his mouth, closed it. Glanced back at the radar screen and flicked some switches. Time for him to get back to work, anyway.

"Be careful on the ladderway," he said. "It'll be slick from the moisture."

"Okay. Thanks for the tour." Donna gave the window one last look.

Beside her, John gasped.

She whipped her head toward him. "What?"

He stood rigid as a statue. Pale, white, his eyes were huge. She shook his arm. "Jesus, John. What?"

He exhaled, shaking his head, and smiled sheepishly at her. "I don't know why I'm so jumpy. I'm sorry. I thought . . ."

When he pushed his glasses up on his nose, his hand trembled.

Donna waited. A dull red crawled up his neck and fanned across his cheeks.

"It was just a trick of the light, but I thought I saw a face in the fog," he said finally, clearly embarrassed. "It sort of dove onto it and pushed itself . . . but it was just the light." He shrugged. "Or my own reflection."

Donna nodded. "Let's go back downstairs," she suggested. "I think we're both pooped."

The foghorn blared. Ramón waved a hand and said, "Ciao."

Donna opened the door, paused, and turned.

"About this Cha-cha," she said.

Ramón made as if to ward her off. "Don't talk to me about that one."

She narrowed her eyes. "Why not?"

"I filed a complaint on him last trip out. Union won't let me talk about it." He checked his watch and picked up a clipboard. "How long ago did we see the radar blip, Dr. Fielder?"

"Is he dangerous?" Donna pressed.

Ramón laughed uneasily. "No. It's just that, well, he's a very bad cook."

"I see." Moving her shoulders, she gestured to John, who went out the door first. She followed after.

They went down the first two flights of stairs at a steady clip. Then John stopped and pressed his hand into his side, panting. He said, "My knees are wobbling."

Donna waited. She kept in good shape; it was part of her job.

"Well, what do you think?" He wiped his forehead with the back of his hand. "Whew, I've got to start going back to the gym when I get home."

"About what?" she asked, leaning over to stretch her calves. "The fog or Cha-cha?"

"Both, actually. But I meant Cha-cha. No one seems to be very worried about him."

"They don't seem to be very worried about anything." 'Cuz they're all stoned, she thought grimly. Then, sighing to herself, she said, "I'll keep an eye on him." Next time she traveled, she was going to tell everyone she was a secretary.

"Thanks." John straightened and continued down.

No problem, that's what she got paid for. Shit.

Donna continued down as well.

The stairs, more properly the ladders, led out into a companionway parallel with the captain's quarters and something called the "writing room," but which was locked and had a No Entry sign on the door latch. Around the leeward corner, a row of cabins stretched toward the dining room. On the opposite side there were more cabins, all of them empty save for a single occupied by Kevin, the surfer.

In concert, John and Donna walked around the corner. Hers was the first cabin on the row and his and Matt's, the last. John was quiet, his shoulders tense and pinched. He seemed to be noodling something around, so she kept her own counsel as they made their way.

They neared her door. Soft curls of fog streamed from beneath it and floated down the companionway.

Joining those that were streaming from beneath Ruth's door.

The cold, white mist wrapped around their ankles and undulated with their footfalls. John grunted and lifted his foot.

"Hey." He lifted the other one, danced around in a circle.

"It's just fog," she reminded him.

He looked up ahead, started to walk-run through the patches that misted by, Kleenex on guy wires.

"This stuff will be bad for Matt. He shouldn't . . . he's on the frail side." He ducked his head.

"There's nothing under your door," she called to him. "I left my porthole open. Ruth probably did, too."

Donna stepped to Ruth's door and rapped lightly. "Ms. Hamilton? You okay?" She checked her watch. Eleven-twenty. She was probably sound asleep. This stuff couldn't be good for an old lady.

At the end of the companionway, John unlocked his door and hurried in. The door shut.

"Ruth?" Donna said with more force. Now the fog was piling around Donna's knees, cold and clammy like a mud pack. She couldn't see her feet.

"Mrs. Hamilton?" After a moment's hesitation, she tried the knob. It turned; the door was unlocked. She'd have to talk to her about that; with all these strangers around (Jesus, with Cha-cha, who looked like a member of the Manson family, around), caution was in order.

There was a funny noise, a thud of wood, or was it a clang? Donna listened. Nothing. Well, the hell with it. She opened the door.

The foghorn blared.

The cabin was laden with smoke-gray fog, so thick Donna couldn't see a thing. It was like being in a snowstorm. She stepped forward and hit the end of the bed with her shins.

"Mrs. Hamilton? It's Donna." Her arms flailed as she bent at the waist and touched the bed. Nothing there but sheets.

Maybe she'd gone out, was sitting in the dining room right now, having a cup of tea.

"Mrs.—?"

The funny sound again. Not a thud, or a clang, but a long, melancholy sigh that seemed to echo past her ears. It chittered; someone playing with a tape recorder to make spooky sounds. It reverbed. Donna swallowed and stepped sideways as she searched for the edge of the bed.

"Are you all right?"

That noise . . .

The edge. She walked forward, dipping to the right to feel the bedclothes. They were soggy.

The ship rolled to the left. Donna lost her balance and fell, not against the bulkhead as she expected but into an indentation. Metal jangled: clothes hangers. She'd fallen into the closet.

Then something shot forward and hit her.

She cried out and grabbed it. Laughed weakly. It was the closet door.

Stepping out, she moved on up the side of the bed.

Someone was standing on it. The faint outline of a figure glowed from a light hip-high to Donna. The source of the light must be on a nightstand, she reasoned.

"Mrs. Hamilton?" No answer.

Donna swallowed fog. She could almost feel it swimming around in her lungs, drifting up and down her windpipe.

The closet door slammed back, forward, smacked against the jamb hard enough to do some serious damage. The fog-horn bellowed.

Thirst, someone said directly into her ear.

Donna whipped her head around. Her knee smacked the night table. The things on top of it clattered. A round, heavy object fell off and hit Donna's toe. It brilled once and bounced against the base of the night table. Alarm clock.

"Ruth?"

The figure made no movements. It stood about parallel with her head; Ruth must be kneeling at the porthole.

To her left, the alarm clock went off again, jangling discordantly. It stopped in midsound as if someone had snapped it off.

Donna climbed onto the bed, which was soft and wet and gave like a fungus as her knees sank into it. A dank odor emanated from it, of something old and unused.

The figure looked too small to be a kneeling woman. In the wavering light, she saw a head too little, shoulders too narrow. Was it Matty Fielder, hiding from his father for some reason? Or just being a mischievous kid? His father would be frantic.

"Matty? Ruth?" She touched the figure. Icy, ungiving flesh met her fingers—

—and her heart lurched as she pulled back her hand. That was a dead person; she knew it. She knew what a dead person felt like. How cold, how hard, like a block of ice.

Stupid, stupid, she told herself, as she jumped off the bed. The figure tottered, swaying left, right, faster, faster, about to fall over. Donna had a sharp, vivid picture of it cracking into a million pieces.

She covered her mouth, pulling herself together. She was acting like a rookie. Like some dumbass baby who—

"Who?" Ruth's voice. Donna sagged with relief, clunked herself in the forehead in embarrassment. Dumbo. Of course it was Ruth. Of course she looked different in the fog.

Felt . . . different.

"Ruth, it's Donna Almond. Are you all right?"

"Yes, yes," the old lady said uncertainly. "I . . . I've been dreaming."

Dreaming? Did she have epilepsy? Donna thought about asking, decided to let it wait. There was enough going on.

"You must be freezing. Let me help you." Donna crawled back onto the mattress. The sheets were sodden. Already her mind made preparations for taking care of the old woman: get her to the dining room, coffee, maybe a shot of hooch.

"I was dreaming," the woman said. She moved away from the porthole of her own volition and found Donna's hands. "I can't even see you, dear."

"It's just fog." Donna maneuvered back to the floor and stood up, bringing the woman with her. "We sailed into it a while ago. It's okay."

The foghorn blared. The closet door rolled and cracked. Rolled and cracked.

"I'm so cold. My nightie's wet clean through."

The reason she'd said she was thirsty, Donna figured. She might be dehydrated. "We'll get you into some warm things. How about a cup of coffee? I'm sure we can scare one up."

"That sounds heavenly."

The sensation of Ruth's disembodied, skeletal fingers grabbing on to Donna's was eerie. Ruth stood directly in front of the light as Donna slowly led her past the closet; an aureole of buoyant wisps swam around her head and shoulders, like she was some kind of winter dandelion shifting in a chill breeze.

Or something underwater, wafting with the currents.

"This is a little frightening," Ruth said with a nervous laugh. "I literally cannot see a thing."

"You and me both." She paused. "What did you dream about, Ruth?"

Beneath Donna's forefinger, the pulse in Ruth's wrist jumped. "I don't remember."

Not so sure about that. Donna worked the inside of her cheek. Maybe it was too personal to discuss.

"We'll get you some coffee."

"That would be nice, dear," Ruth replied. "I'm so . . . I'm so thirsty."

"Yes, you said that. While you were dreaming."

"Oh, I don't remember. The fog just rolled in. I . . . I thought it was ali . . ." She trailed off. "I was dreaming."

"Yes." Donna waited a beat, in case she said more. Cripes, maybe sweet little Mrs. Ruth Hamilton had paid a visit to Dr. Feelgood, alias Kevin the Stoner.

But what about the cold flesh, and the—

She pushed her thoughts away. "Hold on a second. Let me close your porthole." Gingerly, she moved Ruth aside and went along the other side of the bed. Good Lord, the cabin was smaller than hers. She could barely wedge herself between the bed and the bulkhead.

She pressed her hand against the cold surface, feeling for the porthole. Easily found, and just as easily shut.

Just as she latched it, something smacked against it with a wet, sloshy *thwack.* Startled, she pulled away, stared at it. Nothing but fog and the yellow glow from the night table.

"What was that?" Ruth asked querulously.

"A wave. We got it shut just in time."

"I guess so." Ruth sneezed.

Or a bird, lost in the fog, poor thing. That's what it had really sounded like. But no sense telling Ruth that.

Hi ho. In Hawaii, she was definitely going to tell people she was a secretary.

If they ever got to friggin' Hawaii, for God's sake.

5
Arrival

A face.

John lay beside his son, who slept peacefully through the foghorn and the slamming and the creaking, and the voices of Ruth and Donna as they talked in the hallway. Kids never ceased to amaze him. They possessed such capacities, such surprises. He should have been a pediatrician.

Right, his ulcer smirked. Then you could watch not only your own kid sicken and die, but everyone else's, too.

He forced the thought away without arguing with it. A face. Damn it, he had seen something on the bridge. He had seen—

—his own reflection.

The foghorn blasted, and he jumped, though by now he'd heard it dozens of times. He was surprised there wasn't any action over in the next cabin, the van Burens. You'd think she'd be bitching about both the fog and the foghorn. He couldn't imagine they were sleeping through this.

Then again, he couldn't imagine Matty was, either. Matty, his real reflection. John saw bits and pieces of his own features—the straight nose, the broad forehead; bits of Gretchen's—the tender pink mouth, the chin (too narrow now to recognize, but it was hers). And then, the miracle of life: places where the synthesis ended, and something that was neither his nor hers, but Matt's own—the broad planes of his cheeks, his blue-black hair that really was blue-black, the way they drew it in comic books.

There were other traits that were Matthew Samuel Fielder originals: his hatred of potatoes, his nervous habit of pulling on the hairs at the nape of his neck.

His disease.

If Matt died, not only would little bits and pieces of John and Gretchen die, but something that had never been before, and never would be again.

John swallowed hard. He watched his boy's eyelids shift rapidly underneath his lids. REM sleep. His baby was dreaming.

Of what, little boy? Rocket ships? Avenging turtles? Or chemotherapy, and needles forced into his arms while he lay weeping, "Daddy, no, don't let them"? Or sitting on the sidelines while the other boys played an impromptu game of basketball across the street at Chucky's house?

Asking how likely an amputation was.

John swallowed hard and stared at his boy. His stomach was drowning in acid that seared the lining, and he put a protective hand over it. Stuck his hand in his trouser pocket and pulled out a bottle of Tagamet, popped one into his mouth. It wasn't good to be morose. Matt picked it up, even when John thought he was hiding it very well. Kids were psychic. Kids were magical.

Kids were put together with gossamer wire and tissue paper, and even a mild breeze could rip them to shreds.

John muffled a groan. He ached to put his arms around his son but he didn't want to awaken him.

Matt's eyes flickered. More REM. Lots of REM.

Dream, my boy. Dream beautiful dreams, my beautiful little man.

* * *

"Wait. I want to close my porthole," Donna said to Ruth. They stood in the hall on the other side of the old lady's door. During the interlude in her room, the fog in the corridor had tumbled on top of itself to waist height. It stayed bunched together as if it were filling a container whose ends stood parallel with the outer edges of her and John's doors. New bulk cargo for the *Morris,* remaining right where it was put. Shifting cargo, Donna had learned, was one of the major causes of freighter accidents.

"You wait right here and I'll come get you."

"No." Ruth grabbed Donna's sleeve. Using the Braille method, they had poked through the cabin's built-in dresser and the closet, and dressed her in some mismatched clothes and a London Fog raincoat. "Let me come with you."

Ruth's eyes bulged as she gazed pleadingly at Donna. The lady was freaked. What *had* she been doing, staring out at the fog?

Donna patted her hands and said, "Fine. We'll go together."

They shuffled down the hall like an elderly couple. Donna found her key in her purse and stuck it in the lock. Paused.

She didn't want to go in.

Say what, Officer? What are you doing, cowering in front of your own door? Are you afraid of a little fog?

Ridiculous. Absolutely. Nevertheless, she didn't want to go in there. Her heart beat with a vengeance and a muscle beneath her left eye hopped like a jumping bean.

Poised beside her, Ruth looked from Donna to the door and back again, like someone mustering the nerve to jump out of a burning building. Poor old dear was cold. The old lady needed to get out of this damp. Feel the fear, and get your butt in gear. Okay, okay, fine.

Resolutely, Donna turned the lock and pushed open the door.

They both gasped.

There was no fog in Donna's cabin. The overhead light cast a fluorescent pall over the mint-green walls, the brown bedspread, the yellow and green curtain pushed back from the gaping porthole. A mirror over the bureau was sheened with wet, sliding Donna's reflection down its surface like a shredded roll of aluminum foil. The air was clear, if moist, but there was no fog.

Donna frowned and turned back to the door, knelt down and checked the threshold. She had seen fog rolling from beneath that door, fast and thick like dry ice in a horror movie.

"There must have been some kind of air pocket," she said, improvising. "A suction or something that drew it back out of here." She shrugged. "Weird, huh?"

Clasping her coat around her shoulders, Ruth nodded. She said, "Your cabin's so much bigger than mine."

"I know." Donna walked by the bed and shut the porthole briskly. "I was surprised when I went into your room. I busted my shins on everything." She made sure the latch was down and locked. "I hope you don't mind, me coming in like that. I knocked. I was worried about you."

"No, no. I'm grateful that you did." Ruth took a deep breath and checked herself in the mirror. Put a hand to her hair, looked away. "I thought . . ." She pulled the raincoat more tightly around herself, studied her feet. Raised her chin. Looked into the mirror again.

"I thought my husband . . ." Her voice trailed off. If she said anything more, Donna couldn't hear it. After a few seconds she cleared her throat. "You mentioned something about coffee?"

Donna nodded, intrigued but masking it. "And I'll just bet that old coot's got something strong and medicinal stashed in those itsy-bitsy cupboards of his."

The woman smiled sheepishly, as though relieved Donna wasn't going to press her.

"Let's go, then." Donna shepherded her out and shut the door. "We'll have to air out your stuff tomorrow or it might mildew. I think there's actually a dryer on board, if you can believe that."

They moved right, down the hall into the churning fog.

"It's hard to believe you're a lady policeman, dear." Ruth held on to Donna's forearm. "Before I got married, I thought about becoming a social worker. You'd make a good one, I think."

Donna chuckled. As far as she was concerned, there wasn't much difference between the two. She said, "Thank you, Ruth. That's very kind of you to say."

"Not to imply that you're not a good policewoman. I'm sure you are."

"Most of the time."

They paddled on, Ruth pulling back as if she were afraid she'd stub a toe, maybe stumble. Donna tried to stay a step or two ahead of her so she could guide her. Her own grandmother had fallen, broken a hip, and now she was in a nursing home. Not fun, not at all. Donna's mom, safe in Albuquerque from all the difficult decisions, told Donna to do with Gramma what she thought was best. So Baby Donna was the one caught the flak over the rest home, and thanks a heap, Mom dearest.

The fog climbed to their chests, stubbornly remaining within the corridor. Donna wished she'd had the presence of mind to grab her sweater when they'd gone into her cabin.

"Oh, my Lord!" Ruth cried, leaping against Donna and nearly knocking her over. "There's something on the floor. Something huge!"

"Where?" Donna asked. She searched the fog with her eyes. The billows and curls rose and fell back on each other, covering their tracks.

"It's over there!" Ruth hurried her as far away as she could from the direction in which she pointed. "It had pincers!"

"Maybe it's a crab." Donna took a step toward it.

"No! It was . . . gelatinous. I stepped on it." She caught her breath. "Don't you hear it?"

Donna listened.

The foghorn blared.

John Fielder's door opened and he poked his head out. "What's wrong?" Behind him, his son called anxiously, "Daddy?"

"There's something on the floor," Ruth said.

"Oh?" John caught Donna's eye and quizzed her. She shook her head. "Maybe it's the cat." The ship had one, named Nemo, bursting with pregnancy and ready to go at any moment, according to Mr. Saar.

"No. It was . . . it had pincers."

"A crab?" John asked reasonably.

"Let's just keep going," Donna suggested. "How's your son?" she asked John.

The foghorn drowned out John's reply, and Ruth hurried her down the passage so fast she couldn't ask him to repeat it.

"Ruth, I'm sure it was nothing." The woman was shaking. Her lower lip worked, the way old people's lips sometimes did.

"My dream." She shook Donna's hand. "There was a creature like that in my dream. It was . . . hideous. Monstrous."

A creature? "Ruth, you said you dreamed about your husband," Donna ventured, just as they reached the end of the corridor. A metal hatch on the right led to the outside deck, and another stood perpendicular to it, marked "Officers Mess (Passengers Lounge)."

As Donna waited for Ruth to speak, she opened the hatch and started to walk across the threshold. Her toes connected with the lip that extended from the deck. Hard.

"Shit!" she muttered. Ruth screamed. Donna reddened. "Sorry. There's one of those lips here. Step up."

"Mr. Diaz told me they're to prevent . . . things from washing down the hall if the sea comes in." Fearfully she glanced in the direction they had come. Where the Squishy Thing lurked. The Creature.

Donna said nothing, only stepped over the lip. Her toes throbbed.

Elise and Phil van Buren glanced up from two chairs on either side of the kidney-shaped coffee table. Both of them had been reading. As usual.

"Evenin'," Phil said warmly, in his soft Southern accent. His wife said nothing, just put her book facedown on her lap and stared at the two women.

"We've just been through the attack of the killer fog," Donna said.

Ruth let go of her and touched her hair, her face. Poor

lady. No makeup on, and her hair was pretty wild. Donna thought of her perm, and all the wet, and figured she must be one gigantic frizzball. She hadn't really seen her reflection in the cabin.

"It's something, isn't it?" Phil ventured, walking past his wife to gaze out one of the four picture windows. Beyond, gray curled and spiraled. "Captain Esposito was in a while ago. He said it should clear up by morning."

Elise snorted. She picked up a pack of cigarettes and pulled one out.

"That man's an idiot. I can't believe they let him run a ship."

Phil flushed. He came away from the window and crossed to the long, linen-covered table where they took their meals with the ship's officers.

"Cha-cha made a pot of coffee. Would you ladies care for some?"

Donna and Ruth nodded in unison. Donna asked, "Have you seen him?"

Phil jerked his head in the direction of the side door. "Puttering around. He was talking about his fishing lines." Lowering his voice, he added, "There's something very strange about that man."

The flare of Elise's match was like the hiss of a cobra. Her long, perfect nails flashed like stilettos dabbed in blood. Watch it, babe, Donna mentally warned her. If this fog gets any worse, we've already decided to sacrifice you to the gods.

"Why don't you have a seat, Mrs. Hamilton?" Phil finished pouring the coffee and brought the cups and saucers to the two women. Ruth sank onto the sofa and leaned back her head.

"I—I was asleep in my room," she said. "In the fog." Sipping, she avoided Donna's eyes. "Donna came and woke me up."

"That I did."

"There's something out there," Ruth went on. Her voice was shrill.

Donna let the conversation trail away as she knocked on the galley door. There was no answer. It swung open at her touch, and remembering to lift her leg (like a damn dog), she stepped in.

"Hey, Cha-cha?" she called.

A faint smell of gas pervaded the cramped space between the door and a locker-size cabinet of stainless-steel compartments whose once-gleaming surfaces had been reduced to a dull sheen. The gas odor grew stronger near a six-burner stove top. A black pot speckled with blue—home on the range—sat on the back right burner, a cobalt flame winking feebly beneath it. Additional compartments hung over a stainless-steel sink; on the other side of the Formica bar containing the sink, a steel refrigerator-freezer hummed and whirred. Pots and pans hung in nets, were belted on hooks on the walls, rode loose on a large wooden sideboard. A half-open closet to the right of the refrigerator yielded a broom, mop, pail, rags. Five cans of Comet—hence the flat, scratched look of the place.

Donna peered into a drawer. Mouse traps. Rat traps. Sorry she'd looked, she shut it and slung the restraining hook into place.

"Cha-cha?" She opened an overhead cabinet and rooted past maple syrup and pancake mix, powdered milk, sugar. No booze. He had to keep it someplace. Guy like him, you'd think he'd have bottles stashed everywhere. And she didn't mean cooking sherry.

Poor Ruth. She'd been shaking like a leaf. Donna was sure she'd stepped on something harmless. A mislaid mop, one of Matty's toys. Normal objects became ominous in the dark and the fog. That's why cops accidentally shot kids who waved squirt guns in their faces.

But how come there wasn't any fog in her cabin? Not one little tendril, one wispy wisp? Her porthole was open same as Ruth's. Suction, bull. She hadn't bought that one and neither had Ruth.

She rattled around some more. "Oh, Cha-cha-cha," she muttered. "Don't tell *me* you're not a boozer."

The hatch that led to the outer deck flew open and Kevin sailed in, blond locks flying. He had on a white sweatshirt and blue baggies, no shoes.

"Oh, hey, hi!" he said, yanking open a drawer beside the stove top. "Come see this!" He hefted a huge knife in his hand and slammed the drawer shut. "We caught a shark or something!" His hair streamed over his shoulders as he doubled back the way he'd come and leaped through the hatch like a gazelle.

Intrigued, Donna followed him into the wet layers of fog. He melted into them and she walked unsteadily toward the sound of splashes and thrashing and yells of excitement. The containers were singing and droning, the symphony of the damned.

"Yeah! Yeah!" Cha-cha bellowed. "Yeah, baby!"

"Guys?" Donna passed her arms in front of her body. "Guys, where are you?"

The foghorn sounded. The containers droned.

"Here it comes! Yeah!" Cha-cha shouted.

A very loud splash.

"Shit! It bit me!" Kevin yowled. "Shit!"

Donna walked faster. She could see nothing.

"Watch it! Watch it!" Cha-cha again, bellowing wildly. "Oh, baby! Help!"

On reflex, Donna broke into a run, zeroing in on the men as Cha-cha cried, "Baby, baby, baby!" over and over again.

She saw two round circles of light that rattled in the white and headed for them. Then she collided with Cha-cha, who dropped his flashlight.

"What's the matter?" she demanded.

"Son of a bitch bit me," Kevin said, gasping.

His flashlight beamed into his face. She saw his features, all white bones and black angles, the way she and her friends used to frighten each other at slumber parties when they told ghost stories:

Donna, what happened to your beautiful face?
Death and decay, it rotted away.
Donna, what happened to your beautiful legs?
Death and decay, they rotted away.
Donna, what happened to your beautiful golden arm?
YOU'VE GOT IT!

"Come on back into the lounge."

"Our fish!" Cha-cha protested. "Officer Donna, it's in there, eating up all the little babies!"

An image came queasily into Donna's head. Yuck. She tugged on Kevin's arm and said, "If you're hurt, come with me. I'm going back to the lounge." And sit down, goddamn it, and relax.

Kevin walked beside her. He reeked with the smell of dope and she flashed with anger. Christ, did the captain allow drugs on his ship, or was he so incompetent he didn't know about them? She thought she heard a steady dripping on the deck—blood?—and hurried her pace. If Kevin was stoned, he might not realize it if he was seriously injured.

"It's a sea monster!" Cha-cha shouted. "A damn sea monster!"

"Tried to take my fuckin' finger off at the bone," Kevin muttered.

There was a loud splash. The shark must have leapt back into the water.

And a funny, wet *plop* on the deck. Donna thought of the fish in the net, escaping the clutches of the "sea monster" only to suffocate on the deck.

"At the fuckin' bone," Kevin said, groaning.

She sighed. This had certainly turned into a fun evening.

She stepped over the hatch lip into the galley and shepherded Kevin to the sink. He'd wrapped his finger in the corner of his jeans jacket; the denim had soaked to red. Donna's senses went on alert. With that much blood, it had to be more serious than she'd realized.

"C'mon," she said, gesturing for him to unwrap it.

Slowly he obeyed, wincing as he undraped his hand. He drew the jacket away and showed her.

She inhaled sharply. On either side of his thumb, the flesh had been ripped away. A full inch of his first metacarpal gleamed like a piece of ivory; on the other side, the flesh between his thumb and forefinger was severed into two long, bleeding flaps.

Forcing herself to remain calm, she turned on the water and put his hand under it. He cried out.

"You going to faint?" she asked calmly. He shook his head.

"No." Kevin's face was papery white. Behind him, the fog tumbled into the galley, crawling up and over the lip and cascading along the floor. "Dr. John. Get Dr. John."

She cupped some cold water and splashed it on the nape of his neck. "Hold on. I'll be right back."

She dashed out of the kitchen and through the lounge. Phil had his arms around Ruth as she sobbed against his chest.

". . . pincers!" she said, catching her breath. "Sharp, and I stepped on it!"

Phil looked up with a puzzled expression on his face.

Donna said, "Kevin's had an accident. Go to him." Threw an expression of disgust at Elise, who was standing apart from her husband and Ruth, and hopped over the transom to the hall.

She popped on the door. He opened it at once, as if he were expecting her. Maybe he'd heard the shouting; if so, why hadn't he come to check on it? "Yes?" he asked.

"Your turn." She jerked her head. "You've got a chomped-up hand in the galley, and Ruth in hysterics in the lounge. The rules of triage say you should go to the galley first."

"Okay. I'll be right there." He started to shut the door, but she stopped him.

"If you need me, send H.R.H. Elise for me. I'm falling-down tired."

"Okay. Matt," he said over his shoulder, "I need to . . ."

The rest of his sentence was lost to her in the foghorn. With a sigh, she lifted her hair off the back of her neck and continued down the hall. Ruth's monster was there some-where. She kicked the fog, trying to clear a view to the floor. Nothing. As she expected.

Feeling only slightly guilty about leaving all the mess to John, she flopped on the bed. Raised her leg and worked off the sneaker on her right foot with the toes of her left.

The foghorn bellowed.

And beneath it, a *roll, crack. Roll, crack.* Something was loose. Probably the same mop that had scared the bejesus out of Ruth.

Roll, crack. Shit. She'd never get to sleep, listening to that. *Roll, crack.*

A bird beak, she thought drowsily. You could step on a large beak and think it was pincers.

Yeah, so? Did that mean a bird had flown into the companionway, somehow crashed to the floor, and now lay flat on its back with its beak pointing to the stars?

Roll crack. Roll crack. And a funny little *chatter-scrabble, chatter-scrabble,* up and down the hall.

In five minutes, she was gone.

6

Birth of a Legend

April 10, 1797

Thomas Reade, formerly the captain of the *Royal Grace,* in the sea, in his own boat of Charon, dying.

Blackness.

Thirst. The two words echoed through his being; they shook and rattled the water. They vibrated beneath the waves in a titanic plea to the gods.

The sea, alone, all alone, with his death shroud wrapped around him.

And then, a bottle bobbed upon the water.

Blackness, thirst.

The sea, and Thomas Reade; and his lips shredded inside the shroud as he chewed on the canvas, the blood and brains of the boy a dried paste that cracked and peeled off like a second skin. The cabin boy, Nathaniel, his beloved, his darling, his treasure.

Roll, crack! The belaying pin he had dropped when they came for him in his cabin, saw what he was doing. Roll, crack along the deck, like the cadence of the death watch! While they beat him and sewed him into the shroud, deaf to his explanations, his entreaties, his threats.

Nathaniel, his love. Him he had given to her when she asked, Salome to his Baptist.

No, not Salome. Maria. Maria, most holy, virgin of the waters. Stella Maris. Oh, she. She, who gave the ocean life. She had come to him in his dreams, and told him what to do. She had promised so much; she clung to the exquisite vessel of his reasoning like an exquisitely carved figurehead, whispering, pledging. She would not let him down. He knew she would save him.

Reade's cock sprang into an erection. He stopped chewing and grabbed it through his salt-stiff trousers. Oh, yes! Yes! When she came for him, he would be ready.

He wanted with all his heart to fuck the sea.

And know ye, all ye dead men who tell no tales:

Desire is a kind of Spirit.

And the Spirit moves upon the waters.

En route to the Owhyees, and a bottle bobbed beside the boat, beautiful and green, with golden tracings and sparkling jewels, smacking against the side of the dinghy—

—*roll, crack!*—

—as the dying man lay in his shroud. A wave lifted it up, up, up; it gleamed like a crown atop the crest! and tossed it into the vessel—

—just as a huge, white bird swooped down from the sky and grabbed it, cawing with glee.

Then something wrapped around the bird's leg. Alarmed, the bird flapped its wings harder. The leg was ripped off. The bird shrieked in agony. In a spray of blood and tendons, the bottle fell inside the boat

—*crack*—

And Thomas Reade, emerging from his prison, picked up the bottle and shouted, "She comes!"

7
Bottle, Bottle, Who's Got the Bottle?

It was psychedelically beautiful. Green with sparklies, his net treasure.

The minute Cha-cha saw it fall out of the fishing net and roll down the foggy deck, he knew King Neptune had sent it to him. Sendin' out an SOS. And he'd grabbed that sucker and stuck it in his jacket, yessir, all the time Kevin was going ballistic over his hand, 'cuz Cha-cha knew it was a great big secret, just between him and His Sea-ness.

As Cha-cha lay in his bunk, he raised the bottle toward the single bare bulb that swung back and forth from the ceiling of his cabin. Rock, rock, rock, and roll. A memory surged: a vase made out of a 7-Up bottle, purple wildflowers. A house-boat.

Rocking, rocking, rocking. Before the Vietnam Conflict, the house like a baby in a macramé hammock. And he'd been happy there. His scene had been beautiful. Psychedelically beautiful.

Yeah, and if you put the bottle up to your ear, it spoke to you in His Voice.
And it told you what to do.
What to do next.
Come to me, Cha-cha. A thousand times a thousand.
"Yessir, Your Highness," Cha-cha told King Neptune.

8

The Logs:
Diaries
and Messages

en route to Hawaii, past and present

I

April 21

. . . *checked the stitches this morning. The cut was quite severe. Kevin swears something bit him, but there's no sign of teeth marks. Donna told me there was a knife involved, but in all the excitement, it's been lost. Cha-cha said it was his favorite, sharpest one, and has charged "Officer Donna" with finding it.*

That man gives me the willies. He keeps making all kinds of sly comments about something he found in the net. I wouldn't be surprised if he cut Kevin himself.

The fog still hangs around us. We're going into our second night of it and it's making all the passengers edgy. Crew, too, though they're trying to hide it from us. Capt. Esposito ordered us not to move around outside. There's something very unsettling about not being able to see where you're going.

At dinner (steak and pasta; Cha-cha, amazingly, can cook very well), Elise VBH (H, you peasant, H) confronted the captain and demanded he explain why we had all this fog. He just looked at her with contempt and said, "I'm sorry, but I can't control the weather." And she looked at him like she wanted to ask, Why the hell not?

Matty slept like a log last night, but he was listless all day. I think he had nightmares, but he won't talk about them. Cha-cha, bless his bizarre old soul, located Capt. Nemo, who is now curled next to Matt on the bed. Both are asleep. Nemo is purring. I didn't know cats purred in their sleep and I wouldn't have guessed she'd let him near her, pregnant as she is.

Ulcer's flared up again. I'm running out of Tagamet. Don't think the captain's got any in his slop chest.

I think I had a bad dream last night, too. It seemed to have had something to do with a man. Maybe after Ruth's hesitant confession last night, I appropriated the image of her husband. I boozed her up a little to stop the tears and she told me he disappeared eleven months ago, in these very waters. How gruesome! She's going to Hawaii to consult a medium who claims to have received messages from him indicating that he's alive. Poor Ruth. At least she's highly skeptical of the whole thing. On the other hand, she is going all the way to Hawaii to check it out. I guess you do desperate things when you love someone.

I know you do. I'd do anything for Matty. I'd sell my soul if I could.

Dear God, don't let him get sick again.

Dear God, take care of him.

If you listen to lapsed Catholics, God, listen to me.

Later—

Can't sleep. Every time I close my eyes, I jerk awake. I keep thinking I hear talking, something about a bottle? Some kind of dream—nightmare, really. I feel threatened, and then I wake up. I think Matt might be in it. That makes sense, about feeling threatened, with Matt in the dream, I mean.

He and the kitty seem to be snoozing through it all. A while ago, Donna came by to ask for a sleeping pill. Looked worn out. She's a honey. Mmm, been a long time. I think Matty's falling for her, too. 'Course, she lets him win at checkers. She doesn't let the big boys get away with anything. I think Ramón wants her to hurt him. Ha!

Oh, yeah, we never did find anything in the corridor, though Ruth insists something was there.

I almost told her about the face. I know I imagined it, but at the time, it seemed real. But I was too embarrassed—guess I don't want Donna to know I still think about it.

But I do think about it.

II

Assets.

Liabilities.

With a shaking hand, Elise poised her hand over the page of the steno pad she'd purchased from the captain's "slop chest" (charming name) earlier that evening. Continued the list: the condo in the city, the house on Fire Island. The Jag. The stocks, the bonds, the bank accounts. Jewelry, art.

So many assets.

So little love.

Dots of ink marred the paper as she held the pen above the last item on the list. It swung back and forth between her fingers as if on a gimbal.

Tears blurred the ink.

She closed the steno pad and stuffed it in the nightstand, aware that Phil might find it there and know exactly what it was. Her face impassive, she capped the pen and set it beside her pack of cigarettes. She pulled one out and lit it, watched the blue smoke rise. The tears fell at a forty-five-degree angle down her face, dampening her earlobes.

The cabin door opened and Phil blustered in, whistling, carrying a tray loaded with porcelain cups and a coffeepot.

"Cha-cha made hot chocolate," he announced happily, like a kid.

"Great." She took a drag and pushed the smoke out through her nostrils.

"They're going to show another movie later on."
Elise turned her head. "Another one?"
Bastard. Blind bastard. Couldn't he see her tears?
She thought about the list in the nightstand drawer.
She thought about it a lot.

III

Alone in his cabin, Kevin held the corner of the paper in place with his elbow and chewed gum loud and hard while he wrote:

. . . crazy dude. Now he's saying the king gave him a present in the net and "the time is at hand." So I go to the mate and he just laughs. Everybody thinks he's a harmless old guy. But he's scary, man. Only thing was in that net were some fish and some damn shark or something, the one who chomped my finger off, practically.

The lady cop is right about one thing: if something does happen, like if King Neptune tells Cha-cha to go for it, I don't think the crew will be any help at all.

Shit, I'm freaking myself out. We'll be in Hawaii in two days. Just one more night. Since I got bit, I can't work in the galley, which is cool. I don't have to hang around Cha-cha anymore.

I hope I see you again, Sandi.

Fuck, I'm weirding out. Of course I'll see you.

Love ya,
Kev

IV

Blackness.
Thirst.
Loneliness.

V

The ship pitched through the raging storm; waves like cliffs crashed over the decks as the vessel hurtled through the thunder and lightning. The sails were tatters, the masts shattered bone. Banshee wind shrieked, insane and vicious.

"No, no, no," the captain moaned. His eyes as he stared over his shoulder rolled like a calf's on the way to the slaughterhouse. Without looking, he looped a piece of line around and around his wrist, securing himself to the wheel. The lightning danced in his eyes, reflecting back a figure that glided toward him, a tall man in a cape.

The captain sagged against the wheel and sobbed.

The man, the tall stranger who had killed the others—

The demon—

Donna yawned and idly looked out the window at the fog. Monster movies weren't her thing, even if Frank Langella did make a sexy Dracula. (She'd only seen the John Carpenter movie about the fog to please her nephew, Bob, whom she'd been baby-sitting at the time. She used to spend a lot of time baby-sitting her brothers' kids. Other people's kids.)

Well, it was still better than all those Viking movies Ramón watched. He must have had two dozen of them. They were the weirdest damn things, made in Spain with German actors, made in Germany with Italian actors. Dubbed into English and truly wretched. Kevin told her Ramón had posters of Vikings in his cabin, too. Donna had drawled, "It must be some kind of homoerotic thing," and Kevin had laughed so hard she thought he was going to pass out. Watching him she had thought, Fuck singing. She was going for stand-up comedy.

Now Dracula was coming after the captain. Now he was a wolf, hoo-wah. Not her bag.

She got out of her chair and walked to the hatch. She was the only passenger in the dining room; the rest of the chairs and the sofa were occupied by officers and crewmen, leaning avidly toward the TV. The colors played on their faces, rainbow fog.

Ramón saw her. Quickly she waved good night before he could get up. She was too tired to deal with him. That, or too bored. There was nothing to do, and she felt drained and listless. Wasn't sleeping well, tossing and turning. She wasn't a reader, like the van Burens, and she didn't knit, and Matt had declared that he was sick of checkers.

What she wanted to do was run, take a good jog around the ship; but Captain Esposito had ordered the passengers to stay inside the superstructure, where they could be accounted for. No one could see outside in the fog; if you got hurt, or fell overboard, they'd never be able to find you.

So she was reduced to working out in her cabin, and despite the fact that it was larger than Ruth's, it was still awfully cramped. But there was no way she'd exercise in front of the crew.

She pushed open the hatch and meandered down the companionway. It stood clear of fog (finally), and there was nothing on the deck.

She heard crying, from Ruth's cabin.

She got as far as making a fist to rap on the door; then she lowered her arm and walked on to her own cabin.

Despite Ruth's observation, she was not a social worker. Besides, some things—like grief—were private. Okay, maybe not for people like Lady Day. Damn, if she was going to be a singer, she was going to have to loosen up.

The foghorn blared and she barely flinched. They were all used to it.

She faced her door and got her key out of her shoulder bag. Her gun was in there, too—her old .38 and not the natty little Sig she packed on the job. She'd lied to the captain about carrying one—not too smart, she guessed, but she loathed the thought of giving it up unnecessarily. The guys aboard this ship weren't the brightest bunch she'd run across; what if one of them got put in charge of taking care of it?

She faced the door with her key in her hand. Paused. The crying next door was louder. Between sobs, Ruth was saying something over and over. Bad dreams. Again, Donna considered checking on her, again decided to leave her alone.

Let herself in and flicked on the light.

There. That wasn't so bad, was it?

Scratching her head, she dropped the shoulder bag on the bureau and yawned. She pushed off her sneakers and began unbuttoning her blouse. A wave of weariness washed over her, and she left it on, just too damn tired to mess with it. She blinked and yawned, then picked up her Walkman and put on her earphones, pressed Play.

"Strange fruit." Donna mouthed the words softly. She knew all Billie Holiday's songs by heart. Sang them in the bars. Hardly anyone knew who Billie was, but they liked the blues. Only Billie hadn't meant to sing the blues. Jazz. Jazz was where it was at, baby.

Quietly singing, she sat on the mattress and flopped backward like a diver into a pool. Christ, it was a gross song. About lynching black people in the Old South. Stuff about burning flesh. Shit, burning flesh. Donna didn't even use it; why did she even practice it?

Why did she practice at all? There was no call for girl jazz singers these days, despite all that bullshit elevator jazz they played on the radio. Yuppie jazz, she called it. Muzak for the thirty-something crowd. No guts, no glory, no modulation. Just processing.

She sighed and lay still. What did she know about guts anyway? She sang like a piece of cardboard.

Ship sounds filtered through as the number ended and the taped hissed and popped; white noise. She pulled the phones away from her ears for a few seconds and listened to the foghorn, the creaks of the ship, the groans of the containers, the sobs next door. Her mind drifted away; the bed bobbed beneath her like a pool float. The room tipped gently up and down. Donna tried to open her eyes. Had to get up, take off her makeup and her clothes.

Had to get up.

Billie sang in her ears. Donna's lids were stuck to her face. Heavy weights anchored her legs and arms in their places. Her chest rose two inches, fell one. Shallow, shallow.

She was spinning, spinning, spiraling downward into sleep. In her mind she could see herself going under. Okay. No problem.

Her chest rose. Fell. Images of the day washed through her mind as the other side of the tape clicked on. . . . *An ache . . . heavy as stone.* Sing it, Billie, yeah, I know about that. Do it, girl.

My heart has . . .
Not Donna's heart, though. No, ma'am.
an ache
Heavy weights.
Rhyme of the Dutchman, alone, alone. Dead birds in the
hallway. Frank, you sexy vampire. Bite me, big boy. Dutch-
man, haunt me, dude.
Had to get up.
And save the boy, poor boy; and her mom, so humiliated
after Dad left (always smacking her arm, saying, "Don't be a
big baby. Don't be a baby.").
Glenn . . .
Ghosts were people who haunted you, right? Then maybe
she did believe in them. Yes.
Yes.
Spin the bottle. Spin the bed. Spin it. Spin it good, just like
Devo. Spin it, spin it, the champagne girl is up for grabs.
With a slow, languid sigh, Donna sank,
down,
down,
down. Donna in Wonderland.
Alone, alone, all, all alone.
Hold your breath. Hold it good. Oh, yes, because if you
inhale, if you suck it in, if you do that . . .
. . . what?
Deeper, sleepier, don't forget to breathe.
'Night, moon. 'Night, Frank.
'Night, Glenn, my Glenn, wherever you are, good night,
good night—
Dutchman, haunt me.
As heavy as stone.
Something was happening to her . . .
Down,
down,
down. Hold it—
Freeze—
Blackness.

VI

April 13, 1797

She sent the bird to me! She sent it as a sign! I am free from the shroud, and the albatross has succored me!

And now she comes! She comes herself, for me!

From the bottle, for me!

9
Undertow

"Donna, c'mon, wake up!"

Donna jerked awake at once, automatically reaching for the drawer in her nightstand at home where she kept her .38.

She was on her bed in her cabin on the *Morris*. John's face hovered inches above her. Light from the companionway threw shadows onto his face like a jigsaw of bruises. His mouth moved, but a shrill, piercing whistle shot the sounds from the air, blasted the low cow moan of the foghorn. Shouts and footfalls rumbled past the open door. She whipped her head around; he grabbed her shoulder and said, "Donna, wake up. The ship is sinking."

"What?" She jumped up, forcing him to step backward. The Walkman thwacked against the nightstand. John stumbled and elbowed the bureau, knocking over an empty bottle of Coors. Caught in the sound vacuum, it plummeted to the deck and rolled toward the door.

She tore the earphones from around her neck and cupped her ears. She couldn't have heard him right.

"John?"

Sinking. She saw his lips form the words; his mouth was the color of paste, his face gray. Pushing up his glasses, he glanced to the door, where Ruth stood with her arm around Matt. The boy was sucking his thumb and holding her hand. Both of them had on fluorescent orange life jackets.

The bottle smacked the lip on the threshold and broke, the shatter insinuating itself between the whistles and the blaring and the stampede out on deck. The ship was canted, Donna realized. Listing badly, and that meant . . . that meant . . .

"It's going down," John yelled in her ear. She could barely hear him. "Captain Esposito's given the order to abandon ship."

In the corridor, Ramón sailed by, halted, and stuck his head in the door. He, too, had on a life jacket.

Someone lowered the volume outside and Donna was able to hear him. "Donna! Dr. Fielder! Put on your jackets." He eased Ruth and Matt out of his way. They moved as one person, clinging together. "*Rápido, rápido!* The lifeboats are being lowered. You must all hurry."

Donna rose, buttoning her blouse. She'd slept in her clothes and she felt clammy and grungy. "What the hell is going on?" To Ramón: "How?"

He held his hands from his sides and shook his head. "We hit something in the fog."

Ruth covered her mouth with both her hands. News to her, too, apparently. Above his fist, Matt's gaze darted toward his father, who went to him and hugged him against his chest.

"It wasn't another ship," Ramón went on. Under his breath, he added, "At least, we don't think so, *chingada.*"

"But I didn't feel anything," Donna said, watching numbly while Ramón trotted over to her closet and rattled through it. "Something like that, I would've woken up." And that piercing klaxon, that would've woken her up, too. It was inconceivable she'd slept through that.

Ramón turned from the closet and hurried around the end

of her bed toward the bureau. "You got a sweater? Coat? A hat would be very good."

Mr. Saar appeared in the companionway. "Moncho, everything square?"

Ramón opened the top drawer, turned away to address Saar. Donna crossed and put her hands in the drawer, on top of the sock with the bullets in it.

"We need two more jackets, Brian."

"Check." Mr. Saar dashed off toward the dining room.

"Where are the van Burens?" Donna asked, drawing a sweater from the drawer and slipping it on. She lost her balance and Ramón caught her arm.

"They're by the lifeboats. Someone's gone to get Kevin. Hurry." His eyes ticked. His hand was trembling.

He was scared shitless.

"Oh, my God, my God," Ruth croaked.

Donna picked up her purse and hoisted it over her shoulder. "Are you sure it's necessary to abandon ship? Can't whatever's wrong be repaired?"

Ramón bent down and scooped up her sneakers. "We'll take these with. Let's go."

"Ramón, answer my question," she demanded as she picked up the sockful of ammo and dropped it into her purse as unobtrusively as possible.

"The captain would never do a thing like this unless he had to." He lowered his gaze to her hands, looked up again.

"Let's go, then," she said, and everyone activated.

Outside the companionway, they trooped behind Ramón. Men squeezed past them, shouting at each other. Donna understood there was a lot of concern about the pumps, and then someone yelled, "Barney's dead!"

She tugged at Ramón's sleeve. He smiled grimly.

"One of our pumps. We named it Barney Clark." It took her a few seconds to connect the name with the man who'd gotten the artificial heart, how it had wheezed and clicked. She smiled grimly back.

"Brace yourself," Ramón said as they reached the end of the companionway and he stopped at a thick hatch like the one next to the dining room.

"What?" Donna asked, and then he opened the hatch and stepped over the lip.

The deck was a mass of confusion and hysteria. The crew was panicking. Men drenched with salt water flew up from the machine room. Pumps wheezed in counterpoint to the alarm bells and the foghorn. The patchwork castle of containers rumbled and clanged, and the thick metal lines that held them in place strained, ready to snap.

The fog had gotten thicker. She could see no more than a couple inches in front of her. When Ramón stepped away from her, she had a sickening sense that he'd fallen overboard. A thick, sheeny layer of moisture coated her like a facial mask. Her bare feet curled at the sensation of the cold, wet metal beneath them. She flashed on Ruth's Squishy Creature and wondered what it would feel like to step on it without any shoes. If there had ever been such a thing, which, of course, there had not.

"Everyone together?" Ramón's voice carried through the murk. Donna said, "I'm here." No one else answered. Her heart caught and she said, "Count off, everybody. One. Who's behind me?"

"It's me," Ruth said in a shrill voice. Fingers brushed the back of Donna's head. "I've got little Matty."

"John? John?" Donna demanded.

"Yes. Yes, I'm here."

A light flicked on in front of Donna. Vaguely she saw the outline of a man, a globe of yellow floating at the end of his arm.

"Follow the flashlight," Ramón said. "Hurry."

He aimed the beam to his right. Donna walked gingerly toward it, aware that now she was the leader. Walking into space, walking on the friggin' moon. She held her hands out like a tightrope walker to balance herself as a swell of vertigo tipped her right, left. Then his hand grabbed her outstretched wrist. A series of jumbled images—rowing, fishing, enduring —shot through her head, onetwothree, cannibals—

—real deep and back down her spinal cord, real jumbled, desert island and sex—

With a racketlike series of cricks, a shape dropped from

somewhere in the air and dangled parallel with the deck. Boat, wooden, about ten feet. Getaway car. Its silhouette jiggled out of focus in the under-deepsea fog.

"It's okay," Ramón said gently. "We have a radio, and rations and water. We got a man overboard pole. It'll be very safe."

"I'm not afraid," she said aloud, and as she spoke the words, she knew they were probably the biggest lie she'd ever told.

Except for the one she'd told Glenn: that there was nothing she'd do, ever, to hurt Barbara. If she got out of this, damn it, goddamn it to fucking hell, she was going to take him away from her. Life was too short for regrets.

"It's okay, *mi amor.*" Ramón pressed her hand. Saying nothing, she stepped into the lifeboat.

It swayed beneath her weight. The bottom was wet and slippery. Boxes and plastic containers were stored everywhere, and she stumbled over them.

"Here, *cara.*" Ramón handed her her shoes. "They're bringing you a life jacket."

She sat down with her shoes in her lap. The bottom of her jeans soaked through immediately. Her heart lumbered much more slowly than she'd have expected in a major crisis.

Below the boat, the fog pumped and bellowed. The ocean made wet, slurping noises, as if it were thirsty.

Blackness.

Thirst.

Donna whirled around. "Who the hell keeps saying that?"

"Cómo?" Ramón asked. *"Sí, mi hermosa. Sí, como es."* Donna understood enough Spanish to know he wasn't speaking to her. The boat swayed, and white, bony fingers lunged for her.

"Help, help!" Ruth cried. "I'm falling."

Donna squatted forward and took Ruth's wrists. The woman's face was an oval, nothing more. "You're okay. Just sit down."

"There are all kinds of things everywhere!" Her hands jerked in Donna's grasp. "I have to get back out!"

"Now, Ruth, just sit down," Donna said firmly. "Sit." She

reached for Ruth's forearm and steadied her down beside her on the bench.

Ruth hopped back up. "It's wet!"

"It's from the fog. It's all right."

"Matt is coming now." There was a whimpering. Ramón said, "Your papa is coming, too. There, you see? He won't let go of you."

More swaying. Matt got in, followed by John, and they huddled together soundlessly. Donna could hardly make out their shapes in the fog. God in heaven, how was anybody going to find them?

"Hey, dude," she said to Matt. "Gimme five."

Matt whimpered.

"Hey, it's going to be okay. Think about what you can tell your friends back home!"

"I don't have any friends," Matt replied, without a trace of self-pity.

"God, I did this. I did this," John blurted. A thick, deep sob rolled out of him.

"Maintain, father," Donna ordered him at the same time Ruth murmured, "There, there. There, there."

"I never should have . . ." John trailed off.

"It's going to be all right," Donna insisted. She reached for her shoes and forced the right one on, balancing herself with her toes against the bottom. It curved sharply. A solid boat, she told herself. A damn fine solid boat.

The ocean sucked the fog into its mouth, spewed out salt spray. Quickly Donna put on her shoes, all the while thinking that she'd probably stand a better chance if she didn't wear them; excess weight would only pull her down if they capsized.

The klaxon screamed, a shard of sound that sliced between her eyes and the bony ridge above them. Her ears vibrated. Ruth cried, "Why can't they shut that damn thing off? Everyone knows!"

"It's a distress call. For other ships," Donna said. She had to repeat it twice before Ruth heard her.

Another stampede of footfalls, and then Ramón said, "I have the life jackets for Donna and the doctor. Put them on immediately." He spoke to someone, shouted a response, and said "Motherfucker" in Spanish. Prickles of alarm chittered up Donna's arms and feet. What was he pissed off about? What was wrong?

"I am not getting in that thing." Ah, the van Burens had arrived.

"*Señora,*" Ramón began.

"I can't see, Daddy," Matty said.

"Shh. It's okay. It's like Disneyland." John's voice faltered. Matt said nothing.

"Can you imagine what that little boat will do in the ocean? How long is it? Eight feet? We'll capsize in ten minutes."

"Darlin', please." Phil, with his gentle Southern drawl.

"No."

"Elise, sweetheart, we must."

"Shut up!" The sound of a smack. Jesus. She must have hit him. "Shut up, shut up!"

"Listen, *mi hermosa,*" Ramón said gently, "last time I was in my cabin, the water was up to my knees. There's no way the pumps can work any faster. The cargo's starting to shift. That's more dangerous than the water we're taking on." As if to back him up, a scraping, screeching noise of metal on metal filled the air.

"We're a cargo vessel. Those containers weigh tons, *guerra.* Tons. And when tons shift, the load is unbalanced. And when it's unbalanced . . ." He took a deep breath. "It could slide sideways into the ocean and sink without a trace. Real fast."

Elise said, "My cabin was bone dry."

"That's because we're listing," Ramón said. "Come on, Mrs. van Buren. Just get into the boat."

"We're going to sue—"

Donna stepped forward. "Get into the fucking boat. Right fucking now!" she shouted, stepping over feet and boxes. She slung one leg over the side of the boat and anchored her foot on the deck. Reaching out, she found a slender wrist beside Ramón's ball of light and yanked.

"C'mon, c'mon, let's hustle!" Donna said, practically dragging Elise into the boat. "Phil, get your butt and your wife's butt in here!"

"No! No!" Elise shouted, flailing at Donna. Donna made a fist and aimed, and connected hard with Elise's cheek. The woman screamed, sagged, and collapsed into her husband's arms. Shit. Donna hadn't hit her *that* hard. And why wasn't someone besides Ramón helping them, for Christ's sake? Men were running everywhere, shouting orders, bellowing replies; the PA system crackled like a fire but the words it broadcast were indecipherable. If only someone would turn off all the damn extra noise, maybe the captain could make order of this chaos.

As if summoned by her thoughts, someone appeared next to Ramón. She saw the shadow in the flashlight. Phil and Elise sat numbly on the stern end of the boat. They were all facing each other, yet it was impossible to see anyone's face clearly through the fog. Going to sea with a boatload of phantoms.

"Ramón, since you're going first, Cap'n asked if you'd take Nemo." The miserable *rawl* of a cat.

"Nemo," Matt whispered.

"Sure thing," Ramón said.

"I'll hold her," Donna offered, reaching for the shape in the fog.

"Okay." Ramón carefully laid the cat in Donna's arms. The pregnant creature was sopping wet, and she fought as Donna gripped her on her lap. Her belly was distended and knobby. She meowed unhappily as Donna scruffed her behind the ears.

"Just don't have those kitties on the open sea," Ramón cautioned. Catching himself, he said, "We're in the shipping lanes. All the life rafts are equipped with distress beacons. Ours was activated when the boat slipped down the davits. I doubt we'll spend more than a couple hours out there, if that."

"Yes, of course," Donna said as the cat yowled and fought to get away. She dug her claws into Donna's upper thighs, "Shit!" Donna shouted, and held her tight. To her right, Matt was scrabbling into his father's lap. Poor darling. Poor baby. In a tiny boat on a stormy sea . . .

> *Alone, alone, all, all alone*
> *Alone on a wide, wide sea*

"Will you help me watch the cat?" she asked him through clenched teeth. "She's going to be a mommy and she needs a lot of care."

"She sleeps with me now," Matt said. His fingers brushed hers as he petted the cat. "She knows me."

Donna managed a smile. "That's good. Then you can let her know nothing bad is going to happen." And get her to stop shredding Donna's legs.

Matt's head moved. Donna bent down and kissed his cheek. His hand jerked. Then he stroked the cat, who calmed not in the least. Grimacing, Donna looked past him to John, who was clutching his stomach. Uh oh, seasick already.

"I don't suppose there's any Maalox with the rations?" he asked Ramón. "There are rations? And water?"

"Ahoy!" The voice of Captain Esposito boomed tinnily through the fog. "Are the passengers in their launch?"

"Aye, sir, just about. We're missing the *chico*, Kevin."

"We're putting him on the next boat. Prepare to cast off."

"But, sir . . ." There was surprise in his voice.

"Cast off, damn you! Put to sea!" The man's voice rose shrilly. "Get them away!"

Donna half rose, lifting the cat with her. "Kevin! Kevin!"

"Sit down." Ramón scrambled into the boat. "Everybody, sit down and stay down. We're going." He called, "We're off, sir."

Loud bangs hammered the hull as they flew alongside it. Cries inside the *Morris* became shrieks and screams. A loud hiss: oh, Jesus, steam. Donna shut her eyes, trying not to imagine scalded men. *Burning flesh.*

Drowning flesh.

Beside her, John murmured, "Holy Mary, Mother of God, blessed art Thou among women."

A Catholic, she thought vaguely. And she thought he was Jewish.

In her mind she saw drowning men, their eyes goggly like fish as they fought and clawed to get up the ladders and away from the water. Spinning slowly in their orbits, like a floating boy, like the wheel of fortune.

The waves crashed against the hull of the lifeboat. Jesus, how far above the water were they? The passengers tensed like a bunch of rodeo cowboys leaping onto the backs of wild bulls.

"Hold on!" Ramón said. He pressed something else and a loud pop filled the boat.

The cat screamed and clawed Donna's forearms. Donna clutched her hard, and the cat worked her furiously. Elise sat frozen with Phil's arms around her. Ruth twisted in the boat, gripping on to the gunwale. Matt cowered against his father, and John's voice rose—

"Pray for us now, pray for us—"

Donna conjured up a bizarre image of a Neptune Cowboy God, prodding the ocean's flanks with his trident cattle prod, poke that baby, that monster, that sucker, that thrashing mother!—

—and then they hit the water.

They roller-coastered away from the *Morris,* mountain, valley, abyss, Mt. Everest. Matt screamed and screamed and screamed. The boat spun in a circle, around and around like a carnival ride. The cat guttered Donna's arms as she rolled with the frenzy, gasping, "It's okay, kitty. It's okay, kitty. It's okay."

A wall of black and gray, inky and poisonous, earthquaked around them. With a rush of panic, Donna realized that though the *Morris* was five hundred feet long, she couldn't see the hull, or the superstructure, or the hundreds of containers that rattled and roared like caged beasts.

Rub-a-dub-dub, they swirled around and around, shot up, down. They were drenched, screaming, praying. Irrationally, Donna focused all her attention on hanging on to the cat, who fought her every inch of the way. Up and down, roller-coaster city, up and down, almost too far down into the trenches of the waves. The stern dipped underwater, scooping up cold sea and brittle kelp and throwing them into the boat.

Ruth screamed and said, "It's in here with us!" Donna pursed her lips and held on more tightly to the cat.

"It's okay, kitty, okay, kitty, okay, you little fucker," she said over and over. "Goddamn it, stop scratching me."

The lifeboat teetered on top of a wave like a surfer on a board. Donna held her breath as the others shrieked. If it tipped over, they'd topple out. When had she put on her life jacket? She didn't remember doing it. A quick check showed that John's was on, too.

John was groaning like a wounded animal. He sounded like Nemo, in fact. Donna shouted, "Hey, you hurt?"

". . . fine. Just my ulcer," he said between moans. She nodded as though it made sense. *Hey, you okay? Yeah, I'm just swimming around in the middle of the ocean here, and I've got a little cramp. But it's nothing serious. Can't see land, and I'm running out of steam* (oh, God, the steam on the *Morris*) *but hey, don't sweat it.*

The boat pitched and yawed as though taunting them. Then it shot down the front of the wave and splattered into the trench. Gushes of water rained down on the passengers. Elise and Phil were getting the brunt of it, but Elise hadn't said a word. They were hidden from her; she prayed to God they were still in the boat (and not their sacrifice. Christ, she was sorry she'd joked like that. It sure as hell wasn't funny now.).

"Oh, please, oh, please," Ruth murmured as the boat shimmied and shuddered. "Please, if I have to go, let it be here. Oh, Stephen."

"Ruth, honey, cool it," Donna grunted, squeezing Nemo with one hand as she hung on with the other.

"But he warned me. I felt it."

"Mmm."

Abruptly the waves flattened against the surface, slamming everyone against the floorboards and the gunwales. Nemo screeched and tried to free herself; Donna, clinging to her, was bumped off her seat and almost pitched over the side.

Let go of the goddamned cat, she told herself, before it registered that the storm, or whatever it had been, was over.

The fog billowed with sighs, groans, the tabby's claws injecting Donna with cat-scratch fever.

"Everyone okay?" Ramón's flashlight snapped on. He scooted off his seat into the bottom of the boat and fumbled around for a few seconds. "Supplies are still secured," he said. "Everything's fine."

"Bullshit," Elise snapped. Donna found it within herself—a total miracle—to guffaw. The broad was all right! "Oh, you shut up! I'm going to—"

Donna couldn't see her, but she felt a rush of air as Elise threw back her hand for a punch. A brief struggle, as Phil, perhaps, held her arm.

"Sorry I hit you." Donna made herself feel sincere.

"You're going to be sorrier!"

"Listen," Ruth cut in. "Listen!"

No one moved as all obeyed the urgency in her voice.

No foghorns. No alarm sirens.

Ramón shouted, "Ahoy!"

Nothing.

After a few seconds, Ramón crossed himself.

Donna's mouth dropped open. "We can't have moved very far away from it. Not yet."

"Oh, my Lord," Ruth whispered. "It can't have gone down."

John half rose. "There might be men in the water. We should search for—"

"Sit the fuck down!" Ramón bellowed. "It didn't go down. Don't be an asshole. We would have felt the suction. We . . . we would have known."

No one said anything. Donna knew, however, that she wouldn't have known. Not while they were riding the beast . . . and why had it stopped? Was that from the *Morris* going under?

Jesus. Jesus. Tears welled in her eyes. Jesus. That couldn't have happened. It just couldn't. Maybe all of this was a nightmare. Maybe she was back in Tahoe, and the kid hadn't died, either. She'd had a cold; this could be a fever dream. The

John beside her was a doctor; maybe she'd included him in this sick fantasy because a real Dr. John hovered over her sickbed at a Tahoe infirmary. The hospital visit compliments of Daniel, her Caesar's pickup, who was a nice guy after all, happily ever after.

"If it hasn't gone down, why can't we hear it?" Phil said. "We can't be more than fifty feet away from it, if that."

"It's okay, *hombre*." Ramón spoke through clenched teeth. Lowering himself off the bench, he duckwalked toward the stern. Donna scooted herself and the cat aside. Ramón sat next to her.

"We're in the shipping lanes. Another freighter will come by and pick us up soon."

No one spoke. Donna scrutinized the wall of fog for a big, black shadow, a hulk of gray, anything.

"She didn't go down. We'd be able to tell," Ramón insisted.

"How?" John shouted at him.

"What do you want me to do?" Ramón draped his hands between his knees. "What can I do?"

"Turn back," John said.

For a moment the fog blustered in a swirl, and Donna clearly saw the disbelief on Ramón's face. Also the despair. She understood: there was no way for them *to* turn back, even if they knew which direction they were moving in.

Matt sniffled. "Hey." Ramón reached across Donna and John with a hand toward him. Matt flinched inside the protective cocoon his father had made of his own body. "Hey, we gonna be okay. Would I let anything happen to a cool dude like you? This is like how the Vikings sailed. Remember I told you about them?"

"The *Morris* caused this fog," Elise said with certainty. "You were carrying something you weren't supposed to. I know all about it."

There was silence. Donna's lips parted and she turned toward Ramón, whom the fog had once again concealed. She heard him sigh deeply.

"What's this?" Donna demanded.

"The cargo. There was some kind of toxic waste in the cargo," Elise said.

Another silence. Then Ramón finally spoke. "It wouldn't have caused this."

Donna grabbed his arm. "What? *What* wouldn't have caused this?"

"Nothing—"

"Don't try to bullshit me," she said harshly, digging her nails into his biceps.

"*Ay,*" Ramón protested. "It was just some stuff." Gasped as Donna dug deeper.

A sigh. "Who told you?" Ramón asked Elise.

A beat, then: "Cha-cha. Just before we left the ship. He was laughing. He was—"

"Cha-cha?" Phil laughed nervously. "Cha-cha told you there was something toxic aboard? That's just ridiculous, honey."

"But they did, you idiot. You never listen. He just admitted it. Didn't you? Didn't you?"

"We had something . . . that wasn't on the manifest." Ramón paused, and there was confusion in his voice. "But Cha-cha didn't know about it."

"Holy shit." Donna gripped tighter. "Goddamn it, what the fuck was it?"

"Some . . . some stuff in barrels." The fog thinned again, to reveal Ramón's deep-set Latin eyes, studying Donna's shoulder bag. Oh, God, was he thinking about her gun?

She pulled the bag tight against her body and glared at him. "Go on."

He ran his fingers along his thigh. "I told you. It was nothing."

She put her hand in the bag. The others were staring at the two of them. Nemo mewed. Somewhere above them, something made a noise that could have been the shriek of a bird. Beneath them, something bumped into the boat, once, twice, stopped. Elise cried out and moved to a different part of the bench.

Donna glared at Ramón. He smiled weakly at her. "It wasn't nothing, okay?" His accent was thick now, pure East

Los Angeles. She stiffened her jaw and put her hand around the revolver. There was no safety on it, of course. .38 Specials don't have safeties.

She had only shot one man in her entire life, and once was enough. But Ramón didn't need to know that.

"You'd better find some way to tell me we weren't set up," she gritted. "Because what I'm afraid of, what I'm worried about, Mr. Ramón, is that you guys had something you weren't supposed to, and the plan was to dump it in the ocean and scuttle the *Morris*."

"No!" he cried.

"Oh, my God," Ruth said in an underbreath.

"No, it wasn't nothing like that. It wasn't nothing that bad. We had some guys in Hawaii." He hunched his shoulders, started to raise his hand, glanced down at the purse, and shook his head. "Cha-cha didn't know."

"Yes, he did," Elise cut in. She was livid. "He most certainly did."

"Tell me what it was," Donna said.

Ramón shrugged. "I don't know. Honest. It was from a company that works for the military." Sweat trickled from his temple and slid down the side of his chin. "They couldn't get a permit."

"You bastards!" Elise lunged at Ramón, startling the cat off Donna's lap. It darted beneath the beach, meowing. Matt started to cry again. Ruth screamed and cried, "Please, please!"

In a blind instant of fury, Donna began to raise her hand out of her purse, stopped herself. Thank God it wasn't loaded. Thank God.

Ramón raised his hands as if she had drawn on him. "You know what a death ship is?" Donna hissed at him. "They make it look like an accident to collect the insurance, don't they?"

"We didn't do that!" he shouted, looking at the others, for backing, for mercy.

"Is that what Cha-cha told you?" Ramón asked Elise. His voice shook hard. He didn't lower his hands. He'd been arrested before, Donna realized. He wasn't as sleek and suave as he acted.

"Cha-cha," Donna cut in. "How convenient to have a first-class nutcase aboard. Guy who always talks about sinking the boat. Does he have a deal with you? You guarantee him a cut? A room with a view? What?"

"He didn't know. I swear he didn't." Lowering his hands, he held them out beseechingly, gaze darting around the boat, making eye contact with each person. "He always talked like that. We weren't . . ." He quieted. "You'll never believe me."

Donna licked her lips. Someone was crying. "That doesn't matter anyway. We can assume it's been dumped. You did your job."

And the thirsty ocean had swallowed whatever the *Morris* had provided for it.

And what else have we given it, John thought as they drifted, through the years and the centuries? Tons and tons of spoiling food, sewage, half-degraded biodegradables. Embalming fluid. Hypodermic needles dripping with experimental serums; Petri dishes wild with recombinant DNA; nerve gas . . .

Nuclear waste. All carefully cataloged, responsibly contained, legally and safely disposed of.

He knew of many things they should not pour into the ocean. In his quest for a cure, he had created some of them.

God, what a world.

What an ocean. No matter it was angry with them. He thought of another line from the Coleridge poem about the Ancient Mariner: *The very deep did rot.* Ah, yes, with the stink and contamination of the human race, imposing itself upon nature in the classic Western way: subdue the earth. Subdue it.

Ruin it.

He took a breath to clear his head; he couldn't allow himself the luxury of poetic despair. His child was in danger.

But maybe the waste *had* caused the fog. He remembered how it had run over the ship, clung to it for days. And now that they had moved away from the *Morris* (or so one had to assume, or at least pray, was true) the fog had thinned considerably. Oh, it was still with them, and at times it thickened and hid them from each other, but by and large it remained in the bottom of the boat and spilled over the side. Most of the time, they all could see each other, for which he was profoundly grateful. He thought he would go crazy if he couldn't see their faces.

The water began to churn again. Up and down, way up, sliding into the chute of water. Waves shaped like orange slices scratched at the boat and Matt burrowed into him like a monkey, hanging around his neck, their life jackets separating them like two pop beads. John gripped him so hard he feared he would crack Matty's bones.

"Daddy," Matty whispered. "Daddy, please."

"It's okay, baby. We've got our life jackets on and we're in a boat that's sending out a secret code like an SOS to all the ships everywhere on earth. Isn't that right, Ruth?"

Wordlessly she nodded. Come on, come on, help me out, he chided her. She hung on to the side of the boat with both hands, probably a wise precaution. If a wave came up, it might bounce them out, into the liquid disgust they had made of the water . . .

Dear God in Heaven, please. Please, for Matt.

"It's going like this." John covered his nose and mouth with his hand and made his voice low and mysterious. "Double-o seven, come get Matt. He's twenty-six latitude by fifty-one longitude. Got on his raddest shirt. Hair's too long."

Matt didn't smile. His big eyes danced in front of John as the boat bobbed over the waves.

John shifted his gaze from his child to Donna, who was swiping blood off her arms. Good Lord, the cat had done a job on them. Long, angry cuts a quarter-inch deep ran from the insides of her elbows to her wrists.

"Salt water," he said.

She took a long look at the water. Made a face. Something down there, maybe, something you couldn't get a permit for, and he was telling her to clean her wounds with it. He tried to form an explanation about parts per million, dilution; he knew she'd tell him that was a load of crap or horseshit or something else equally demure. Cops possessed amazingly crude vocabularies.

"Well, shit," she murmured, turning around on her knees. With an elbow over her purse, he noted. She started splashing the ocean onto her arms. Grimaced but said nothing.

"Next time, go directly across the wrists," he advised. "It'll be quicker."

She even managed a laugh. She was a pistol. She and Ramón had made a truce of sorts, at least for the duration of their stay in the lifeboat. There was something in her purse that made Ramón nervous and her more secure. A gun. Of course.

"Well," she said briskly, getting comfortable again and wiping her hands on her shirt. "What shall we do? Play charades? Sing 'Row, Row, Row Your Boat'?"

"You are so low class," Elise spat. "So—"

Phil put a hand on his wife's arm.

"Let's just settle back, shall we?" Ruth suggested. "We can sing later."

The cat warbled plaintively. Matty shifted on John's lap. Slid between his legs onto the bottom of the boat.

"The kitty's scared." He reached toward the shadows beneath the opposite side of the bench. A paw slashed; the cat yowled long and low and hard.

John had a horrible thought:

If the food ran out . . .

Kittens for breakfast.

His stomach burned as if he'd swallowed a flaming torch. He caught his breath and laid his hand across it.

"It's okay, dear," Ruth murmured to him.

Grace under pressure. He admired that.

Envied it.

Needed it.

When does a man have to be more than a man?

Right now, buckwheat.

Right now.

His stomach, a lava bed. He clenched his jaw and nodded at Ruth.

"I'm fine."

And you're finer, lady. We get out of this, I'm going to marry you. And Donna, too. Matt and I need as many mommies as we can get.

He looked at Donna through the fog. Her hand was in her purse and her fingers were moving around. He could see the ripples of her knuckles in the leather.

Jesus, Mary, and Joseph. She was loading her gun.

II
TREADING
WATER

10

On Course: Damp Bodies

Not alone, not alone, not alone at all, on the wide, wide sea. The sea that is ruled by invitation only; the sea that awaits your RSVPs, a thousand times a thousand.

Yes, you are not alone.

As you sleep in the lifeboat, dear, dear Ruth, with your crew mates; as you drift merrily along (quoth he, a most, heh-heh, inviting man, oh, captain, your captain), as you sleep as I once did, open your heart and let me read it. And listen, me beauty, as I have listened to you. Attend to the message in the bottle that is for you, just for you. The one your fogbound heart has been praying to read. The one I have written just for you, because I heard you first,

oh, my dear Ruth, the one that is just for you:

This is how it will be when you drown:
You won't inhale any water. That doesn't always happen.
When you drown dry, your glottis reflexively closes tight—

airtight—and, ironically, you can't breathe at all. No air goes in, nor out. It's only later, much later, that the water creeps into your lungs,
>on little
>cat
>feet.

Peaceful, and purring, and gentle, it doesn't hurt at all, my darling. And the undertow doesn't yank at you. That's a misconception. You never feel a thing. The water curls around you, fuzzy cattail, a harmless garden snake. As the panic sets in, remember that, Ruth, my love: the snake is a friend.

And the garden is beautiful.

Remember the marshes where . . . we . . . went bird-watching? The reeds and the cattails. The fog-gray pussy willows. Remember how you and . . . I . . . brought a bag of Fritos and somehow, the Coppertone bottle got uncapped, and we joked about dipping the chips in suntan lotion?

We capsized the boat with our laughter. It tipped right over, and your coat spread over the water like a sodden pair of wings. I called you the yellow-hooded water-treader. And we laughed, though the weight of the coat dragged you under, no matter how hard you treaded. You grabbed the Coppertone bottle as if it were a life ring, and we laughed and laughed—

The boat tipped over, Ruth. That was how he—

How I—

But look, my darling. Look. This is how it will be when you drown:

And suddenly, Ruth was gliding into veils of pale jade and cat's-eye green and henna that parted as she floated through them, tissues and oval tubes, and flat, silky ropes. The water around her shimmered deep blue, sparkling with golden sun, gilding the backs of her wintry hands, the autumn leaves of kelp.

Beautiful, beautiful.

The sun filtered through the curtains; they lifted, and she gasped. Kaleidoscopes of colors spun in slow motion as she descended toward them: carpets of orange, violet, scarlet, pink, yellow, fans of carnation and white; fuzzy velvet shapes like hands that waved at her, tender crimson, shy, muted lavender. Hello, hello. Hello.

And fish, in riots of color no marsh bird ever sported: parrot-red and forest-green; robin-scarlet; the iridescent cobalt of a peacock; tendril fairy coronets like those of crown cranes. Jellyfish washed with the peach-blush of cockatiels.

Welcome. Welcome, Ruth, who desired.

And desire, being a kind of Spirit, anguished yearning, and prayers made of tears were enough to bring her to this place. It was enough to call him to her side; him—

Ruth shifted, hazily aware of her own confusion. Who? Who, Stephen? Was it Stephen who spoke?

Oh, but see the walls of coral, curving through the water into inlets, coves, and forests; and harems and grottoes, reclining and opening before her. Glossy towns, and cities; and in the center of the universe, shielded by a lacy canopy, nestled on a pillow of rainbow anemones, a green-colored moray eel coiled in repose.

A bottle-green eel.

A glass snake.

The creature's skin glistened like wet lips as the water caressed it. Waves of light rippled on its scales. As Ruth drew near, it opened its eyes. Rubies, rare and perfect, glittered in the sockets as it sleepily raised its head and watched her. She could see through its body, see the spinal cord, the teeth.

It reached toward her.

The snake is a friend—

A man's hand moved through the dreamsea beside hers. The wide, flat back, the long, tapering fingers. On the ring finger, a simple gold band—

—inside, inscribed simply, *"Forever."* It was his wedding ring.

We will laugh again.

Stephen. Oh, Stephen. Tears rolled from Ruth's eyes and skinnied down the aqueducts of her heavily lined face. She put her hand in his, warm and wet and hard fingers sliding against her palm. In the world beneath the surface.

Beneath the water.

*   *   *

And a voice said unto her, in her dream:
Christen the vessel, Ruth.
What?
And everything flashed away from her, in a cloud of dust on the ocean floor.
Give Her a name, and a shape, and a form.
Groggy, she opened her eyes. She lay in the lifeboat, her shipmates sprawled around her. Donna's curly black head rested on the shoulder of John, the doctor. His glasses had slid to the base of his nose. Elise and Phil sprawled like puppets whose strings had been severed. Ramón, his head drooping over the side of the boat, his chest arched as if for that last, final breath.

Matty, curled against her breast, sucking his thumb in his sleep, and Ruth held him tightly—

No, she didn't. That was part of another dream. Matty was actually across the boat, too far away to touch.

The world went hazy, as though she were peering through a cloud, a gray mushroom cloud of fog. Like the light the doctor shines in your eyes during an exam, and the world dandelions around the brilliant yellow, as you peer into a black-hole sun.

You're dreaming, she told herself, but she didn't think she was. Hallucinating, then, of Stephen, or maybe of someone very like him. It was confused now, and no wonder. The terror of their situation must surely be the cause of it. Incredible to accept, that she was cast adrift on the same sea—that vast mouth of sea, hungry and . . .

No. No. She blinked, hard. She was so disoriented she didn't know what was happening, and what she was imagining. As in her cabin that day.

Yes, as in her cabin that first foggy day, when *someone* had told her to open the porthole, and she had seen . . . what had she seen? She couldn't remember. But she did remember how the desire—

—even now, something about desire clung to her mind—

—to leave the ship had almost been insurmountable. She

could never have told Donna she had been dreaming about jumping off the *Morris,* could she?

Within the lifeboat, the world swam with dark silhouettes and a shifting gauze of gray; like a bad pair of binoculars or a movie projector lens out of focus. Images shifted fuzzily before her:

In her hand, she saw, but didn't see, a bottle. It was, but wasn't, green. And it was, but wasn't, encrusted with chunks of precious stones around the neck.

And there was a note inside, addressed to her.

Oh, yes, there was. Of that she was suddenly sure; as she looked down at her hand everything shifted into hard, true reality and she saw that she actually did hold the most beautiful of bottles. It must have fallen into the boat, or perhaps one of the others had brought it along—some treasure, an expensive perfume bottle, a champagne bottle for a celebration.

Or to christen a vessel.

She jerked. Why had she thought of that? Why did it sound familiar?

She peeled off the gooey outer coating—wax?—and shook out a piece of thick, yellowed paper. It was decorated with a skull and crossbones, and there were words in an elaborate scroll that read,

The Captain, H.M.S.?

As she puzzled over this, she heard a voice inside her head: *We need a name. We need a life.*

Then something flapped hard against the back of her head, oozy and ice-cold; she screamed and fell forward; something dug into her skull with a sharp, piercing cut that made her grunt low in her belly. With a limp hand she flailed behind her; but her head was so cold; her brains were freezing; she was losing herself, going

down,

down,

down, into the hazy place; she saw, and couldn't see; smelled, and couldn't smell; touched, and couldn't touch—

—the neck of the bottle as it slipped through her fingers and wound around her waist, spiraling in a slow dance around and around; it raised its head and looked at her with jeweled eyes, opened its mouth. A waxy coating of yellowed white dripped from its teeth—no, its fangs—in large bubbles toward her lap—

The world turned, around and around. The bubbles bounced inches from her face; floated sideways past her nose; stretched down, down, toward her forehead—

And the bubbles popped above her as they reached the surface that glowed above her once more, above her sea-dream world and the man of her dreams. And there he was. There, he was, and she was joyful, in a loose, disconnected way. Her happiness was expended practically before she felt it; it was diluted, dissolving.

But there he was. And as she reached for him, the world rippled and she saw—

Yes, she saw—

But Stephen, what happened to your beautiful hand?

Death and decay, it rotted away.

No. No, no, no. She writhed in horror as the gold band sank into the black and purple and the bloat—

She turned her head and saw his face, a horror of rot, and the lips that chunked from the skull as they spoke, and the purple-black fingers pointed to the bottle in her hand:

Ruth, quick, Ruth, hurry. Christen us. Dip us in the water with the force of your need; baptize us in the name of your Spirit and make it so, make it real—

She looked toward the surface and effortlessly rose to meet it. And then, just as effortlessly she was inside the life-boat, dry as a bone. Steaming through the fog, the huge car-cass of the *Morris* bleated and bellowed. Layers of mist rose from the water and strangled the ship, smothering the hull and the outside deck and the superstructure—

—And a huge, grinning face dancing in triumph at the top of the bottle, the huge glass bottle that had entrapped the *Morris.* Gazing down at its wild work, then out at Ruth, with eyes that were whirlpools; and in them, fleets of ships strug-gled and sank: square-rigged vessels and gray frigates and pleasure yachts, and rafts and kayaks and deep-sea vessels, drowning in a pirate skull and crossbones that tipped its head back, tipped it back to show the emptiness inside it, and laughed and laughed.

The fog gathered and thickened until the ship was invisible. The bottle pitched and rolled, and the sound of something huge battering its sides buffeted Ruth's ears like the explosions of bombs. Screams and shouts and wails rose like a single membrane of smoke toward the stopper on the bottle, and pushed, and pushed. Cries for help, and prayers, that pushed, and pushed.

The cork popped out. And something streamed out with it, black and grotesque, tentacled and clawed, reeking of the grave; something flew into the fog and spread itself over the horizon. A single howl, like that of a wolf.

A caw of a bird. A dead man's laugh.

Ruth quailed. Evil, evil. A demon genie had escaped. The ills of the world . . . an old story popped into her head. That woman, the curious one, the Greek—

Pandora? Done!

Immediately, the bottle shattered. Walls of glass shot into the fog and rained into the sea, churning the depths. Sheets of glass, rods of it, chunks as thick as cars, as sharp as guillotines, plummeted within inches of the lifeboat. The water frothed as pieces like transparent knives pitched headlong beneath the surface. Gulls shrieked like harpies across the rising waves. The ocean boiled with agony.

We will laugh again, Ruth.

And everything vanished.

Ruth—in a dream that had to be real, a delusion that had to be happening—sank into stillness.

And you, Dr. John Fielder? Do you dream of us as well? Can the fog creep inside you and make you set sail for us? Let us see what dreams may bring you bobbing to our harbor:

Beneath the surface, John huddled in the white box. The sides flaked mint-green paint that caught and eddied in the water. The fit was tight; he could hardly move, or breathe. That didn't matter; he was afraid to do either—although somehow, he could breathe if he wanted.

Something undulated at his temple. He jerked, forced himself to remain motionless. The something crawled along his skin. Inside his head, he managed a weak, sick laugh: the dark brown thing, so threatening, was a lock of his own hair.

Christ, he thought, and then he had no thoughts, only a sliding fear as the light appeared, parallel with his chest. A hundred fathoms away in the water, or maybe just an inch, it glowed dimly in the icy blackness. His stomach clutched and he flattened himself against the frigid, hard surface. He'd prayed he'd be safe there.

He was a fool.

The watery light made a circle. His heart contracted and he held himself rigid. Ice floated around his knees, his belly. His bare skin glistened a pale blue, as if throwing off a reflection of sky and clouds.

But the things that bobbed overhead weren't clouds; they were icebergs, a field of rock-hard thunderheads. Thousands of sparkling dots rained from them, ocean snow, diffusing the light into a poisonous yellow mist. Moving only his eyes, he watched the things. His hair wafted in the water, and brought images of tentacles, and air hoses, and heavy, weighted chains.

Will this be how I drown? Yet he breathed; he lived.

A stinging jab pricked his shoulder; another, the inside of his elbow. Another, another, another. At the perimeter of his nipple, blood welled into a pin dot. He winced, forcing himself not to squirm. Spots of blood rose on his body like a disease—

like that disease—

—then ran together to crease into long, paper-thin cuts. The sharp-edged things bounced off his arms, his legs, his feet, drifted downward. One landed on his cheek, pinched, swirled in a current. Shards of glass, hundreds of them, razor-sharp.

He flailed at them, and found something jutting from the sides of the box. Handholds. A shelf. He tried to hold on to the outcropping. Beneath his palms, wood splintered and softened. It broke into waterlogged chunks that pirouetted in upward spirals past his shoulders, mingling with the glass and his blood. The bits of wood separated into fibers; he found himself thinking of tuna and the way it flaked when he made sandwiches for—

for—

The fear slid thickly into his guts, spreading through his veins. Oh, God, where was Matty?

His heart blasted against his spine. His pulse roared. The skin on his face tightened as he pressed his lips together. The hard surface chilled his backbone. Vibrations roiled through the water, sending the bone-soup into a counter-current.

His boy, his boy, where was his boy?

Daddy, here I am!

Matty appeared before him, chubby-cheeked, blooming with health. He stood in the water, and yet he didn't; he stood on the deck of a ship, a sleek white ship whose deck was varnished wood, and yet he didn't. Behind him, a rail coursed around tiki torches that cast warm shadows on his face; neon lights set into the deck lit Matt from below.

But the figure beside his child remained shadowed, dark, indistinct. It held Matty's hand and looked at John.

Matty waved excitedly. *Here I am!*

Healthy and happy and full of life.

Full.

forever.

Ah, yes, good doctor. A noble desire. A passionate yearning. Yes, that will suffice.

Laughter reverberated over the water.

And you others:

Here, Ramón Diaz. This can be how dying can be for you, if I so desire:

Like a stream, trickling down the center of your heart. Wearing away the earth of your life with a wet, sugar tongue and a gentle tickle; until you cave in from the breastbone, and all the clay that you are mixes with the sea. Your guts, like man-of-war jellyfish, disembodied hearts pulsing along, along, along.

For you, Phil: like a still pond of water, into which you knowingly step, lie down, and cross your arms. Our martyr, our Ophelia. Or will you become a man at the end, and fight?

Or for you, Elise, you who savor your seething discontent like those cigarettes you smoke: a death like the ocean, brutal, fierce, and merciless. Sweeping over you in galvanic fury, flinging into your face your insignificance as you thrash and go under. Your helplessness. The fact that you have no power, that you can be torn into pieces so easily, so wonderfully. Think of it. Think of your arms, wrenched from their sockets. Your eyes, ripped from theirs. Or perhaps your skull will be bashed into a pulp, and the bits of your brain extracted like seeds from an overripe papaya, and fed to the sharks.

Yes, or we will hang you from the side of the ship, yes, hang you so they can leap from the water and gnaw at you. Shins first, toes. Or upside down, so they will mar your beauty first. Have you ever seen a woman whose nose and lips have been chewed off?

Have you ever met the kind of man who could do it?

Who has done it?

Yes, yes, oh, yes.

So nice you can join us. So nice.

And as for you, Donna Almond . . .

Half-asleep, Donna put her hand around the barrel. Happiness was a cold gun. When she pulled herself together, she'd unload it. Everyone was behaving very well, no chance of mutiny or cannibalism with this set. Of course, they'd only been at sea for a day, and the belief in being rescued was strong at this point.

Her gun ferried ammo across the ocean, but the safety was on, even though a .38 Special didn't have one.

She was the safety.

Her cheekbone fitted nicely against John's shoulder, and she sighed, allowing herself to drift closer back toward sleep. Plenty of food and water, and flares, and the signal would lure someone to them. Everything was copacetic, as Glenn would say.

Glenn. Fuck it. When she got home, she was going to ask for a transfer. It was the only answer. Okay, that was okay. There were other shoulders in the sea. Even now, she was vaguely horny, nuzzling John, young Dr. Kildare. He was a bit timid, but he had such a capacity for caring. And he could patch her back together whenever the streets got vicious. She bet he sewed stitches tight and small, less chance of scarring. Yeah.

Back to sleep now, Donna. You can sort all this later. Now listen, this is how it will be when—

That fucker, Ramón. She would get his ass and get it good. Sue the hell out of them? She'd get them put away for life. Life imprisonment. Yeah.

This is how it will be—

Ramón in a cell. Yeah. Ramón in a big glass box. Ramón under glass, his nuts in a fingerbowl. Right on. Right on, right on, right fucking on.

Sleep, now, old girl. Sic him later. She chuckled to herself, silently, because sic sounded like suck, and after all, she was a cop with a nasty mind. A sleepy, incoherent, but still nasty—

LISTEN!

Sleep now. Yeah. Man, she was cold.

GODDAMN YOU, LISTEN TO ME! WHEN YOU DROWN, THIS IS HOW IT WILL BE WHEN YOU DROWN. AND YOU WILL! YOU WILL DIE!

Sighing, she let herself go.

YOU BITCH! LISTEN—

Swimming parallel, with the safety on.

11
Boarded

Swim parallel.

Dreaming, Donna fought her panic down as she kicked her arms and legs, but it was hard to stay calm when the world was nothing but endless, heartless gray. She made a circle in the water. There was nothing to see. Water, water, everywhere, no lifeboat, no *Morris,* no people. Nothing to cling to, nothing to save her. She was alone, alone, all, all alone.

She took a hard breath as the undertow grabbed her ankles and yanked her into colder, thicker water the color of lampreys and sharks. Wind whipped her hair from her forehead, frozen and harsh; if she didn't drown, she would freeze. She shook so hard the muscles in her legs and stomach twisted into throbbing cramps.

The waves surged around her, crashing over her head and forcing her under the surface. She choked down filthy, icy water that shot down her throat and stung her lungs; it gathered in her abdomen like an anchor and dragged her down,

down,
down.

There was death in there, a million parts per million's worth. She must get out, or it would kill her.

She tried to tread water, but she was too tired. Never in her life had she been so exhausted. She couldn't raise her thighs, couldn't move her wrists. As she surveyed the gray sea, the gray sky—

—why, it was fog, all around her; she was swimming in fog!—

—she knew she was going to go under once too often, and not come back up, and then it would be over, all over.

No! She stirred. Dreaming, she told herself. She was only dreaming. The realization should have comforted her, but it did not, as she struggled and gagged and slipped under again.

Something bumped her hip.

What do you want? The same voice she had heard on the *Morris* and yet, not the same. A voice to fear.

But not as much as that other voice. That other, that one that had spoken of thirst and darkness.

Or had it been a different voice?

What was happening?

Bile rose in her throat. Something cold slithered over her. In her sleep she imagined it was a shadow crossing the sun. She tensed, balling her fists. Or dreamed she did. The coldness crept over her face, over the top of her head, and then someone drilled a hole in her forehead and poured ice water over her brains.

Evil, evil. Something grotesque seeped inside all the cracks and weakest places; God, it was going to fucking kill her with its stinging, razored ice.

What do you want?

"Nnnothing—" she managed, as her brain froze over.

Then she heard a scream, followed by a gurgle, and she whipped around on top of a huge wave. Disoriented, she cried out. Water rushed into her mouth. Dreaming, she reminded herself.

The little Lake Tahoe floater struggled at the base of it, eyes huge with terror. He sank; for a moment, she saw his red mittens, the hood of his black and red ski jacket, so lost, so hopeless, as the wave rose up, up, like a wall of gray stone, and folded back on itself, and crashed over him. Donna was carried with it, and she flailed for him as she slammed back down. But seaweed tied her hands and feet; she was helpless, and then something hard smacked her at the base of her skull, and all faded from whale-gray, to pewter-gray, to the blackest of black terror, grief, remorse.

"Unh, unh," she stammered. Dreaming, damn it, dreaming.

And yet, *real*, as she pulled herself free, arms and legs wrenching from the kelp of the undersea forest, and sped toward the surface, unhindered. The boy was not her fault, not; these things happen—

NO! someone shouted, at the same time that she forced her eyes open and raised her head off John's shoulder.

In the fog, a shape the size of a sea serpent hurtled toward them. Muzzily, she gripped the side of the lifeboat and tried to make sense of the image. Silently it sped toward them. She glanced around; everyone else was asleep. Matt's mouth hung open, slack—they all did. They looked as if they'd been drugged.

Huge, sleek, a monster. Donna swayed as adrenaline shot through her veins. Christ, get it together, she thought; despite her terror, she couldn't seem to focus—

The blast of a klaxon—

"Jesus!" she shouted. It was a ship!

A huge, sleek cruise ship bore down on them. The fog evaporated as the bow sliced through it, fading into wisps that evaporated into nothingness. The sky above the vessel beamed clear and blue. Deck upon deck of sparkling white loomed above a hull of white striped with aqua. On the stack, a green figure of a mermaid sat on a rock, her arms open wide.

"You guys! Hey, wake up!"

The klaxon blew long, short-short-short and plowed toward them.

"Ahoy! Ahoy!" Donna shouted, waving her arms. The fog rolled away, sank into the water and crawled into the clouds, revealing the figures of hundreds of people as they hung over the rails and waved back. Faces peered from portholes that opened in rapid succession along the lower decks. The passengers cheered and waved. Rolls of toilet paper streamed into the water. The horn blew again.

Around her, the others finally stirred. Froze, stared, and burst into cheers. Phil grabbed Elise, then Ruth, and kissed them both. Matty threw himself against his father and jumped up and down. John started to cry and buried his face in his son's hair.

"Thank you," he croaked. "Thank you."

Then John hugged Donna, and Ruth kissed her cheek, and they laughed and cried and sat down quick and hard to avoid capsizing the boat. Elise and Phil huddled at the stern, Phil with his arms around his wife. She made no move to embrace him. John sat to Phil's right, turned sideways to stare at the ship. Matt sprawled half on his lap, half off, picking excitedly at his father's wet shirt, chattering and laughing.

"It *is* like Vikings!" he called to Ramón. The man smiled weakly at him. Yeah, right, buckwheat, be scared, Donna thought, as she sat down on the bench—called a thwart, she remembered Ramón telling her. We're saved and you are big-time busted, friend.

On the other side of the thwart, Ruth covered her mouth with both hands, looking dazed.

No one embraced or congratulated Ramón, Donna noted with bitter satisfaction.

"Ahoy the lifeboat. Is everyone all right?" someone called over a public address system.

"Yes!" Donna and Ramón both shouted. Donna nodded vigorously and gave a thumbs-up. Ramón scrabbled past Ruth to a plastic sack filled with flares, pulled one out, and shoved it back into the bag, as if realizing it wasn't necessary. He sat back and dangled his hands between his knees.

"We'll help you aboard. Sit tight."

With one arm around Matt, John cupped his other hand around his mouth. "The *Morris*," he called. "Is it all right?"

There was no answer. The ship bore down on them with

the seeming speed of a 747. Donna looked nervously at the oars, thought about getting the lifeboat out of the way.

"My God," Elise said. "They'd better slow down."

Ruth moaned. Donna dropped to her knees beside her and touched the woman's cheek. The old lady was white and sweaty. Her fingers were gnarled balls of bone and vein, gripped around each other as if she were fighting off a mugger who'd grabbed hold of her purse.

"Are you all right?"

Ruth nodded slowly. "Yes, I think so. I . . . I'm so relieved." She caught Donna's hand. Her flesh was ice-cold. "But I feel . . . I'm . . ."

God, she might have had a stroke. Donna held her hand and waved to John. "Can you check her out?"

He duckwalked toward them, rising up to climb over the thwart. Back on the massive ship, a large, square door close to the waterline opened and something like a cart was wheeled to the edge. Men in black scuba gear appeared and crouched beside the cartlike object, gesturing.

Elise dug in her purse, produced a comb, and started raking it through her hair. Tears chained like pearls from her bloodshot eyes.

The object unfolded. It was a bright yellow raft. The divers pushed it over the side and jumped in after it, splashing into the water. Next, men bolted something onto the edge of the open area. A long suspension ladder unrolled the length of the side and tumbled into the water. The divers caught hold of it and made signs to the men waiting above them.

"Can you row to us?" the public address voice queried.

"Yes!" Donna called. Ramón was already setting the oars in their oarlocks.

"Told the captain to get an outboard," he grumbled.

Everyone looked at everyone else. Was the captain still alive?

John finished taking Ruth's pulse and studied her pupils. Donna noted the way he smoothed her hair from her forehead. Patting, touching her. An errant quip about bedside manner fleeted through her mind.

"You feeling better, kiddo?" he asked.

Uncertainly Ruth nodded. "I . . . I dreamed again," she said, as though she were confessing. "It was so vivid . . ." She put her hand to her hair. Her eyes jittered back and forth. "But now I don't remember any of it. I don't remember a thing!"

Donna paused. She had dreamed, too. But she also remembered nothing.

"That's how dreams usually are. Everything is fine now. We're safe now." Ducking his head, he grabbed Matt and snuggled him under his arm like a chick. Matt's thin fingers gripped his back, white dabs on his father's life jacket.

Donna took her place beside Ramón on the bench in the middle of the boat. He took the left oar, she the right, and without speaking, the two began to row toward the ship.

"Why can't they get any closer? Why did they stop all the way over there?" Elise said, pawing through her purse. She found a cigarette and lit it.

For God's sake, they were rescuing them, weren't they? Donna wanted to tell her to shut the fuck up, but she knew Elise was just upset. Anger was fear's twin brother.

John let go of Matt. "I should do that," he said, indicating the oars.

Donna made a snorting sound. "Oink, oink. Stay with your kid."

A couple of minutes later, a diver popped up a few feet from the lifeboat. The other two stayed with the raft. The man checked out the boat, asking if everyone could make it up the ladder or if they should order a hoist.

"A hoist, I think," Donna replied, thinking of Ruth and possibly Matt. The boy was wrung out. Circles ringed his eyes and he was sunburned. He couldn't have lost a significant amount of weight overnight, but his bony wrists seemed bonier. John appeared to have noticed it, too. His dark eyebrows showed through the tortoise-shell frame of his glasses.

The diver nodded and swam alongside the boat, urging it toward the ship.

"Have you been looking for us?" Donna asked.

"Yes." He grinned. "I get a gold piece for spotting you first."

She smiled, figuring this was some kind of reference to sea
lore she didn't understand, especially when John guffawed.
Damn, she was going to have to get around to reading some
books one of these days.

But not today. Today she was going to sleep and drink and
make a lot of phone calls.

"You've got ship-to-shore?" she asked, and for a moment
the diver looked confused. Probably hadn't heard her. She
mimicked putting a phone to her ear.

"We're almost there," he said, and turned back into the
water.

"Of course they have a phone system," John said. He gave
Matty another hug. "See? We had an adventure, didn't we?
And we're fine now."

Matt didn't smile or agree. Instead, he scooted closer to his
father and sucked his thumb, and pulled at the hairs on the
nape of his neck.

The lifeboat bumped softly against the hull of the ship like
a water spider dancing on the surface tension. Dodging the
rolls of toilet paper that careened out of the portholes,
Donna smiled and waved at the onlookers and glanced up
the field of white, searching for the ship's name. "Yo, baby,"
someone called; she laughed and gave the high sign.

Ah, there it was. *Pandora.* In bold black letters that seemed
twenty feet tall.

Pandora. Wasn't that the name of the woman who let all
the evils into the world? She had a box—

Behind her, Ruth gasped. Donna started to turn her head
but at that moment, three men in white officer's uniforms
and hats appeared at the edge of the opening and called,
"Ahoy! Are you able to board now?"

"Yes," Donna said as John leaned over her shoulder and
said, "The *Morris*! Is it all right?"

"You'll have to speak with the captain, sir," one of them
replied. "We don't have that information."

"Well, where is the captain?"

"He's on the bridge, sir. He'll debrief you after you come
aboard."

"Let's get off this thing, all right?" Elise asked shrilly,

pushing past Donna. The three divers positioned the boat and held it while Ramón secured the hoist.

Donna gave her a hard look, the same one that withered seasoned gang members. "Ruth first," she said.

Elise squared her shoulders, opened her mouth. From his seat, Phil took her hand. "C'mon, darlin'. We're safe now."

Elise glared at him. "Who does she think she is? She's not in any kind of authority over us. She's not—"

"Darlin'," Phil murmured in his soft Southern voice. "We're safe now."

Elise exhaled and plopped down beside him, studiously avoiding eye contact with Donna. Donna shook her head and held her hands out to Ruth, who gingerly sat on the strap while they fastened her in.

Ruth was slow, but she made it. Everyone cheered, in the lifeboat and on the *Pandora*. Matt was next, glancing down anxiously at his father. Then the Alphabitch, then John, then Phil, then Donna.

Halfway up, as she hovered in the air, a sick, dizzy leadenness wrapped itself around her. She hugged the straps of the hoist as her head spun. She tried to focus on something—the lifeboat, now small and toylike, the sparkling green and purple water, once so gray and forbidding. The anticipation of a shower, and bed.

Her stomach lurched. She was positive she was going to be ill.

Someone spoke through the cheers and the hoots. People were banging things: pots and pans? Cameras clicked and flashed.

Someone spoke, and she swore she heard a familiar voice —whether man or woman, she couldn't tell—heard the voice say, *She's the one.*

"Donna? Donna?" John queried her. The hoist quivered as it raised her to deck level and stopped. He reached for her hand.

"I'm okay." She shook her head to clear it. "I'm fine." Took a breath and unbuckled herself as hands reached to help her.

So many faces. She put her left foot on the deck and her

right knee buckled. Someone, not John, caught her arm and supported her; in the crush of well-wishers, she never did see who it was. The cheers in the cavernous space were deafening. Despite the fact that this was some kind of service entrance—a forklift was parked on the other side, and on the walls hung signs about union rules and OSHA and workman's comp—a throng of passengers had pushed their way in. Camera shutters whirred and clicked and the ship's horn rattled the metal posts that divided the room into halves. The press of bodies was suffocating.

"Stand back, stand back, please," an official voice boomed. "A little air, please."

The passengers obeyed, moving to either side of imaginary barriers and leaning over them to smile and wave and take pictures.

A crewman in a black jumpsuit stepped aside as a bearded man in a startlingly white uniform and a black-billed hat trimmed with gold braid approached the group. He had epaulets on his shoulders.

"Welcome aboard," he said heartily. He had a British accent. "I'm the staff captain, Edward Smith. And this is Chief Officer Lorentz Creutz"—he gestured to a tall, older man— "and Dr. Hare, our ship's doctor."

The doctor, a short, rotund man, stepped forward. "Are any of you in pain? Have there been any injuries?"

As he spoke, a woman dressed in a starched nurse's uniform with a square cap on her head pushed a wheelchair toward them. A man in hospital greens followed with another.

"I don't think we need those," Ruth said firmly. Bemused, Donna slung her weight on her hip. Somehow, she'd imagined their rescue would be more dramatic: hauled dripping from the ocean, hacking and coughing, blankets thrown around their shoulders as they limped or were carried from the pitching deck of some old steamship. It was vaguely disappointing.

"Nevertheless," the doctor replied, "I would prefer it if you'd ride in one to the infirmary. I want to check you all over." He reached down and chucked Matt under the chin. "You thirsty, tiger? Like some orange juice?"

"I'm no . . ." Ruth began, and collapsed.

John pushed his way to her side. "Get a gurney!" he called. He leaned over Ruth as the doctor knelt beside him. "I'm a physician."

Hare pressed two fingers over Ruth's neck. To the wide-eyed nurse, he said, "You heard the doctor. Gurney. On the double."

"Aye, aye, sir." She whirled on her heel.

"Ruth?" Donna chafed her wrists. "Honey, you okay?"

Ruth's eyes fluttered open. "I dreamed . . ." she whispered. Donna put her ear to the woman's lips, but she said nothing coherent. A long, sibilant *sssss* issued from her mouth, like the kiss of a snake.

Two more men dressed in hospital greens lowered the stretcher to the ground. John put both his hands around Ruth's hip while the doctor slid his around her upper arm.

"We're going to move you onto the stretcher," John said softly.

Ruth started, took in the men holding her. Her hands waved in little circles as she tried to make them set her down. "I'm all right now," Ruth protested. "It was just . . ." She looked puzzled, as if she couldn't recall what she'd been planning to say.

"Here we go," John said as he and the doctor eased her onto the stretcher. Deftly accomplished. Donna silently applauded.

The metal legs of the stretcher unfolded as the men in the greens pulled the stretcher to hip height. Wrapping his hand around Ruth's, John said to Donna, "Could you take Matt for me?"

"Sure. That okay with you, big guy?"

Matt's eyes widened. "Captain Nemo!" he cried. "We forgot about Captain Nemo."

"*No problema,* kiddo." Donna headed back toward the edge of the opening as Ruth was spirited away. Ramón trailed after. Donna glared at him over her shoulder and he slowed up, looking abashed.

"I want all of them in wheelchairs," Hare told the nurse. "Stat."

Matt ran to the edge before Donna had a chance to stop him. "Hey, mister!" he called down. "Mister, get my cat, please!"

Queasily, Donna joined him at the side. Two divers were directing the lashing of the lifeboat to a large hoist, which was connected to the floor by a winch. One of them flashed a thumbs-up and crawled into the lifeboat.

"She'll be scared," Matt directed.

Ramón sidled up, tousled Matt's hair. "She will be fine, *hombre.*"

The diver straightened and cupped his mouth. "She's here. We'll bring her up inside the boat, okay?"

"Thanks!" Matt smiled up at Ramón and her. "Whew. That was a close one."

"Yeah." Donna's knees wobbled some more. "I gotta lie down," she said to no one in particular, and sank into Ramón's arms.

She woke up staring into the face of the nurse.

"Hi," she murmured groggily. "What happened?"

The nurse dropped something into a Dixie cup and set it on a white lacquer nightstand. "You passed out," she chirruped. "We brought you to your stateroom."

Donna lifted her head. She lay in a king-size bed in the middle of a room the size of the dining room on the *Morris.* The walls and carpet were a soft beige trimmed with a border of brown and blue seashells, and the furniture was white lacquer. A watercolor seascape hung on the wall across from her, and it wasn't just a print. There was another smaller one beside the lacquer dressing table, which had a full-assault makeup mirror bounded by lights.

"This is our Proteus suite," the nurse said. "It's our best quarters. You have a stereo, a VCR, even your own balcony. It wasn't booked, so the captain ordered you put into it."

Awkward sentence. Made it sound as if the captain had ordered Donna to stay there. Donna yawned. "Thank you. It's very nice." Touched her forehead. "I feel dead."

"I should imagine." The nurse lifted her wrist and checked her pulse. Donna looked down at herself. She wore a light blue nightgown. Her gazed flicked to the nurse, who angled a thermometer in the light from the lamp beside the bed.

"Ship's boutique," she said. "We're washing your clothes."

"Thanks."

Donna yawned and the nurse slipped the thermometer under her tongue. Donna pulled it back out.

"How's Ruth?"

"Absolutely all right," the woman said. "We pumped her full of salt water."

"What?"

"She was a little dehydrated." The nurse reached for the thermometer. Donna held on to it.

"The *Morris*?"

The woman hesitated. "I think you'd better wait to speak to the captain."

"But—"

The thermometer went in. Glowering, Donna rolled her tongue along the smooth surface.

"He's very anxious to talk to you."

Around the thermometer, Donna asked, "When?"

"As soon as you feel up to it." She picked up a metal medical clipboard and made some notes. Pulled out the thermometer and read it. "Good. Let's check your blood pressure." From the white lacquer table beside the bed, she picked up a cuff.

Waving her away, Donna sat up. "I want to talk to the captain now."

The woman smiled calmly. "After the doctor examines you."

"Now. I want to talk to him now. The *Morris* was taking on lots of water. If you haven't found any other survivors . . ."

"The captain is questioning First Officer Diaz right now," the nurse said.

Donna huffed at herself. She didn't know shit about ships, and here she was demanding to throw in her two cents' worth. Taking on water. Get out, who the hell did she think she was? Doing her typical bossy cop act. Right, Ms. Macho, who had fainted like a Southern belle right there in front of God and everybody.

The nurse wrapped the cuff around Donna and squeezed the rubber ball attached to it. "But the captain does want to speak to you," she emphasized. "Very soon." She spoke as if the man had personally singled her out to discuss weighty matters with him. Donna smiled at her own vanity—or her obvious need to be considered important—and lay back.

"I'll pencil him in," she drawled. Sat up again. "I need to call some people, let them know I'm okay."

"Relax." The nurse urged her back against the pillows. "No one's heard about it."

If she knew that, she must know something about the *Morris*. "Look—"

"You must be hungry." The pressure on the cuff increased; Donna could feel the pulse in her arm, hear it as it lurched toward her ear. Boompa, boompa, a little sluggish, perhaps?

"Yes, I'm hungry. But I'm also concerned about what's going on." Donna yawned. The room rocked. Natural, she told herself, after being in the lifeboat for twenty-four hours.

"What do you mean? Nothing's going on." The nurse squeezed the ball. "We'll bring you a tray. What would you like?"

What do you want?

"No, no, I'll get up." Hell with her. She'd talk to the captain soon enough, get her answers from him. Boompa, boompa, wasn't that enough? The cuff constricted her arm painfully. Donna frowned at it.

"Almost finished." The nurse squeezed the ball again. Again. Her arm throbbed. "And the doctor wants all of you to stay in bed for the rest of the day."

Donna flashed with irritation. "But I'm all right."

"Now, now, doctor's orders." That professional smile. That officious voice. Donna knew them both from a hundred visits to the emergency ward. Usually reserved for the patients, while, as a law enforcement officer, she got to deal with the real people behind them. It was galling to be on the other side of the sheet.

Damn, that thing really hurt. And there was something

forced about the nurse's bedside friendliness. Didn't like her, Donna guessed. No big deal.

Her stomach growled. The nurse ripped the Velcro fastening and folded up the cuff, put it and the ball in a plastic box.

"The doctor will be in shortly." With a snap, she shut the box and picked up it and the Dixie cup. Something rattled in the bottom of the cup, like a nail or a marble, and Donna was about to ask her what it was when another wave of dizziness washed over her and she lay back against the pillow.

"I hope you enjoy your stay with us," the nurse said, and trotted out of the room. "I'll order a tray for you."

"Wait." Donna tried to raise her hand. It lay at her side, tired and heavy.

Fuck it. Closing her eyes, she let herself sleep.

In the darkened stateroom, John cuddled Matt as the boy snored loudly. Captain Nemo curled at the foot of the bed. Barely awake, John smiled and sighed against the back of Matt's head. The cat licked the big toe of his right foot, pushed from beneath the bedclothes; her rough tongue tickled and he shook his foot to discourage her. She batted it with her paw. He shook it again. She raised herself up and caught it, giving him a remonstrative though restrained nip before she settled down to licking it again.

Nibbling, nibbling, mousie. Who's nibbling at my housie? John had been reading *Hansel and Gretel* to Matt; there was a picture book somewhere on the bed, open to the page where the witch caught them. Nibbling, nibbling, catsie, who's nibbling at my toesie?

John, his eyes heavily closed, smelled his son's hair and started to drift back down into dreams. Nemo licked his toe.

All was right with the world, and his stomach didn't hurt too much. Hare had given him some Tagamet. They were safe, and he could sleep.

Drip.
Drip drip. Drip.
John opened his eyes again, to darkness. Rearranged his glasses and rolled onto his back, smoothing his hair away

from his forehead. The porthole was open, the moon soft and pink in the frame of the metal circle. Light brown curtains rippled in a tropical breeze.

Drip drip drip.

Damn. They'd told him the captain would be in in a few minutes to talk with him. That must have been hours ago.

And what was that dripping?

Gingerly, he slid his arm from beneath his son and sat up. Put his hand on the nightstand beside the bed.

There was something wet on it. A flat piece of cork—a bob, a coaster?—and he picked it up at the same time he turned on the light.

In his hand he held a glass ashtray, perfectly dry.

Confused, he cocked his head. A long, metallic echo shuddered through the room, *drrrrrr*—

from one corner,

—iiiiip

from another. Then a steady trio of drips just above his head. Louder, so loud he covered the crown of his head with his hand and gazed up as he swung his feet to the floor.

Right into a deep, cold puddle. The water splashed on his arches, so icy it stung, and the floor beneath was scaly and crusted.

"Hey," he blurted, lifting up both feet.

"Daddy?" Matt bolted upright, squinting. The Hansel and Gretel book fell off the bed, landing with a splash.

"Oh, my God!" John cried. He leaned over and groped with his fingertips. Sinking! Sinking. Jesus Christ!

"Daddy?" Matt shouted, rising on his knees.

John's hand touched the smooth, soft carpet. It was dry.

And the dripping had stopped.

There was a muffled knock on Ruth's door. She looked up from the old Agatha Christie paperback the nurse had thoughtfully brought her. Though she read the text, her mind was working on another mystery altogether. Something about Stephen, something very real, yet unreal, if only she could remember it . . .

Another knock, insistent yet not intrusive. "Yes?"

"It's the captain, madam. May I come in?"

Oh, my, the captain himself. Such a deep voice. And a lovely British accent, like that other man's, the subcaptain or whatever he was. Ruth primped her hair and rearranged her bathrobe, also provided by the nurse, who had given her a sponge bath as well. Thank goodness. She wouldn't want someone as important as the ship's commanding officer to see her in the condition she'd been in after twenty-four hours in a lifeboat.

"Yes, please do," she said brightly. "Please, Captain, come in."

The door opened.

12
Spin It Good

Pain roared through Kevin as he sobbed with terror. Oh, jumpin' Jesus, how did he get here?

Kevin had snuck into the hold of the *Morris* with a big black sailor named Eskimo, to buy an O.Z. of the best buds this side of Maui; and they stayed down there testing the merch and getting pretty wasted. The next minute, water smashed in every which way, the sea blasting over their heads. Fish smacking him and seaweed and cold, gray water; and the fog rollin' in, man, like a son of a bitch; and he stood there screaming while Eskimo shouted, "All hands turn to!" totally freaking out, and the next minute—

Holy fuck, the next:

He was writhing on the wet deck in a soot-black section of the hold that reeked of sweat, grime, and oil. The overhead was so low the group around him had to—

—*the group around him.* Seamen in tatters, their faces dried up like forgotten apple cores. He couldn't tell if some of them had eyes in their shrunken heads. They hung like string puppets abandoned in an attic, their chins tipped downward.

Those chins streaked with blood as they stared at him. Light flickered over their faces; the sound of an explosion rattled the floor beneath him. Christ, the ship was blowing up!

In agony, Kevin tried to sit. The flare light played over his body. He was naked. His bare stomach was gouged with cuts and scratches; black dots and rings covered his arms.

His head throbbed and fell back on his neck, bashing the floor. Grunting, he raised it again.

Welts—burns—whorled around his pelvis. Thick, open sores rimmed with charred hair. New flesh, raw and bloody and marbled with muscle.

The muscle. *The muscle.* Where . . . ? His gorge rose as he strained himself up on his elbow. Stomach acid sloshed into his chest cavity and his heart stopped, literally.

Jesus, it was gone! His dick was gone!

Shrieking, he collapsed onto the deck. His fingers stuck into his thigh. Sank into it up to his wrist. A geyser of black blood shot into the air, splashing the men who loomed over him. It sprayed the ceiling and dripped down in viscous dribbles.

And they dove for it, they fucking bolted and started licking it up, and slurping it and—

"Getta doc!" Kevin grabbed at himself. A pulsing rope slithered between his pointer and middle fingers, oozy and slimy; holy fuckin' Jesus, it was an artery.

Kevin screamed. He yelled and bellowed, making noises he had never heard a human being make.

And then the screaming rose with the geyser of blood until a hurricane pummeled those withered, zombie faces, and they tipped back their heads and opened their mouths, because his blood was gushing in a tidal wave, a fuckin' tsunami, and it was his life shooting out of his body; right out, pooling on the floor. It ran and pumped, though his shaking hands clamped down as hard as they could, which wasn't very hard at all, 'cuz he was dyin', man, dying.

NO! He had to do something, had to do . . .
had to do . . .
His head thudded hard against the blood-drenched deck.
Holy fuck, he was going to fuckin' die.
Across the hold, someone sniggered, low and cruel. Lips
parted and air sputtered in a series of soundless, plosive
chuckles.
Laughing at him. Laughing 'cuz he was hurt bad,
gonna die gonna die gonna die gonna—
His dick, oh, Christ, his dick—
The laughter grew. Kevin vomited a stream of bile. It
steamed, mixed with his blood.
Laughing, laughing, laughing.
"One must be sacrificed, for a good voyage," someone
said.
"Gaaa," Kevin managed. The pain, rolling over him,
waves, waves. The terror, oh, God, bad trip, bad, Officer
Donna was right, bad drugs; tripping and . . .
"I'm sorry," said another voice, and through his clenched
lids, Kevin saw a man covered with sores, with blood—*his*
blood—eyes so sunken, a knife—oh, God!
"We sank. *Trinity*. SOS. SOS. Mayday, Mayday." The man
sobbed. "SOS, I'm alive. I'm still alive."
He raised the knife and held it to Kevin's throat. "Best you
die. I'm still alive. Best . . ."
"No!" cried the first voice, and the man with the knife
halted. He threw back his head and wailed, "Let me die! Let
me go with him!"
Fresh agony lurched through Kevin. The blood and vomit
hissed like acid, eating a hole in the deck underneath him;
and it collapsed into rotted planks of wood that floated up
around his shoulders as he plummeted into a place that was
darker, fouler, deader . . .
Freakin' out. His brain, oh, God, he was hallucinating because—
because—
Mwahhhhahhahahahhahahhahahhahahhahahahhahahahah
The laughter chased him down and slapped him hard. It

was going to bash his skull in. That fucker had done this to him! Had killed him!

In his mind, as he fell, Kevin raised his arm and gave the bastard the finger.

Back in his body, he did nothing.

But smash to the bottom and get on with dying.

Back on deck, Edward Curry, former captain of the *Trinity*, sprawled on the deck, in the blood, near his reward.

"Please let me die," he pleaded. "Please."

The captain—the present captain, the one who ruled the waves—sat in his chair in the corner, shrouded by the dark. His hands rubbed the soft wooden armrests, worn down by the centuries of his flesh upon them. A young boy knelt between his legs, nibbling, nibbling fishie, so sweet, so young, his Nathaniel.

"Please. Use someone else. Please. I can't stand it anymore, I can't do it again." Curry barely moved. But his hand, the captain noted with satisfaction, stretched toward the little sausage afloat on the Sea of Death, meatlet, cutlet of Desire.

"Harder," he whispered to the boy, his little cabin boy. Surges of pleasure ran through his cock. Ah, ah, why not let Curry die? The sacrifice had been made. The captain no longer recalled why one was required. He didn't even know why those words sounded so familiar. Something in him refused to remember; there was much that was blank these days. He sensed he had struggled against something, and prevailed. Something had tried to . . . to rule him. To make of him a slave . . .

. . . a thousand times a thousand, it had tried . . . but he was the captain, he was, was, *was*! It was he who commanded, he who was the god!

He no longer remembered how he had come to be a god, and to rule the dead of the sea. Nor why it was exactly that all those living, save himself, enraged him so. Why it was such sport to pull them down

down,

down, but it was the way of his holiness, his worship, in this temple he had fashioned with his magic.

Nor why, exactly, everything seemed . . . renewed, or remade, even he . . .

NO!

No, all was as it should be. All was as he ordered it to be. Life was under his control.

He knew he needed Curry, until he chose another acolyte to take his place.

He also knew he would not allow Curry the blessings of immortality. The man was a coward, and the captain would not suffer cowards in his crew.

"Please, please," Curry begged. His hand curled around the morsel. The captain kept him hungry; he was easier to dominate that way.

"It shall be as you desire," the captain promised the other, vanquished captain as he stroked the head of the little boy, who in turn stroked him. "But not yet," he added, as Curry's head jerked up hopefully.

"Not yet," and he leaned back in his chair.

And what had happened to the body of that other young one? As it fell into the hole? Whence that hole?

Not to ask. The captain's mind shut hard, watertight, as a black, thirsty fog rolled toward it. He began to shake. Not to ask! Never, never, for he was the captain, he!

But the power,

and the glory, and there was a

there had been a

"Ah!" he shouted, and strained against the culmination of his ecstasy, of the swell of the tide within him, the galvanic, joyous fury of his power; and as he sweated and shuddered, his mind roved over the waters, and the seafarin' winds, seeking out the newest ones; and he thought:

Come aboard, come aboard, me hearties. I shall have you all, I shall take you all, even I shall kill . . .

. . . that bitch . . .

"Nathaniel!" As the cabin boy sucked it down

down,

down, and the depths were sweet, and the eel of his body slithered into the murk of paradise.

* * *

Donna looked at herself in the mirror of her suite. Well, hey howdy, get a load of this. Cinderella is going to the ball.

A much nicer dress than anything in her absent luggage hugged her waist and hips. Low-slung and red, a real Corvette dress. It was very nice of the captain to authorize some credit on board, and the boutique franchisees had been happy to donate some clothes to the survivors.

A ghost of a chill kissed the small of her back. Survivors. Answers better be on their way, or she was going to kick some butt but good.

Well, answers *were* on their way, officer ma'am. Cool your smokin' jets. She picked up the cream-colored invitation that reminded her of a graduation announcement.

At the top of the stiff paper, an anchor.

Below it, the words, *Captain, the* Pandora

A few spaces, and then:

The Captain respectfully requests the pleasure of your company at the Captain's Table for dinner this evening.

Damn straight he'd get the pleasure of her company. It was overdue, to her way of thinking.

She'd tried to call Ramón to see what the captain had told him—and vice versa—during his debriefing, but the ship's operator said no one had told her his cabin number. Donna requested an outside line and the operator—with the same style professional bullshit voice as the nurse's—replied that no one had authorized charges for her room. So Donna had sworn and sputtered and dug out her MasterCard and given her Glenn's number, and the operator had finally consented to give it a try, only to report that something was wrong with their satellite connection and that they'd have to try later.

Hell and damn, and back again. You'd think on a boat like this, you'd be able to make a phone call.

Then a clerk from the boutique had come in with a rack of clothes, which didn't mollify Donna much but gave her something else to do. The invitation from the captain had arrived shortly after that, and then John and Matt had popped by with their invitation, all excited. Matt had told his father he wanted to write a book about his adventure, which got John thinking about movie deals. Donna was surprised at him; he didn't seem the greedy, starstruck type, but when he began talking about being able to take off some time from work with the money he'd make, things clicked: he wanted to be there for his son when whatever was wrong with him got worse. Happily enough, though, the boy was looking much, much better.

"I tried to make some calls, too," Donna said, frustration creeping back into her voice as she recounted her inability to do so.

John frowned. "I got through. Reached my housekeeper. No one's heard anything about us or the *Morris*. She was shocked. I asked her to keep mum until we learn more from the captain. No sense upsetting everybody." No, indeed: what if they were the *only* survivors?

"Well, I'll try later. I guess with fiber optics—" She made a gesture with her arm as she realized she didn't know what the hell she was talking about. She knew about satellites and signals bouncing wrong and like that, though, so it made sense John had lucked out and she hadn't.

The doctor came to check her, from stem to stern, which necessitated John's and Matt's exit. He asked her about her dizzy spell, and she lied to him and said she felt one hundred percent, and he gave her his permission (gee, thanks, your highness) to leave her stateroom. In truth, she was fagged out; who wouldn't be after a day and a night on the high sea? But she'd be damned if she'd stay cooped up in bed.

Then a steward told her it was almost time for cocktails in the captain's quarters, and if she'd dress, someone would be by to escort her.

Now a chime rang, followed by a patter of knocks on the lower third of the door. When she opened it, a dark man dressed like a waiter stood aside as Matt tumbled into the stateroom, his father following behind with a stuffed green dinosaur the size of a heart, and a single long-stemmed red rose. Father and son were both dressed in suits and ties, Matt's with short pants, and Donna felt a bit outclassed. Her duds were a tad casual, maybe.

John's eyes widened and he faltered charmingly before saying, "Nice dress." He looked down at the rose as if he'd just discovered it and held it out to her.

"For you."

"She can have the dinosaur, too," Matt ventured, staring up at her. "You look like the lady on MTV," he told her.

She smiled at her suitors. "Well, gee, thanks." She took the rose and dinosaur with a little bow. "How keen. I'll have to put it in water—"

Something mushroomed behind her eyes. Gray filmed over them; she reared backward and dropped the dinosaur as she touched her fingers to her lids.

"Donna?" John said.

Tendrils of darker gray waved in front of her fingers. The fog, she thought distractedly, rubbing again. "Jesus, I can't see a damn thing!"

Hands grabbed her shoulders. She could feel them but she couldn't see them. Where someone should have stood, a darker gray swam in front of her. She cried out.

"Hold your head still." Frightened, she jerked as John cupped her chin and pried her lid open as far as it would go.

Cobwebby lines of black and pewter undulating directly in front of her. And a—she tried to focus—a

"Are you in pain?"

She shook her head. "No, I . . . I just can't see you."

—quick quick, a flash, a semidiscernible image—

"Sit down." John led her to a chair. She groped like a blind woman.

"Shall I get the doctor?" asked another voice.

—an image of a—

The room flashed back into place. John's glasses were pressed against the bridge of her nose as he stared into her eye. She blinked hard to clear the tears that were streaming down her cheek.

"Okay," she said. "It's okay now. I can see." She raised a hand as he continued to stare into her eye.

Examined her other one, pulling the lid. "Could you see anything? Anything at all?"

She thought for a moment. What had she thought she'd seen? Or almost seen? She didn't know.

She made a gesture. "Gray, wavy lines."

His face took on a distanced, thoughtful expression. Processing the medical computer. And from his look, either coming up with nothing or something he didn't want to share.

"Should I call Dr. Hare?" The voice belonged to the steward.

Donna shook her head. "I'll see him later." John's lips parted in protest. She raised her chin a notch and said, "I'll see him later."

"You blacked out earlier," he said gently.

"I just spent twenty-four hours in a lifeboat, too." She eased him away. He rocked back on his heels and stood.

"I really think—"

"MYOB, John," she snapped. She looked past him to Matt, who had picked up the dinosaur. The rose, too. His eyes were huge.

"I'm okay," she assured the two of them, softening.

"That happened to me once," Matt murmured, still staring at her.

John flushed, muttered, "During chemo."

Donna said, "I think you'd better hang on to that dinosaur for me, okay? I'll go put the rose in some water."

Water. What she had almost seen had had something to do with water. Or something in water. Something shiny. Something green.

Something borrowed, something blue. Let it go for now, Donna. It was probably stress.

"Ma'am?" The steward held his hand out for the rose and carried it into her bathroom. He turned on the tap. Donna picked up her purse and room key from the end of the bed.

"I'm fine," she huffed at John.

The steward returned with the rose, clipped to a stubby-stemmed blossom in a drinking glass. He set it by her bed, turned, and made a little bow.

"I'm Adalberto, your cabin steward." He smelled of heavy, musky after-shave and his hair was oiled. His nails stabbed a quarter of an inch above the ends of his fingers, like a cheap hood in an old gangster movie. "If you're ready, I'll escort you to the captain's quarters."

John held out his arm to Donna. "You insist?"

"I insist."

He sighed.

"Lighten up," she chided, then put her arm around his to soften her tone.

They moved toward the door. "By the way, have you heard anything?" she asked. Matt nonchalantly circled around to her other side.

John shook his head. "Not a damn thing." Lowered his voice. "I keep wondering about Kevin. And Cha-cha." He glanced down at Matt, who held the dinosaur in his arms. He was pretending not to listen, but Donna knew people pretty well. Chemo. Oh, dear God, the little guy had cancer.

"Wait'll you see the ship," John said in a different tone. "It's fabulous."

They went out of the room. The hall stretched before them like an endless fun-house corridor, so long it dipped in the middle. The carpet was a wavy pattern of blue and black and green, a vague sea-life motif, with dots of darker blue that resembled fish in a Rorschach kind of way. The walls were white, and light fixtures that looked like hurricane lamps glowed starkly and rippled between their footfalls on the carpet. Shadow and light, the carpet swayed and the fish darted behind ropy ladders of seaweed. Donna looked up; the illusion made her queasy. What if something was really wrong with her? She cast a wary glance at Matt. Something like *that*?

"We're reading *Hansel and Gretel*," Matt told her as he walked beside her.

"Really?"

"Yeah." He nodded earnestly. "But my dad fell asleep before we got to the good part."

"Good being synonymous with gross," John added dryly, rolling his eyes.

"When the witch is gonna eat them."

Donna raised and lowered her brows. "The dark side of childhood."

"Yes." He leered at her. "And some of us never grow up."

Behind them, the steward made a noise. They turned; he dropped his gaze to his hands and murmured, "Please turn left up here."

"Hard a port," Donna said, executing a military-style turn. Giggling, Matt imitated her.

They came to the foyer of the ship. Potted palms fanned silhouettes onto the walls, where silhouettes of black creatures, half horse, half sea serpent, coiled and reared at teardrop chandeliers. Inlays of blood-dark wood trimmed with brass paneled the registration desk and purser's office in a panorama of maritime vessels that began with a crude raft, paraded through galleys and medieval ships, to the sailing ships of different ages, and finished up with what had to be the *Pandora* herself. The scenes were bordered with crushed-glass mosaics of mermaids frolicking with dolphins and whales.

"Wow," Donna said. "How . . . busy."

A man seated in a white chair looked up from his newspaper and smiled at them. Across the room, a woman turned and pointed, spoke to her companion, a Japanese man. A third person joined them, dressed in the *Pandora*'s staff uniform. Looks and murmurs ricocheted through the room like the Wave at a baseball game.

"They must be going for art deco." John gestured toward the chandeliers. "Those are wrong, but everything else could've been on an old thirties ocean liner. The furniture in our rooms, too. All the lacquer." He looked embarrassed. "My . . ." A furtive glance at his son. "My wife was an interior decorator."

Oh, no, was she dead? Donna filed the question away. Wife dead, son half-dead?

How could she be so glib?

"So, this is like an old ocean liner?" she said, to cancel out her bad thought. "Like the *Titanic*?"

John smiled. "The *Titanic* was earlier. Though you could've found those chandeliers on the *Titanic*."

"Maybe they got a deal on them," she said.

"The captain picked those out himself," the steward observed frostily.

Donna grinned behind her hand. "They let him help decorate? I guess he was pretty sure he'd have the job for a while."

The steward's smile got nowhere near his eyes. "Oh, yes, ma'am. Pretty sure." He held out a hand in a bullfighter gesture and everyone swung right, toward a quartet of elevators.

"Oh, Cha-cha has to see this," Donna said.

Lacquered on the face of each door, ol' King Neptune sat on a throne of shells. He was magnificent, steady-eyed, barrel chest thrust out, trident in hand. A coronet radiated beams of light and his beard and hair streamed in the sea air.

"He's got a crown like the Statue of Liberty," Matt said. Donna and John chuckled.

The elevator doors opened without a sound and the group stepped in. The walls were covered with the same pattern as the carpet. The ceiling was mirrored; Donna could see straight down the front of her dress. Casually, she covered her chest with her arms.

The steward stood at parade rest with his hands folded over his belt, watching the numbers. Twelve decks. Donna wondered if there were actually thirteen. That happened in hotels. Got damned confusing when you were trying to answer a call.

"Have you heard anything about the ship we were on?" she asked the steward. "We're very concerned about it."

"No, ma'am." The steward unfolded his hands and licked his lips. Stood straight-shouldered, like a soldier.

The doors opened. On the other side of the corridor, another lacquer portrait covered a door, this one of Neptune in profile, riding a sea serpent. He looked fierce, godlike, and Donna hoped he was on Cha-cha's side, and that the two of them were off somewhere safe, having a great conversation.

They waited while the steward tugged at his white jacket, cleared his throat, and rapped on the door.

"Donna? John?"

Phil van Buren's voice. The door opened and he smiled at them and jerked his head for them to come in. In a fluid motion, the steward disengaged and glided down the corridor.

John stood aside for Donna. Elise van Buren-Hadley lounged on a plaid sofa in a tight black dress that had to be silk. Her blond hair was up and she had on serious gold jewelry. Phil wore a dark blue suit.

After the grandeur of the main hall, the room was unremarkable. The only interesting item was a large model of a fully rigged sailing ship encased in a bottle. It sat on an ornate stand on a coffee table. A brass plaque placed across the legs of the stand read "H.M.S. *Royal Grace,* 1792–1799."

"Cool." Matt peered at it. "This one's real. Not like the *Morris.*"

"Yes," John murmured. He had to be thinking what she was: that that hideous decoration in the *Morris*'s dining room might now lie at the bottom of the ocean.

Donna glanced around. In the corner at a wet bar a steward stood deferentially, surrounded by liquor bottles of every description.

"Where's the captain?" she asked, making for the bar. The bartender inclined his head.

"He's been detained, madam. He'll be here shortly. May I take your order?" He had some kind of accent, German maybe.

"Scotch, straight. A double," Donna requested. Elise's eyebrows shot up. Whatever was in her glass was clear; champagne, probably. She watched as the bartender served it up. Donna thanked him, stepping aside while John asked for a piña colada and a 7-Up for his boy. The bartender began shoveling ice into a blender at his elbow.

"Where're Ramón and Ruth?"

Phil waved his drink. "Ramón's been sent off somewhere. I think they actually threw him in the brig. Ruth didn't feel up to coming."

Elise lit a fresh cigarette and blew out the match, searching for an ashtray. She muttered something, but the whir of the blender drowned her out.

John handed Matt's drink to him. "Is she okay?"

Phil shrugged. "The steward told me she wanted to sleep."

"Maybe I should take a look." John checked his watch. "I could meet everyone in the dining room afterward."

"If she doesn't sue, she's an idiot," Elise said.

Donna tapped the beads of water on the varnished wood bar with her finger. "Maybe they've got Ramón on bread and water."

The lights went out. The blender stopped.

"Hey," Matty said.

"It's not you," John said quickly to Donna. "They're really out."

"Oh, great, great." Elise huffed in the darkness. The red light of her cigarette flared as she took a drag.

"Darlin', it's all right." Poor wiener-man, he just put up with it, didn't he? Donna wished he'd just haul off and belt her. "I'm sure it's just a fuse."

"On a *ship*?"

"Excuse me." The bartender brushed past Donna, fumbling his way to the door. "I'll see if . . ."

His voice trailed off; a door squealed open, and his footsteps sounded in the hall, which was also dark.

Uh-oh, what about the elevators?

And the engines?

"Oh, for God's sake." Elise's voice rose.

"Daddy?" Matt touched Donna's fingers, jumped away. She reached out and slipped his hand into hers.

"Boo," she joked. "Now we can hold hands and no one will ever know." He grunted. A noise like rustling silk: he was probably fingering the hair on the back of his neck. She'd noticed that he did that whenever he got tense.

There was a pause. Everyone stood around quietly. Elise's cigarette winked like a beacon.

Suddenly Matt murmured, "Oh, no . . ."

"Well, hello."

There rustle of clothing as everyone turned in the direction of a deep English voice.

A man framed in soft, flickering light stood on the threshold of a door to the left of the wet bar. There was a candle in his hand, which he lifted as he pushed the door out of his way and came into the room. He was of medium height and build, snappy in a white officer's uniform, with short, curly red hair. Something white was pressed to his lips. A handkerchief. The flame flickered, flickered, flickered over his face, carving a deep shadow on the left side of his face. Donna strained. No, no shadow. A black eye patch covered his eye socket.

He walked into the room. His lips were full and bowed into a faint smile. Donna found herself smiling back, though the man couldn't see her.

"I'm Captain Reade," he said.

He raised the candle toward the bar, dimly lighting the area where Donna stood. Over her shoulder, Elise's smoke trailed like a tendril of yellow fog.

"I see the steward was using the blender. Well, that would do it. My apologies. There's a short in this room, and I've warned him not to plug . . . Ah."

The lights flashed on, revealing him more fully. He was scrubbed and clean and neat. Green eye. A sprinkling of freckles on his cheeks, softening the sinister appearance of the eye patch. Otherwise, he was a regular guy, nothing special.

His gaze lingered on Donna. "I'm Donna Almond," she said.

"Somehow, I knew that," he replied. He cocked his head. "Are you feeling ill, Miss Almond?"

She blinked. What, didn't she look okay? "I'm fine, considering."

"Please, Captain. Let's introduce ourselves after you tell us about the *Morris*," John said urgently, coming up beside Donna with Matt in tow.

"Yes, the *Morris*. Please sit down."

No one moved. Elise puffed on her cigarette. Reade cleared his throat and said, "I'm sorry, but I don't allow smoking in here."

She blazed, opened her mouth, closed it, and finally said, "I'll be glad to put it out if you'll give me an ashtray."

Phil flushed. Reade reached over the bar and handed her a cut-glass dish. Wordlessly she tamped out the cigarette.

"Thank you. Now." He remained standing. Everyone

craned their necks. He leaned against the bar and faced them.

"Captain," John pressed.

Reade held out his arms. He smiled brightly. "It was a false alarm."

John and Donna looked at each other, at Phil. Elise shut her eyes and bit her lower lip.

"They found a small hole in the hull, patched it, and pumped out the water. The *Morris* docked in Honolulu a couple of hours ago."

Elise goggled at him. "By God, I'll—"

"Shit," Donna groaned. "I mean, that's great, but here *we* are."

John held up a hand. "But we must be close to Hawaii, too. Is that your destination?"

"Well, it's very odd you should ask that," Reade said in a bemused tone. "Because we're on our way to Australia, and we've already passed the Hawaiian chain. You drifted over a thousand nautical miles in twenty-four hours. That's one of the reasons we were so busy on the bridge, trying to make sure the *Morris* hadn't made an error about her position."

"Wait a minute. Stop." Elise jumped to her feet. "Are you trying to tell me . . . are you . . ." She reached down and batted Phil's shoulder. "Do something!"

Donna scratched her cheek. "But is that possible? Does that make any sense?"

"All we can surmise is that you were caught in some kind of massive current," Reade said as he perched on the edge of a bar stool and hung his hands between his knees. He folded his handkerchief and put it in the inside breast pocket of his uniform.

"Like a riptide?" John asked.

The captain nodded. "Something like that, yes. Now . . ."

"Well, you're taking us back to Hawaii, aren't you?" Elise snapped.

"It would make more sense to continue on to Australia. We can take a plane from there. Right, Captain?" Phil rose. "Let me get you some more champagne, sweetheart."

"*Australia!*" she screamed.

"There's a problem," the captain cut in. "Unfortunately, another lifeboat was launched from the *Morris,* and we've been searching for it all day."

"Who . . . who was in it?" Donna crossed her fingers.

The captain pulled a sheet of paper from another pocket. "I have a manifest." He handed it to Donna. It was on the same creamy stationery as the invitations.

Donna grimaced. "Cha-cha's on it," she announced. "Kevin isn't." She handed the list to John, who scanned it and offered it to Phil, who studied it and gave it back to the captain.

"Ol' Kev's probably hitting the surf by now." John took Matt's glass and popped an ice cube into his mouth. Chewed down hard. "God, I hope the others are all right."

The captain put the list away. "We'll keep looking."

"Coast Guard?" Donna queried.

"Everyone's doing everything they can. I must say, I was quite surprised by the size of your boat. It was uncommonly small for a freighter. And ill equipped."

"What a surprise," Elise said acidly.

The captain clapped his hands together. "But at least all of you are safe, and we'd like to celebrate that. Shall we go to dinner now?" He picked up his cap.

Donna moved her shoulders. A *thousand* miles? Poor Chacha. He must be out of his mind. More out of it.

"Listen," she said. "The *Morris* was involved in some kind of illegal dumping. Something dangerous. Ramón—"

"Officer Diaz has told me all about it." Laugh lines formed around his single eye. "He was afraid you'd get to me first and I'd keelhaul him."

"Keelhaul?" Matt looked at the captain, clearly smitten.

The captain gazed down on him fondly. "An old-fashioned method of punishment."

"Execution, more like," John put in.

The captain nodded. "Yes, it was usually fatal."

"Cool." Matt slurped his straw. "What did they do?"

Just then, the steward wheeled around the corner. "It's all ri—" Saw his superior officer, and skidded to attention with a salute. His face was white as chalk. "Sorry, sir. It . . . it was the blender."

The hand that held the salute trembled violently. Jesus, the kid was scared half to death.

Reade saluted him back, said, "Don't let it happen again." He pointed at Matt. "That little fellow would like to see someone keelhauled." Smiled, to show it was just a joke.

"N-no, sir." A line of sweat trickled down the steward's temple.

"Well." Captain Reade stood. His eye narrowed as John came over to Donna, combining the two of them into a couple.

He led the way to the elevators. The nervous steward stayed behind to clean up. In the back of the group, Elise was whispering fiercely and Phil was doing his best to calm her down.

"Do you steer the ship?" Matt asked him.

The captain smiled. "In a way. Would you like to see how?"

"Yes!" Matt looked up at his father with a puppy-dog expression that might have melted even Elise's heart, had she been paying attention.

"That would be great," John replied. "Thank you."

"Oh. Oh." Matt was about to burst.

"Tomorrow." The captain's mouth twitched. "All right?"

"Sure! Cool!"

"That's quite a boy you have there," he said to John. "Maybe someday he'll grow up to be a sea captain."

"No! An astronaut!"

"You're behind the times, Captain Reade," John said.

"Don't I know it." The captain traced the gold braid on his cap with his forefinger. "Boys make men feel old, don't they?"

John sighed theatrically and rolled his eyes. "Absolutely."

The elevator came, and they all got in. Donna flashed: Hope no fuses blow while we're in this baby.

The captain looked up at her reflection in the mirrored ceiling. The fluorescent haze turned him gray. "You're safe," he said. "With me."

13
Feelers

Phil was the last one out of the elevator, to prove he wasn't afraid of another blackout. Then he lagged back from the herd to watch his wife, who sashayed her way up to the captain's side, practically pushing Donna Almond out of the way like in some old black-and-white movie—Move it, sister—and now the captain and Elise chatted like two naughty children plotting a murder.

Phil sighed heavily. The doctor, John, glanced at him. So did the captain, with a smirk.

Fuck him.

When they trooped into the vast dining room, everyone rose and applauded. Phil caught up to Elise as the captain eased away from her and entered stag, probably to look more heroic. Elise tensed when Phil took her hand, and her fingers lay in his grasp like a catch of cold, dead trout.

The room was magnificent, all crystal and gold and silvery pink. It reminded him of an opera house. On a dais gleamed

the white and silver of the captain's table, complete with an
ice sculpture of a mermaid on a rock, arms open, and small
bouquets of flowers. All the chairs were empty, though the
table was large enough to accommodate twenty easy. Apparently, the captain had invited no one else to his table, just the
survivors, minus Ruth and Ramón. None of his own officers,
either.

They began to select their seats—there being no place
cards—and Donna lowered herself into the one on Phil's left
as the steward held it out for her. She flashed the man a
flirtatious smile that he impassively ignored. Phil wasn't sure
she understood what an honor this was. Heavy makeup,
plunging neckline, she was definitely blue collar, a "worker,"
as Elise would so sweetly put it. John, however, thanked the
captain for singling them out. You could tell he was an edu-
cated man.

Phil frowned and sat down. Lord, under Elise's tutelage,
he'd become such a snob. When they'd met, she'd laughed at
him and called him a cracker. Now he was a rich, cultured
Southern gentleman.

At the time, it had seemed like a fair trade: he would give
her money, and she would give him class. Elise had been a
storybook heroine, beautiful and genteel, and mired in poverty. Over the years, she'd conveniently forgotten the poverty
part, but she'd always remembered that when they met, he'd
owned silver services that should have been in museums but
had no idea which fork to use at dinner.

His fortune came from real estate, and all by accident. He
had been a simple insurance salesman in a two-man office,
kept score for the bowling league, and rooted for the Atlanta
Braves. After his mama died, he took his share of the inheri-
tance and purchased a dilapidated Piggly Wiggly grocery
store in Charleston. He'd bought the land on a whim, just
because it was located near Van Buren Avenue (no relation),
and then the developers had approached him less than six
months later, laughing and clapping him on the back and
asking, How did he know that was exactly what they were
looking for for their mall? Pure dumb luck, with a capital D.

He'd gone on from there, buying more when he felt led to, and selling it for a killing. Gettin' rich, but still not sure why.

Elise would have known what she was doing. Oh, yes. As she knew now, lounging and posing for the sake of Captain Reade, a devilish temptation with his eye patch and his British accent, like that good old boy in the Brenda Starr comics, Basil somebody. Captain Basil, who poured wine with his ding-dang pinkie sticking up, and every time he uttered a syllable Elise creamed her hundred-dollar silk panties.

Maybe it was his telling her not to smoke that had done it. Oh, she'd sputtered, but that was what she really wanted. By the time they'd gotten into the elevator, she'd zeroed in on him like a cruise missile. Phil understood that it wasn't so much that she found the man attractive, although it was obvious as mud on a lamb that she did, but that she wanted to rile him, Phil. Get him to macho up, take command. Slap her around and act like Rhett Butler.

He would always disappoint her. He wasn't the kind of guy ladies read about in romance novels. He was nice, and he was a sort of a wimp, and that, Miz Scarlett, was that.

Passengers constantly interrupted their dinner, shaking hands with them, telling them how happy they were that they'd been saved. A varied mix, old, young, Japanese, Mexican. Bright-eyed, having a marvelous time, excited by the rescue at sea. Surely now it would be news back home, folks calling their folks, and families would worry. Elise had phoned "all the people who mattered," with requests to contact those who mattered less.

Donna should try her calls again ASAP; he was just about to tell her so when a tragically obese woman waddled over and told them all how grateful they should be to the captain: he'd spent an entire day searching for them, remaining on the bridge for thirty hours straight.

"He's wonderful," the lady gushed. "He's the best captain in the world."

"Now, now, Mrs. Reinstedt," the captain murmured modestly, but it was clear he was flattered.

Many others simpered over the captain in the same way, almost as though they'd been coached. The captain's the best.

The captain's the most fabulous. The captain, the captain, the captain. Not that the captain seemed to mind. Ol' boy kept shifting that one eye toward him and the others, as if to make sure they noticed how much the paying guests worshiped him.

With a heavy heart, Phil surveyed the room—the widows, the young couples, the families. Beyond them, an immense dessert buffet from which ice sculptures rose like glaciers. Banks of big, wide windows, and the black night beyond.

Last night in the lifeboat, he'd wept with fear. She had heard him. Everyone had. She probably wouldn't fuck him for a week.

He took a swallow of the excellent port, which tasted like it was at least fifty years old (Elise had drilled him on vintages; he was quite the expert now, a regular oenophile). Elise was not going to screw the captain of a cruise ship, for mercy's sake. Even though she had gone to bed with his tax attorney and tried to with Hunter Bennett, his former insurance partner and ex-best friend.

Even though the damn captain was acting like she should.

A band on a dais started up an innocuous, catchy song.

"Oh, I'd love to dance," Elise trilled. "Phil's got two left feet." She laid a hand on the captain's arm. "Would you do me the honor?"

The captain looked at Phil. There was something cold and mean in that one eye, and Phil felt a chill in the small of his back. The man kept looking at him, and the room tipped to the right just a bit. Straightened out. Phil's head swam. God, he was exhausted. Wasn't everybody else ready for bed? They'd just been fished out of the sea, for God's sake. What were they doing at a goddamn debutante ball?

The captain gazed at him. Phil regrouped and smiled evenly, waved his hand. Go ahead, boy. Take her. I'm man enough to take it.

Elise set down her champagne glass and pushed back her chair. Phil didn't assist her. Instead, he drained his glass (supposed to sip it, you cracker) and motioned to the steward for a refill.

Elise and the captain melted into the growing crowd of

dancers as others took the floor. The captain glanced once over his shoulder, and Phil shot a glance toward Donna, not quick enough to miss the man's shit-eating grin.

Well, hell, the *Morris* had made it, so maybe this damn boat would sink instead. That'd solve everything, wouldn't it?

The steward bent over his glass. Phil grunted. What a terrible thing to think. He drained it before the man left and held it out. Donna started to say something, shut her mouth. Good woman.

Dizzier now, and with good reason, damn it, Phil studied the crush of dancers. So many. You'd think the boat would sink under their weight. The thought made him queasy. Milling around in a slow-motion circle as everyone slid their feet along like ghosts dragging their chains. Step, slide, step, drag.

Drag,
down
down
down—

He shook his head, bleary with alcohol. Stupid, stupid. But then he was pretty stupid, wasn't he? Stupid with a danged ol' capital S.

Drag,
down
down
down—

Across the room, a woman swiveled her head and smiled in his direction. She was a brunette with a soft, sweet face, shell-pink lips, and eyes as big and gentle as a Thoroughbred's. Kind of woman he should have married. When he didn't look away, her smile grew and she lowered her eyes demurely.

Blood rushed to his face and he put his glass to his lips. She looked up through her lashes, a bit flustered. Oh, darlin'. His face grew hot. What a lady.

Someone walked past the panes of glass, casting the lady in shadow. Light flickered back over her features as the passer-by moved on.

Phil blinked. For a second, for a moment there, she looked like she—

That she was—

Elise and the captain returned. She was cheery and horny; he knew the signs. He decided he'd seen an optical illusion— the woman's face was there, and in perfect condition—and guzzled his fourth glass of port. Donna's and John's gazes ticked from Elise to him—damned gossips—and he feigned nonchalance as Elise sat beside him. He envied little Matt, oblivious and unconcerned, picking apart a cream puff and dipping his fingers into the filling like an islander eating poi.

"Matt," his father reproved, and the boy guiltily glanced up. Phil winced. Christ, he looked terrible. The bones in his face glowed through his skin. Suddenly Phil didn't envy him quite as much. In fact, he was damned ashamed.

"Captain Reade has invited us on a tour," Elise announced to everyone, as if she had personally arranged the treat.

The man bowed as if this was the ultimate sacrifice, but one he would make to please them. "Yes, if you're amenable." He cocked his head at Phil, raised his brow questioningly. Goddamn, he'd better not embarrass himself, Phil thought. Ease up on the moonshine. Don't give that man a single reason to feel superior.

"Yeah!" Matt cried.

John Fielder tapped his mouth with his napkin and laid it beside his plate. "I don't know. It's been a long day."

Matt pouted. "I took a nap. And I don't even have to anymore."

The captain laughed, deep and rich and assured. Romance-hero laughter. "Then you should be rewarded. Positive reinforcement and all that, eh, Dr. Fielder?" The lone green eye beamed at the doctor like a jewel in the forehead of an idol.

John acquiesced. "Okay, okay. How can I win when he's got the navy on his side?"

Captain Reade held up a finger. "Just one ship, Dr. Fielder. Nothing so grand as an entire fleet."

Elise basked in his cleverness.

Oh, fuck you, Phil thought sourly, standing up with his glass in his hand. Fuck you, both of you, you dang assholes.

As they left, he avoided the captain altogether. And flamed

at the mingled laughter of the man and his wife. Plotting their little murder, plotting their bullshit.

Ballrooms, bars, a disco, a peek inside a glittering casino. John hid a smile as Donna's eyes widened at the luxury and murmured, "Fu-uck," in an awed voice. Elise's spine went *boing!* ramrod-straight at the utterance of the horrid F-word, and then he did chuckle aloud, covering it with a cough.

The ship was large; Reade recited figures about tonnage and length and weight, but the figure that most impressed John was that there were a thousand people, more or less, aboard the *Pandora*. It was a floating town.

"As you see, we refer to the water myths of ancient Greece throughout the *Pandora*," the captain explained as he led them through the Danaë deck. "Danaë was the mother of Perseus, as you may recall, whose father shut her in a bronze box and threw her in the sea."

"Trippy," Matt said, and John shook his head at Donna, who, he saw, was looking uncomfortable. He began to watch her. Pontus, Nereus, Glaucus—each time the others nodded knowingly when the captain mentioned a name, she drew a blank, glanced around to see if the others could read her ignorance.

"Ah, Glaucus, there's an interesting story," the captain said as he led them past a billiard room. A trio of teenage girls giggled over the balls and waved their cues as they hefted themselves over the table, trying impossible shots.

"As you probably know, Miss Almond, he was a young fisherman who became a merman. And he fell in love with a maiden, Scylla, and begged Circe to make her love him."

Donna nodded, and John's heart went out to her.

"But Circe loved him, too, as you may recall. And she poured a potion into Scylla's bath that turned her into a hideous sea monster."

"And what you're leading up to is the beauty shop is called Scylla's Place," Donna shot back, and John realized how condescending he was being. This was one lady who didn't need pitying, or protecting. Maybe she wasn't book smart, but she was street smart. A pistol through and through.

They saw the immense kitchens, where the bakers stayed up all night to make the breads, rolls, and pastries for the next day. A line of short Filipino men chopped vegetables with evil-looking knives. Their fingers were etched with scars. Could you tell how long the men had worked there, by counting the scars like the rings of an oak tree?

Beyond the banks of ovens was a room of nothing but deep freezes, stocked with anything one could imagine, from filet mignons to buffalo steaks. Matt lit up and was about to beg for buffalo when John nudged him and he fell silent.

They left the frigid room lined with its coffin-sized freezers. Anything one could imagine. John knew ships like this carried body bags, and he also knew they kept one or two freezers empty and waiting.

A rush of panic flooded him and he took Matt's hand, who made a face but didn't say anything. It took a lot to kill a human body, he reminded himself, but the thought did nothing to soothe him. His stomach spread itself over a barbecue grill an inch above fresh, white-hot charcoal. He palmed his vial of Tagamet and popped one.

Up and down staircases of marble and brass in the quasideco style; past an open door that revealed a charming room built like the interior of an old sailing ship, with weathered planks and chests and a half-rotted mast dead center.

"What was that?" John asked the captain.

"Oh, just a playroom," Reade replied with a wave. But there was an odd look on his face. He was an odd bird, anyway, and he certainly had been enjoying taunting Phil, the poor asshole. John had watched Reade watching Phil, as if to gauge the man's reactions as he moved in on his wife.

"Where? Where?" Matt demanded, but they'd moved on.

"Here's the library," Reade said, pausing before a door. He looked at Donna. Now he wore an even stranger expression, one of . . . elation? Surprise? Satisfaction? John couldn't figure it out. "We have practically every maritime book ever written. Fiction and nonfiction."

She swung around the corner and studied the books while the others barely glanced into the room. "What's it called?" she asked, scanning some of the titles. "The Merlin Room?"

The captain smiled. "Just the library."

They walked on. Matt yawned widely, started, and ticked his gaze up at John, probably to see if he noticed. John played along, but his mind had begun to shut down. Too much, too frightening, too many hours. Kids must be more resilient than adults. Or did the others feel like stopping and screaming as memories of what had happened crowded in on them?

"And here we are." At the end of a long corridor, Reade halted in front of a milky white glass door marked "Museum." A Closed sign hung from the doorknob. "The treasury."

With a flourish, he unlocked the door and flicked on the lights.

Slashes of fluorescents illuminated rows of glass cases. Overhead, dozens of ships in bottles rotated slowly as the captain stepped into the room, followed closely by Elise van Buren. Phil tottered in. He'd taken advantage of the two bars they'd passed, and now he was really soused. Elise was furious, and practically humping the captain in retaliation.

The captain flicked on a second set of lights set deeper into the room. On the far wall, a stairway zagged to a second level, like a balcony, and a line of faces glared down at the newcomers, harsh and painted and . . .

"Figureheads," John said, startled. A crowd of Greek ocean gods and bare-breasted women, a knight, some Indians.

Mostly babes with huge boobs, and Matt's eyes were about to fall out of his head.

"We have one of the largest collections," Captain Reade replied. "Some of them are quite lifelike, don't you think?"

More than quite, John thought. They looked positively human.

"They're eerie," Donna said behind John.

"The boatswain's mates hate to clean up in here at night." The captain put his hand on his hip and admired the figures like a father pleased with his children. John tried to estimate what a collection like that must be worth, especially so well executed.

Extremely well executed.

Matt and Donna edged through the door. Elise and Phil hadn't moved away from the threshold and were creating a jam. Elise realized it, walked to the first case on her right, and said, "Oh, Captain Reade! This is from the *Titanic*?"

"Your favorite ship," Reade said to Donna, who looked startled. She brushed past him and joined Elise at the case.

John tapped Matt on the shoulder. "Now, don't touch anything."

"Oh, please, Dr. Fielder. He may touch anything he wishes." The captain hunkered down to Matt's level. "You may treat the museum as your own."

Matt raised his chin and pointed at the hanging bottles. "Are there ships in those?"

"Yes. Remember the model in my ready room?"

"There was one on the *Morris,* too. Only it wasn't real."

"Not real?" the captain echoed. "Well, all of mine are. They certainly are." He crossed to the women. "We bought that from the French expedition that went down."

John joined the group. In the case, the head of a bisque doll stared sightlessly at them. His heart tugged; children had gone down on the *Titanic.* He'd known that, but it hadn't really penetrated. Babies screaming in the dark, choking in the freezing ocean.

His stomach wrenched and he shied away, only to collide with Donna, who muttered, " 'Scuse me," in a raspy, troubled voice. The head bothered her, too, and he wondered which of her horrific experiences as a police officer was running through her mind.

"And in the next case, something a bit less . . . unusual."

It was an old captain's uniform, a blue tailcoat and white breeches on a wire form, capped with a white curly wig and a tricorne. A pair of gloves hung from one of the pockets of the coat. Surely a re-creation; it was in far too good a shape to be authentic. His vision blurring, John scanned the typewritten card that gave information about it, but his mind failed to process it. Too tired, and his glasses were dirty. And the shock of their day was making him quiver with fear again. They could have died. In a million ways, they could have been lost forever. A shark attack, the lifeboat capsizing. Donna's wounds growing infected . . .

No. Not in one day, John.

Yes. Yes, because no one can travel a thousand miles at sea. And yes, because death can come like a snap of the fingers. That was what had crushed his spirit as a practicing physician: the randomness of death. The specter fell across your path: you had sex with one wrong person; you breathed in too much CO_2; you slipped in the bathtub, for God's sake . . .

You took the wrong ship . . .

He rubbed his glasses on his shirt as the captain showed them more treasures. China plates with blue willow trees on them. A rusty sword.

A pair of dog tags. A semidecomposed bathing cap that had belonged to the first woman to cross the English Channel.

A tall case near the center of the room that contained a skeleton.

"Of a mermaid," Reade whispered to Matt, smiling.

John blinked. From the pelvis up, a full skeleton twisted on a string like a hanging victim. But connected to the back of the pelvic girdle, a long, articulated spine dangled in the harsh blue light and coiled on the velvet-covered bottom of the case.

"Wow," Matt breathed. "Wow, that's bodacious."

"Has to be What's-His-Name," Donna announced. "Glaucoma."

"You're so amusing, Miss Almond," the captain said, silently applauding. Elise sniffed.

Reade winked at Matt. "And here's my pride and joy." He walked to a case in the center of the room and waited for the others to arrange themselves around it.

The case was covered with a black velvet drop cloth. With a flourish, the captain whipped off the cloth and draped it over Matt's shoulders like a magician's cape.

A green bottle gleamed on an ornate gold stand. It was made of glass, run through with veins of gold. Hefty chunks of red and green circled its neck, reminding John of running lights. A covering of waxy yellow, perhaps tallow, coated the end.

Matt was clearly disappointed. John, too. The skeleton was far more interesting.

"This is mine, actually, not the museum's," Reade said. He looked around the group, found Donna, and talked straight at her. To his own surprise and amusement, John felt a pang of jealousy.

"It belonged to my great-great-great-great-grandfather, Thomas Allen Reade." He tapped the case. "That bottle is hundreds of years old."

"Cool," Matt said as he edged back toward the skeleton.

"Were you named after him?" Elise asked, putting her hand on his arm. Jeez, she could be more discreet. John slid a sidelong glance at Phil, but he'd meandered to the back of the museum and was studying the figureheads.

"In a manner of speaking." He, too, watched Phil. "Many of his descendants have born bits and pieces of him. Of his name," he added, grinning at Donna again, who dutifully focused her gaze on the bottle while she struggled to conceal a yawn.

"I'm Thomas Alexander Reade, however. We've generally been a maritime family. Thomas Allen was on a ship, the *Royal Grace,* when this bottle came into his life." He paused dramatically. "It's quite a story."

Matt perked up. "That's the ship in your room! I saw it! The sign said '*Royal Grace.*'"

"You're quite observant," the captain said. "My father built that model."

"Tell us the story!" Matt demanded.

"Matt," John said automatically.

The captain rubbed his hands together, palm to palm as if he were forming a ball out of clay. "Thomas Allen was put to sea in a boat, all alone, without food or water. Why, we have no idea. He never told. It's been generally agreed among us Reades that he was accused of some crime. And that he was meant to die on the high sea. A wretched way to go. But he drifted for months. Caught rainfall with a leather cap, killed fish and seabirds."

His voice softened and he looked past them, to the row of figureheads. "The empty sea. The nights. The thirst. Imagine how he must have felt."

"And?" Elise urged. Donna, too, looked expectant.

The captain shrugged. "Eventually he got back to England. The only thing he had with him when he returned was that bottle, and it was sealed up exactly as it is now. He wouldn't allow it to be opened, claiming that some mystical properties about it had allowed him to survive. And to this day, no one *has* ever opened it . . ."

Donna shot him a faint, mocking smile. Matty, on the other hand, was agog.

"Aren't you the least bit tempted?" Elise tilted her head as if offering her neck for a nibble.

"We've been an enormously lucky family," Reade said, patting the case. "I'd hate to be the one who broke the spell."

There was a silence. John cleared his throat. "Speaking of breaking spells, I think it's time to hit the sack, matey." He cupped Matt's head.

"Oh, Dad." Matt's shoulders rose and fell with exasperation. Mean Dad Fielder, the quintessential party-pooper.

Donna stretched her arms above her head and yawned. Her boobs rose with the stiff bodice, and John stirred. Since Gretchen's leave-taking, he had remained celibate. The pope would be so pleased.

"I guess I'll turn in, too," Donna said. To John, "Walk me back?"

Yes, yes, yes. "Sure," he replied, croaking. Geesh, what a big kid.

"Thanks so much for the tour," Donna said to the captain. "And the stories."

He regarded her steadily with his one green eye. A current sizzled through the air between the two of them, and John was a bit dashed.

"There's a lot more to see. And hear."

Donna moved her head back slightly, a challenge. "Then we have something to look forward to."

Elise cleared her throat. "I'm really keyed up. I don't think I'll sleep for hours."

Reade regarded her. "The doctor can give you something, if you'd like." He checked his watch. "I should get back to the bridge."

To watch for the other lifeboat. John shivered. Second night in the dark, on the water. At least they had their lanterns and flares. Flashlights.

Knowing that didn't cheer him up.

Filling the silence, the captain said, "The boat was loaded with crewmen, who've been taught survival procedures."

"Yeah, well," Donna muttered. "Some of those guys weren't the sharpest tools in the shed."

The man chuckled. "You're very forthright."

"So I've been told," Donna replied. She glanced at John.

"Well, we'd best go," he said. "Thanks very much for showing us around. It was fascinating."

"Yeah, thanks," Matt put in, without any prompting. "Um . . . ?"

"Tomorrow," the captain said. His hand hovered over Matt's head as if to tousle his hair; at the last moment he drew it away.

"Mr. van Buren?" Reade called.

Phil turned around. A light shone directly down on him, washing out his color. He looked like a figurehead himself, of a beached husband, maybe. Someone's swashbuckler once— or never—but now nothing but a weather-beaten shell. Visibly upset; all eyes and a lavender-bleached mouth that moved to say something pressed into a line. He swayed as he came toward the front of the museum, bracing himself against the glass cases. Elise breathed sharply through her nose, turned away.

"Are you all right, Mr. van Buren?" the captain asked, humor in his tone.

Phil jabbed his finger over his shoulder, back toward the figureheads. Then he shook his head and lowered his hand, and staggered toward his wife.

Ignoring him, Elise swept out the door. They all trooped out, Donna last.

The captain pulled her aside and murmured something to her. She smiled lazily and joined the others, and John tried to decide what to do about that dress, and his itch, and the pope.

Donna was feeling pretty good as they left the museum and headed down the corridor. First John and now the captain. And there'd been Ramón, of course, but he didn't count because he was on a mission from El Pocket Rocket, Hispanic god of sex. Back home she was impervious to flirtation because it was just the guys, just the cops she worked with, and it was like flirting with her brothers.

With one notable exception.

Anyway, the captain had invited her to be his guest at breakfast, and she'd agreed.

She caught up with John and strolled alongside him, suppressing a desire to whistle the theme from *The Love Boat*. Matt trotted ahead, chattering about rediscovering the sailing-ship playroom his father, but no one else, had seen, and Phil and Elise trudged behind like two hanging victims on the way to the gallows. Must be lotsa kicks in their bedroom. On the other hand, this could be the kind of stuff that got them off. Donna had handled enough domestic situations to expect anything.

The corridor was dimly lit, the lights yellow against the white walls. That hideous carpet. Officer, issue this boat a design citation. Put that rug in the *Guinness Book of Bad Taste*. Better yet, throw the decorator in the—

Suddenly John crowded close to her and hunched down as if the ceiling were too low for him. She waited, expecting him to scratch his leg or tie his shoe.

"Your ulcer hurt?" she asked. To her surprise, he ignored her.

Behind them, Phil and Elise crowded each cheek by jowl, walking like hunched old ladies. Matt minced stiff-legged with his arms close to his sides, pulling in his shoulders as if to avoid something.

"Guys?"

"What?" John said, and they all spread out again, filling up the corridor.

"Did I miss something?" she asked, glancing around.

John looked at her. A beat, then, "I'm sorry?"

She held out her hands. "You all squeezed in. Like the hall had gotten smaller . . . oh, forget it," she said at their confused expressions. "I must've imagined it." She made a gesture with her hands. "At least I'm seeing things, instead of not seeing them." Before John could say anything, she held up her finger and said, "First thing tomorrow. I promise I'll see Dr. Hare."

"Good. I'll come, too, if you want." They walked on. He asked casually, "What did the captain want?"

"Huh?" He pulled her out of her reverie—the way they'd scooted in. As if the hall had gotten smaller. Maybe the shadows had fallen just so, and they'd reacted to the optical illusion. Christ, who knew? Who cared? It was just so peculiar.

She waved her hand. "Oh, breakfast," she said airily. His face fell. To be kind, and also because it was true, she added, "I wanted to talk to him about this thousand-mile thing. That sounds bogus, don't you think?"

Glumly he nodded.

Men, she thought. They walked on.

But they *had* bunched up. She knew they had.

"He's an asshole, isn't he?" she added.

John brightened. "Yeah, he is."

Donna smiled to herself.

Men.

At the elevator, Phil said, "I think I'll have a nightcap, darlin'. I'm too keyed up to sleep."

His wife shrugged. The elevator came, and she went in with the others, leaving him in the hall.

"I won't be late."

"Good night," Donna said. The doctor and his son chorused the same. The doors closed on Elise's cool, composed, uncaring face.

He shouldn't, he knew he shouldn't. He was already drunk. But he didn't want to go back to the stateroom, not with her, and lie back to back in the dark, knowing that in her mind she was trying the captain's cock on for size. Just for yucks, and his stupid-ass heart would break all over again.

He noted a door he assumed led to the promenade deck. He was fairly certain there was a bar out there, a few steps down and to the right. The longer he was married, the better his sense of direction when it came to places where he could forget his troubles.

Yes, the promenade deck. It was enclosed with a thick wall of glass or plastic on the water side to keep the bad weather out. Empty deck chairs lined the bulkhead, a colorful green and white blanket folded and lying on each one, and the deck was a varnished lane of teak. Very pretty, with an old-fashioned feel to it. You could almost imagine ladies in bustles and floppy hats strolling by for the benefit of young men in derbies and spats, one eye on the girls and the other on a pair of dice or a deck of cards.

He walked to the center of the deck and stood with his feet apart, admiring the fat, pink moon that glowed through the barrier. Even on this immense ship, you knew how danged insignificant you were. It was like riding a button down the Mississippi. Did God care?

You'd think she'd have some sense of mortality. Some need for him. They could've died.

Tears ran down his face. All he wanted was to be loved. But the longer they were married, the more she hated him. She was so cruel, leaving them notebooks everywhere, her goddamn lists of all his material goods.

The tears fell harder. He couldn't help it. Couldn't help it. His cock wasn't twelve inches long and his chest wasn't shaped like a washboard, and he got rattled around strangers and he didn't like it when she screamed at the help. Was that so terrible? Was that grounds for . . .

for . . . her not loving him anymore?

All he wanted was to be loved. Poor old Glaucoma. Woman he loved turned into a monster.

Knew exactly how he felt, poor cracker.

The moon sparkled on the water. He thought he heard the rush of wings—

—could birds fly this far out? Where the hell *were* they, anyway? On the way to goddamned Australia?

The deck rocked, and he made four little running steps to

the left. Goddamn, he was drunker'n a skunk. Moonshine in the mountains, boys, Phil's ridin' a comet, yeah, boy.

All he wanted. All he wanted was a sweet girl to love him. The rush of wings—

Whoosh. Whoosh-whoosh.

Phil lurched right with another swell. What was that? *Whoosh-whoosh-whoosh.* Like something cutting through the water.

And way back in his ear, a soft hoot whispered, an echo-memory of something that made him murmur "Dixie." It played a poignant counterpoint to the *whoosh-whoosh-whoosh.*

And way, way back, just about too far back to detect, another noise: a . . . no, it was gone.

He listened for a moment. Everything was gone. His eardrums probably had the D.T.'s. Well, a beautiful night like this was wasted on a melancholy man. Time to get happy.

He staggered to the right. Saw the glow of yellow light farther down. Yes.

His footsteps were lonely on the deck. He was surprised no one else was out tonight. Ah, but someone was: he heard footfalls behind him, coming up fast, practically beside him now. He turned his head.

There was no one there. He cocked his head. Must have been mistaken.

Something brushed his hand—

—nothing.

He came to a door. It was shut, but the light he had seen beamed from a transom above it. "Smoking Saloon" was painted in the center of the door in elaborate curls of gold.

Whoosh-whoosh, whooooo.

Then the undersound.

He went in.

The red-flocked walls glowed beneath the oil lamps, and the oil painting of a naked woman over the bar seemed to undulate with the shifting light. Her breasts were huge and perfectly round; she had a Victorian tummy. With a jolt, he saw that her legs were spread open and everything painted in, the rosy little conch shell and all. Only then did he see her face, and he knew he'd seen that gentle face before: deep-set brown eyes, a small, upturned nose, a cupid mouth with a charming overbite. A demure wanton, Virgin Mary and the rock star Madonna. Every man's dream.

And then he noticed the woman who was sitting at the bar. The hairs on the back of Phil's neck rippled. Yes, he'd seen the face in the picture before. It was the face of the woman who now sat before him—

—and whose lacquered eyes had blinked in the museum (had *blinked, yes, they had!*)

—and who had smiled across the dining room until the shadow of a passer-by had dipped it in decay, and it had turned gray and mottled and the flesh had slid—

Dang, he was drunker'n a dead possum. He couldn't think straight, sure as hell couldn't see straight. His gaze returned to the painting. Had to be her. Had to be.

"Good evening, sir," the bartender said, and Phil jumped, not having noticed the man before. The man had a spectacular handlebar mustache and he looked vaguely familiar, though Phil couldn't place him.

The woman flattened her palm against the bar and gave herself a half turn so that she directly faced him. Her dress was pink, soft and silky, clinging and hinting, nothing sharp, nothing dangerous.

Whoosh.

"Um, may I sit down?" he asked. She dimpled.

"If you like."

Phil put down his empty port glass and eased himself onto the stool beside hers. Well, it was sure enough that he was much drunker than he felt, that much was clear. Self-conscious, he licked his lips and asked for bourbon and branch.

The woman crossed her legs. Her upper thigh pressed against the fabric of her dress and displayed the tone of her muscles. Good tone, as good as Elise's. Better, he thought defiantly.

"So, you're a survivor," she said.

"Aren't we all?" he quipped, his voice slurring.

She picked up her drink. It was a hurricane glass—

—no, it was, had been a martini glass. Hadn't it?

He frowned and stared at it. Something, a wisp of green—some kind of parsley? A flash of red. His lips parted. He pointed.

"There's a fish, a fish in your—"

He looked again. No. It was a plain martini glass, tinkling with ice.

"Yes?" she said. He shook his head. God, he'd better get to bed. He started to slip off the stool—

—had a sensation of falling, a thousand fathoms down, of sinking, and sinking and sinking—

—he caught his breath and steadied himself against the bar.

"Here's to ships," she said in a soft, husky voice. Her deep-set eyes bored into him, looked shyly down. "Ships that pass in the night."

He raised his own glass and sipped.

"I—I was hoping you'd walk in here," she confessed.

Phil warmed. His body quivered. She was attracted to him! In her own sweet way, she was flirting with him.

"So was I," he replied.

"The captain told me I'd meet someone nice on this cruise."

Phil glowered. "What would *he* know about it?"

The bartender pushed his bourbon toward him. The woman smiled at Phil and raised her glass. "To victory at sea."

"Damn straight." He socked it back.

And inhaled.

"Well," John said to Donna. They stood close together in front of her door, close enough if he got up the nerve, but then Matt yawned. The green dinosaur rested in his arms, and both were ready for nighty-night.

"Well," more briskly. John crossed his arms over his chest. "I guess we should go. It's very late."

"Nemo might have had the kitties," Matt added.

"Call me if she did?" Donna asked.

Matt nodded. "Good night."

The two trooped out the door.

"See you tomorrow." She shut it after them and pressed the lock. Turned and faced into the stateroom.

Something was not quite right.

Cops have a sixth sense, and a seventh, when things are out of whack. A strange feeling rattled up the backs of her legs and tapped her on the nape as she surveyed the room. The white lacquer furniture, the pictures. The bedside light on, the covers turned down. Did the steward do that, or was there a maid? No matter. That wasn't what was wrong. That worked. The rose in the water glass worked.

What didn't? The feeling gnawed at her. Anywhere else, she'd assume it was a prowler.

Anywhere else, she'd have her gun. It lay inside the nearly empty bureau, revolver in one drawer, bullets in another, hidden under extra towels and a box of Kleenex.

She held her breath, listening. The *Pandora* was much quieter than the *Morris,* but there were still creaks and groans. She thought she heard a band, some kind of Dixieland, and figured she must be above a club or bar. There were several on the ship, and Captain Reade had spoken proudly about a "West End–caliber" revue. So that was all right.

Maybe it was the memory of her sudden loss of vision that was freaking her out. Reluctantly, she touched her right eyelid. Terrifying. John was right; she should get checked. But she wasn't sure the ship's doctor would know any more than John did. He didn't strike her as a Harvard grad kind of guy; just what caliber of doc ended up tending sunburns and seasickness on a cruise ship, anyway?

She took a step into the room. The hairs on the back of her neck stood straight up. Donna shivered, cast her gaze left, right.

Nothing.

In the bathroom, then.

Swallowing, she forced herself to move across the room and go in, flick on the lights, and look.

Towels, sink, toilet, tub. Mirror on the medicine cabinet. Fluffy white bath mat on the floor.

She pulled back the shower curtain.

Nothing.

A cold sweat broke out across her chest and her face. She shivered, rubbed her arms, crossed back into the stateroom. This reminded her of her jitters on the *Morris* when the fog rolled in and turned Ruth Hamilton into a—

—a—

Say it, Donna: a dead, stiff little boy.

God. She shuddered hard and rubbed her arms. Her heart hammered. She could hardly bear to stay in the room. Anxiously she glanced at the door. Where else could she go? Was she going to demand another stateroom because she had the creeps? For Christ's sake, Osmond, get it together. There's nothing here. Nothing that shouldn't be, except you, you lunatic.

"Shit," she whispered. Turned—

—gasped—

—her own reflection.

Shit. Scowling, she reached behind and grabbed the dress's zipper and pulled it down. She'd be damned if she'd tiptoe around like some bimbo afraid of the dark. Battle fatigue, that's all it was. Hell, twenty-four hours in a lifeboat was enough to shake up anybody.

Pulled off her bikini underpants and stood naked in the air-conditioned room. No wonder she was shivering. She had on hardly any clothes and the room was very cold.

She walked into the bathroom and washed her face, swabbed off her makeup. Getting old, lady; lines and wrinkles.

She padded back to the bed and regarded the pulled-back covers. Something about the angle reminded her of a mouth. She folded her arms over her elbows.

She was afraid to get inside it. Something about the way the sheets encased you, something about lying prone. Something about turning off the light.

Something about losing your marbles, Donna. Get the hell in and stop this.

Gingerly she pulled back the sheet. Her pulse thumped in the hollow of her throat. Her face tingled with prickles. She swallowed again, hard.

Put one leg on the bed, sank down on her rump, and pulled

her knees up. Reclined, heart pounding. Uneasy inside her ribs, which were uneasy inside her skin.

She set the alarm. The captain ate breakfast at seven. She should get up by six-thirty at the latest.

Hesitated a long time, and then she turned off the light. The petals of the rose brushed her wrist like a tissue of skin.

In the dark she listened, eyes wide open. It was a subtle sensation, but you could tell you were on the water; not like the *Morris,* of course, or in the lifeboat. The captain had explained about the stabilizers that made the ride smoother. Neptune's shock absorbers.

Those poor men, out there somewhere. At least, she hoped they were out there somewhere.

What was that? Her ears pricked. Her skin tingled hard.

A creak. The ship. Footfalls in the corridor.

Something . . . no, nothing else.

Nothing else.

Breathed in, out. Willed her limbs to feel heavy: toes, feet, ankles, shins. Her heart beat fast and her skin prickled.

Knees, upper thighs, thighs, puss. Butt. Abdomen.

She yawned. Encouraged, she took more deep breaths. Thought about being heavier, made of lead, made of the heaviest thing on the planet. Something that dropped to the bottom like a stone and stayed there—

Christ. She tensed.

Sleep, Donna, sleep, whispered a voice deep inside her head. *You are exhausted.*

Exhausted? She was practically dead. Every atom in her body was drained to the max.

Flexing her leg muscles, she snuggled under the covers. Big breath in, hold it, hold it, toes, feet, ankles, shins . . .

Yes. And sinking, down deep, plummeting down, so heavy you could never, ever come back up . . .

But that's okay. That's okay because you can't hold it forever. That's okay.

Her lids fluttered as she melted into the mattress. Her anxiety detached itself and floated free with the tide. There was nothing wrong, nothing whatsoever. All she needed was rest. Tomorrow would be a better day.

The voice replied very quietly, so quietly she knew she had created it from the vestiges of her uneasiness:

Tomorrow? Don't count on it.

14

Enough to Shake Up Anybody

And from the depth of the ocean, King Neptune whispered:
No one else can see me, Cha-cha. Only you.

"Right on," Cha-cha whispered back. It had always been
that way. Only now, it was more so. He had never heard the
king better, since that bottle had showed up in his fishing net.

Since the paper inside it said something like, Do it!

"What'd you say?" Mr. Saar asked in a tight, clipped voice.
His head was a glowing, broiled apple and his lips were peeling. A gash along the side of his head was like a scratch on a
nickel on a sky-tray of dusty pewter.

They'd been at sea forever, and their still to make water
was broken, and something was wrong with all the bottled
water and food. There was a total of sixteen men in the boat,
and they were freaked out, and Cha-cha was sorry King Neptune wouldn't appear to them and comfort them. But he'd
always been the one, ol' Chach, right on, baby, and he alone,

because he was sorry about Nam. Just following orders, that's what everybody said, like the Nazis, man, but you knew it was evil to spray little kids and pregnant women with bullets and napalm. You knew it no matter who told you to do it. He'd forgotten about that, until the boy, Matt, had come aboard. It'd been a long time since a live kid walked the deck of the *Morris.*

Plenty of dead ones, though. Zonked-out, yellow kids with charred faces, stumps for arms. Wandering through the bulkheads, floating on the overheads, crying for their mamas and never finding them. Cha-cha had watched one run begging to that police lady, that Donna chick, but she'd just gone about her business without seeing him.

And the ghosts of the women, with blood running from between their legs and their titties slashed off for souvenirs, man; they howled and wailed and no one heard them 'cept him.

And what they did to the Viet Nam dudes, man. Back in Nam, what they did to them . . . Cha-cha had the hardest time of all with their ghosts. 'Cuz there was no way you could relate to all that brutality, all that torture . . .

And this was the same generation that went to Woodstock. Peace and love in the good ol' USA, and fucking up their karma in the world's worst way over in Indochina, and you couldn't straighten it out no matter how many Grateful Dead concerts you went to.

So Cha-cha stayed at sea forever on the *Morris* ('cept for the trips to the VA hospitals, but the ghosts cried for him and he came back, always came back), from the time the *Morris* was called the USNS *John J. Abernathy* to the time it was the *Moonfish* to now. He was a live ghost, man, and that was all you could do about it.

Damn straight, Cha-cha. You were the only one who understood the evil of that ship. You were the only one I could trust to do the right thing.

Mr. Saar was glaring at Cha-cha, so he covered his mouth and whispered, "Right on, King."

So far so good, Cha-cha.

Right on, King.

Now watch, I'm going to make something happen.

Water rippled on the flat sea.

"Oh, my God!" Eskimo shouted. "It's a fish! Oh, Jesus!"

Everyone held their breath and watched the row of fishing lines. A dozen were set with the flies that came in the survival boxes. In the entire week, they hadn't caught anything.

Watch, Cha-cha.

The line nearest Mr. Saar jittered. A hushed cheer rose up; Mr. Saar motioned for everyone to stay quiet as he pulled in the line, very, very carefully.

A grouping, gasping black fish flapped onto the deck and started to jive-dance itself to death. Open, close, open, gasping, the large fish was drowning in oxygen; its blank eye wide and unblinking, bursting with fatality.

Righteous, Your Majesty.

You believe in me, don't you, Cha-cha? You believe I have your best interests at heart?

Aye, sir. Yessir. Cha-cha saluted. Nobody on board noticed; their attention was riveted on the fish. Hands grabbed it, held it down. The men were about to rip it to pieces, and why not, dudes? It was going to die one way or the other.

You know I would only tell you to do the right thing.

"For sure," Cha-cha whispered, watching the men and the smothering fish.

And you would do it.

Yes, sir, King, sir. You know it, baby. You know it, righteous Neptune-god. I'll follow orders, oh, yes, I will, because you're my karmic commander in chief.

And if you pass this test, you shall be my new acolyte, Cha-cha.

"Oh, far out," Cha-cha murmured, though he wasn't sure what an acolyte was.

In a blaze of glory, the king heaved his beautiful sea self out of the waves and floated beside the boat, and with his trident he pierced the fish in the side. Its mouth convulsed and then it stiffened. Dead. And the men knew it, and began tearing its head off.

Then he pointed his trident at the boatful of men and said,
in his ringing sea king voice:
Kill them, Cha-cha.
Kill them all.
I'm hungry, too.

15
Surface Tension

It was late, too late. The handsome captain had visited Ruth hours ago. They had talked about her harrowing experience, and about Stephen, though she hadn't meant to. Most embarrassing, she must have dozed off in his presence. Cool breezes had washed over her from the open porthole when she awakened to the night, with a terrible headache that throbbed as if the inside of her head was frozen.

Then she must have dozed off again, and in the bathroom of all places! Or sleepwalked, for she was standing upright, staring into the mirror. A hazy shape smeared across it, distorting Ruth's face with a series of afterimages, Vaseline on a camera lens. Something drifting away—colors, shapes, a golden radiance—swimming away, languid and lovely, so beautiful, so beautiful, up slowly, so very deliberately, and up and up, toward the—

"Come back," she whispered. Air rushed from her windpipe and she jerked up her head. Her lids fluttered. She blinked at the mirror,

and saw only herself.

Her face was dripping wet. The sink was brimming with water, the faucet not quite off, trickling into the overflow.

"I've been dreaming," she said aloud. "I've been dreaming."

She stood naked in the bathroom, with her old woman's pendulous breasts and belly exposed, her large-boned thighs, and tried to comprehend what she was doing there. Her eyes stared back at her, bewildered. Her body was rosy and happy, as if she'd been having . . . as if a man—

Stephen.

Her hand over her breasts, she lowered herself onto the toilet seat. A drop of water hung suspended from her chin, splashed onto her abdomen. Self-consciously she covered herself, as if someone else were in the room.

Were still in the room.

"Stephen?" she whispered. A flutter of anticipation and fear behind her knees, at her elbows, the nape of her neck. Her heart pounded and she cocked her head, listening, attempting to sense a presence. Why was her face wet? She tried to think, but her mind was reeling, her attention outside herself, not inside her head. Washing her face? She used cold cream, didn't put water on her face at night. Too drying.

Water, too drying. How odd that was.

She listened hard. Things like this only happened in books or movies. She had never believed—

—she had always believed he was alive. Alive. She hadn't believed in things like this.

Things like what?

Breathing in, her lips rippled like fins. She began to tremble all over.

Why was her face wet?

"I've been dreaming." Her words seemed to reverberate off the tiles. "Dreaming."

Somewhere in the distance, the sound of dripping water. Her gaze ticked to the sink taps. Nothing. The tub. Also nothing. Then it stopped. Perhaps she should tell someone. If it was a leak . . .

Don't be foolish, Ruth, she told herself. Her next-door neighbors were probably showering or taking a bath. On a ship the size of the *Pandora,* a thousand things could be going on.

She wiped her hands together, over and over and over.

Why was her face wet?

And why, beneath the anxiety, was she marvelously, soaringly happy?

"Donny-O! Jesus, I'm glad to hear your voice."

The connection was not the greatest. But Donna had awakened an hour after she'd drifted off, with a major case of the willies; and it occurred to her to try Glenn again.

His voice gave her good, deep shivers. "Yeah, well, I guess it's pretty good to hear yours, too." She pulled at the sheet that covered her breasts.

"They said you almost bought it. Newspapers've been calling the station. Randolph's pissed."

Donna closed her eyes and shook her head. "That's our boy. One of his men nearly buys it and he gets pissed because of the extra work it makes for him." She shifted under the covers and stuck her arm under her neck. "I wonder if they've been blocking the calls here. We haven't had any. Their phone system is for shit. I can hardly hear you."

"What's the tub like? They said it was a new one. It's got an un-American name."

"*Pandora.* Like the woman with the bottle?" She paused. Oh, so that was the ship's logo? A mermaid with a bottle? "No, wait. This one had a box."

"All women have boxes, Donald."

"Oh, fuck you." She scratched her thigh. The ship creaked and rolled. "Listen," she said, "they been talking about the illegal cargo?"

"Say huh?"

"Some kind of crap they dumped, or were gonna dump, in the ocean without permission. In the lifeboat, the first officer confessed . . ." She stopped herself. Screw it. She was talk-

ing to the man she loved, not her coworker. Her heart quick-
ened and her voice grew soft. "I'll tell you about it later.
Glenn . . ."

There was a pause. Glenn cleared his throat.

"Donny, I had a talk with Barb. She . . ." He cleared his
throat again. "I'm gonna get a new partner, babe."

Wham. Donna closed her eyes.

The whiskey voice of Lady Day crooned through her veins,
swirling, weeping, through the veins, *no, no, no,* the keening
of the lost, of losing, of pain that you couldn't even feel, it
hurt so much, and you needed someone else to feel it, and
that was why Billie had died crazy, junk crazy. 'Cuz you
needed something to dull it. You couldn't believe how bad it
hurt . . .

the pain . . .

Oh, God.

My man.

Oh, I love him so . . .

"Sweetheart?" The first time he'd ever called her that.
"Donna?" First time in a long time.

"You . . ." She swallowed down hot tears. Goddamn it,
she wasn't like this. She didn't care. "You've got a really
fucked sense of timing, Boelhauf." Her voice cracked.

"Donna, you know why. You almost said it yourself, when
you left. You know I love—"

She hung up, stared at the receiver.

The world is all despair . . .

It grabbed you under the tear ducts and tore you down the
middle and peeled you back, so you sat there gaping, one big
wound, all the hoses around your heart pumping out your
life. And inside, the life-saving cut-off systems didn't work,
not too good; the pain slipped in over the flanges at the
bottoms of the chambers. The sea washed over them, trailing
in the things that swam and lurked beneath the surface;
bringing in the stuff that made you sink, made you drown,
made you.

The phone sat there, staring back smugly. Take that, it told
her. You wanted to talk to him? You thought maybe his
woman would be out and the two of you could have a cozy

pillow session? You thought just because you lived through a shipwreck you could have him?

God, the pain . . .

Oh, my man. My man, I . . .

My man.

Her eyes were dry as sandpaper. The tears wanted to come. They begged to come.

But big girls don't, and neither did she.

Ninety-nine bottles of blood on the wall.

Phil looked up from his drink. It was near dawn, and he was alone.

In a storeroom, with an empty bottle of—

—*bourbon,* beside his port glass. Bourbon, yes, and an odd, confusing feeling of relief washed through him as he focused in on the Kentucky Thoroughbred on the label.

Bourbon, not—

—anything else, and with a woman, not with a—

—a ghost or a monster or something—

His head pounded unmercifully. Groaning, he grabbed it in an attempt to keep his skull from fragmenting with the pain.

Brooms and pails leaned against a wall and covered most of a poster of a woman in high heels and a bathing suit. Shelves containing large brown containers marked "Industrial Strength. USE AS DIRECTED" lined the other. Above him, a light bulb hung from a cord and fizzed like a moth.

His head sang and he shut his eyes as he forced down a stream of upchuck. Tried to smile at the awkwardness of his thought—down, upchuck—but didn't make it.

Vomited hard into the nearest bucket.

And as he did so, his hand pressed the deck, and it was covered with something bumpy and scratchy, and the room stank of decomposition, salt, rotten things. The room went dark, completely black—

—and as he finished and squinted into the darkness, the bumpiness smoothed out, and the smell faded, but the light did not come back on.

"Hmmpf." He rocked back onto his butt and pushed himself up. The darkness crested around him; he rocked back and forth, teetering to catch his balance, and flailed for the wall. Grabbed a pipe—

—no, a broom—and pictured himself in the pitch-black storage room, swaying like a damn pendulum with a broom in his hand.

Sidestepped toward the door, found the knob, and let himself out.

He stood on the promenade deck, right about where he had let himself into the bar. Where the moon had glowed, the yellow sun rested on top of a fluffy cumulus cloud.

But there was no bar. Only a storage room. He must have gotten turned around. Good Lord, he'd stumbled around the ship, drunker than a danged ol' skunk. He didn't remember a thing. Everything past the first drink in the bar was a blank.

Sagging, he turned left and headed down the promenade. Looked back. Darn it, the bar should be there. Right there.

He scratched his head, and even that hurt. It hurt to think. So he put his questions on hold and walked back toward the foyer and the elevators.

Elise wouldn't be worried about him, but she would be angry.

Maybe he should sleep it off in the storage room. Him and Betty Grable.

The very deep did rot.

Donna's own hand, floating white beside her as she swam the black, frigid depths. The ribs of a monster—

—no, no, of a ship. The ribs, and nothing else, nothing but the ribs and her hand. Her hand, which was nothing but bone. Her hand, around which flaps of skin, bone-white, transparent, and empty of blood, wafted and drifted.

Bobbing and drifting, she swam within the ribs of the ship, like something that had peeled away from it. A piece of living tissue, floating inside a prison of rib bones.

No, no, the ship wasn't alive. Its ribs were wood, rotting wood. She narrowed her eyes. Rotting, and impregnated with worms. The ribs were a writhing mass of them.

The worms go in, the worms go out. The worms, the snakes, the serpents.

No, no, the ship wasn't alive.

And it wasn't waiting.

For her RSVP.

Reply, if you please.

Hours went by.

In her bed, Donna cozied up to the warmth beside her. Her bare ass dipped into the valley created by the weight of *his* body and slid against some part of him, probably *his* hip. Oh, Glenn, oh, darling, please, yes, do it. Yes, do it.

Reply, if you don't please. Tell me what you want. Is it the man? Have I got it right this time? The boy, or the man? Or something else? Name your poison. Name my bait.

Name it.

Donna rolled over on her back.

Ice water into her brain, freezing it. She gritted her teeth with pain, grunted, forcing herself to stop it, stop it.

"Stop it!" She sat up and looked wildly around. Through the open porthole the sun was rising over the water, stippling the sky with turquoise and salmon.

And the other half of her bed was warm.

She thought nothing of it—who wouldn't toss and turn, after a phone call like that—but despite her desolation she was struck by the irony of it: now that it was over (whatever "it" had been), she'd had a wet dream about Glenn.

And you go on, Donna thought wearily, as she was escorted by a steward into the officers' dining room. Wan, a little shaky, you say Fuck him and you make it through the morning, because you do. And maybe that's why he could say good-bye to her; that inner strength of hers, or denial or whatever the hell kept her from begging, and maybe he thought that was evidence that she didn't need him. While Barb did.

So she tossed her hair, loaded on the makeup, went to breakfast. Good morning, heartache, take a seat in my soul.

And jeez, she thought, better seat Captain Reade up on a dais, on a throne with a papal canopy, for all the deference the other officers gave him. He was king of the bounding main on the *Pandora*, sitting in state at the head of a long table, smack dab in the center of a long, narrow room. All four walls were painted white and covered with a row of dark paintings of ships and seascapes. There were no portholes; it was an interior room. Donna added another square to her mental map of the *Pandora*.

The space at Reade's right was reserved for Donna with a little white place card (OFF. ALMOND, comforting choice of words and phrases), the one across from her empty, and other officers filled the places in long double rows. So much crisp, starched white, the uniforms, the tablecloth, the napkins. She was snowblinded.

A steward, a young black man, approached with a silver coffeepot. "We should begin," Reade said, checking his watch. "My day usually starts earlier than this, Ms. Almond."

"Oh? You didn't need to hold off on my account."

"But I wanted to have breakfast with you." He put his arm around the back of her chair. His cheek was smooth and smelled good. His eye glinted and he smiled as if he had a really good secret.

"What I meant was, I could've gotten up earlier. I didn't . . . sleep well last night."

He looked concerned, peering at her very seriously. He said, in a low undervoice, "Has something happened?"

"No, no. It's nothing."

"You don't seem yourself." That single eye, like some laser beam. What was that old TV show? *Battlestar Galactica*. The Cylons had a single red eye that pulsed and pulsed, just before they cremated you.

"It's nothing, really. Thank you," she said to the young steward as he poured her coffee.

"Well, if there's anything I can do."

"You've done enough already," she said quickly as she

sipped. Seeing his bemused smile, she added, "Saving us and all."

"It was nothing," he answered, the hero's ultimate cliché. "Let me introduce you to the officers. I believe most of the ones you've met are still on duty."

Bell, Jaros, Baker, Kelly, a dozen others. Nice guys, easygoing, seemed competent; and all a bit familiar, she supposed from their having been around the ship. They appeared fond of the captain, but he was clearly The Old Man, alone at the top. Didn't seem to mind.

"What's for breakfast?" she asked.

"Steak and eggs," Reade told her. "We prefer . . . simpler fare than what they eat in the passengers' dining room. I hope you don't mind."

"Mind?" She unfolded her linen napkin and spread it over her lap. "Can I eat here every day?"

He also unfolded his napkin. "If you like."

"That'd be very nice, ma'am," Kelly said. Hmm, giving her the once-over. Her red T-shirt was on the tight side. She returned the favor and he let her, with a swagger.

"Ma'am, how do you like your steak?" the steward asked Donna as he refilled her coffee cup. She had trouble understanding his accent, some kind of Rasta thing, African, she didn't know.

"Rare." The steward nodded and brisked away. "That's the only way to eat meat," Donna said.

Reade took his arm from around her chair and picked up the sugar bowl, offered it to her. She shook her head.

"I eat it rare, too." He put three heaping spoonfuls of sugar into his coffee, stirred. "So rare it's practically raw. With the blood oozing . . ."

"Juice," Donna cut in, grinning. "Call it juice."

"Lots of juice, then. To your health." He inclined his head as he drank his coffee. The others raised their cups in a toast.

"And yours. You-all's." She sipped. Marveled at how well she was doing, considering that what she really wanted to do was mourn the loss of what she had never had.

"Any word on the lifeboat?" she queried as a number of

stewards put steaks and fried eggs in front of each diner. Grilled tomatoes, how British. Sausages.

The officers looked at each other, then at the captain, as though there were a tacit agreement among them that only he should discuss the subject.

"Not so far." He cut his meat with a very sharp knife, slashing it; blood dribbled around the perimeter of his eggs. "I must say, the passengers have been quite civilized about it, our using up their vacation this way. This is quickly becoming a cruise to nowhere."

He chewed lustily, talked with his mouth full. "There are such, you know, for people who are rather jaded about cruising. They've seen all the ports . . ." He snapped his fingers at the steward. "More marmalade," he said harshly.

"Aye, sir." The steward scurried away.

"So they just sail around in the ocean?" Donna finished for the captain.

"Yes. To play and to feed. It's astonishing how much we go through on a ship this size."

"'To feed'?" Donna laughed. "You make them sound like horses!"

"Or cattle," Jaros offered. There was general laughter around the table.

"Well, what are you going to do today?" Reade asked her, coming close again. "There are so many things to do. We have films, and video, and of course, there are dance lessons and lectures and cultural activities."

Cultural activities? God spare her. "I don't know. Maybe go swimming." She'd get a bottle and hole up in her room, cry and scream until she threw up.

He slashed another bite of meat and chewed it thoughtfully.

"What are *you* going to do today?" she asked him.

He made an expansive gesture with his hand. "Keep things going. Show young Matt how to steer the ship." He looked over his shoulder. "Keelhaul a certain steward for forgetting the marmalade."

Donna nodded sagely. "A capital offense."

His face hardened into a mask of anger that set her back in

her chair. The single green eye narrowed, his nostrils flared; his lips pulled back from his teeth in a feral grimace. "On this ship, it is," he said in a low, menacing tone.

The others stopped eating. Tension rose in the air like hysteria. Jesus. Donna sat still, feeling out the situation. Her stomach tightened as he glared; not at her, she knew, but she couldn't help her reaction.

And then it was over. The captain picked up his knife and severed another chunk of meat, incising it from the bone. Quick, and neat, and deft. He brought it to his mouth and a droplet of . . . juice . . . vibrated on his lower lip.

Everyone began eating again. Donna raised her brows and scooped egg and toast into her mouth. Damn. How bizarre.

"Have the newspapers been calling the ship?" she asked, trying a new tack. "TV? My partner back home said they're flooding the station with calls."

Reade shook his head. "We've moved out of range. There won't be any more calls for a while. Incoming or outgoing."

"Really? But I talked to him just a couple hours ago."

"We've traveled quite a distance since then," he replied. "We're trying to find the lifeboat," he reminded her.

"When will we get back to a port?" she asked. "I only have a three-week vacation."

"Oh, you'll make it."

She frowned. "But I need to—"

His smile was firm. "You're beginning to sound a bit like that van Buren woman, Ms. Almond."

Donna was flabbergasted. Speechless, for a moment, and then she said icily, "I really don't think that was called for, Captain Reade."

He stood his ground, lifting his chin and pursing his lips together. "It's just that you sounded remarkably unconcerned about the fate of those aboard the lifeboat."

He was right. She made a moue of apology. "Point well taken."

He raised his brows. Her stomach caught at the sight of the left one, peering above his eye patch. So to speak. But it reminded her of other hidden things behind it. "Oh, I wasn't trying to score points off you, Ms. Almond."

"Donna, and I know." For something to do, she grabbed a Danish and tore a section of it off. "It did sound pretty shitty."

His laughter burst out of him, a surprise. He scratched his chin and cupped it with his palm, leaning on the table as he regarded her.

"You're not the usual fish one catches out of the sea."

"I guess most cops like to think they're pretty unique."

"And unpredictable?"

"Oh, I think once you get to know me, I'm fairly predictable." She popped the piece of Danish into her mouth.

"You're difficult to read, then. Very difficult. I'm having one hell of a time."

She posed. "That's because I have a metal plate in my head. From Nam."

His mouth fell open. Christ, he believed her! She guffawed —Glenn called it braying, said she sounded like a donkey— and was about to tell him it was a joke when a bleary-eyed man in uniform appeared at the dining-room door.

"Sir, the watch would like a word with you," he said.

The captain half rose from his chair. "The lifeboat, Huntsinger?"

"No, sir, nothing like that."

Reade sighed and touched his lips with his napkin. "I'm sorry."

Donna cut herself another piece of meat. "No problem. Thanks so much for inviting me."

"Perhaps we could do it again tomorrow?"

She shrugged. "I'll have to check my busy social calendar. Can I let you know later?"

He shook his head in amusement. "Don't forget to wait an hour before you swim. And watch out for sharks."

She gave him a mock-salute, which the other officers seemed pleased with, half-hidden smiles going around. Brother. Get a life, boys.

You know of oysters, Cha-cha, how they lie panting in their iced half shells. Fresh, not rotted, you know when men swallow them, their hearts still beat, and they dissolve slowly, painfully, in stomach juices.

These men must be our oysters, Cha-cha. And you must harvest them for me.

Fresh.

From his seat in the lifeboat, Cha-cha made a half salute and murmured, "Aye, sir."

"For God's sake, what the hell are you mumbling about over there?" Mr. Saar demanded. His fingers stank of fish guts and blood; they'd devoured everything, even the eyes. One fish among sixteen was not enough, not nearly.

Think about the Indianapolis, *Cha-cha. She was in the Second World War. One thousand men aboard her, and they all went down. Some drowned. Oil fires raged for weeks.*

"Oh," Cha-cha whispered, twisting his fingers around each other. "Oh, man."

Schools of sharks attacked them, Cha-cha. Ripped off their arms and legs and their heads, Cha-cha. Tore open their stomachs.

Think about that, Cha-cha. The blood in the water. The bloodred water. And then think of Nam, and the Morris, *and if only you'd known me then.*

"Oh, oh." Tears welled in Cha-cha's sunburned eyes. "Yeah, man."

"You're always fucking mumbling and muttering." Mr. Saar's face was shriveled with sunburn; his arms swollen and covered with blisters. The other men were skulls painted red.

"You crazy old bastard," Eskimo said. "We ought to . . ." His eyes narrowed as he looked at the others. His teeth were yellow and sharp as a weasel's, and his fingers were black talons. "We oughta throw your skinny ass overboard."

As one, they leaned forward, suddenly alert, suddenly cruel. Cha-cha swallowed and scrabbled into a corner at the stern, kicking a box of flares with his heel and tangling himself in a coil of line.

Fear not, Cha-cha, I am with you.

I will help you.

Think of this, me hearty hardy: They are nothing but oysters. Blood-rare belly timber.
All of them.
All.
Even your precious Officer Donna, and she is delicious.

16
Cracked in Four Places

Alone, alone, all, all alone
Alone on a wide, wide sea!
And never a saint took pity on
my soul in agony.

John tiptoed onto the veranda of his and Matty's suite (the Odysseus) and shut the sliding glass door behind him. The moon flamed as it set, bleeding through the water. John stared at it as his heart beat fast, faster, too fast. He bit his knuckle until he drew blood. It was always darkest just before the dawn.

Yes, it was. It was pitch-black; you couldn't see anything, black as a gunshot wound, as a grave hole, as the future without . . . without . . .

The sobs burst out of him. He held his blazing stomach. His torso convulsed and his head missed the rail by a quarter of an inch as he fell to his knees and stuck his face between the slats.

Matty was getting sick again. He didn't need tests to tell him that. John had awakened and rolled over, and seen him, and it hit him all at once, really hit him for the really truly very first time, that his boy could die. Like a shaking slaughterhouse calf, he had come to the fact that there was something worse than chemotherapy, or radical surgery, or the whimpering of his child, too weak to cry. No one ever wanted it. When they said they wanted it to end, they meant the pain.

No one wanted to die, ever. Least of all his baby.

It was a punishment for daring to believe it was over. For going on a vacation out of reach of their medical safety net. The sin of pride, of daring to believe God's hand didn't fall on those in peril on the sea.

"Oh, please. Please." His glasses fell off his face and clattered on the tiled flooring. One hand clutching his stomach, he buried his face against his arm and lost track of words and prayers and sank into abject fear. Drowning in it. He couldn't anymore, he couldn't, couldn't.

Matty. Oh, Matty.

He couldn't.

It was just a panic attack, he told himself, over and over. It wasn't real. Night terrors. It was always darkest . . .

He shook.

He couldn't give him up. He would never give him up. Oh, sweet Lord, sweet Jesus, please.

He cried until he was out of tears, but not out of grief. Then he lay curled on the chill tiles, his glasses twisted beneath his side. His chest rose now and then with an exhausted sigh, like a dying fish.

Matty. Matty. He reached for the bottom of the door, as if he could will himself through it and touch his son.

The moon drowned. The sea oozed red, persimmon, chartreuse. It gleamed with silver, the underside of a rotten fish.

Then the world shrank into a pinprick. His senses alerted him with a sudden, sure knowing that he was not alone on the balcony. Someone actually stood behind him, within the railing. Not Matt, though. He knew that as well. His child lay sleeping.

It was John who was in danger. He felt it creeping through him like ice water. Something very wrong, menacing. Something that watched, and . . .

. . . and wanted. It wanted something.

The world spun on the head of a pin, a needle; John's attention focused to a point at the back of his head. Somehow he knew he mustn't look, mustn't turn his head to look at it. That if he did . . .

. . . what?

Nonsense. He tried to roll over, or even to move his head, but he was paralyzed. His lips moved, but he could say nothing. Many thoughts rushed through his head: of fleeing, of confronting the intruder, of doing something to protect himself and his son.

And another thought, that had begun before the feeling that he wasn't alone, and that continued despite it: *I will do anything, I will do anything, I will do anything.*

And another sure sense:

Of the intruder replying, *I know.* "It is natural for men to indulge in the illusion of hope. We are apt to shut our eyes against a painful truth, and listen to the song of that siren 'til she transforms us into beasts."

Your Patrick Henry said that, John, Father John, and I am saying it to you now.

And you are listening, Father John.

You are all ears. And heart. And ripe for reeling in, yes, most ripe and ready.

And Ramón, what do you want?

What is your desire? What calls you to me?

"Hey!" Ramón yelled again, pounding on the door of the dim cabin. He couldn't believe they'd locked him up. What about you had to be proven guilty first? *Chinga tu madre,* Donna Almond. It was her fault, the bitch, for sticking her nose in his business.

He wiped sweat off his forehead. He was worried. Hell, he

was *scared.* They were going to get him no matter what Captain Esposito had promised. Pin the whole thing on him, boot him out of the merchant marine, damn it to hell, *coño, macho,* and probably throw him in prison. Real prison, not juvie. With fudge-packin' bench-pressers and dudes who had nothing to lose.

This would kill his mother.

He got up and paced the cabin. The floor was dusty; there was the same poster of Guns N' Roses on the plain white wall that one of the Ordinary seamen had had back on the *Morris.* A rack, and that was all. Hard to believe there was spare cabins on this ship; he'd never been on a vessel before that wasn't packed to the gills with freight and bodies.

Where was someone with some food? He was starving. And he had to piss like a racehorse. *Chingada.*

Hijo, he didn't even know what had been in the barrels. Never had. He just untied the lines and rolled them overboard. He'd done it a dozen times, gotten the extra thousand a dozen times. Twelve thousand dollars, and now his ass was in a sling, *hombre.*

He put his head in his hands. "Big man," he could hear his *mamacita* taunting him. She would stand before him in her white ruffled apron, her hands on her hips, and shake her head at him: "Big man, you think you're a big man now, Moncho?"

Now that you've belonged to a gang?

Now that you've been busted for drugs?

Now that you've been arrested for breaking and entering?

Now that your blood has trailed through your mother's house, and the boy who knifed you lies in a coffin?

Now that you have ruined your career with the merchant marine, and ruined your life, and broken your mother's heart?

Big man. You always wanted to be a big man, eh? Like some Viking warrior on those stupid movies of yours?

Ah ha.

17
Red Sails in the Sunset

The second day aboard the *Pandora* was almost over. The sun was a dark red ball that shimmered as it drowned.

As she leaned against the rail of the Nereus deck, Donna let the sunset breezes waft through her hair. The water churned, dark green and orange, purple and scarlet, deep and unfathomable. Water, water, everywhere.

Her gaze flicked now and then to the aerobics class on the far side of the varnished deck, separated from her by a pool tiled in blue and green; a scattering of men among mostly svelte women, although there were some real sad cases. A towheaded child in pj's bouncing up and down with a teddy bear in her arms. Beyond, an impromptu group had gathered to dance to the taped music, *Jump, jump, for my love*. Bouncy, peppy stuff. Fuck you, cellulite, and the thighs you rode in on. Oh, and have a nice day.

On a raised platform behind the aerobics class, two Asian men performed tai-chi exercises. Their faces were dark in the twilight, but serenity was evident in their sliding, meditative movements.

Donna had on her red dress, and she was lonely, but she was sending out the signals smart men set their band widths to monitor: Don't look at me, don't approach me, don't speak to me. She was thinking about Glenn, and how bitterly ironic the music was as it bopped along, a mindless counterpoint to the mindless, numbing dirge inside her. A private soundtrack that made the blues sound like Paula Abdul. She flashed on a piece of gallows humor. At least now maybe she could really sing out the pain. Get those gigs in this tight red dress. Maybe her guts hurt enough . . .

No. She clamped down hard and the walls slid up; and she felt . . . foggy. Odd, how she could accomplish that. Big name for it was disassociation, happened to abused kids; that was how psychos and multiple personalities got born. The pain was so bad they made someone else feel it.

My heart has an ache . . .

She watched the exercises, the tai-chi men, and her mind wandered. Saw the Tahoe boy, pondered those stupid what-ifs: if Glenn had been there; if Daniel had slept through it; if she'd had one less drink and hadn't picked him up in the first place. If she hadn't fallen—

—been pulled—

—down the embankment back into that freezing water. Little boy, little boy, is there a heaven and do you spiral through it?

Her mind shut out the questions, floated on. Christ, what now? Was she supposed to date? It took so much effort to be nice to somebody you didn't know. Sometimes she just didn't know how. Cops were generally emotionally retarded; they all acted so childish because they didn't know how to behave like grown-ups, except in emergencies.

Except then.

A tall blond man glanced her way. She cranked up her repulso ray. Let her guard down now, she'd end up with a sympathy fuck, and he was probably some slime like Daniel.

My heart . . . heavy as stone.

Okay, so fuck a known quantity, Donna. Mentally she

shook her head. John was nice, but like her, he had someone else on his mind. The captain was interesting, but he just wasn't right. The ego there was monumental, and she felt every time she talked to him she was dealing with the proverbial seven-second delay. Earth to Cap'n Reade, breaker, breaker, c'mon?

So. So that left the sun going down, and Donna trying to get up the energy to buy herself a drink.

An ache.

The sky was a neon rainbow, orange and turquoise and purple. So beautiful. Such an adventure, the *Morris,* the lifeboat, this. But now she felt isolated from it, like a widow, the perpetual spectator. When she got back to San Diego, things would be very different.

But at least she could go back. At least she hadn't died at sea. She smiled dryly, thinking what Glenn would retort to that: "Yeah, I wept because I had no hat. Then I met a broad who had no head."

Her darling smartass. Oh, her man, her man, she loved him so.

She wanted to toss some flowers into the water. That's what they did at a funeral at sea, didn't they?

And how thick is our sense of melodrama today, Officer?

She sighed and leaned her head in her hands. Maybe she'd go buy that drink. Maybe she'd

jump, jump, overboard for my love

"What?" She straightened quickly and looked around for the joker. Paused. It must have been a glitch on the tape, somebody mouthing off.

"Oh, one of the *Morris* people," she heard someone say, in a voice tinged with awe. Two old ladies sauntered along, towing an elderly man in a golf cap. He shuffled awkwardly. Stroke victim. God, she'd never want to go through that. When she went, she wanted to go quickly. Not like the boy, though. Not unnecessarily. Not 'cuz of being stupid.

And he hadn't gone quickly. Oh, no. Drowning took a good while. Had taken.

A quartet of young Japanese men took pictures of each other, of the American chicks making it burn in spandex.

Their enthusiasm was endearing as one of the girls waved at them in midhop and they laughed and waved back. Life goes on, don't it, Kemo Sabe?

That it does. That it does. She wrapped her hands around the rail and stretched her back, lifting her face to the red sun. The seas spewed behind the ship in an impressive display, misting her face. She ran her tongue around her mouth and caught up the salt.

Life goes on, and the parade passes you by, sometimes. Such a beautiful night, and so much romance in the air.

With a sigh, she left the deck and took the elevator to the next deck down, the Amphitrite deck, intending to nose in the ship's boutiques. But after she got off the elevator, it occurred to her she had no idea who or what Amphitrite was, and she didn't even have the slightest idea how to pronounce it. That pissed her off, in her current mood. She didn't like feeling rejectable on any grounds, and she'd never ascribed to the idea that ignorance could be an attractive trait in a woman.

She stomped over to the nearest ship's map, done up like an unfurled scroll with Greek designs at the top and bottom, and located the library. It was close by. Good.

"Mind if I join you?"

Donna looked up from *Flotsam: A Maritime Encyclopedia of Trivia.*

The captain perched on the arm of her brown leather sofa. She'd kicked off her shoes and curled her feet underneath her, realizing for the first time that they'd gone to sleep.

"Hey, it's your ship."

He smiled. "Aye, that it is." He craned his neck and scanned the page she was on. "Ah, you're reading 'The Rime of the Ancient Mariner.'" She nodded. "What do you think?"

She decided she might as well be honest. "I don't like it much. A lot of the rhymes sound forced. And he just keeps throwing more and more stuff in."

"Oh? Such as?"

"The woman. This Life–in–Death person he says was on the other ship. What's she there for?"

He looked at her strangely. Okay, she was dumb. So sue her. For every penny she had, she added wryly, thinking of Elise van Buren-Hadley.

"She's the one who curses the mariner," he said. "She invents his punishment. She was gambling with Death for his fate."

Donna considered that. Didn't get it. "So either he could die, or sail around forever?"

He inclined his head; she couldn't see his features. "Yes, with a dead crew."

Donna frowned. "Then what about the Spirit? The one he pissed off when he shot the albatross?"

The captain licked his lips. A bead of sweat formed at his temple. Interesting.

"His . . . strong emotion," he said, as if he were having difficulty speaking. His eye took on a faraway gleam. "It calls the Spirit."

"Well, so like . . ." She wiggled her feet. Caterpillers crawled up her insteps. She thought about an old *Star Trek* episode, where a creature fed on the emotions of the crew and made them all fight with each other. Cops as a rule loved science fiction shows. She had no idea why.

"It will give him what he wants . . ." And he was gone, somewhere else. Donna watched his face. A muscle jumped in his cheek and the sweat bead popped and slid underneath his eye patch. Eeuu.

But that wasn't what the poem said, she wanted to point out, decided against it. She waved her hand. "I see. I get it now. Thanks." She flicked the pages. "I was looking through this, and just got to reading it because John and Ruth were reciting it on the *Morris.*"

"Ah," he said. A curious smile wiped away his dreamy stare. "*They* are the poets."

"I guess."

"I'm not much for that poem, either," he went on companionably. "I prefer the exploits of Odysseus."

"Golden fleece?" she ventured.

He chuckled. "That was Jason. No, Odysseus was the one who wandered over land and sea for decades. He was a great sailor, a godlike captain."

He sat straight and raised his chin. Saw faraway things she could only guess at: the great, godlike Captain Reade, on a quest fraught with fabulous dangers.

Donna snapped her fingers. "He was the one who tied himself to the mast so he could hear the . . . the mermaids."

His features softened, and he said, almost in a whisper:

" *'I have heard the mermaids singing, each to each.*
I do not think that they will sing to me.' "

He jerked, hard, paled.

"Who said that?" she asked, probing. God, was he mental? He made no response. "Captain?"

"Odysseus," he murmured. Then he added slowly, "No. No, that was someone else." To her surprise, he took the book from her and slapped it shut.

"That was Mr. T. S. Eliot, and it's too lovely an evening to coop yourself up in here, like Penelope at her loom. I'm on my rounds. Would you like to accompany me?"

She frowned slightly. Damn it, she wanted to finish reading the book. She held her hand out for it. "I'd like to take that to my stateroom, if that's okay with you. And yes, thanks, I'd like to accompany you."

She rose, her hand outstretched. He rose, too, clasping the book against his chest. They faced one another. Incredibly, it seemed he was warring with her for possession of the book. Well, fuck you, she thought stubbornly. She knew how to care for nice things.

"Captain? The book?" she pressed.

Saying nothing, his lips pursed, he handed it to her.

"Let's go," he said.

First they walked along the outer decks. The wind riffled his hair, and as he looked out to sea, she studied him. She wondered how old he was, and why he just didn't strike her as genuine. He could be a real charmer, then in a flash turn into a tyrant. He liked people to kowtow to him, pay him compliments. She observed the way he puffed his chest when the other passengers stopped and chatted, fawning over him. How he snapped at the crewmen, making her wait while he berated a young Asian man in a navy jumpsuit because he didn't squeeze his mop hard enough.

"Do that again, and you know what'll happen," Reade threatened him. Donna wanted to ask him, what? Would he keelhaul him? Make him walk the plank?

The poor kid bowed and scraped and scurried off like some kind of water bug, mop and bucket slamming together at his hip.

Reade took his hat off and ran his fingers through his hair. "It weighs me down, sometimes. All this responsibility."

"Ah," she said noncommittally. Mothers who smacked their kids around sometimes told her the same thing.

Above them, a large bird wheeled through black, tumbling night clouds; its wings cut the moon into silhouettes of pointed fingers. It cawed and perched atop the stack, then fluttered upward and hovered as if observing them.

"I didn't know you could get birds so far out," she said, then realized she didn't know how far out they were.

"This ship is my world," he said, not hearing her. His eyes were on the bird. His voice grew dreamy, distracted. "The years sail by us, and we stay in the same place." He paused. "Or so it seems."

"A captain without a ship is like a fish without a bicycle."

"Just so," he said with a quick smile as he continued to watch the bird. It cocked its head and chittered like a monkey.

"A ship is born with a soul, and her master must learn her heart. He must learn if she is tender, or if she is stable; he must know how she does in following seas. He must know if she wants to dive. He must learn how her engines do, and if her boilers are good-natured; he must learn if she is fearful, or wrathful, in the gale. All this he must know, and that is why he is called the master."

"That's nice," she said. "Who wrote that one?"

The bird screeched and flew away. Reade rubbed his hands together and crossed them over his chest. "Wrote it? I just made it up."

"Oh." She was impressed.

They walked on, saying little. After checking the promenades, he took her through the empty dining room, and the busy kitchens, the shops, still open; the spa, the infirmary.

Then he led her down the bowed companionways past innumerable unmarked doors to one he selected without hesitation. Once through it, they stood in a space that reminded Donna of an airlock in a science fiction movie. He pushed a button and a door slid open; behind it gleamed the steel box of an elevator.

"We're going to the bridge," he explained.

They went up. The doors opened on a large, square room dominated by a series of flat metal control panels laden with digital readouts and a bank of windows looking out on the dark water. Five or six uniformed men bent over screens or wrote on clipboards; one man spoke into a telephone receiver. They snapped to and saluted as they sighted the captain.

He held the salute for a moment, snapping his wrist, said, "As you were." They relaxed.

"Evening, sir. Miss," said a tall man Donna recognized. Through force of habit, she checked his name tag. Lorentz Creutz.

"How does she run?" Reade asked.

"Like a dream, sir." The man bit off the words, raising his chin as he gazed levelly at Reade.

Reade stared back without blinking. Almost in a drone, he said, "Even a young ship holds many masters in her hull of many hulls; in her staterooms and holds, the captains of a hundred ships live on. And now and then, when their souls are strongest, they long for what they've lost, not their lives, but their commands." His eye blazed. "It's a fierce, good thing, to be the master."

Creutz thrust forward his jaw, turned on his heel and walked away. Reade chuckled.

"He's a hot one, that. But I've tamed him."

Donna blinked, said nothing. What *could* she say?

A few moments later, Creutz returned, dragging a wooden captain's chair beside a more comfortable-looking office chair. "Madam," he invited, gesturing for her to sit.

"Thank you," she said as Reade stepped in front of him and made a show of bending over the back of it, as if there were somewhere to scoot her to. She knew he was peering down her front. Damn dress.

"I have some business to attend to," Reade said. "I'll be a few minutes. Enjoy the view." He gestured at Creutz.

Donna settled in and tapped the book. "Thanks. Maybe I'll read."

Reade hesitated, then inclined his head. He sure was hung up about the damn thing. Grinning, she opened it randomly as the two men walked toward the other side of the bridge.

But the sight of the lights on the deck below was magical. The lines were illuminated for the night, and the crow's nest was like a little crown of diamonds high in the darkening sea sky. People chatted and milled around the pool; others danced. Tiki torches around the perimeter burned and smoked.

Dark gray shadows lurked on either side of the water—something under the surface? Whales? She turned to ask Reade.

But he was staring at charts and printouts, speaking to them in sea talk about degrees and millimeters and knots. They responded in kind, garble-garble.

She sat back and looked for a few more seconds at the deck. Then she settled back and flipped the pages of the book.

Something caught her eye. She stopped. There was a listing for a Creutz, Lorentz. A drawing that resembled the man on the bridge. What, was he famous? She raised the book closer to her eyes, compensating for the low light, and—

Reade slipped into the chair beside her.

"Sorry," he said. She shrugged and shut the book. She'd check it out later.

Stars peeked out from layers of gray on gray. Almost as

they watched, the sky blackened and the diamonds glittered. Donna found herself thinking of ice, and she shivered, suddenly uneasy. Ice, what was there about ice that could bother her?

The *Titanic* hit an iceberg, she thought. The sucker cut a gash in its side like a can opener. The bisque doll's head lolled at the bottom of the sea inside her mind. She shook herself and listened to the captain.

"The stars are clear and bright tonight, aren't they?" he asked. "You can see the sky voyagers. I'm an Ophicus. The astrological calendar is actually comprised of thirteen signs. Did you know that? That was discovered some time ago, but no one's bothered to get it right. This era is so lazy."

"You don't believe in astrology," she said with faint dismay.

"Oh, I'm quite the occultist," he replied. He cocked his head at her. "I think you'd be surprised how valid it is in our situation. I mean, in this day and age," he added. "People think of the occult as some medieval nonsense, but there's really a lot to it."

"Like 666 and that?"

"Oh, that's Satanism, not occultism," he said seriously. "I'd never make a pact with the devil."

"That's reassuring," she said dryly.

"I'd never jeopardize the *Pandora* that way," he went on, and she wasn't sure he was joking. "I carry precious cargo." He leaned toward her with a smile. "Would you like something? A drink? Some champagne?"

"Oh, please . . ."

"No trouble. That's what the crew are for." He chuckled. "Oh, yes, that's what they're for." He raised a hand.

A man Donna hadn't noticed before glided silently toward him. He inclined his head and for a moment she thought he was the same steward who'd walked her to the captain's cocktail party. He bore a close resemblance, but it was a different man.

"Champagne," he said, and checked for her agreement. Nifty.

"Yes," she said. What had happened to her bottle on the

Morris? And the fake bottle, with the thong in it? It seemed like years since she'd left Long Beach.

"At once, sir."

The man glided away. Reade said offhandedly, "Being the captain of a vessel like this is sometimes like being a country squire." His smile grew. "Or maybe even Odysseus."

"Must be nice."

"Oh, it is."

Behind them, something made a beeping noise and something else clanged. A man spoke into the telephone and said something about degrees lat and long. The helm was nothing more than a joystick, and that was disappointing. She'd expected some kind of wheel, not brass and wood, to be sure, but something more dramatic.

The captain moved his chair closer to hers, but she barely registered it. She rested her cheek on her fist and gazed at the stars. Astrology and astronomy both were beyond her. She never saw the silhouettes of bears or bulls or archers. What she saw was what was there: a pile of stars. Beautiful in their own right, and no need to gussy them up with mysticism.

"Do you believe in life after death?" Reade asked her.

She pulled herself back from her reverie. "I'm afraid not," she said without looking at him. "I wish I did."

"Maybe someday you will." He paused. "Someday soon."

"Mmm."

More shadows moved over the *Pandora,* moon clouds and moonbeams. Gradually thickening, they crossed one another over the bow, the water, until they appeared substantial. The people who walked the decks below reminded Donna of flies caught in a web, and she and the captain were the spiders.

"I believe in life after death," he offered. "In fact, I have proof of it."

Donna tensed. He wasn't going to lay some Christian testimony on her, was he? She hated that kind of shit, people pushing their religion down other people's throats. She didn't suppose that went with studying the occult. Well, she didn't want to hear about his crystal-gazing, either. As far as she was concerned, all the people who meditated on their belly buttons could do a lot more good for their karmas if they'd get involved with their communities, help a kid to read or set up a Neighborhood Watch program, something like that. All this other jazz was a bunch of time-wasting mind candy.

To her relief, he said nothing, stared out to sea.

The bulky shapes in the water glided on either side of the ship.

"What are those?" she asked.

"Torpedoes." She blinked, and he laughed. "Shadows of the conning tower, that's all. From the moonlight. Ah, here's the champagne."

In silence they watched the steward pop the cork in a napkin. He filled two glasses and handed one to Donna, the other to his captain.

Reade raised his glass to Donna. " 'That the rude sea grew civil at her song.' "

She accepted the compliment with a nod and took a sip. "It's nice," she said.

"Moët and Chandon," he told her, and she smiled faintly.

"I brought a bottle of that on board the *Morris.* They've probably drunk it up by now."

"How did you happen to be aboard the *Morris*?" he asked.

"My vacation. A sister-in-law of someone I know works at a travel agency. She told me about freighters and I thought I'd check it out. I thought it'd be fun."

"Were you in for a shock."

She smiled ruefully. "Well, I thought the damn thing would float, at least. I mean, on a regular basis. But it was one damn thing after another. Things were pretty weird aboard without the accident." She finished her champagne and he poured her another glass, listening intently.

"Such as?"

She wasn't sure if she should go into much of anything, not wanting to embarrass Ruth. "A general tension. People had lots of bad dreams, and—"

"Did you?" he cut in, leaning toward her.

Across the bridge, Creutz lifted his head, turned slowly toward her. She almost gasped: a ghastly green light from the radar monitor washed his face into glowing green bones that floated in the darkness. His face shifted, seemed to dissipate. He moved his mouth as if he were trying to tell her something.

"Did you?" the captain repeated.

Startled, she paused. The captain, with his back to Creutz, had not seen.

Seen what? She thought of John and his stress-created face in the fog. Mentally shrugging, she said, "No." Not on the *Morris,* anyway. Last night . . . *The very deep did* . . . did what? She couldn't remember it now, but she knew she'd had a bad one.

Creutz's face dissolved as he turned back around.

"They got really jumpy when the fog hit," she added.

"Ah, the fog. Captain Esposito mentioned how thick it was. Freaky, that."

She nodded. "You couldn't see anything. It was just like being blind." Her stomach did a loop as she remembered her blackout in the stateroom. Freaky *that.* Shit.

"You traveled alone?"

"Yup."

"Ah. I thought perhaps you were married to Dr. Fielder when you first came aboard."

She hid her grin with a sip of champagne. "No. Just shipmates, passing in the night."

A curious expression lit up his face—recognition, pleasure, she wasn't sure.

The black shapes moved along, moved along, like dark escorts or bodyguards. The moon hung in the sky, fat and orange. A glowing cloud encircled it.

She gestured toward it with her champagne glass. "Look at the moon. Doesn't that ring mean it's going to rain?"

"That's a harvest moon," he told her. "That's what we seamen call a moon like that."

"But it's April," she said.

"The sea doesn't know about seasons. Or time. It only knows about one thing."

"And what is that?"

"I'll tell you later." He filled her glass again. "In the morning."

"Uh," she said, and closed her mouth. She could wiggle out of this without a direct confrontation. She didn't want to hurt his feelings.

"Yes?" he prodded.

She yawned. "I'm afraid I *will* have to wait until morning to find out what it is. I'm totally fagged out." She moved her head in a slow circle; it cracked as she lowered it to her chest. Tight, constricted, sore. What she wouldn't give for a backrub.

"Ah," the captain said again, and there was understanding in his tone. And good humor. Good. It was nice to have a thick-skinned man around, and that he didn't take the rebuff personally.

"Well." She rose. "Thank you for the champagne. And the company."

He, too, stood. "I'll walk you back to your stateroom."

"You don't have to."

He took up her hand and placed it on his arm. "Please. I do. I'm British." Picked up their champagne glasses, handed hers to her, and hefted the bottle over his shoulder.

"What a load of horseshit," she said, laughing. He flinched, and she ignored his reaction. If he didn't like her swearing, fuck him.

So to speak.

They went down the elevator. Once out, he turned her this way and that, until she began to suspect he had no intention of taking her back to her stateroom. The Protozoa Suite. Who the hell was Proteus, anyway? She'd have to look it up, too.

When they reached the museum, she was sure he was taking a more circuitous route than necessary. He lingered by the closed door, cupping his hands around his eyes and pressing his nose to the glass.

"Checking on your bottle?" she queried, stifling a yawn. She was becoming very drowsy. Her hands weighed a thousand pounds each. She wished he'd hurry up and let her get into bed.

In the stateroom. The *weird* stateroom. A ripple of unease danced underneath her breastbone.

That was last night's weirdness, she reminded herself. Survivor's weirdness. Everything was fine now.

Past the disco. The captain peered in. Gyrating couples bounced aimlessly around; no one over twenty-five really knew what passed for dancing anymore. A Madonna look-alike sang some old song that was vaguely familiar; a spotlight blasted her directly in the face, draining the color from her skin so that she was dead-white, eyes and cheeks and lips. A mask of paper; it was very unattractive.

"Do you ever have jazz singers?" she asked.

He raised his brows. "Are you applying for the job?"

She was startled, assuming that he knew her secret. Then she realized he was teasing her. She shrugged.

"Just curious."

"We always have room for a good singer."

She twisted her mouth in a half smile. "Well, I'm not a good singer."

"That I doubt. I'd like to hear you, madam mermaid. You must, soon." He puffed out his chest. "A command performance."

"You'd keelhaul me."

He guffawed, and she walked on. But it occurred to her she could do something like that; hell, why not try? Not on the *Pandora,* maybe, but when she got back, why not go for it? Glenn wasn't . . .

Glenn . . .

"Miss Almond? Are you all right?"

Wordlessly she nodded, her clenched fists at her sides. She was all right. She was.

They passed the library, where a few people sat reading or writing letters. Donna peered over the shoulder of an elderly man who sat at a desk near the door. He wrote, *We're so excited to be aboard on her shakedown cruise. Nothing could ever sink this marvelous ship.*

Donna raised her brows as she turned to the captain. "Is this your ship's first voyage?"

He made a gesture for her to lower her voice and steered her down the corridor.

"That's Mr. Hare," he said. "He's a little confused."

"Oh?" She thought for a moment. "I though the ship's doctor's last name was Hare."

Reade laughed quickly. "Mr. Hare is his uncle."

Donna nodded, said nothing.

They went past some closed doors. A low, sad note crooned through them, mournful and lonesome and . . .

"Yes?" the captain was saying.

She tilted her head.

And nothing. No note. She shrugged. "I thought I heard something."

"Some people think the *Pandora*'s haunted," he said. "I myself didn't hear anything, just now."

"Neither did I," she shot back, grinning, and walked on.

And then finally, they were at her door.

"Well," she said, "thanks again." She paused. "Good night."

His mouth turned up on one side. Very charming, very gallant. He took her wrist and steadied her glass as he poured her one more glass of champagne.

"For the road," he said. Then: "I hope you're feeling better tomorrow."

"I feel . . . thank you," she amended. If that was the game—that she wasn't up to it—that was fine.

"Good night. Sweet dreams."

"Thanks." She fished in her purse and found her key, unlocked the door. Hesitated.

Once again, she didn't want to go in. The hairs on her forearms stood on end and a stripe of ice coated each cheek, her scalp, the small of her back. She didn't want to go in, not at all. Haunted . . .

"Officer Almond?" he said.

She shook hands and held up her glass. "Good night."

Pushed the door open to a dark room. Stood on the threshold. Swallowed.

Looked back toward Captain Reade. He was already walking away.

She took a step inside the door. In the light from the companionway, she saw something moving around her feet.

Wispy, and smoky and insubstantial, something that curled around her ankles on
little
cat
feet,
pussy willow-gray.

"Jesus!" She jumped back into the hall. Her heart jackhammered her rib cage as she peered into the blackness. She glanced left and right. Now what?

"Shit," she muttered, darted forward, and felt along the left side of the wall for a light switch. Her forefinger nudged the edge of a switch plate and she hurried to find the switch itself, suddenly sure that if she didn't move fast, someone—or something—was going to grab her hand—

—or chew it off her wrist—

Damn it! Somehow she missed the switch. Huffing, she tapped the wall with her palm.

Heavy breathing. And a waft of heat against the back of her hand, oh, fuck—

She pulled back her hand; and as she did so, the lights magically snapped on. She cried out, heard herself, and made a tight, angry face.

Because there was nothing in the goddamned room, no dry ice on the floor, no monster salivating over her wrist. Christ on a crutch, what was the matter with her, and did it have anything to do with her blackouts?

And then goose bumps flooded over her like an ice-water waterfall as she walked into the room and slammed the door shut. She trembled violently, from head to toe, as she stomped across the room,

and she swore to God something moved as she passed by the foot of the bed to the closet; she could almost see the covers ripple.

But when she yanked them back, there was nothing there. Because there *was* nothing there.

Of course.

Chatter-scrabble.

The captain froze. Listened. What *was* that bloody noise?

On occasion, he heard it; on occasion, his heart raced at that sound. Its familiarity, its . . . treachery.

No. An engine. Nothing more. It was nothing.

Chatter-scrabble.

No, he was

> *Alone, alone, all, all alone,*
> *Alone on a wide, wide sea*

and between him and the gull he had summoned with his magical incantations, yes, together they had ripped open the shroud, and uncorked the bottle he had caused to appear.

He touched his chin. Singing. Had someone called to him, sung a lovely song—

No. That was Donna Almond, on the other side of the door, practicing her music because she wanted to be a chanteuse. It had always been Donna.

And so *strong.* He sighed, smiled. How she fought against the lines he drew around her. He would keep her a long time; as long as forever proved to be. But tonight he had other fish to fry, as they said nowadays.

As *they* said.

Chatter-scrabble.

"Nothing there," he said in a booming voice.

Nothing there at all.

18

Rubbing It

Ruth had been correct, back on the *Morris:* something had lurked in the companionway outside her cabin door.

And now, in the chimera-black mirage of night, it lurked outside Elise and Phil's suite on the *Pandora.* It slithered within the fog that blanketed the companionways and forecastles and stacks and cabins, in the gray mass of dreamcloud wherein it had its being; as it moved, *chatter-scrabble,* as it curled and crawled with its bird-beak pincers; as it sought out the flesh and the blood; and the dreams, and the traitor,

chatter-scrabble, chatter-scrabble,

its hunger fierce, its yearning terrible, its agony unbearable.

Its anger, a crucible.

* * *

Elise sat in bed, surreptitiously fondling the invitation a steward had delivered to her while Phil fussed in the bathroom:

Meet me.
T.R.

The paper was thick linen, luxurious to the touch, romantic. She smiled to herself. Of course she had no intention of going, but it was nice to be asked, all the same.

If Thomas Reade wanted to ignore her publicly in favor of that meter maid, let him suffer the consequences. All day, she had made herself available, sunning by the pool in the most outrageous bikini, and he had never come by, not once.

Phil's electric razor buzzed and hummed, and her smile slipped. Her husband was hoping for sex. He went through the same precise rituals whenever he wanted her, and in the same order: combed his hair, washed his face (the only man she knew who did so), shaved, brushed his teeth. God, God! Maybe if he'd do something different—comb his hair last, or not comb it all; Jesus, if he'd just stop being so predictable, and so goddamn spineless—he never came and asked her, or told her, that he wanted to make love. He just combed his hair and primped like a woman, hoping, she assumed, that it would arouse her.

With the anger came the guilt. She was horrible to him. Last night she'd practically grabbed the captain's crotch right in front of him. Why did he put up with it? Any man would—

Any man would do what her father used to do. Reflexively, she touched her jaw. It had hurt worse when the doctor pushed it back into the socket than when her father dislocated it.

Oh, was she screwed up. To equate such sadism with manliness . . .

The razor went off. Now he was gargling. New fury seethed through her, though she didn't understand it. On their honeymoon, he had folded his clothes as he had removed them, garment by garment, aligning the creases in his trousers, rolling his tie. Would've folded hers, too, if she hadn't ordered him to leave them on the floor, for God's sake.

The cap of the deodorant bottle.

The *fsst* of his breath spray.

By the time he came to bed, she was so angry she wanted to slap him. And when he shyly tried to mount her, she gritted her teeth and said, "I'm not feeling too well."

"Oh, I'm so sorry, darlin'," he said, climbing off without a protest, though his erection was jabbing her in the thigh and surely he must be ready to explode. "Can I get you anything?"

Meet me.

Raging, she shook her head.

Within an hour, he was fast asleep. He was making her do this, she told herself. You didn't go looking for it if you got it at home, and it was a male conceit that women were more likely than men to remain faithful though unsatisfied. Lots of her friends back home had something going on the side, with the pool man or the gardener or their kids' soccer coach. It was part of being married to worker bees: even if their husbands owned the hive, they were drones, and a queen bee needed a special kind of jelly to keep her royal.

No, she didn't believe that. She knew she was a tramp, treated him abominably. But why the hell didn't he kick up a fuss?

Yet even her shame could be exciting. Dressed in white slacks and a cashmere sweater, and nothing underneath either, she pulled open the door and darted into the hall, shielding the light with her body. She stood for a moment, assuming he would come to her. Surely he didn't expect her to know *where* to meet him.

Only what to do when she found him.

She took a few steps to the left and looked down the hall. The passageways were so long they dipped, which gave the *Pandora* a less-than-solid air she found unnerving after her ordeal at sea. Once they landed in Australia, she would never set foot on any kind of vessel again.

"Captain?" she whispered; and, more softly, "Thomas?"

She heard a creak behind her. Thought he could sneak up on her, eh? She stayed as she was, allowing him to enjoy the element of surprise. *Creak, creak,* and the tread of shoes on the carpet.

The lights lowered, throwing her into sudden shadows. A thrill of anticipation made her shiver once—goose walking over her grave—and she took a couple casual steps forward, to make the game more interesting.

The soft, sure tread of footsteps in the gloom advanced. She lowered her head and tried to peer out of the corner of her eye without giving away that she knew he was there—

—and the carpet moved.

She blinked. It *moved.* The vinelike traces eddied and whirled, and whirled, and the red shapes floated among them, and a

face

She cried out just as a hand cupped her mouth. Then she whirled around and the captain stood before her, laughing silently.

"Got you," he chortled quietly.

"God!" She took two steps backward. "I—I saw—" She jabbed her finger downward. "I saw—"

"What?" He followed the direction of her hand. "A spot?"

She thought for a moment. What had she seen? She could no longer remember. What had frightened her?

"I creep in on little cat feet," he whispered, nuzzling her under the chin. His hands stole around her waist. Rolling, liquid warmth circled her thighs and her sex. Her nipples hardened, and she gasped when he pulled her against his body.

He kissed the nape of her neck, pulled her around to face him, and opened his mouth.

Something moved behind him, at the end of the corridor. A tall shadow? Her gaze flickered past his ear—

—and then there was nothing, and he was kissing her. His breath was hot and his tongue probing and thick; his erection pushed into her belly and she became very, very wet.

"Come on," he whispered, grabbing her hand. He hurried her down the corridor.

"Where are we going?"

He smiled though he looked straight ahead. "To play spin the bottle."

Together they hurried down the passage. He had a death grip on her hand that was painful, but they moved at such a breathless pace she couldn't manage to tell him. He was strong—she could tell he didn't mince around, but took what he wanted—and all her icy shame melted away. She was built for more than Phil could give. Love was giving you what you wanted. Fulfilling your needs. Ergo, Phil did not love her.

So there was no need to be faithful to him.

The captain's grip was an iron band over the back of her hand, and it clamped down hard, making her cry out. They were practically running. She put her other hand on his wrist, started to ask him to slow down, ease up, when he whipped her around the corner and the—

—the *difference*—

—struck her mute.

It was the same ship, wasn't it? She had walked down this same section of hallway a dozen times. But she had never noticed—never *seen*—the royal red carpet, the flocked walls, the elaborate crystal lamps hanging from the ceiling. She had never seen how dirty it was, with cobwebs dripping like diamonds from the teardrop coronas of the fixtures; the green mold on the thick oak baseboards.

A mirror, splattered with raised, round bumps—

—barnacles?

"Captain," she said, "what . . . ?"

Around another corner. Now she halted, throwing him off balance, and turned violently left, right.

The walls, the ceiling, the floor, were made of dull gray metal, low and slick with moisture. Papers were strewn on the floor, and they were wet; and everything smelled rotten and dead; and something gritted beneath her shoes: sand, and shells, and the skeleton of a large fish. The spine curved around her left foot and the skull crunched beneath her heel as she jumped back.

"What?" she cried.

He frowned at her. "What's wrong?"

And the room—the metal, the papers, the fish skull. Her knees turned to jelly and she grabbed hold of his shoulder to keep herself from falling to the filthy deck.

"Don't you see it?" she asked, raising a trembling hand to take it all in. But it wouldn't go in; her brain refused to process the images she knew she was seeing. She looked, looked hard; and then—

—the white walls, the ugly carpet, the hurricane lamps.

"But," she said stupidly. She covered her mouth. "But I saw—"

He stared at her. Stepped backward. "What?" he asked, and his voice was low, dangerous. "What did you see?"

She pointed. "The room. The whole place! It was . . . it's . . ."

He looked at her with a wild grimace, showing all his teeth, like a fish she'd seen in the museum, something long and dark and wicked—a viper fish, all head and tail, and sharp, sharp fangs.

"Thomas!" she cried.

"You saw what?" he shouted. "What? Tell me!"

"I—I thought I saw, that I was somewhere else." She licked her lips. "I don't know, I had a hallucination."

He was silent. He looked away for a moment. His head averted, he caressed her cheek with his nails, trailing them down her neck, her chest. With great care, he enfolded her in his arms and held her.

"Forgive me for being short with you. Now," he said against her hair, "Elise"—his voice was honey—"what did you see?"

She thought for a moment. Her heart pounded wildly as she realized she could no longer remember what she'd seen. What she *thought* she'd seen. It had been a mistake anyway, whatever it had been, for here they were, where they should be.

"I'm all right now," she whispered.

"Of course you are." He kissed the crown of her head. "Do you think I'd let anything happen to you?"

She closed her eyes, and felt him trembling.

* * *

"Hey, let me out!"

In the dark, Ramón pounded on the door. He'd been in there for hours, maybe days, without food or water, without the chance to use the head, *orale,* and with the setting of the sun he'd realized they hadn't turned on any lights for him, and he couldn't find the switch.

"Hey!" He pummeled with both fists, kicked the jamb for extra measure. Shit, they couldn't do this! He was an American citizen! This was, like, violating his civil rights.

"He-eyy!" His voice grew shrill, cracked.

"Don't," said a voice behind him. "Being feared is *his* desire."

Ramón whipped around. "Who said that? Where are you?" There must be another door, one he hadn't noticed. All right, and now they'd let him out and—

"It's his sustenance," the voice continued.

Ramón reached out his hand. "Hey, where are you, man?"

"At the bottom of the sea, I pray to Christ and all the angels." The sound of weeping. "SOS, this is *Trinity.* Curry, SOS. Mayday."

Ramón burst out a nervous laugh. "Cha-cha?" He shook his head. No, not Cha-cha. But someone else who wasn't put together too good, maybe, or just some sailor who liked to talk in riddles.

The weeping grew faint.

"C'mon, man, you freaking me out, bro," Ramón said, his accent thickening with his unease. "Did you come to let me out?"

There was a long sigh. Then nothing. Ramón waited.

Nothing.

"Oyé, oyé, amigo!" he called, stepping to the center of the cabin. He ran into the cot and almost lost his balance. Moving away from it with his arms outstretched, he looked like a kid ready to whack a piñata. "You still here?"

Silence.

"Hey, man, c'mon!" He found the opposite wall of the cabin and began to feel along it for the other door. The guy must have left.

"Hey, I'm an American citizen!" Hand over hand, he slid

his fingers over the walls, cried out when he touched a knob, then understood it was the original door. There was only one.

The guy could not have gotten in, nor left, through any other.

A trapdoor, then? A hole in the ceiling?

"Hey, goddamn it!" Ramón bellowed, getting mad now, because he was getting frightened.

Then someone else said, "Diaz?"

It was the voice of Captain Esposito, skipper of the *Morris,* who should be in Hawaii.

Who should not be here.

In the Proteus stateroom, Donna looked up from her book and stared into space.

Lorentz Creutz was the name of the captain of the *Kronen,* a Swedish warship that sank in 1676. It was also the name of the *Pandora*'s staff captain.

She tapped the page. Maybe she remembered his name wrong. Or maybe he was a descendant. Things like that happened. She'd ask.

Shut the book, and turned out the light.

Ignoring the prickles that skittered over her body, and the urge to look under the bed, and the funny feeling that she was being . . . not watched, but . . .

not watched. Time for sleep.

She turned on her side and fluffed her pillow. Thought: *Dufus, no one can be descended from a dead man.*

As they grappled in the deserted cavern of the indoor swimming hall, the captain cupped Elise's breasts and saw Nathaniel's sweet face, and sent out his thoughts:

Consider this, Donna, my beautiful whore, my slut, my temptress, my siren:

Ajax the Greek lost his ship and in the tempest swam to the cliffs. He would have lived had he not in his arrogance cried out that he was the one man Poseidon could not drown. The god was furious—as he should have been, Donna, as he should have been—and he broke off the rock Ajax clung to. Ajax fell; the waves swept him away, to his death.

It would do well for you to find some humility. For soon, I promise, I will break off the reality you cling to. And then I will break you, before I drown you.

And I will drown you. I swear it.

You are the only one who does not let me in. You have fought me, and for that, I will make you pay, a thousand times a thousand.

And as for this woman, who had seen . . . how had she seen? He would let her see a little more, before he crushed her.

He smiled, and kissed her, raging inside because Donna would not hear him.

But Elise would.

Oh, yes.

Oh, yes; Elise knew she had done the right thing; and the guilt evaporated and so did the odd memory of something gone wrong, as she and the captain writhed in a tiled Jacuzzi beside the indoor swimming pool. The air was cool and smelled of chemicals, but the champagne was delicious. He had planted an ice bucket and glasses before he had come to fetch her. A man thought of these things. A real man, that is.

In the center of the high plaster ceiling, a single, low-watt bulb struggled inside a white metal cage. Shadows did the hula on the white plaster, and on the diamond-shaped tiles of blue and green that bubbled in the boiling pot of sprays, jets, arms, and legs.

The water moved like a solid oval with the subtle roll of the ship and spilled into the pool; steam rose from the pool like jets of champagne bubbles. The heat and the bubbles made her dizzy; and she vaguely recalled that something had frightened her, terribly, but now everything was more than fine. Poor girls learned much of sex and a bit about shame, oh, yes.

His body was rich; and they slapped together, making waves, long and hard and tight and hot. He was inside her, thrusting, and Elise gasped and dug her nails into his buttocks. He was unending; he was the biggest man she'd ever had, so big it hurt, but it hurt sublimely, and she stretched her legs open as wide as they could go.

"The snake is a friend," he said huskily, and she laughed and threw back her head.

She was getting close to coming, everything constricted, quivering, juicy; she was almost there, and she hadn't had an orgasm in months that wasn't self-induced—she'd been faithful since Phil had found out about Hunter—and she teetered on the brink of ecstasy with a full-out hunger that made her feel like she was drowning. Clinging, clinging to him, riding with him, up, up to the crest of the wave—

languidly, she rolled her head to the side—

—*the snake is a friend*

—and through the steam, saw faces.

She screamed and jerked backward, but he kept at her, pushing and thrusting.

Withered faces, eyeless and slack, and unseeing. The faces of skulls, bleached, pitted; barnacles on strips of flesh; an eel trailing through a jaw. Blackened, charred faces; and with them, the face of a child, smiling wickedly. Their eyes met and the child sniggered.

"Look!" she shrieked, pounding on his back, flailing her arms and legs in blind panic. But he ignored her, or couldn't hear her—how couldn't he hear her?—as he pushed and pushed and pushed.

And suddenly he hurt her; his cock was no longer a cock, but something that sliced into her womb. Screaming, arched backward, toward the faces. He had a bottle between his hands, a green bottle, and he was ramming it into her, over and over and deeper and deeper—

—the faces opened their jaws, and they had teeth,

barbs,

harpoons

—and the boy crouched at the edge of the tub now, behind the captain. He laughed low and cruel and delighted; and his face broke apart and slid into the tub, chunks of flesh and gouts of blood; his nose, his lips, plopping into the boiling fleshpot. His face throbbed raw and glistening, and it laughed; a thing watched her, a thing laughed, with no nose, no jaw, but rows of gleaming ivory teeth.

She struggled wildly, smacking the captain's hips with her thighs, shrieking, screaming, pleading—

—and the captain shouted with pleasure and plunged into her.

He was cutting her open, rendering her down. In a haze of unendurable agony, she started to black out.

Then he chortled and said in a mocking voice, "That's how we play spin the bottle, Ms. van Buren-*Hadley*. That's how we win."

The boy-thing's laughter joined his, the child cartwheeling around the tub, his face bobbing around her in a bloody stew. For a moment, the wind whipped around her, and she was freezing, and the cold was almost worse than the pain, but that could never, ever be.

Elise woke up in her own bed, beside her clean-shaven, sweet-smelling, mild-tempered husband.

She was unhurt. Untouched.

She was in her nightgown, and there was no note anywhere.

She went into the bathroom and vomited, and when she came back to bed, Phil rolled over and slung an arm over her hips. She lay there, shaking, and tried to convince herself it had all been a dream.

Elise.
Phil.
John.
Ramón.
Ruth.
Cha-cha.
Cracked in six places; and when it's full of water, it will go down,
   down,
   down,
   ah, Nathaniel, how I loved you, child! How it hurt me, to hurt you!

Down,
down,
down,
and it won't be airtight.

19

Bottling Plant

The door to the museum gaped open. A woman in a white dress and jacket sat at a card table, reading a book. Donna cleared her throat and the woman glanced up.

"Are you open?" Donna asked. It was noon of the third day aboard the *Pandora,* and this was the first time she'd seen anyone inside the museum. The door was always shut.

"Yes. Please come in. I'll be happy to give you a tour." The woman half stood; Donna indicated that she should stay seated.

"I came in here the other night with the captain," Donna explained.

"Oh, with the Captain?" the woman echoed. Capital C Captain. "Oh, but of course. You're one of the survivors."

Jesus. That's what John should make them call his movie. *The Survivors.*

"I was in the lifeboat, yes."

"Oh, my." The woman stood. "My. And the Captain has been showing you around."

"Mmm-hm." She wandered toward the nearest aisle. The woman trailed after her.

"What is it like?" Her eyes shone with excitement and she clasped her hands over her chest.

"Not that much fun," Donna retorted. She made a point of staring hard at the objects in the case before her. Cups and saucers. The typed card said they were from the *Bismarck.* She cast back; there'd been something about that in the *Flotsam* book. That guy who found the *Titanic,* he'd found the *Bismarck,* too. She turned to the woman—

—whose face was strangely blank. She stared straight ahead, as if Donna weren't there, a robot turned off. Wooden, Donna thought, and cleared her throat. The woman jumped, hiccuping a nervous laugh.

"I'm sorry. I . . ."

"I didn't know they salvaged anything off the *Bismarck,*" Donna said.

The woman grimaced. "I'm sorry, I wouldn't know. I wasn't here then."

Say what? Donna hid a smile. She nodded and walked on. Irritatingly, the woman continued to follow her.

"If you have any questions," she ventured.

Donna stopped at the case containing the captain's bottle. The cloth had been redraped, a dramatic, if silly touch.

"Is it true it's never been opened?" Or weren't you here then? she added silently.

To Donna's surprise, the woman took a step backward. She shook her head vigorously, jaw set, fists clenched at her sides. "Absolutely not. Never. It's never been opened. It—"

"Donna?"

John and Matt stood just inside the door. Donna sidled away from the woman, who was still swearing on her mother's grave that the bottle had never, ever, ever been uncorked (and who was supposed to really give a shit, Donna wanted to know), and came up to them.

"Hi." She made Groucho eyes at Matt. "Hey, big guy, you're looking good."

Matt's eyes widened and he gazed at her very hard, very hungrily. He was holding his green dinosaur, practically folding it in half in some kind of urgency. John put his arm around his shoulder. Matt stepped close to him.

"What's up?" Donna asked. Her first thought was that maybe they'd heard about the lifeboat; from the looks of them, it would be bad news.

"We were wondering if you'd like to have lunch with us."

Matt moved away and walked to the back of the museum, toward the balcony where the figureheads perched. John's eyes followed him.

"He looks terrible, doesn't he," John murmured, the agony in his voice an agony to hear.

Donna scratched her shoulder. "Are you kidding? He looks terrific."

His smile was grateful, martyred. Obviously he didn't believe her.

"No, really. I think he looks the best since I met you guys." A pause. "Don't you?"

Tears welled in his eyes. "I think I'm . . . I'm losing it, Donna." He covered his forehead with his hand and took a shuddering breath. "I . . . I . . ."

"Hey, big John. Hey, big guy," she soothed, placing her hand over his. She squeezed hard. Harder, as he trembled. "It's okay. It's really okay."

Matt returned. His eyes were narrowed and full of questions. John averted his gaze, made a show of examining the case with the bottle inside. Donna tweaked Matt's nose playfully and said, "What's up?"

He jabbed his thumb over his shoulder. "Those statue things? Figureheads? I seen a lady who looks just like one of them. Just like it."

"Isn't that neat."

Matt held his dinosaur under his chin and rocked back on his heels. "I really did." His gaze flicked toward his father. John's shoulders bounced up and down and he put a hand on the case as if to steady himself. Silently weeping, oh, poor, dear man.

"C'mere," Donna told Matt. "I want to see that skeleton

thing again." She guided Matt with a hand on his shoulder, urging him along when he started to turn back toward his father. "It's cool, don't you think? Do you think it's real?"

Matt nodded soberly.

The lights hit the bones hard, mean. How did they join the tail to the rest? Donna searched for glue, wires, tacks. Nothing. It was a good job.

Matt jumped backward. "It moved!"

Donna made claw hands and advanced on him. "Boo!"

He pointed at it. "It really did!"

"The ship's moving," Donna pointed out. "So it would sway back and forth. Isn't that right, honey?" She rapped the glass. Matt's lips parted. "Yoo, hoo," Donna called. "Hey, Lorelei, I'm talkin' at ya. You know who the Lorelei is, Matt?" She made come-hither motions with her fingers. "I read about her this morning. She's a hot German babe who lures ships onto the rocks. She sings to them." She smacked her hands together. "And they crash."

Matt wrinkled up his face. "Not really."

"Oh, yeah," she said earnestly, but when she saw he was a little confused she laughed and feinted a tap on his nose. Coloring, he ducked his head and peered at the case through his lashes. He was still thin, still pale, but his cheeks were pink and the rings under his eyes had disappeared. John had nothing to worry about. Or rather, less to worry about.

They stood in silence for a moment. "You were right," she said, in case he was still confused. "There's not really such a thing as a Lorelei."

"I know." There was a defensive edge to his voice.

"I thought you knew."

John approached them. Behind his glasses his eyes were red and puffy, but he'd gotten himself back together. He looked with them at the mermaid skeleton.

"I wonder where they got that thing," he said. His nose was stuffy.

Donna yawned. "P. T. Barnum."

The museum attendant hovered a few feet away. Donna said to John, "Shall we go?" To the woman, "Thanks for showing me around. I'll come back later."

"Yes." The woman smiled brightly and slid behind her desk. Picked up her book.

"And back she goes, into stasis," Donna intoned, once they were out of earshot. John wasn't listening, or else he didn't think it was funny. He had her hand in a death grip, clearly still upset, but self-possessed. Maybe she would tell him about Glenn, and he would have someone to comfort, take him out of himself. She was feeling better herself, having him to worry about.

Halfway down the hall, John moved in closer to her. On her other side, Matt did the same. Now just a minute, she thought. Hold on, you're doing it again. But she said nothing, let John drag her along toward his own destination. Matt trotted beside her, looking good. Real good.

After a lot of twists and turns, they ended up topside next to the pool, where a lunchtime barbecue was in progress. The ocean shimmered a stunning dark blue as the *Pandora* breasted it. The sky was clear and bright. A thousand miles. Fog and terror, and now, a haven.

Beside the pool, stewards manned huge grills and stood sentry at long tables of salads and desserts. The greasy smoke burned Donna's eyes and she rubbed them hard. Gotta protect the old eyeballs, especially after they'd taken unauthorized leave. A line of passengers waited for burgers and hot dogs, jostling and chatting, some waving in Donna and John's direction. The celebrity survivors.

Donna turned to John. "Check out the way they . . ." She trailed off. His face glowed chalk-white as he stared at a cluster of unlit tiki torches. Beside him, Matt watched his father with a worried frown.

"You okay?" Donna whispered to John.

He pushed up his glasses and shook his head.

"Hey, Matt, can you get your burger yourself?" Donna asked him cheerfully. "We'll go stake out a table."

The boy gazed at her with the same intense expression, begging her to do . . . what? Bobbing his head, he took his place at the end of the line, behind the fat woman who had gone to pieces over the captain at dinner the first night aboard. Renquist. Reinberg. Reinstedt. Yeah.

"Oh, hello, little one," the woman exclaimed. Matt drew back slightly.

Donna smiled wryly. He was on his own.

She steered John to a table far away from the other diners and sat him down. On a dais on the opposite side of the pool, a steel drum band played a calypso.

She scooted next to him. Took his hand again.

"Talk to me," she urged.

He lowered his gaze to their hands. "I'm having a panic attack. Another panic attack," he amended miserably. "I woke up and I saw how bad he looks, and I guess I lost my mind." When he looked at her, he tried to smile. His upper lip trembled and she wished she could hold him. But you got tough being a cop, and she knew he'd break down if she did. So she kept her grip on his hand. Made him go on.

He took a shaky breath. "He might die. I've known it, but I've never really known it."

She frowned and patted the back of his hand. "John, he looks fine. He looks very well."

"To you. But you should have seen him when he was . . . he was . . ." He looked over his shoulder. "There's something about those torches. This place. Déjà vu. Or a dream." He rubbed his temples. " 'All we see or seem, is but a dream within a dream.' "

"Kicky."

"Poe." He exhaled. "I've been thinking about dreams lately. I . . . I'm so upset I'm hallucinating. The other night I thought someone was following me or something. I even thought the ship was sinking." He laughed hollowly. "You know, if you had the same dream I did, it wouldn't be the same dream."

She scratched her arm and waited for him to go on. This conversation didn't come equipped with a road map.

"Filters. Our reality filters our . . . unreality." He blushed a little. "I could describe everything I'm seeing and feeling and you still wouldn't . . . I don't suppose you've done much experimenting with, um, drugs."

"Don't suppose," she retorted. "Because why?"

"There really is no such thing as a shared experience. It always comes back to the individual." He laughed hollowly. "You must think I'm going crazy."

"That's okay. Crazy men are so much more appealing."

He smiled. "I think sometimes I imagine people are thinking, 'Well, if I were in your shoes, if he was my kid . . .'"

She smiled gently. "John, you've been under a terrible strain. Still are."

"God, don't I know it. I'm so damned jumpy." He made an unconscious, shuddering gesture.

Donna caught her cheek with her teeth, thought a moment. "Jumpy?"

"Things don't feel right to me. Or they *aren't* right. I don't know. I'm just so anxious. Not just with Matt."

She shifted, crossed her legs. "You're not alone there. I've been feeling jumpy, too. Things haven't seemed right to me either."

His eyes widened. They sat for a moment without speaking.

"I think it's from being in the lifeboat," she said. "You know, it's hitting us now that we're safe. It was pretty freaky." She waited for him to agree.

"Maybe," he said slowly. "Or maybe it's something else." He leaned his head on his free hand and stared at the table. "I've been seeing a shrink, Donna. I obsess. I can't stop washing my hands sometimes. Or washing his sheets. Things like that."

Poor guy. Poor, poor guy. "Well, *I* don't obsess. And I've been having the willies so bad I can hardly sleep." She decided not to tell him what Reade had said about the *Pandora* being haunted. A, because it was bullshit, and B, because she didn't want to load the dialogue with extraneous ballast.

Behind them, Matt secured a burger. The Reinstedt woman jabbered on and on, put something on his plate, leaned over, and asked him something. He shook his head.

"Maybe you're right," John said. His gaze lingered on his child. "It's just the aftershocks of a life-threatening situation." He hesitated.

"Or?" Donna said.

"What was the *Morris* carrying?" he asked. "The toxic material. Did you ever find out what it was?"

"Huh?"

His gaze returned to the tiki torches. "Maybe whatever was on the *Morris* has, ah, like a hallucinogenic factor." He considered. "Some kind of chemical toxicity that affects perception."

She pulled in her chin and frowned, puzzled. "That's pretty farfetched."

He hunched his shoulders, lay down his arm, and blew a puff of air from his cheeks. "Not as farfetched as you might think, Donna. A lot of the stuff I handle in my lab has frightening side effects." He let his shoulders go. A buff of shine glistened on his broad forehead. "Everyone talks to you. Has anybody else been feeling strangely?"

"There's Ruth," she said. "But she's been feeling strangely ever since we pulled out of Long Beach. Remember how she insisted something was in the hall?"

They looked at each other. "And I found her at her window, just staring into the fog. She said she'd been dreaming."

John considered. "Maybe she's epileptic."

"I thought of that. But *I'm* not. I'm basically a levelheaded cop. And I don't scare easy, usually, but I've been going to pieces whenever I see my own shadow." She paused. "On this ship. On the *Morris,* I was fine, strangely enough. Most of the time. There were a couple times, a couple things."

A couple words no one spoke, an old lady too small and dead-cold. A dream?

All we see or seem
Is but a dream within a dream.

Shit, what was this, Poetry 101? Dreams and ancient mariners. What a combination. Dreams by ancient mariners, for ancient mariners, of ancient mariners.

Something chittered up her spine, very like a chill. But why?

John started to speak, closed his mouth. The way his eyes darted around the table, she knew he was suppressing something he wanted very much to tell her. At length he cleared his throat.

"I'll look in on her in a little bit." It took her a beat to realize he was talking about Ruth.

"I'll go with you. After lunch," Donna suggested.

He shook his head. "Captain Reade's invited us up to the bridge again. We're due to meet at two." His watch read one-twenty. "After that?"

Donna shrugged. "Sure."

Matt walked up. His plate was heaped with a burger and macaroni salad. No fries; she remembered John telling her Matt hated potatoes in any form. "There's ice cream, too," he said happily.

"You'll never eat all that in a million years," John goaded him.

"Will too."

"I'll bet you five bucks you can't clean that plate." John pulled out Matt's chair. "Deal?"

"Deal!" Matt set down his food.

"Well, get ready to fork it over while we go get some food. Ha ha." John wagged his finger at his son. "And no fair throwing it overboard."

"Da-ad! I do not cheat!" Matt said indignantly, shoveling the burger into his mouth.

"And I hope you don't welsh on bets, either." John took Donna's hand again. "Come on. If we don't go now, there won't be any left."

They joined the end of the line. "He's fine," Donna said.

"I just hope I lose that bet," John murmured wistfully.

Dressed in a violet silk jumpsuit, Elise approached from the shuffleboard side of the pool, held up a hand, and stomped toward them. Donna made a face and muttered, "Here comes trouble."

"Have you seen Phil?" Elise demanded as she neared, looping her hair behind her ears.

Donna put some sweet pickles on her plate. "Nope."

Elise slumped, glanced left and right.

"Is he missing?" Donna asked sweetly.

"Never mind." Elise made a funny swooping motion—digging into her purse, Donna realized, fished out a cigarette, and lit it. She hovered around for a few seconds while Donna and John inched forward in the line, adding potato salad and chips to their meals. She inhaled hard, turned her head, and blew out the smoke. Shifted her weight. Scanned the crowd, the deck, glanced up high at the bridge. Looked away quickly, her face strained.

Donna took this all in while pretending not to notice anything. But it was clear Elise was upset. A nicer person, a softer person, would have felt sorry for her.

"How long has he been gone?" Donna found herself asking, and gave herself a mental slap. Shut up, bitch, you're off duty.

"It's . . ." Elise drew on her cigarette again. Her attention shifted to a point past Donna; her eyes widened and she took a step backward. Another.

"Never mind," she said again, and walked away.

Donna looked over her shoulder. Reade stood directly in her line of vision, and he had an odd smile on his face. He was patting his mouth with a handkerchief. He caught Donna's eye and saluted her with two fingers. She waved back.

"Your date's here," she told John.

"What?" Donna pointed. "Oh," he said. He held up his plate and Reade nodded, pointed to the bridge.

"Yes," John mouthed. The captain signaled that he'd understood and turned away.

A steward asked Donna how she liked her meat. "Rare," she replied. To John: "Do you like him?"

"Medium well," John said, then laughed. "Sure. He's fine. Matt's totally under his spell. The captain's 'radical,' you know."

"So he seems to think," Donna said. "He himself, I mean. Where's the ketchup?"

"At the end of the table, madam." The steward pointed with his chin.

"Well, he gets the job done," John ventured.

"*Some* jobs," she shot back meaningfully. As she expected, John's face perked up.

"So, we'll go see Ruth later?" she pressed. "Maybe we'll go for a drink after?" Hell, why not? Her dance card was empty, so was his, and they were both adults. She was sure he could handle being the object of a rebound, given the certainty that their shipboard romance would be brief. What the hell, what the hell.

Oh, hell.

"That'd be nice." John's face reddened. He pushed up his glasses and she wanted to bat his hand away, tell him he looked like a nerd when he did that. There was something so vulnerable about him that she wanted to strap a bulletproof vest on him or something. He and Phil were a pair, weren't they? On the other end of the macho scale, on the other hand, stood Reade and the sleazy Ramón. She'd take John or Phil over either of them anyday.

And did guys think about sex this much?

Need you ask, Officer? Need you really? And were you thinking about sex, or were you proving you don't care about Glenn?

"Penny for your thoughts," John murmured.

"Oh, no, these are worth a dollar." She picked up the ketchup bottle and turned it upside down. "At least a dollar."

"Okay." He smiled faintly. Not sure how to take her, she supposed. She kind of liked that.

"I was wondering if Nemo had had her litter yet."

John frowned dubiously. "Donna, that was not worth a dollar."

She shook the ketchup bottle harder. Nothing came out. "Damn. What's in here, anyway?"

The ketchup slid out, thick and chunky and gooey, coiling on top of the seared meat. "That's more like it."

"Donna," John pressed.

"Okay, okay." She handed him the bottle. He set it down. "I was wondering how often guys think about sex, if you want to know the horrible, unvarnished truth."

To her delight, he broke into a wolfish grin. "All the time," he replied. "Every single moment of every single hour."

She grinned back at him. "Oh, I see. Then there *is* such a

thing as shared experiences." She gave her hips a swing as she led the way back to the table.

I have cast the net, I have played out the fish. The moon is red, and it's time to harvest this newest catch. She goes first, as I promised. For seeing through my set-pieces, she dies first, and perhaps, worst (as we speak of poetry here, you moderns who are so primal, so terrified):

After ten minutes of walking, Elise slowed down, turned around fearfully, and scrutinized the faces around her. She was being foolish. Of course Captain Reade wasn't following her.

Of course none of . . . that had happened. She hadn't snuck off and she hadn't, they hadn't . . .

Dim memories sprang up and she fought them away before they could take shape. Something about pain, and faces, and a child. And her screaming.

No . . .

She walked along the promenade deck, the one with the thick glass sea wall that protected strollers from salt spray or rain during bad weather. The surface of the water sparkled and danced; as she watched, a gray shadow perhaps five feet long swam beneath the waves, faded. Dolphin? she wondered, as tears welled in her eyes. She stopped and searched the horizon.

Was she overreacting? No. While she'd been dreaming that she had snuck out of bed for a rendezvous with the captain, Phil had actually done it. But that wasn't like him. Had she finally pushed him too far?

And those dreams. God. Had she said something in her sleep? Had he heard her? Maybe he thought she was playing around again. Maybe he got so angry he went off to a bar, as he had done the night before.

Well, the hell with him; was it so much to demand, what she asked? That he be a man, that he . . .

How disappointing their first time together had been. How diffident, how tentative he'd been. And he was *tiny*. She honestly had trouble knowing when he was inside her. That made her angriest of all, but she didn't understand why. Except that she felt cheated; that being with him made her less of a woman. That she was being wasted.

And the captain. The captain had . . .

She shivered and shook her head. Dangerous shoals there. Uncharted territory. She'd had a bad dream that seemed very real. But it hadn't been real, because she was here, and she was fine, and . . .

She closed her eyes and put her hands on the thick glass. She wished to God they hadn't set out on the *Morris.* She hadn't wanted to; now she couldn't figure out how she had acquiesced after they'd seen that damn rust bucket. He had his ways, now and then. Money wasn't his only charm.

The boat rocked. Though she felt dizzy, she kept her eyes shut. Beyond the glass, the water rushed like a caress. Footsteps sounded around her. People laughing, talking. Distantly, a piano tinkled something like "Camp Town Races"; or was it a calliope? Very *Natchez Belle;* oh, God, she hated the South, all that magnolia-sweet-potato-pie crap. Peachtree this and Tara that, and half the people were so ignorant they couldn't even spell "confederate." Small-town small minds, called you honey with one side of their mouths and tore you to shreds for being a Yankee with the other. And the men were so wrapped up in themselves, in their glory of being a good ol' Southern boy. They were terrible lovers . . .

The sound of the water caressed her. A coldness swirled around her, and she opened her eyes as something—someone—

—a man—

—spread-eagled himself behind her and pushed her against the glass. The hard chest, the hard thighs, the penis—

"Wh—" she gasped, and the man said gruffly, "Look." She struggled; he squeezed her against the barrier and clamped one hand around the back of her head, forcing her to face straight ahead. She tried to scream but no sound came out; she blinked rapidly in her panic, trembling violently. The other passengers walked by with apparent disinterest. This couldn't be happening. This was another dream.

"Look, damn you."

Snails covered the wall now, dozens of them, in a wide circle, sluglike, brown, and oozing; and each time she blinked they got bigger, and bigger, until she could see that they were taking each other from behind, each one, in a long chain of sex.

"Each one is male and female," her captor said in a low, languid voice. "Each one fucks the one in front, gets fucked by the one in back. Look."

He forced her head to the left. Black mussels clung to the glass. "Hermaphrodites," he whispered. "They release their jelly into the sea. Queen bees require special jelly, do they not?"

Elise gasped. Her knees buckled, but he held her hard. His penis pushed against the small of her back and a wild roar of fear thrust through her.

He turned her head up and to the right. A crab clicked sideways along the top of the glass, carrying another crab in its claws.

"The ocean seethes with sex," the voice said. Was it the captain? "It seethes. You will be happy in it. And I'll wake you and fuck you from time to time, and you'll live."

Bile shot up from her stomach and trickled down her chin.

"It's time for you," he went on, squeezing her. "I'm tired. Perhaps I'm growing old. You saw through the *Pandora*. You saw my other lives. My ships. I wasn't prepared for that."

"I . . . I . . ."

"If you die aboard, you're mine," he whispered in her ear.

She heard the tinkle of the piano; the man's hot breath, growing rapid; and then, a single woman's voice, singing, a clear, sweet soprano. Elise's eyes rolled back in her head.

When Elise woke, she lay on the floor of the museum, flat on her back with her legs spread apart. And he was there! On top of her, again, the dream, again; and it *hurt*.

But he was so real. Solid, as he leered and laughed at her, as he thrust through the crotch of her jumpsuit.

"Ss . . ." She tried to push him away; and he pushed in hard; he rent her. Blood streamed out of her, pooling around and steaming, etching a hole in the floor where she lay. The linoleum warped beneath her like a badly tied hammock.

With a voiceless gasp, she shrank from him as he thrust again, slid a shaking hand between their bodies to his cock, hard and thick and

glass.

She hadn't known you could hurt like this and live.

Her hand pushed at him, stop, stop. There was a roaring in her body, a wail like a burning animal; and then she couldn't tell if she was pushing it in or pulling it out; and behind him, around them . . .

the faces. The faces. Then, no faces.

His laughter. And incredibly: singing. Someone she knew. Donna. Donna, *singing!*

"God!" she shouted. "Help!"

The glass.

The agony.

Time, or no time. Space, or no space. Elise was, and wasn't awake.

She was, and wasn't alive. But alone, yes, alone.

all, all alone.

"Oh," she groaned, rolling over on her side. A sound of a bottle, rolling on the floor. Her legs slapped together and hot pain rolled through her sex organs. She moaned. The room tipped and swirled, dissolved, returned—

—for a moment she was sure, absolutely sure, that she was on some kind of long, flat barge, stretched out next to the wheel of a car, or a pile of dead fish—

She struggled to awareness. The fogginess receded, and she lay in the museum. She faced the back of the room where the figureheads were kept. Indian chief, bare-breasted Columbianna, ancient Chinese demon—

She screamed. They were—

No, no, they couldn't—

—in a long chain, up and down the stairs, one in front, one behind, one in front, one behind, one—

—and then she was surrounded by writhing bodies, black

men in chains on the floor, grabbing at her, screaming, claw-
ing.

"Hell! Help!" she shrieked, and rolled hard to the right.

The men disappeared. She lay on the deck of a large yacht,
the sails full with sweet breezes. A man sat in a chair at the
wheel, and he was singing:

" 'Sailing, sailing, over the bounding main . . .' "

"Wha . . ." she rasped.

Then someone clutched her ankle and pulled, hard; she
shrieked as she tumbled down into a whirlpool, down,
   down,
   down,
and around, raging on black panthers' paws, sucking her
below, to the deadly deep, forty, fifty, sixty-nine thousand
leagues; and the sharks came for her, the gray shadows half
as long as the *Pandora,* serpent sharks smelling the forbidden
fruit of her. They seized her with rows of teeth like broken
glass bottles, and dragged her

"Phil!"

under, and out

of everything.

*And also harvesting him; the male and female of the pair,
though they are actually so sexless that I shall remember them as
figureheads. I will use their faces and their memories, but I shall
never give them knowledge of sex again. Adam and Eve before
the Fall, poor sad and tasty duet:*

Phil staggered on with the lovely girl on his arm. It didn't
matter to her that he was in his pajamas, nor to anyone else
who passed them by. On this sunny spring morning, the other
passengers smiled and waved, the bustled ladies twirling their
parasols, the men raising their top hats.

Phil shuffled on the steamboat deck, and he knew this was
all wrong. Didn't he? He knew he was on the *Pandora,* but
this was a paddlewheel, wasn't it?

"What . . . ?" he murmured.

A flash—

a flash—

—and he was standing on some kind of catwalk, sur-rounded by blackness, and she was, oh, God, she was—

—like in the dining room, nothing but rot—

—beautiful, and smelling of the magnolia behind her ear. Her hair was loose, how daring, and it draped the creamy lace of her dress like a cape of shiny black—

Water! Black, foul water swirled around his knees! The *Pandora* was sinking! It was—

"Come," she urged, and stepped into a metal cage. No, an elevator. Yes, up to the surface, before the water got them.

He jumped in. "I'm, I'm all mixed up," he said, grabbing her shoulders.

Her shoulders of bone, her spine of bone, her skull. She dangled from the top of the cage like a puppet, a skeleton, whose jaw opened, closed, whose bony arms reached for him.

Whose *tail bones*—

Phil screamed and threw himself against the back of the elevator. She reached for him—

—it started to go down, down, into the water.

Jump overboard, Phil. Jump now.

"Gahh!" he shouted. His jaw locked open as he dug his heels into the floor and hurtled himself against the cage—the glass case—the cage—

"What's wrong?" she asked, her deep-set brown eyes large with worry. Her hair fell in a curtain as she raised her hand and touched his sweaty cheek.

His jaw hung open and he made gagging sounds. He couldn't think. Couldn't make sense. Where was he? Dream, dream. Pajamas, a dream.

Whoosh.

That sound! He swiveled his head.

Whoosh. Whoosh.

The tinny plunk-plunk of a piano, a banjo.

"It's all right. Just jump," she said softly.

Whoosh, whoosh, whooshwhooshwhooshwhoosh

And Phil saw, but didn't see, a white wood column grow behind her, and he felt, but didn't feel, the floor bow upward into a curved wooden deck. And heard, but didn't hear—

—the whoosh of the paddlewheel—

—the cry of the steam whistle shrieking, shrieking, too much steam, too much, the engines, racing; and the riverboat swerved to avoid something dead ahead, a black shape in a bank of fog huge as a cathedral.

Someone bellowed, "Reverse! Reverse engines!" The whistle blew; bells clanged.

The shudder of gears; squealing like dying pigs. And a crowd of passengers stampeding toward him, pointing and wailing and screaming in fear. And one of them was Mrs. Reinstedt, the fat woman who had come by at dinner, only now she wore strange clothes, old-time clothes, lace and a bustle . . .

"Please," Phil begged. She waddled past him, pointing. She fell to her knees. Phil turned and something hit him in the forehead, something small and hard and green;

and he screamed as he stood on the edge of the top deck of a steamboat painted fresh and white, and a score of old fig-ureheads posed like religious icons before the columns that held up the roof, and the wheelhouse; he really stood there now, really did—

—too much steam, the boat was rumbling like a volcano—

—and he jumped just as it blew, grabbing the girl beside him and throwing them both over the side. The deck blasted into a thousand flaming pieces, up into the air, and he grabbed on to the girl, whose dress burst into flames, and the two plummeted toward the blazing inferno, and the steam.

And into some kind of huge metal container like a drum or a kettle. And at the last, the very last as the steam boiled him alive, flaying the skin off his beet-red body, he hung in a silent scream in her arms, her charred arms that moved around his back and held him tight. Her skeletal rib cage punctured his chest and boiling blood oscillated out of him.

At this last, as he held on, held on, unable to believe any-thing, least of all that a man could live through this, a man could sizzle like a griddle and still draw breath; the skull kissed him on his lipless mouth and whispered, in the cap-tain's voice, "Fresh, hot belly timber. Ah, yes."

20
Feeding Time

The captain stood on the bridge, staring out to sea with his hands folded behind his back. He was tired, though he was never tired; his bones ached, though they had never troubled him through all the centuries and shipwrecks and harvests.

Something was wrong.

The sea, his sacred lady, stroked the hull of his vessel.

I was a mariner, he brooded, *a captain, and they shoved me in that boat with my treasure about me. My books, my uniform. The hand of glory; no, the head, Nathaniel's sweet head of glory, so superstitious were they that they wouldn't allow him to stay aboard the* Royal Grace. *Nor would they commit him to the sea.*

It were a boon, that his little head was there. I was so hungry.

I was so thirsty. And that taste, that taste, that was mana from the sea, the beauteous sea, who suckled me with the milk of Nathaniel's brain. Ah, Stella Maris! Giver of life!

*It was so black, so dark, on the high breasts of my beloved
Oceana. And I Wanted,*
I Desired,
I Dreamed and
And suddenly, Creutz beside him was no longer Creutz,
but a mossy stick figure dressed in wafting tatters of silk and
ribbon; a thatch of blond hair wove above his head, floating
like a sponge. And from his mouth, a tentacle waved Hello,
Goddag, in Swedish; and it begged
Let me not be,
let me not be . . .
The captain panicked. That couldn't happen! He whirled
around. He stood on the bridge
alone, alone, all, all
Everyone was gone! The wheelhouse was a wreck, sand
and detritus littering the floor—
Losing his touch. Losing his strength. His vision.
"No!" he shouted, and it all came back.
Creutz, leaning over a chart. Adams, late of the *Benicia,* at
the wheel, the wooden wheel that—
No!
at the plastic joystick. And the others, at their stations.
Their battle stations.
It was *their* fault, he told himself, and thought of the survivors aboard. *Her* fault, for he still had not learned the nature
of the hook that would impale her heart. She was confusing
him, dissipating his magical power. He must pull the nets in
faster.
Yes, he must.
He smiled, and sent out his thoughts to the young Mexican, the one who would be a big man. This one he would do
with élan.
He closed his eyes and dreamed.

On the water, in the fog, Ramón stood with one leg on the
hull of the longboat and faced into the bitter English wind. *Yo
soy,* he thought. I am. *Yo soy vikingo.* I am a Viking, and I'll
cut these weaklings down! I'll bash their skulls in and drink
my mead from their bones!

He grabbed his erect cock with both hands and laughed into the gale that rocked the longboat. Thus blazed his kinsmen into battle, loving the fight, thrusting with pride in their prowess and savagery. What did the English plead?

From the fury of the Norsemen, good Lord deliver us.

Yes, the fury! The fury!

He stood at the prow, clad for battle in his leather and metal. Kraken, his fabled longsword, was drawn and pointed downward. His crew rowed through the mist, their arms corded with muscle. There would be spoils to take, and dark beauties to rape, and priests to torment and torture.

What a fine day. What a day to be alive!

"Captain, strong seas ahead," his lieutenant warned. Indeed, as the boat slipped between two tall, chalk-white cliffs, the waters swelled beneath the boat and crested.

"Evade!" Ramón commanded, holding on to the dragon figurehead. The weight of Kraken dragged him forward; as he sought to right himself, two long, white hands shot through the surface of the water and grabbed the tip of his blade.

"By Odin!" he shouted.

" 'Tis one of their water witches!" one of his comrades shouted. "Let go of your sword!"

The two men closest to him abandoned their oars and grabbed hold of his waist. But the long, white hands wrapped around the blade and yanked. The steel sliced through them but they did not bleed.

Despite the strength of the two men holding him, Ramón plunged into the frothing waves.

And into the arms of a creature with a stark-white face and hair the color of bleached bone. It was naked and it had the torso of a woman, but beneath, it curled white-rotted tendrils around him, legs, hips, arms. Tighter, tighter, until he was swaddled in its stinking flesh. Beneath his sword arm, something jerked Kraken from his grasp.

The creature cackled. He heard the sound distinctly through the water; and then it was obscured by a stream of bubbles that Ramón understood was the air in his lungs, which it was squeezing out of him.

He jerked his body hard. It laughed again. Violently he wriggled back and forth as his brain filled with blinding panic.

Above, oars stabbed into the water from the hull of his boat. His mates, trying to save him, though none dared dive in after him, although he was their captain and they loved him. His eyes rolled as he saw how close they came, and yet never touched the monster.

His eyes began to cloud and his lungs ached with emptiness, but he kept his mouth clamped shut. He mustn't try to breathe; there was nothing to breathe, except death.

The monster roared with glee and rubbed its breasts against him. Its tendrils curled around and around and around. Shouts filtered from the surface, but they were moving on; the dragon's head began to move past.

And then the creature began to sing in a clear, sweet voice. Its rib cage vibrated against Ramón's as it trilled words he couldn't understand. Perhaps it wanted to lull him into surrender, or it was a spell of some kind. Odin protect his men, he thought, if the English had command of such a being.

It sang. Ramón's lungs shook. Leader of such a fine ship, and the first son of a chieftain, and he was dying an inglorious death. If only he had his sword, or any kind of weapon.

Then something moved through the murk behind the monster. It was a flask, he thought, yes, a flask, of green, some treasure of the English. He willed it to hit her, knock her unconscious. Willed it, willed it . . .

Tantalizingly, it bobbed just behind her, and he lost all hope as it stopped and hovered harmlessly. A vain wish, that such a thing could harm his enemy. A vain hope, that he would survive her evil embrace.

He could contain himself no longer. Better to die in a manner of his own choosing than in whatever way the monster intended.

He opened his mouth to take a breath that he knew was not there—

—and the creature crushed her mouth over his and spewed something into him, something horrible and cold and clotted. He knew that taste. It was blood; she was drowning his lungs in the blood of her body.

Nei, he roared in his mind. He struggled in the cocoon of her body, whipping his head back and forth, demanding of the gods a chance to fight. A chance for Valhalla.

The bottle flew at her, crashing across the back of her head. Her skull cracked and blood gushed up from the fragments, toward the surface. Going limp, her arms fell from around him. As soon as the tendrils loosened, he ripped them off himself. Grabbed his sword from her fingers, raised it back in the water, and cut off her head.

Down, it tumbled in the water,

down,

down,

down,

At his feet, the head of Elise van Buren.

Ramón screamed and leapt away from it. No, he had not— *No.*

Fog rushed around him, gray, dirty, cold. It billowed toward him, an onrushing tide of wind and stink.

He spun left, right. Dropped the sword. Ran through the cloud. About ten feet from him what looked like an old wooden mast pierced the sweaty clouds, and from it jittered a tattered Union Jack. The fog grappled with the top right corner like an animal worrying a bone.

"Nahhh . . ."

The fog swirled downward and scraped itself away, revealing the hulking wreck of an ancient sailing vessel. Pirate ship, Ramón thought, trying for an answer where there could be none. Schooner, clipper, part of a movie, part of a dream. An intricate sign above the companionway that led below decks read *"Royal Grace."*

Ramón staggered backward, directly into Elise's head, and with a shout he fell, sprawling over a rotted deck.

A stench rose from beneath his elbow. He crabbed on his backside and palms, put his hand into the warm guts of a rat whose head had been crushed and smeared against the splintered, pitted deck.

The fog careened toward him. A face poked out from it, smirking, laughing, a sharp, cruel face with an eye patch, and the mouth opened and it was full of blood and meat, and it chewed so that he could see that it was—

—it was—

Ramón rolled over on his stomach and vomited.

Someone stood in the distance, at a ship's wheel. A tall, wiry figure with long, flowing blond hair.

Kevin! Ramón crawled toward him, trying to call, unable to speak. He crabbed on his hands and knees, straining to outrun the fog and Captain Reade. Nails and splinters pierced his kneecaps and tore the skin in long, tortuous lines; he grunted, felt nothing, hurried toward Kevin.

The fog slipped around him.

"Kkkkk—"

Reached him. Ramón reached him. He put out a hand—

—and Kevin's ruined body slumped over the wooden spokes, fell to one side, and splattered onto its back. His face was a motley of gray and purple. Large, crusted wounds covered each side of his face. Like a large, withered flower, his nose was crushed against his cheek, white shards like stamens stuck in the gore.

As Ramón screamed and jumped away, he caught that something was wrong with Kevin's eyes, something horribly wrong: they looked like cartoon eyes; they were nothing but outlines of navy-blue—

—they were drawn on his lids. His eyes were closed and someone had drawn eyes on his eyelids.

"Jesus!" Ramón shouted; somehow this was more horrible than—

No. No, it wasn't.

Reade's boots stood beside him. The man bent down and offered Ramón a hand. In his other hand he carried Elise's head by the hair, like a handbag.

"See how easy it is?"

Ramón whimpered, shuffled away, and flung himself against the base of a wooden mast.

The captain had a handkerchief over his mouth; he wiped daintily and drew it away. His lips were covered with blood.

"Fresh, not rotted," he said. The head dangled in his grasp.

Her right cheek was missing; Ramón could see her teeth through the hole.

The captain smacked his lips. Ramón looked from the head to him and back again. No. No.

"Now we'll render her." He pointed above Ramón's head.

Elise's corpse was strung upside down from a hook that dangled from the crow's nest. The body was sopping with blood, which no longer ran, no longer dripped. The flesh from between her legs to her throat had been sliced open, and entrails hung like sausages.

Ramón sobbed.

The fog billowed down, broiling, roiling, wringing itself around him like wet sheets. Ramón sank to his knees and punched at it like an angry child, tears splashing over his cheeks and scattering like spittle with each futile jab.

"And you wanted to be a big man," Reade scoffed, stepping through the fog to stand before Ramón. "You thought to presume."

He still carried the head. In the other, he held a Viking longsword. He raised it up and scrutinized it, slashing the fog idly. "Isn't it beautiful? It's a museum piece," he said, showing his teeth as he smiled. "Your dreams are entertaining. Childish, but entertaining."

Ramón couldn't speak. Nor could he stop crying. He couldn't have cut off her head. He couldn't have. He couldn't . . .

"Oh, do shut up, or I'll cut off yours," Reade snapped, brandishing the sword. Ramón flinched, and the captain shook his head in disgust.

"You're a poor piece of work, aren't you? A peasant." He jabbed the sword upward. "Render her. Now. Your mates will want their dinner."

Ramón sobbed harder. Reade exhaled. "What do you think, that I can keep you alive with my imagination?" He waited, as if Ramón could manage to answer. The only sound was Ramón's gagging as Elise's body dangled above him. Her fingertips grazed the crown of his head and the blood on them smeared his hair in a mockery of baptism.

"I can kill you with it, though," Reade continued. He made

a lacy wave with the handkerchief. "My imagination. As they can attest."

The fog billowed down and swirled around Ramón. Desperately he gazed at the sword. If he could just get it away from him.

The guy was loco. Ramón didn't know what kind of *chingada* shit the guy was taking, and had probably given him as well, but it made you freak out bad, *hombre*. Very bad.

Yeah. Wild hope rose inside him. That was it; he was drugged, and none of this was really happening. C'mon, man, a wreck of a sailing ship? And . . . and the lady, the *señora*, she wasn't there. It was a bad trip, like LSD, yeah, that was all. It was . . .

The fog thickened and unrolled like a hatch, and figures appeared in a vague haze, walked through the opening.

Ramón wet his pants.

Men with red scarves tied around their heads and gold hoops in their ears; men with dark blue uniforms and caps; men with doughboys; with tricornes:

And their faces were black and yellow and green and purple, and dead ice-blue; and they had no faces;

and their eyes were round slanted and cloudy; and they had no eyes;

and their lips

their lips dripped with blood that splashed

down

down

down,

their lips spoke words he couldn't hear because he was screaming and vomiting and slipping in his own urine.

They staggered and shambled toward him in a mass, like a single tentacled creature, and Ramón, despite the fact that his mind was drowning, skittered away from them.

"No fear," said a sad voice that penetrated the din. "I told you."

No fear. No fear. Fear is his Desire.

And he saw a man with red hair, a living man, tied around the mast. His face was covered with bruises; his skin was bleached white; he had no teeth.

"Cut her down, then cut her up," the captain said to his crew.

A sharp *roll, crack, roll, crack* accompanied their footfalls. *Drugs,* Ramón told himself, and *hit him. Stop him. Kill him.*

Roll, crack, foul, walking death.

Roll, crack, and a *scrinch, scrinch, scrinch,* as somewhere a windlass turned, and the body dropped lower toward the deck.

Ramón got to his feet and ran. With his head turned toward the captain, and the dead men, and the—

—the fog—

He ran for all he was worth.

And slammed into Captain Esposito. Hard, and solid, and Ramón threw his arms around him.

"Help! Help!" he begged. "They're . . . they . . . eat us, eat us," he managed. "They—" He sagged against Esposito as the world started to go black.

When he woke, he was tied upright to some kind of pole. Hard metal; that much he could tell though the area was lit a dim and sickly green. That much, and that the soles of his shoes were soaked.

A dream, he thought muzzily. No sailing vessel wreck, no body, no fog, no death crew. No—

He opened his eyes. His head was bound in place, and he was staring into some kind of hole, some—

—a periscope. *Periscope.* His mind thrashed some more. Submarine?

Water seeped through the sides of his shoes and reached his ankles. Sub, and sinking!

"Help," he murmured. His head wanted to fall back, but he was held tightly in place. The water sloshed as if something moved near him, and he blinked, his lashes brushed the eyepiece.

And he saw:

Captain Esposito, barefoot, with lines tied around his ankles and his wrists, crying and gesticulating to the figures around him, who held the ends of the lines in their fists. The death crew. No dream. No dream.

Esposito stood on the bowsprit, just above the figurehead of a woman, and shook his head. The ropes dangled from him like a giant spiderweb. The crew stared at him impassively, as dead men would, and waited.

Esposito stumbled and almost tumbled off. The crew waited, holding the other ends of the lines slack in their hands.

Reade appeared and gestured with the sword. Esposito shouted something back.

"*Capitán,*" Ramón groaned. "*Nuestra Señora, ayúdale.*" Help him, Our Lady. He blinked, could not look away.

Reade moved the sword again. Again Esposito shook his head; again, nearly lost his balance.

How could he be seeing this? Ramón wondered. How could—

The figurehead moved. In a graceful gesture, it raised its arms above its head, and then its body grew long, long, like a snake's, and while Esposito argued with Reade, it coiled around on itself and slithered toward him. It opened its arms—

—Reade folded his arms, and the dead men stared—

—and hurled Esposito into the water. It stood on its tail and watched as he splashed down, disappeared, his location betrayed by the tangle of lines that stretched as he sank.

The men gathered the lines and began to walk on either side of the deck. The ropes draped over their shoulders, tautened, slackened. It didn't make sense; the bowsprit was in the way of—

It couldn't happen. It couldn't be happening.

The men walked the length of the ship, the old sailing ship *Royal Grace,* while Ramón gasped, "No, no," over and over and over.

The figurehead slithered back below the bowsprit, and lowered her arms, and she became a half-naked woman once more.

The men reached the bow, and Reade issued more orders, and they began to hoist whatever was left of Esposito.

Which wasn't much.

And directly behind Ramón, a woman sang:

Row, row, row your boat
gently down the stream.
Merrily, merrily, merrily, merrily,
Life is but a dream.

Reade danced a hornpipe, placing one arm over his stomach, one across his back, bobbing, weaving, jibing, and tacking.

"Oh, God," Ramón rasped. "Oh, no, please."

Soft laughter.

Then nothing.

Reade stopped and stared directly into the periscope's crosshatches, walked closer, closer, until his face filled the sight.

"They underestimated me. They should have killed me. How? How, you ask?" Reade cocked his head. "Does it matter?"

Ramón wanted to faint. The water rose around his calves.

"You wanted to be a big man?" Reade continued. "A captain? Only captains serve me." He gestured with his thumb over the bits of meat and bone attached to the lines.

"Only captains serve me, and I serve only the leftovers. The boneheads."

He turned around, addressing the men who now shuffled toward the carcass. "Did you see how he jumped into the stewpot? Phil van Buren, I mean? Did you see him boil with the fish bones? And the woman. Elise. Did you see her take the bottle, and attack herself? She thought it was me. She thought it was my *cock*."

A white bird schreed and landed on Reade's shoulder. "That man had a dream of a steamboat, but he was really in the kitchen, walking over the burners. He thought he was belowdecks, but he dove into the stewpot like a swan."

Fresh bile urped into Ramón's mouth. Phil van Buren, dead? Esposito?

The *chiquito*, Matty?

"Do you know who I am?" Reade demanded. "Do you know what I want from all of you? What I'll have?"

But Ramón could not answer.

He could not do anything.

"Don't you wonder where you really are? What you're really seeing?"

Reade caressed the bird's wing, its foot, its beak. "The Greeks, they knew that ghosts drink blood," he said. "And my ghosts are always hungry. I am the Captain, Ramón Diaz. I will always be the Captain, and those who serve me are strong-willed men who hate me. Hatred is a kind of Spirit, and it is that which keeps them from ceasing. But those who are weak . . ." He jerked his head toward the remains of Esposito's corpse.

The bird flew over to it, settled on it, and launched into the air with part of a foot in its beak.

"Do you know what, Diaz?" he said to the periscope. "The damndest thing is, Esposito was already dead. And my men didn't kill him. The first time, I mean. They couldn't. They can only harvest the dead, though I can lure the squirming belly timber into the nets for them. Only the living can kill the living. Like you and I, Ramón. You and I."

The captain put out his arms and whirled in a circle. The bird flew around his head, orbiting like a moon, and the captain sang the awful song the woman (what woman?) had crooned behind Ramón.

"But now that he *is* dead, he's mine," Reade proclaimed. "Mine. And they can kill him again and again. Whenever I wish.

Whenever I

Desire."

And more fun, and more.

"Of course, you want what's best for your son," Captain Reade said in a low voice.

They sat together at the back of the bridge while the cruise director, a sprightly young woman with dark hair and brown eyes, amused Matt by moving a toy boat along a chart that hung on a bulkhead on the starboard side of the room. Matt laughed, but lines creased his forehead and his eyes were ringed with black. John thought miserably of the moon encircled by clouds: storm on its way. Bad weather. Bad days. Donna had been kind, but Matty looked like . . . death.

"A boy like that is a prize worth fighting for," Reade added, and John shifted in his chair. He didn't appreciate the captain's comment. His son wasn't a "prize."

"Do you know that Dr. Hare used to do research on parasites?" Reade crossed his legs and nodded for emphasis. "He worked on *sacculena.*"

John crooked his neck forward to hear better, although he didn't particularly care to discuss medicine with the man. He'd simply requested that the captain allow him to radio Sydney and have a cancer team waiting by, and to contact his doctors back home. The phone in his room wasn't working, nor was anyone else's. Something to do with the satellite again, or so Reade claimed. John was beginning to think they had inferior phone equipment, and the staff had been instructed not to admit it.

"I'm sorry," he said distractedly. "I've never heard of that. What is it?"

"A kind of barnacle. You haven't read his papers?" Reade looked mildly disapproving. "*Sacculena* is a kind of barnacle that actually lives inside crabs"—he waved his fingers—"can't remember which kind. At any rate, they extend a mass of rootlike fibers through the crab's body, rather like tentacles. It grows saclike protuberances." He shivered. "Castrates male crabs and makes them into females. Rather gruesome, don't you think?"

John made a face, though his gaze was focused on Matt. "Rather."

"But Dr. Hare made an interesting discovery. If you chilled the crab, you could kill the *sacculena.*"

"And eat the crab," John said dryly, managing a weak jest.

Reade chuckled. "If you pleased. But what I meant was, the crab survived. You froze the . . . cancer, and the host lived on."

John's gaze ticked toward him. "Captain, why are you telling me this?"

Reade shrugged. "Of course you want what's best for your son." He clapped his hands and rubbed them together.

"What say we adjourn and tap the admiral, ey?" When John didn't respond, he said, "That's sea talk. Lord Nelson—our British naval hero? Horatio Nelson? His body was pickled in brandy for the voyage home. So we call having a brandy, tapping the admiral." He pantomimed pounding something. Tapping a keg, John translated.

"Matt," he called.

"He'll be all right with her," Reade assured him. "She'll treat him like her own."

"I just want him with me." For as long as possible. John's hands shook and he clenched them hard.

Captain Reade rose. "As you please. You know best. I, too, want what's best for your son." He faced John as John stood.

"Have you been having dreams, Doctor?" Before John could answer, Reade turned his head and watched Matt with the woman.

"Because dreams can come true, Doctor. Believe me, I know." He looked back.

"And perhaps there's a little something I can do to help them come true."

John raised his brows, unsteady with the conversation. The atmosphere on the bridge had just transformed. It was charged, flickering with a new energy. Or was that a result of his own anxiety?

"You may have noticed that things aboard the *Pandora* can be different."

John took a half step backward. "Beg your pardon?"

Reade smiled and rubbed his chin, half shutting his eye. "Come now, I know you've felt things. Perhaps seen things?"

The water on the floor. The cork, or bob—

—or glass ashtray, John. Just an ashtray.

"I'm not sure I know what you mean," John said. "Matt," he called, a bit harshly. The boy said something to the woman and walked toward him on spider-thin legs. He was so pale and wan John thought the boy might keel over.

"If you don't know what I mean," Reade said, "then open your eyes, your ears, and most especially your mind." He clapped a hand on John's shoulder. John jumped.

"God sent you to this ship, Dr. Fielder. He knows your

inner heart, what you pray for. God sent you here, so Matt could live. I know that in my soul. In here." He made a fist against his chest.

As John gaped, the captain turned on his heel and headed for the elevator.

Through the looking glass, through the magic periscope that Reade had somehow fashioned, Ramón watched as the crumpled form of a man sagged at the feet of Captain Reade. The man wept and mumbled. Reade laughed.

"Curry, I must thank you for your latest service to me. You have been a worthy acolyte." He looked straight at Ramón. "And now I must ask you, do you truly wish to die?"

Sobbing, the man named Curry picked up the sword Ramón had so recently dropped. "Goddamn you," he whispered, and lunged toward the captain. But he was weak; the momentum threw him face forward onto the deck with a sharp crack. A cloud of blood bloomed around him and the sword clattered from his grasp.

"Try again," the captain taunted as he picked up the sword and held it out to him.

"Just kill me," the man begged.

"No. You must do it."

Bastard, Ramón thought. Fucking *chingadera* asshole. He was going to kill that man; why not just do it? Reade was a fucking sadist, tricking the *señora* into killing herself with a bottle. And her husband, making him jump into a pot of boiling water. Why did he have to fool with them? Why not just fucking do it?

"Ay, Dios." His mind numbed: what had Reade said? Only the living could kill the living.

"Oh, God, oh, God," he said in English, over and over. He shook, hard.

Maybe Reade couldn't kill them because he was not alive.

And if he couldn't kill them. If he wasn't alive . . .

He had to get free. He had to tell the others. He had to save them, save himself. *Jesús Cristo,* maybe Reade could do nothing to them. Nothing, unless they let him. If they didn't believe what they say . . . if they understood it was all fake . . .

"*Ayúdame, ayúdame.*" Help me. Help me, God.

But God was not listening.

Perhaps He was dead, too.

Or a fake.

21
Through a Glass, Darkly

Ruth cried out. In the tub, why was she in the tub in her stateroom? Why was her face under the water?

Why did it seem that something was pressing against the back of her neck? And what was she seeing? Beauty, beauty, fading—

The image of the captain's face, when he had come to visit her, loomed large, burst like a bubble.

What was she doing?

Beauty, beauty; ah, no wait . . .

A knock on the door.

Ruth sat up. The water streamed off her face into the tub. But she couldn't have bent low enough to put her head under the waterline. She was too old, too stiff, too . . .

The knock came again. "Yes?" she asked timorously. "Yes, who is it?"

A shape on the other side of the plastic curtain. A shadow,

moving among the red and blue fish, the printed forest of seaweed.

A voice that she couldn't hear, but suddenly she knew whose voice it was:

"Don't go," she pleaded, lurching forward. "Stephen!"

The doorbell.

The shadow faded.

Ruth put her hands to her head. Dreaming? Or awake? Why could she no longer tell?

"Ruth? Ruth!"

It was Donna. Ruth flattened her hand against the shower curtain. "Come back, come back," she said.

"Ruth!"

She was alone now. She felt it, knew it. Carefully, she hung on to the railing above the soap dish and hauled herself to a standing position.

"Coming!" Her voice screeched, an old lady's voice.

She grabbed a towel and wrapped it around herself. Stepped cautiously out and reached for her bathrobe.

The doorknob rattled. "Ruth? Ruth!"

She faced the tub. Was there anything in the room that could have cast a shadow against the shower curtain? A chair in the next room, perhaps, or the way the light fixture was adjusted?

For now, hearing Donna's voice, she understood how . . . jumbled . . . she had been. Imagining all kinds of things. A gullible old woman's hopes, amplified by the excitement of being lost at sea. Foolish hopes. No one had been hovering behind the shower curtain, least of all her missing husband. There was no supernatural force at work; there were no messages coming to her from beyond.

But what about what had happened on the *Morris*?

And why had she been sitting in the tub? She'd taken a shower not an hour before, in preparation for lunch.

And there *had* been a shadow on her curtain. A moving shadow.

"Ruth!"

Stirring herself, she walked out of the bathroom and

crossed her stateroom. Glanced at the clock as she passed the dresser, and caught her breath.

Either the clock was wrong, or she'd sat in the water for three hours.

She opened the door.

"Hi," Donna said. "I was getting worried about you. You all right?"

I don't know, I don't know, she wanted to cry. She nodded and said, "I am a little hungry, though. I . . . I missed breakfast."

"Lunch, too, I'm afraid. It's almost dinnertime." She peered around the door. "Has John been by to see you?"

"No, dear. Ah, can you give me a few moments to dress?"

Before Donna could answer, she slammed the door shut and fell against it. Her heart spasmed; she was covered with goose bumps.

"Oh, God," she whispered, and turned her head toward the bathroom.

A shadow on the curtain, moving slowly, slowly.

Waiting.

The icy water chilled his knees into two brittle disks of throbbing pulses as Ramón stared into the magic periscope and saw:

The captain and Dr. Fielder, walking, talking. Fielder looked guarded, yet he was clearly interested in whatever the captain was telling him.

Lies, *señor*. Lies. Take your boy and leave the ship. Leave, leave, as soon as you can.

Saw:

The museum, and a skeleton stretched within a cage of glass; she a creature of exquisite beauty, who raised her arms toward Ramón and sang. And Cha-cha with his old metal bowl, and spoon, and he was stirring a mixture of fingers and eyes; God, he was stirring.

Saw:

A woman with Matty. They were walking across a fog-laden deck of some kind of barge, some Egyptian-looking thing, with velvet hangings and tassels and torches. The torches, something about them. Ramón flexed his knees, relaxed them. The torches. Fire. Heat.

With her arm around Matt's shoulders, she raised her other hand and pointed to a cloaked figure who glided through the black torch smoke. He rode in a boat, and he guided it with a long pole. Ramón heard the woman murmur, "Charon." Only that.

The figure raised its head. And Ramón felt a flash of shock that there was anything left that could terrify him.

But death terrifies everyone, even the dead. And the captains of the dead.

And the Desire of Death moved upon the waters, something bigger than they knew about; something beyond the captain . . .

Wanting.

22
Message for Donna

The captain stood on the bridge. The sea opened her arms to him. He grit his teeth and thought about diving into her, and sinking deeply.

Do you hear me, Donna? he called, though the bitch wouldn't listen. *Do you hear me? I am gathering them, all your friends. I am putting them under*

(way under; way, way under)

my spell, which is the ocean's spell: a dream, a hope, the ebb and flow of their lives, which is the tide of their mortality.

And you can do nothing about it, you with your near-perfect imperviousness. You have a hard shell, but I shall penetrate you. I shall have you, and I shall take you, and I shall keep you. You will be Life–in–Death to my Ancient Mariner, the beautiful woman who never dies, but brings death. The captain's woman.

You are the one. Do you not remember me, my darling? Whose hand pulled you to the slumber-deaths, with the boy I loved, the little boy in the cold, bottomless lake?

My lady of the lake, do you not know me? The companion in your watery grave, who calls to you with the song of a tempter? How you fought, my lovely, as I sought to keep you. How you hated me for taking the child.

And was it only fate that when she called me, the old widow called with her Desire, and gave form to Pandora, *that you came back to me? Fate, or destiny?*

They're taking longer than I expected, your death throes. Much longer. How tired you must be. And how you fight me still! How you deny me!

But you shall tire. Everyone eventually does. And you shall accept my invitation. You shall come aboard. And after you've done with kicking and screaming and fighting to keep your head above water, we shall come together and I shall fulfill my Desire.

Do you know this poem?

Implacable I, the Implacable Sea
Implacable most when I smile serene
Pleased, not appeased by myriad wrecks in me.

Melville. It's in that book, which of course I let you have. And of course, you've been too thick—thus far, at least—to make any connections: Bruce Smith was the master of the Titanic. *Creutz commanded the* Kronen, *which sank in 1767. Such an odd name, yet you passed it off as nothing. The two times I used Marcus Hare, who went down with his ship* Eurydice—*a double clue, nay, a triple, as Eurydice herself went down to the Underworld—no matter. It was elegant, but lost on you. No matter. I am amused. That is why I bring them back, again and again. For my amusement. I would grow lonely without them, and I am fated—for I have sworn—to sail with a dead crew.*

And after you cease to amuse me, the deluge.

So learn the poem, me beauty. Learn it word for word, because I shall make you say it, Donna me lass, Donna you bitch, you cunt you filthy whore I shall wound you I shall cut you I shall torture you and I shall make you sorry I shall drag you down a thousand times I shall I shall

Implacable

III
GOING DOWN

II

GOING DOWN

23
Here Comes Trouble

It was five-thirty in the afternoon of the fifth day aboard *Pandora*. Donna sat cross-legged on her bed with a glass of Scotch in one hand and the other on the phone. She was becoming seriously concerned.

Everyone was behaving strangely. Ruth crept around like a thief, obviously upset about something but afraid to discuss it. She hadn't seen Ramón since they'd come aboard, and he apparently was never in his cabin when she phoned. Now Elise and Phil van Buren were missing. Or at least avoiding everyone they knew with the skill of a Mafia informant. One little, two little, three little Indians.

She told herself the van Burens had reunited and wanted to work things out in privacy: it would be easy to lose yourself among one thousand other people. That's what she told herself, but it didn't quite assuage her nagging doubts about their safety.

The thing that bothered her most was the change in John.

Spacy, preoccupied, and distant, he kept a clamp on it, whatever it was, and the closeness they'd begun to share as friends, confidantes, potential lovers, was gone. Matty appeared very troubled, and he seemed to want to talk to her, but John never let him out of his sight.

Donna felt isolated, as if everyone else had some secret that she wasn't allowed to share.

And she'd just told herself a lie, to help herself sleep at night: the thing that bothered her most was that the lifeboat hadn't been found. When would they call off the search?

Oh, Cha-cha. Crazy old man.

She took a belt of Scotch and rested the glass against her cheek. Started to dial Glenn's number. Heck, they could still talk like two cops, couldn't they? He could set her mind at ease; tell her if anything was coming out in the news about the dumping, for instance. Give her something to do; make her feel less useless.

But was that really why she wanted to call him? Huffing, she took another sip of Scotch. And if Barb answered the phone, well, that would be pretty damn weird, wouldn't it? Believe it, white girl.

There was a sharp rap on her door.

"Yeah," she said. Maybe it was John.

"It's Tom."

Captain Reade, her mind filled in. Well well well. He'd made the leap to first names. She got off the bed and went to the door.

"Hi," she said. "I'm glad you're here. I think it's time we talked about a few things."

He didn't hear her. "Come quickly." His tone was urgent. "We've found the other lifeboat."

"Oh, God. Just a sec." Donna stepped into a pair of sandals and grabbed her room key. He was already halfway down the hall by the time she shut the door.

"This is great! I was just thinking about them. Just wishing we'd find it."

Reade flashed an odd smile at her. "Really? It was sighted five minutes ago on the radar." He strode down the hall, arms pumping. "We should be on it within the hour."

That long? "Have you called the other rescue vessels?"

He nodded. She was on his eye patch side. "And I'm filing a report on their sheer incompetence. It must have passed a dozen vessels, and none of them saw it. Claimed the fog was too thick. Ridiculous!"

"Fog?" It had been clear and beautiful ever since they'd come on board. She remembered how the fog engulfed the *Morris*.

"The weirdest shit is going on." She started over. "I think there was something really wrong with that stuff the *Morris* dumped. I think it might have contaminated us."

"Oh?" He shot her a look as they strode along.

"Captain Reade, to the bridge, please," a PA system voice announced. "Captain Reade, to the bridge."

"Would you care to accompany me? Watch the operation from up there?"

"Sure." Okay, okay, one thing at a time, and the lifeboat took precedence. For the moment.

A woman dressed in a long, white lace dress and a floppy hat with feathers on it waved from down the companionway. It was Mrs. Reinstedt again. Jesus H. Christ, she had a big butt. Donna blinked. It wasn't her butt. She was wearing a bustle.

"Captain Reade! Hello! They've been found! It's so exciting."

"Yes," he called back, waving. Half turned toward Donna as he kept walking, and did a double take.

"Do you see her?" he asked, with an odd, high-pitched squeal. "Do you see?"

"Huh?" Donna scratched her arm. See her? Of course she saw her.

"You do." Reade broke into a wide smile. His eye jittered like he was on crack. Donna took a step away from him as Mrs. Reinstedt waddled around a corner and disappeared.

Covering his mouth with his hand, Reade burst into a gale of laughter. He fought for composure, succeeded, and straightened, wiping a tear from his eye. Saw Donna's blank look and explained, "She's getting ready for the shipwreck party." Chuckled.

"Although I don't know why she's starting so early. She always wears the same thing. She's a frequent traveler with us," he added. It was clear he was straining not to laugh again.

"The *what*?" Donna asked, astounded.

"The shipwreck party." He waved a finger at her, gesturing for her to follow him around a corner. "Haven't you been reading your Daily Program?"

"No. You mean, like on *Gilligan's Island*? Should you have one of those on a cruise?"

"We have one every time we sail," he replied. He beamed at her. "We've been doing them for years and years."

"But . . ." She shut up. What did she know? But would an airline host a crash party? How absolutely bizarre.

"You'll have to have a costume," he told her. "You're the guest of honor." And this time he did laugh, a short, harsh guffaw.

"Huh?"

"Well, all of you, of course. Since you're our real people. Shipwreck people," he amended. His mouth twitched.

"Am I missing something?" she asked irritably.

"No, no, *au contraire,*" he said. *"Au contraire."*

She rang a hand through her hair and put it on her hip. "Well, what's so funny?"

"Nothing. I'm sorry. It would take too long to explain. Perhaps later, after we've got those men on board."

She let it go. They hurried along until they reached the elevator and went up to the bridge.

"Captain on the bridge," a man with a handlebar mustache announced. All the men stopped what they were doing and immediately saluted Reade.

He returned it, said, "What've you got?"

"It's moving in very fast, sir," said the man. He looked familiar to Donna but she couldn't place him. He pointed to a radar screen. "Just like the other one."

Reade cocked his head. "Curious."

"Yes, sir. If you hadn't recalculated, we'd have . . ." The man cleared his throat.

Reade looked at Donna. "We'd have missed you," he finished.

Say huh? A ship like this would've missed her lifeboat? She didn't get it, but she was more interested in watching the radar blip. The line whipped around and around on a field of glassy green. A blip appeared each time on the lower left quadrant. How did they know that was the boat?

"Jesus," she said, "I hope everyone's all right."

Reade left her and walked to the semicircle of windows.

"So does he," the other officer confided. "He hasn't slept more than an hour at a time since your boat was first reported. And then, when we heard about the second one . . ." He sighed and shook his head. Donna wondered how you got that kind of loyalty. She thought her own big boss was a total asshole, no matter how many sleepless nights he put in for the good of the department.

"They're coming!" the other officer cried. "Sir! We're practically on top of them!"

"Steady on, then," Reade ordered, coming over to the radar screen.

The keel of the *Pandora*, slicing through the water.

You must not acknowledge me, Cha-cha, when I rescue you.

"But you're my big kahuna," Cha-cha murmured, surveying the fog. The king was nearby. He could hear him so clearly. But he couldn't see anything, man, not even the cargo that lay at his feet.

You have done everything I've asked thus far, Cha-cha. Don't disobey me now.

"Yessir," Cha-cha murmured, chastened.

Good, Cha-cha. Very good. Now listen: one of them is still alive. The black man. Quickly.

Surprised, Cha-cha sat up very straight and listened. Sure enough, he heard a sad little moan. He nodded.

"Yessir."

Down on the main deck, John, Ruth, and Matt stood together, straining to see. Ruth had rousted the other two from a nap and they'd run to the railing. Now John held Matt tight, preparing himself in case he was needed. Dr. Hare had gently but firmly refused his offer of assistance unless he found himself confronted with something he couldn't handle. John prayed he wasn't needed.

The *Pandora*'s horn blared and a cheer rose from the assembled passengers and crew. John leaned over the railing. "I don't see them."

"There! There!" Matt jumped up and down. "Look!"

And suddenly John *could* see them, where he thought he'd looked and seen nothing before. Figures moved inside the boat, standing and waving.

"Yes!" John shouted and flailed his arms above his head, laughing when the woman next to him threw her arms around him and gave him a big kiss. He picked Matt up and hugged him; and it didn't register when Matt pounded on his shoulder and said, "That's the lady, Dad. The lady that's a statue."

Beside him, Ruth dabbed her eyes with a Kleenex. Touched, John put his arm around her and gave her a squeeze.

"I know you'll think me callous," she said, so low he could scarcely hear her, "but just now, I was sure that . . . that Stephen would be in that boat."

Her words jolted him: a thought had flashed through his own mind, quicksilver, like a school of anchovies: *Now Matt will live, like the captain said.*

The captain was a religious man, maybe even a fanatic. That was all there was to it. But when John had been with him these last couple of days, when he was near, he could almost envision Matt running and playing and growing up. He could almost feel his ulcer healing. A form of paradise, some kind of mild, unrealistic euphoria, filled him when he was around Reade. Or was that called hope? Was it in such short supply in his psyche that he'd forgotten how it felt? And if it was this good, who cared where it came from?

My son is full of barnacles, he thought, squeezing Matt's hand as the boy danced with excitement.

And the cold can kill them, a voice replied down in his brain where he couldn't detect it, but he heard it just the same.

* * *

Donna accompanied the captain to the landing and watched them hoist up the boat, men and all. There were sixteen, laughing and joking, shaking fists of triumph. A big black man clapped Mr. Saar on the shoulder. The white man's face was bright red, but otherwise he appeared fine.

Cha-cha saw Donna and stood up. "Officer Donna!" he called. "It's me! Don't shoot!"

Reade chuckled and nudged her. "That must be Cha-cha."

"Absolutely." She cupped her mouth with her hands. "Hey, Chach! How are you?" God Almighty, his skin was red as—

red as—

a rose.

"Cool, baby. Cool as ice! Right on!"

"Well, sit down or you'll kill yourself!"

He flashed her a peace sign and plopped back down.

"Jesus, he looks like he's been skinned," she muttered.

"A bad sunburn," the captain agreed. "Dr. Hare will have something for that."

The boat was hauled up even with the landing with the men still in it.

"How come you didn't bring us up like that?" Donna asked the captain.

"This way is more dangerous," he replied, as if that should satisfy her. Which, of course, it didn't, since it only led to more questions in her mind.

The crew was carefully helped out. Men in greens arrived with a squadron of wheelchairs and a stab of vertigo rattled Donna for an instant as she remembered her arrival on the *Pandora: She's the one.*

Ice water in her brains.

Whoah, girl. She took a slow, deep breath.

"Shit, we don't need those things," the black man said. "We're a little burned, but we're fine." As he climbed out of the boat, he held his hand out to Cha-cha. "Sorry I gave you such a hard time, brother."

Shaking with him, Cha-cha wagged his head and made a peace sign. "Hey, Eskimo baby. Peace and love." He winked. "King made that fish come. Told me a lot of groovy things."

"Fish?" the captain queried.

"Yes," Cha-cha began, and then he paled. His mouth dropped open. He staggered a little and said, "Your Maj—" Cupped his hand over his mouth and bobbed like a pigeon. Backed away and started whistling tunelessly. Poor old wacko, Donna thought. He must have had a real time of it.

Suddenly he said, "We knew how to get here 'cuz we heard you singing, Officer D."

Donna jerked. "What?"

Saluting, Mr. Saar stepped forward. "Our supplies were defective, sir. We were starving."

Reade knit his brows. "But you were only at sea for six days," he said.

"No way!" Eskimo interjected, looking incredulous. "No way!" The others nodded.

"We *were* starving!" one of them said. "We wouldn't starve in less than a week."

"I want to get these men to the infirmary," the doctor said impatiently.

Reade rubbed his chin, lowered his hand. He said to Donna, "I'm afraid I'll have to see you later. I'll be accompanying these men to sick bay."

"We were gone twenty-three days," Mr. Saar insisted as the group moved away. He sounded more hurt than puzzled that no one was agreeing with him. "I counted them."

Donna chewed the inside of her cheek. "Welcome to the Bermuda Triangle," she murmured. Bad counting and phantom songs. Well, hey howdy, things were curiouser and curiouser.

The crowd drifted away once the men had left for the infirmary. She stood around for a while, monitoring the scene. Twenty-three days, and the guy was positive. One little, two little, sixteen little Indians. Holy moly. And Cha-cha knew she liked to sing, too.

Maybe it was time to do some real digging.

John walked over, Matt in tow. He looked sheepish as he said, "Are you going to change for dinner now?"

She regarded him. Pink on his cheeks, eyes cast downward. Too sweet for words.

"Yeah." Maybe he'd open up on the way to the stateroom. The still-weird stateroom, where her heart still thundered for an hour or two before she fell asleep.

"We'll walk you, okay, Matt?"

The boy silently nodded; his eyes huge and round and pleading. What, baby, what? Donna tried to ask, but his attention was distracted as John urged him along and the three began to walk.

"How you been, kiddo?" Donna asked.

"He's fine," John said shortly.

Those were the last words anyone spoke until they reached Donna's door. Then John muttered, "See you at dinner," and split.

Ah, geez. She took a deep breath and let herself into her room.

Her heart thundered, but she got dressed anyway.

Up periscope, later, and privately:

"Cha-cha, I'm so pleased with you."

Cha-cha, on his knees before King Neptune with his hands folded across his chest, nearly wept with joy. He couldn't believe all this was happening to him. It was too psychedelically supercalifrage.

Up in the crow's nest, the two of them surrounded by fresh red canvas—red sails, how cool—the yards vibrating with the force of the gale, Cha-cha raised his face to the darkening sky as the rain began to fall. Captain, his king-captain, in a ball of golden light. Cha-cha could and couldn't see him, but he knew he was there. The light danced up and down the yards like Tinker Bell, but he knew it was the king. It was the gold of his aura, yeah, baby, the halo crown of the god of the sea. *Hare rama, hare Krishna,* oh, yeah.

"Rise, Cha-cha."

Cha-cha stood easily, rolling with the ship on his old sea legs. The ocean rose, swelled, pregnant with life that swam and slithered and plunged. And ate. Dark shapes burrowed through the black water on either side of the ship.

Below, on the black, black deck, men dressed in old-time clothes cowered on the poop. One held a small, chestnut-haired boy in his arms and rocked him. Beneath the lightning, something rolled along the deck, *crack, roll, crack.*

"There are more tasks that you must accomplish for me, Cha-cha, before you can come aboard. You know that, don't you?"

Cha-cha grunted. "Aye-aye, sir. Yessir."

"And then I'll let you have a reward." Cha-cha brightened, and the king smiled. "And what would you like?"

Cha-cha toyed with the end of his rainbow T-shirt. "My ghosts, king baby. I want my ghosts. I thought they'd like, come with me, but I think they stayed on the *Morris.*" He swallowed hard. "I don't think all of them can swim."

The king waved his hand over Cha-cha's head like a magician. At least, Cha-cha thought it was his hand. It could have been his scepter, or a sword, or the sparkly green bottle he'd found in his net. His mind jigged. *Had* he found something in his net?

Had he sunk the Morris?

"Your ghosts have been on my mind, Cha-cha. I sent lifeboats for them, and they're on their way. So you must hurry and do everything I tell you, so you'll be ready for them."

Cha-cha rubbed his hands together. "Right on. Right on."

Come.

Blackness.

Loneliness.

Cha-cha started. "Say what, Your Maj?"

The ball of light fluttered and for a moment, a very brief moment, Cha-cha thought he saw—

That there was nothing but a handful of—

No. No, there was the king now, coming into focus, oh, yeah. Cool. Trippy. Yeah.

"I am the captain," the king said, and Cha-cha thought he sounded just a bit freaked out. That freaked *him* out.

"What? What's wrong, Your Majesty?" he pleaded.

"I am the captain," the king murmured. Then he whispered it. "I am the way, and the power, and the light."

Cha-cha flashed his brown teeth at the lightning, and the ball of gold karma that was his cosmic commander.

"Hallelujah. Right on," he said, shaking with cold. He

wished he had his denim jacket. There hadn't been time. The rain splashed down, down, down, filling the crow's nest, covering the deck to the gunwales, submerging the hold where the livestock and chickens were caged. A pig squealed.

"Sacrifices," the king said. "The sea demands many, and is still not appeased." Then he leapt out of the crow's nest and stood on the yardarm. Jumped up, down. Began to dance.

"I've cracked her head open, Cha-cha. She feels the ice water, now and then."

The lightning flashed around him, and Cha-cha clapped his hands in time to the music
  that was, and wasn't
  there.

Ramón had no idea how long he'd been tied to the periscope, but he judged the water was rising at a slower rate. It had remained at his lower thighs for some time and—

"Help! Help!" he shouted, losing control. He couldn't stand there and analyze how fast the sub was filling with water, *hijo de puta*, not when he had to stop it, stop the curse, stop the dead men and the dead captain, and stop everything.

"Help! *Ayúdame!*" He shouted the words over and over and over, until they ceased being words, and then he felt the first thrust of the knife as it sliced open his arm. Tissue and muscle ripped and tore in a white-hot waterfall of blood.

Ramón screamed. Now it came, now death came, oh, dear God, *Madre de Dios*, was he imagining it?

"Bad, bad," a voice said as the knife thrust back into the wound, deepening it. Cha-cha? Could it be Cha-cha the cook?

"Nnnnno! Cha-cha, no!" Ramón thrashed against the pole. "It can't be you!"

Cha-cha's face was covered with his blood. The old bandanna, sopping with it. "King says to tell you it's this or drowning. You can, like, choose."

Pain, hot as coals; so much pain. Mama, Mama. "Fight him, *viejo*. He can't do anything to us. He can't alone, he . . ."

And more pain. And more.

"King says choose."

But Ramón couldn't answer. He couldn't do anything but hang there, and bleed.

Down periscope.

Sprawled on her bed, Donna glanced idly through *Flotsam*, at the clock. Turned a page. Mmm, guy named Wagner wrote an opera called *The Flying Dutchman*. A girl named Senta throws herself in the sea to redeem the soul of the damned man, who, as far as Donna could tell, had gotten in trouble with the devil for boasting he could round some cape.

"Senta, you bimbo," she muttered, closed the book. No way would she ever sing opera. Would she ever be able to. Jazz, now. That was natural. That was your real voice.

That was your real suicide. And maybe your redemption. Not for Billy, though. Never made it to heaven, to the other side of the hurt . . .

Enough sea lore. Dinner was in twenty minutes.

Stretching, she got up and headed for the bathroom. Spied her Daily Program under the door, where every night someone slipped it, and every day she tossed it—cultural activities, no way!—in the trash. She picked up the Program again and read it again:

> *Shiver me timbers! Soon the ol'* Pandora *will go a rockin' for our ever-popular shipwreck party! We've got some real shipwreck passengers aboard this year, so ask them for tips on how to dress! We'll be honoring them all: Mr. and Mrs. Philip van Buren, Mrs. Ruth Hamilton, Miss Donna Almond, Dr. John Fielder and his son, Master Matthew, and many of the crewmen from the freighter,* Morris.
>
> *Ask your steward what it's all about. He'll be glad to help you with your preparations. So put on your duds, man the lifeboats, and join us at dinner for a rollicking evening of good (wet!) fun!*

Yo ho ho. She couldn't believe it. Not *her* idea of good wet fun. She'd be damned if she'd wear a costume to a thing like that after what she'd been through. For that matter, maybe she'd have room service that night. Whenever it was. Didn't say.

She'd like to stay in her room tonight, too. She was feeling so *odd*. Tired and woozy, disoriented. But she wanted to see if Phil and Elise showed.

"One more time for the little red dress," she grumbled, and set about getting ready.

Tonight was French cuisine night, and Mrs. Hamilton and Captain Reade were both eating snails. Matt thought that was about the grossest thing in the world.

"Dad, c'ai have a hamburger?" he asked. It was cool on this ship to order anything you wanted. They still hadn't had their buffalo steaks, but Captain Reade had promised they would before they left.

"Dad?" he repeated. His father gazed off into space and said nothing. Matt knew he was worried about him. That terrified him. Dad was a doctor, and he knew all about the germs that had made Matt sick, and if he was upset, then that meant the germs were acting up again.

And that meant Matt might get sick again.

Visions of hospital beds, needles, and machines twisted inside his head with the gross (and rad) wax statues in the Medieval Torture Museum on Fisherman's Wharf, where they had gone after Matt's last visit to the hospital. Guys getting pulled apart on racks, ladies being buried alive with bags of cats tied to their stomachs—at the time it had all seemed so great.

But the hospital could be like that. And what was the difference if your hair fell out because you were locked up in a dungeon, or 'cuz you got zapped by the radiation machines?

And the witch, eating up Hansel and Gretel. Wouldn't it be gross if grown-ups did eat little kids sometimes? Like if you were starving, and there was this baby, and . . . he shivered. Sometimes he managed to gross even himself out.

What was dying? He knew he didn't understand it, 'cuz his dog, Julie, had died the last time he was in the hospital, and sometimes he thought she'd be waiting for him when he came back from somewhere. He had looked at the pictures of bodies in one of his dad's medical books, but they didn't look real. In his head, they were mixed up with horror movies and comic books, and the stuff other kids talked about in the hospital. Like how you rot, even though they fill you up with formaldehyde.

That word was cool and scary at the same time.

"Daddy?"

His dad started. Matt said, "C'ai have two hamburgers? I'm really hungry." He was trying to reassure his dad. Because the first thing to go was always his appetite. Especially when he had to stay in the hospital.

There was a trick to it: if *he* could convince his dad he was okay, then his dad could convince *him*. And then, maybe, he would be safe.

Matt's dad looked down at him for a long time. Then his lips curled downward and he cupped Matt's cheek.

"You are so good," he said in a choked, funny voice. "I don't deserve you."

Matt was more afraid than ever.

"Would you like three hamburgers?" Captain Reade asked. Matt shrank. He used to like the captain, but he had changed his mind. Captain Reade talked to his dad a lot now, about Matt's cancer, and Matt knew it was upsetting his dad. He wanted to tell him to shut up about it, but Captain Reade was an adult and anyway, Matt was too nervous around him to say much.

And that lady, the statue lady who was the cruise director. No one listened to him about her, but she was strange, too. Not just because she looked like the figurehead in the museum—Matt understood about resemblances—but because when she was around him, sometimes he fell asleep and had dreams, saw things. He couldn't remember much after he woke up, but he knew they had to do with being on the *Pandora*.

"Hasn't Nemo had those kitties yet?" Donna asked him. She had on her red dress and she looked so pretty. He wanted his dad to bring her home with them. He hated the thought of never seeing her again.

"We'll hit Australia before she does."

Australia. Kangaroos. Wallabies. Matt couldn't wait to get there.

"I—I don't know," Matt stammered. For some reason he didn't understand, he wanted to go sit on her lap and have her hug him. That was a real baby thing, but the urge was so strong he almost did it.

Then he heard his dad murmur something to the captain and Matt got quiet. Sometimes his dad said a funny thing: Don't rock the boat. Matt sort of knew what it meant, and he sort of knew he'd better lay low. He just didn't know why.

"Matt, won't you come sit by me for a few minutes?" Mrs. Hamilton asked warmly. "My seat mates are gone and it's kind of lonely on this side of the table."

The old lady sat between two empty chairs. The funny thing was, it almost seemed like there were people sitting in them, shimmering, like; people he couldn't really see. He didn't want to get anywhere near those chairs, but all that was baby, too. Like seeing a heap of clothes in a chair and thinking it was a monster. Or being so sure the closet door was opening, and it wasn't.

Or imagining the captain was some big bad guy. All baby stuff.

Manfully, he scooted his chair out and walked around the table. She smiled and patted the empty chair next to her. Oh, no, he'd have to sit in it. He swallowed hard and slowed down. There wasn't someone there, was there? There really wasn't.

He got closer. A blur of white, a . . . a hanging, a thickness.

He stopped. Stared at the chair.

The captain was watching him. Now his dad watched, too.

"Matty, go on," his dad said gently. "Mrs. Hamilton is lonely over there by herself."

It wasn't empty. There was a . . .
a . . .

"I gotta go to the bathroom," he blurted, and ran-walked away from there as fast as he could.

* * *

"You scared him," Donna mockingly accused Ruth. "Really, Ruth, you shouldn't flirt with younger men."

Ruth spread her hands and made minute corrections to the placement of her silverware. "I didn't mean to. Frighten him, I mean."

"I know." Donna sighed theatrically. "I'm always scaring them off, too."

"Well, here's one man you haven't frightened." Reade touched his napkin to his lips and laid it beside his plate. "Won't you dance, Miss Almond?"

"Now?" She looked around, startled to see several couples on the floor.

He pushed his chair away and came to her side with his hand extended. Donna flashed with dislike—he was like Daniel, pushy, arrogant—but what the hell, maybe she could finally get him to listen to her.

She put her hand in his, and rose, and he escorted her to the square of wood at the other end of the room. Mirrors gleamed back the candlelight and twinkling ice sculptures on the dessert tables; in the far distance, the huge picture windows gleamed with moonlight. It was a stunning effect.

The music was slow, and Reade took her in his arms. They danced for less than half a minute before Donna said, "I'm worried about the van Burens. John and I have a theory—"

"The van Burens aren't in your jurisdiction," he interrupted, and it took her a moment to understand he was gently chiding her. His features softened. "It's hard to go off duty, isn't it, Miss Almond? You should learn to relax. Enjoy life. It's a very precious thing, life. One never knows how long it will last."

She said nothing, because she hated sermons like this. She knew how to relax, damn it, and as for life being precious and uncertain, all she had to do was think of Tahoe to remember that.

"Okay," she said after a beat. "Okay, but I have something else to talk to you about. The toxic dumping? John and I think we're having some kind of reaction."

"Oh?" He looked concerned. His eye patch wasn't centered and for a moment, she scrutinized it with the revolted fascination people saved for traffic accidents. Knock, knock, Captain. What's in there?

"Yes," she said. "We're so damn jumpy. And John . . ." She trailed off, squared her shoulders. "Everyone's having bad dreams, or something."

"A stress reaction," he stated.

"I don't know. But I'd like to talk to Diaz, find out just what was in those barrels."

Reade made a moue of apology. "He doesn't know. Captain Esposito claimed he didn't, either. But they're working on the case in Hawaii. You can discuss it with them when we get to Australia. And besides," he went on, "Dr. Hare examined you all and found you in good health."

Yeah? Well, what about her blackout? She pressed her lips together in frustration. The guy was smooth; you had to give him that. When he didn't want to talk about something, he didn't.

"I wouldn't worry, if I were you." He pulled her a little closer and a tang of sexual tension came into the air. She flashed on an image of him and her together in bed and rejected it instantly.

His face clouded with disappointment. What, could he read her mind?

"You're irritated with me," he said disarmingly, smiling.

"Yeah." No sense lying. "This could be really important. We might need special treatment."

"Oh, if you did, we'd make sure you got it." He led her in a circle.

"No offense, Captain, but you're not a doctor."

"And neither are you." A beat, then, "You're a puzzling woman. I would really like to know more about you. Your experiences in Viet Nam, for example."

"My—" Oh, God, she'd forgotten all about that. She choked back a guffaw and kept a straight face. Glenn would love this.

"I don't really like to talk about it," she said.

"The metal plate."

She couldn't help it. She was wound up and tense, and his gullibility struck her so funny she started to laugh.

He raised his brows. Hairs showed above the patch. "I say. Were you having me on?"

"I'm sorry." She made herself stop, wiping her eyes and sniffing. "I'm known as a practical joker back home. No one ever believes anything I say."

"I, as well." He inclined his head.

"Really? I'd never guess it."

"No?" His smile was slow to grow, long-lasting, as they moved around the room.

"What will you do back home?" he asked. "Does someone wait for you?"

Oh, hey, a bit too personal. She cocked her head. "That's classified. Sorry."

"I like a woman who keeps her options open," he rejoined. "People who are receptive to . . . possibilities are always more interesting."

"Mmm. I don't know if I'd say that about myself. I have a fairly one-track mind, and right now, it's on those barrels."

"Perhaps that's why," he said, half to himself.

Donna waited. When he said nothing more, she said, "Why what?"

He jerked back from some reverie. "Why I can't . . . figure you out." He smiled slowly. "Very well."

She turned her head. "The music's . . ." She paused. The music had stopped, but it hadn't . . .

"Miss Almond?"

She ignored him, listening. And for a moment . . .

Pain, and a suffering that didn't go away, not ever, not even when you put time on your side, and whiskey in your gut; and not even, not ever; and it was a kind of failure on your part . . .

for a moment, a dusky voice that sang you toward it, and promised you if you just came down, got down, lay down, it would free you. And you would float . . .

Donna stiffened and eased herself away from him.

"Donna?" He waited.

She shook herself. "I'm sorry. I was thinking about something."

"Well, I hope you'll stop taking on all these unnecessary

responsibilities," he said. "You should enjoy what our ship has to offer."

Asshole. She'd have to do her own investigating, that was clear.

"Hmmm?" he drawled, taking her elbow.

She roused herself. Walked a bit fast, so she lost contact with him.

"Donna Almond, you're a challenge," Reade said, trailing after her. "The biggest one I've had in a long time. I like that."

Thomas Reade, was she thrilled. It was her dream in life to be his number-one challenge. She pretended she didn't hear him,

just like that other voice; she didn't hear that either and joined the others at the table.

24
Bottled Up

The French dinner segued into drinks, with Captain Reade in a wanky, squirrelly mood, alternately gazing at Donna and staring off into space with a loopy grin on his face. No one else seemed to notice, which Donna found almost as unsettling as his Captain Nemo act.

The group broke up after about an hour of that, and by then Donna was as fidgety as Reade. Goddamn, she was geared up to set a few things straight. She'd had just about enough of the twilight zone, much grass, hombre; and it was about time she rounded up her Indians and made sure everybody was okay. Then she'd go back off duty, until she got the hell back to San Diego and went back on duty. Shit. Some vacation.

She listened to the clack of her heels as she marched along the wooden deck. The moon and stars were out; beautiful, distracting. She kept her eyes open for those old familiar faces, didn't see them. But the sea was silvery black and

inviting
nice, real nice.

She clacked on. Her Achilles tendons were beginning to ache and she almost missed the incredible ugliness of her cop clodhoppers. Yeah, well, hard to accessorize a nightstick.

Past people who bobbed their heads at her, past open hatches, shut doors. Shiny white railing. No rust on this lady.

Damn; she had to get these shoes off. Okay, back to the stateroom. She could call Phil and Elise from there, too. If they didn't answer, she was going to find them, if it took all night and she had to tear the ship apart to do it. There were too many weirdnesses: twenty-three days, and psychic solos for Cha-cha, and one by one, everyone was disappearing. Reasonable cause for search, right on, as Chach would say.

John had excused himself about three minutes after Matt left for the bathroom, and neither had returned. Ruth said she was tired and going to bed early. Donna would call them, too, and to hell with it if they were already asleep.

Through the corridors and down some stairs, whoopsie doopsie, what a maze; and finally Donna stood in front of her stateroom door and fought down the dread, got the door open, and shut herself in. Stood, as always, and took in her surroundings. Bed covers drawn back. Porthole windows closed. Drawers shut. Book—

She frowned, crossed to the white lacquer nightstand.

She had closed *Flotsam.* She remembered doing it. But now it lay open.

Dropping her purse on the bed, she flicked on the lamp. Drew back. Someone had been reading about the *Titanic.* A two-page black-and-white photo of the wreck gleamed on the glossy paper. No caption, but she knew it was that big expedition, the Ballard one, that she'd read about the other day.

She didn't recall any photo like this in the book. And she was certain she would have, when flipping through it. The paper was different; the book fell open naturally to these pages.

They gave her a chill. Cold down there; and if you were trapped, you felt the thunder of the descent; you knew it was curtains as the icy depths rushed at you. Did you pray? Did you panic? Did you try to hold your breath?

"Damn maid," she muttered, and decided to check her gun. If they felt they could mess around with her stuff, then there was no telling what they'd paw through.

Angrily, she yanked open the drawer and pushed the box of Kleenex and the towel out of her way. She caught her breath.

The .38 Special was gone.

She reached for the phone, stopped. No, she wouldn't inform the captain just yet. Thus far he shined on everything she told him. Hell, he probably took it.

But he was in charge here; she had a duty to tell him.

She ran her hand through the drawer again, just in case she'd made a mistake. Started searching the entire stateroom: drawers, closet, under the bed. Nightstand. Not there.

A sick, queasy anxiety flooded through her. This was one of the things cops dreaded; that someone would take their gun, shoot someone with it. That had happened to Martinez's old partner: perp grabbed it, fled, shot a bystander in the mouth. Young runaway, probably one of the perp's girls. The round blasted the back of her head off. Brains everywhere. The partner had drunk himself off the force.

The bullets. They were missing, too.

"Goddamn, goddamn it," she said, reaching for the phone. Cleared her throat to talk to the operator. She had to tell Reade, even if he was acting like he was on drugs.

There was no one there. There was nothing, no dial tone, no buzz, just dead air.

"Hello?" she demanded. She clicked the plungers. Nothing.

Dead phone, missing gun. She took a deep breath. Listened, felt, waited.

Nothing.

"Christ," she said, yanking off her heels.

Sometimes death comes in disguise:
as shallow water that you dive into because it looks deep.
as a smooth glass surface that rears up like a monster.

As ice-cold, death-cold, when all seems warm, and safe, and inviting.
Come to me, Donna. Look for me.
Solve me.
Come aboard, and be my life.

There was a ribbon-candy ice cream parlor, red, white, and pink; and John and Matt sat in one of the booths, eating banana splits instead of snails and hamburgers. The place was half-empty, but there were lots of kids, moms and dads, and their laughter was a constant irritation to John. He fervently wished he and Matt could have had this talk in their stateroom, but the vibes hadn't been right.

When he'd found Matt in the head, sobbing into the sink, he'd pulled his boy against his legs and cried, too. And it was a long time coming, the ability to speak, and Matt was the first to say anything:

"I want to be a real kid."

Real kids ate banana splits. As soon as they could handle it, they left the bathroom and went to the ice cream parlor.

Now they sat, both finished and slightly ill from all that sugar on empty stomachs. Matt's legs dangled in the air and he swung them back and forth, trying for nonchalance, but his face was twisted with unhappiness. Didn't want to talk, John guessed. Neither did he, but he supposed they should. It was past time.

"Matty." His son looked up at him, and John faltered. What to say? How did you be a father? How did you be a man for your boy?

"Matty," he tried again. "I want what's best for you."

"I don't care what's best," Matt blurted. He doubled his fists and smacked the shocking pink Formica tabletop. "I . . ."

John covered Matt's hands with his. "Son, I know it's not fair. I know you're afraid."

"So are you," Matt accused. "And I wouldn't be, if you weren't."

John bowed his head. Ashamed, he withdrew his hands,

heard Matt's breathy protest. Took his small fingers in his and squeezed, not too hard.

"I'm trying not to be." A damn tear welled in the corner of his eye. He couldn't wipe it away, and it spilled down his cheek, in plain view of Matt.

"You're crying because you think I'm going to die," he accused with a tremor in his voice.

"No. No, I don't. I—"

"Dad," Matt said sternly, "don't bullshit me."

John's mouth fell open and an automatic parental rebuke flew to his lips. He stifled it in time, and nodded.

"All right. Yes. I am afraid." He paused, squeezed. His heart skipped a beat. His ulcer went into overdrive.

"I can't help it, sweetheart. I . . . I . . ." I'm supposed to make you live, he wanted to say. I'm supposed to heal you.

Physician, heal thyself. Do whatever it takes. You said once, you'd sell your soul. You said you'd do anything.

Had God sent them to the *Pandora*? Jesus, he was crazy if he believed that. But wasn't he a Catholic, lapsed or not? Didn't he believe in the magic of the mass? Weren't miracles and mysteries possible?

He took a breath. He didn't know what he wanted to say, but what he *did* say was, "Matty, have you had any . . . do you think there's something about the *Pandora* that—"

Matt stared uncomfortably at the mirrored wall adjacent to the booth. "I think we should check on Nemo."

Matt's thin face. His stiff, set jaw that looked like it might crack. Oh, dear God, where's the fairness?

"Yes. She's been alone an awfully long time." He thought for a moment. Did females feel alone when they were pregnant? They carried life inside them, such a miracle. A miracle, or a tragedy, that living creatures carried the means of their death inside them as well.

Maybe they could talk in the stateroom, without all the people and bustle.

"Okay, matey." John saluted smartly. "Ready to cast off."

"Oh, Dad." Matt smiled patiently, and John felt a little better.

* * *

Succulent sacculena. Soul on ice. Flesh on ice.

The ice water washed over Curry's face and roused him from his torpor. He cried out and moved the fingers of his left hand, the ones he hadn't broken in his fall to the deck.

He lay in fetid darkness, somewhere close, where the bulkheads pressed on his shoulders and feet, and the floor was strewn with garbage. He gagged; had two simultaneous thoughts: that he was freezing, and that the captain had lied to him, because he was still alive.

"Mother," he whispered.

And something nearby did, and didn't, answer him. Boots echoed on the deck. He closed his eyes and tensed. His face throbbed. His broken fingers ached.

Curry hefted himself to a sitting position. He was drained; there was nothing left of him. He was sinking into the ship, the cursed ship; he was dying and Reade would have his soul. Damned, and deserving of it; Curry had murdered a hundred people, and he had devoured their flesh to stay alive.

A noise, distant, a piece of death.

Dead fish float, he thought incoherently. If he died, dear God, don't let him sink. Let him float, far away, out to sea, where Reade couldn't touch him.

Three hours of searching, and no one knew where the captain was, and they wouldn't let Donna go onto the bridge, and no one seemed to give a good goddamn that her gun was missing.

She shook her head and folded the map she'd taken from the stateroom. She'd conscientiously gone through all the public areas, and a few reserved for the staff. Now she'd meander, in time-honored police tradition, and hope something came of it. Jeez, she had to bump into somebody sooner or later: the list of people she was looking for was growing by the minute: Phil, Elise, Ramón, Reade, anybody in charge.

What was that ship she read about in *Flotsam,* the one where everybody disappeared? *Marie Celeste,* something like that. Yeah, well, the *Pandora* was proving to be her sister ship.

Scowling, she took some stairs marked "Crew Only." They were steep, and dirty; she hoped she didn't get her red dress too scuffed up. She must look great, sandals and satin. Glenn would—

Her heart became a fist. Fuck Glenn.

The stairs dropped her below decks into the bowels of the ship. It wasn't so pretty there; no carpets and white walls, no quaint hurricane light fixtures. Just rusty, greasy guardrails and metal steps, loops of electric wires and utility lights clipped to them. No need to play dress-up for the crew, who knew what ships were really all about: grease and oil and lots of cogs and gears meshing together, and a hull that cut the water into two parts: the surface, and everything else.

The thunka-thunka of machinery slathered the air with a greasy tang of diesel fuel as Donna descended another flight of stairs and stepped out onto space on a catwalk perhaps two feet wide. The sides were flimsy and painted with Rust-Oleum, and the whole thing shook as she walked along it. To her left, riveted sections stuck out from one another like the cutaway of a dirty stereo cabinet: big shelves, little shelves, junk inside them: wrenches, Coke cans, beer bottles, paperbacks. Wadded-up cigarette packs.

A pair of snazzy bikini underpants, ice-pink with lace inserts. New, expensive. Maybe Elise van Buren-Hadley was slumming?

Donna walked on, keeping to the shadows whenever possible so she wouldn't get busted and sent back to Go. Voices drifted by. The catwalks and cables extended in both directions; it was like being inside a blimp. Somewhere below her, the cavern must be divided into neat watertight compartments. All she saw when she leaned over the side were more catwalks and hundreds of pipes and valves. Christ, if you wanted to hide out on the *Pandora*, it would be a cinch.

She didn't have a watch because it was on the *Morris*, but it had to be almost midnight. The air rose and fell around her like breath, and the handrails were sweaty and slick; now and then she almost heard a deep, shuddering sigh; and though she chalked it up to machinery, the sound prickled her scalp. She was snooping around in the innards of the ship, in the greased-up guts, with the catwalks intersecting each other like hundreds of feet of intestines; the oceanic space was a giant stomach cavity. Voilà Officer Osmond, bobbing through it like some dot of bacteria.

After a second of indecision, she chose the right-most of two stairways (ladderways, she corrected herself; on ships they were ladderways) and clomped down it, *clang, clang, clang,* attention, please, here I am. Wondered idly if Captain Nemo was a mother yet.

Someone else walked down a ladderway: footfalls clanged against hers with a discordant metallic ringing that made her grimace and run her tongue along her front teeth. It was like listening to someone run their fingers down a chalkboard. She saw no one, though. She went on.

Down, farther down, where the shadows lengthened despite the lights; and the dank living smells grew stronger. Donna ducked her head beneath an electrical cord silhouetted in the gloom; and another, looped and roped haphazardly across the catwalk. Wires and cords dangled every which way, coiled around metal posts, trailing over the catwalks, punched into square blocks of extension cords. If she wasn't careful, she would fucking hang herself.

Then from down below, a set of rolling vibrations expanded into the silence, whum, *whum,* WHUM, whum, *whum,* WHUM. They rumbled through her palms as she held the rails; the soles of her feet, her knees. Her groin. It sounded like a huge, unbalanced washing machine, or a flywheel when the timing was off.

Or a boy, spinning on a lake . . .

Donna peered below. No light shone at all. The vast blackness spread beneath her feet like a maw, and she hadn't brought a flashlight.

Okay, time to go back up. She imagined herself a scuba diver, tapping a watch at a dive buddy and pointing her thumb toward the surface: See ya at decompression, bro.

She turned around. Saw the double stairways and decided to go up the left one this time.

Chips of ice flow with the current of the glass-clear water; ice packs the spaces between the mountains; rivulets of opaque water like rivers of solid water in a world of liquid ice.

The frigid water and the absence of salt preserve. Centuries of wood lie scarcely blemished; rusted metal only rusts.

Fish move in and out with the ice. They dart into the holes, the wounds, the shattered windows. They swim into the porcelain sinks, the bathtubs, the toilets, and out again. They trail the broken masts and coil around the anchors.

Above, the sun glides over; the moon.

The ice glistens. The fish shimmer.

The silverware sparkles. The glasses fill with sand, empty with tide.

Jewelry glitters. A fragment of fabric waves.

In the captain's chair, a body sits. It is dressed in a black suit and it wears a black cap, and an eye patch. Its hair is red and its eye, its single eye, stares through the ice. It lifts slightly with the undulation of the current; the fish swim around but do not light upon it. It sits, it stares, it dreams.

It dreams for—

COME.

"Shit!" Donna cried, sagging against the railing. She whirled around and hung over it. Her hair fell forward, momentarily blinding her.

Panicking, she brushed it away. She was shaking all over. She was on the verge of wetting her pants.

Goddamn, what was *that*? Hallucination?

"Goddamn. God*damn.*" Something at her, something in her—ice water in her brains—*she's the one*—

the one

the one

Bile rose in her throat. Her hands trembled badly as she wiped her hair from her face and fought to control herself.

the one

"Fuck," she spat harshly, and started up the stairway fast,

hard, though her muscles lurched and her mind was screaming.

Screaming.

COME.

Cha-cha stepped from the shadows as Officer Donna ran up the ladderway, for a moment diverted by the idea that he could see up her dress.

COME.

Then he turned his attention back to the hatch, oh, yes, baby, yes; maybe she'd heard it, too, and that was why she'd stopped dead and then started cussing. Oh, yes, 'cuz there was something in there, something psychedelically supercalifrage, and Cha-cha had whooped like a fire horn when he found the hatch that would lead him to it. He had spent hours looking for it, down,

down

down

in the bowels of the ship, the good, empty belowdecks, after he had . . . after . . .

He couldn't remember, but he knew whatever he'd been doing had had something to do with a knife, which he had dutifully put back in the museum.

Now he ran his hand along the exterior metal plate. There was a slash about three inches wide near the bottom of the door on the left side. He got on his hands and knees and peered into it. Knock, knock, who's there? Why, it's Cha-cha, baby, ready to go down the hatch. He giggled high, very high, like a teakettle.

He saw nothing, so he stuck in his hand. Was something there? Did he hear a strange slithering noise?

"Rats," he said worriedly, and withdrew his hand. He rose and ran his hands over the door. Not rats, no, baby. Something was in here, and it was good.

With a sigh, he laid his cheek against the metal. Never mind the grime and dirt. Diesel residue was part of nature, man, and he was into nature.

"Here I come, ready or not. Here I come." He wrapped his hand around the handle.

And then another voice swept into his brain:

Cha-cha, Cha-cha, me boyo, me bravo. Cha-cha, move away from that place. Move

away from it!

Cha-cha cocked his head and jerked up his hand, to show it wasn't loaded. "King? That you, baby?"

Away from it. Away away away. Intense, heavy, worried.

He looked around. "Your Majesty?"

"Cha-cha!"

Cha-cha ducked down and whirled around, shielding his eyes from the harsh beam of a flashlight.

"Cha-cha, what are you doing?"

"What?" He looked over his shoulder at the hatch. He had wanted very badly to go in there. Hadn't he? There was a treat in there.

Wasn't there?

He reached again for the latch.

"No!" the figure shouted. Cha-cha jumped. It stepped into the light, and sure enough, it was King Neptune in his captain's uniform. "You may not go in there."

Cha-cha squinted at him. "There's someone in there," he ventured.

"No." The king slung himself over the rail and walked toward him. Halted when he was about fifteen feet away. He made a half turn, standing in profile. Such a king. Such a big guy. Cha-cha admired him, began to forget where he was, and why.

COME.

"There!" Cha-cha cried. "Did you hear that?"

"I . . . I don't hear anything." King Neptune pivoted on his heel, slow motion. Stared at the door. He shook so hard Cha-cha could see it. "I am the captain," he whispered. "I am."

"Yeah," Cha-cha said, confused. "But—"

"Cha-cha, come with me. Fast." His Supreme Oceanic Majesty held out his arms, and Cha-cha shuffled through the rat poop and the trash and the stinky, slidy stuff toward him.

"But there's—" He jabbed his thumb over his shoulder, then rubbed his hands together. "Isn't there someone in—"

"No!" His arm around Cha-cha's shoulders, he bounded to the railing and flung one leg over. The way he pulled on Cha-cha, he almost fell over.

"But we should—"

The king ran up the ladderway, dragging Cha-cha behind. Below, something called:

COME COME COME COME COME COME COME COME.

Called urgently. Tantalizingly.

And someone groaned. Cha-cha looked over his shoulder.

"Hurry, damn you!" King Neptune shouted.

Cha-cha and his cosmic karmic commander headed for the surface of the ship.

At the top of the ladder, the captain stopped. Under control, stay under control . . . why this mindless panic?

There was nothing in that room. In that room, that dying room, where he sent the dead men. The sacrifices. Nothing in there.

He was the captain! He was the way, and the power, and alone, alone, all, all—

and the waters had churned as Captain Reade, late of the Royal Grace, *reached for the bottle and uncorked it, dear God, he was so cold; he had drifted into ice floes, and the waters churned and from the depths arose*

"Come, Cha-cha," he said in a loud voice, drowning out—

drowning out

a bad dream, and nothing else.

"My love."

Gasping, Ruth raised her head from the sink. Her throat ached. Blood gushed from her nose and ran down her chin. Her hands were clenched around the porcelain sides and as she threw back her head and gasped for air, her knees buckled and she fell to the floor.

She sprawled on her back, staring up at the light fixture as her chest worked spasmodically. Her fists opened, closed, opened again.

She coughed and a jet of watery vomit gushed from her

mouth. She rolled over on her side, marveling distractedly that so much could have collected inside her.

And the blood! A torrent from her nose, a bucket of it as she got to her hands and knees, slipping in the wet, and pulled herself to a kneeling position at the sink. The water was the color of rust. Was there any left inside her head?

Hacking hard, she rested her cheek on the sink. Sweet Jesus. Dear, sweet Jesus, what had she been doing?

My love.

"Oh," she gasped. "S-Stephen?"

Unsteadily she rose, not daring to let go of the sink to wipe her mouth. Fresh blood plopped into the sink. Her wet hair streamed into her shoulders; she knew when she looked into the mirror she would see an aged crone, a bloodied skull-thing that would terrify Matty if he saw it.

She closed her eyes as she lifted her head, because it would terrify her as well.

And then she opened her mouth to scream, though no scream came out.

Because she was no longer holding on to the sink. Her hands rested in someone else's.

Stephen Hamilton, lost at sea these eleven months, stood before her.

"Ruth," he said, pulling her to him. "Ruth, my darling."

She put her arms around his neck and began to cry. Her blood smeared across his white Windbreaker; he held her head and rocked her. His heart beat in her ear; his sun-leathered hand cupped her under the chin.

"Ruth."

She couldn't speak. She only nodded. He was here. He was here and he had been here all along. She knew it now. She knew. She knew.

They stood for a long, long time, in a fuzzy darkness that was somehow soothing. She didn't know where they were now; she didn't understand how; she didn't care. There are more things on heaven and earth. There are more things.

There is Stephen.

He stroked her hair, her cheeks. Daubed her face with the silk handkerchief in his breast pocket. After a time, she seemed to awaken as if from a doze; she started and he said, "Shh, shh, it's all right now, dear."

He took her hand and led her—

startled, she looked around—

—led her through a maze of tables in an immense and beautiful ballroom. The walls were paneled and lacquered with art deco figures of the sea gods and goddesses; and above the dais where band instruments were arranged, a golden statue at least twenty feet tall watched over them. Robes flowed around the figure in streamlined grace, and his hair coursed down his shoulders. In his left hand he held a trident; Neptune, Ruth supposed, though he reminded her more of God. The features of his face were pleasant, though modeled with a heavy hand, imbuing them with an underlying sense of power.

No, not Neptune, for he was missing an eye. And his features were those of another man.

"Captain Reade," she breathed. The unmoving form gazed down on her like a guardian.

"He brought me to you, Ruth," Stephen said.

Past tables draped with jade and salmon, glittering with silver, he escorted her, easing her along on her sore legs. Her knees were bruising; her stomach was upset and her nose had begun to bleed again. With her free hand she wiped fiercely at it, rubbed her fingers on her nightgown. It was covered with blood and vomit; he didn't seem to notice.

"Sit, darling." He eased her onto a padded chair at a table for two. "Sit, and I'll order drinks."

He raised his hand. A steward appeared at the far end of the room, on the other side of the dance floor, and floated toward them. Floated, his feet inches above the ground.

Ice poured through Ruth's head and she doubled forward and grabbed it. Questions, terror flooded in—what was happening? Dear God, how was he here? And how—

"Champagne for my love." The steward nodded, floated away. She knew that man. She knew him. He was . . . She blinked hard. Her head ached with the cold. He was Kevin! The surfer boy on the *Morris*!

The room spun around and around. A strange rattling

sound orbited her, *chatter, chatter, chatter-scrabble.* Her closet door, on the *Morris.* She was kneeling by her porthole and dreaming all this; and someone had whispered in her ear:

Jump overboard, Ruth.

Jump now.

Before it's too late.

Her heart stalled. Then Stephen slid his hand over hers and squeezed between her fingers, the way they used to do when they first got married. He liked to see their wedding rings side by side. His gleamed on his hand—

his hand of black pulp—

No, on his wonderful, tanned hand; his strong, brilliant hand.

The steward reappeared with a tray. On it sat a bottle in a silver bucket and two champagne flutes.

"Kevin?" she ventured.

He winked at her. "Hi, Mrs. Hamilton. Surf's up." With a flourish, he presented the bottle. "Retrieved from the *Titanic.* Never opened."

It didn't look like a champagne bottle. It was green, with gold stripes running through it, and there were jewels around the neck.

Kevin wrapped a towel around the top and pushed at the cork with his thumbs. Stop, she wanted to say. Stop; this is a dead man's bottle and it holds a dead man's potion; it will kill me if I drink it. It's a libation; they used to pour blood on the deck to ensure a good voyage; and that was a symbol of the earlier days, when they would kill someone, actually kill a living person. A slave—

How did she know that?

What was he doing here? What was she doing here?

"Oh, Stephen," she blurted in a flash of panic. "Stephen, Stephen, I don't understand!"

He faced her and wiped her wet hair away from her face, caressing her cheeks.

On the dais, a dance band began to play "Always." Lush strings, a clarinet, the flash of brass as the trombones droned.

The cork strained against the top of the bottle. Kevin smiled and pushed, smiled and pushed—

—and she remembered her dream of the *Morris* inside the bottle, and the laughing face. Captain Reade's face.

"No, no, my darling." Stephen took her hands in his and kissed the knuckles. "It's a garden here. It's paradise. We can be here forever."

The room filled with people, women in slinky satin and furs, men in tuxedos. Beautiful, and handsome, candlelight gleaming on their faces and necks. The tinkle of ice, low, husky laughter; a swish of silk as the woman at the next table rose with her escort and they headed toward the crowded dance floor. A sultry brunette, with dark, deep-set eyes, who put her hand into her companion's and her arm on his shoulder, and swiveled her head toward Ruth and smiled.

The couple began to fox-trot. Above them, light bounced off the golden statue and cast diamonds on the lacquered walls; the diamonds blurred and rippled and the entire room shimmered, as if it were underwater.

The cork popped. Ruth jumped. Stephen held her hands tightly, tightly, leaning over a glass candleholder and a bouquet of exquisite fish—

—no, not of fish, but the bright colors of kelp forests, and seaweed prairies, and the ice-blue sweetness of the underside of icebergs; oh, the beauty, the beauty, the riot of sponges, the jewels of anemones, the wonder of eternal life beneath the sea.

and Kevin poured champagne, not—

—not anything else—

into their glasses.

Ruth stared into the eyes of her husband. She had missed him so much. She loved him so much. Young people couldn't feel love like this. It was only after years, decades, half a century—

"To you, my beloved," Stephen said, raising his glass. Letters were engraved around the base, but she couldn't read them. "To us, together forever."

He waited for her to touch her glass to his. Without moving, she lowered her gaze to the glass Kevin had set by her hand. *"Normandie,"* the engraving read. Another museum relic; the *Normandie* had burned in New York harbor when she was sixteen. She remembered her mother's distress; she'd always wanted to travel on it.

Tulip glasses from the *Normandie*. Champagne from the *Titanic*.

She brushed the glass with her fingers. Anticipation rose throughout the room. The couples around her stopped chatting and watched. The dancing couples slowed, focused on her.

The reflections of the mirror ball rippled and danced, rippled and danced, as if everything were—

—underwater—

"Oh!" Ruth cried. She leapt out of her chair, breaking contact with Stephen. He cried out in despair—

—and her head flew up and out of the sink.

And the shadow in the mirror that was, and wasn't, there—

The shadow misted into steam and rolled away on a nighttime sea.

"Stephen!" she cried, slamming her hands against the mirror. "Stephen, come back!"

Just one moment of courage, my darling. A minute, and then it will be over.

And then it will begin.

The water in the sink swirled with the blood from her nose. Tentatively she dipped her shaking fingers into it. It had seemed so real. So very real.

She looked into the mirror.

"Will we really be together?" she asked aloud.

"Of course, darling. I said we would, didn't I?" Stephen replied beside her, his warm, gentle hand resting upon her shoulder.

"I'm just so afraid."

"There's no need. You wanted to come to me, Ruth. Didn't you hear me? Back on that other ship, I called to you."

"I thought you did!" Her eyes misted. "I was too afraid. I thought you were warning me against something. I heard you tell me to . . . to . . ." She frowned. What had he told her? To jump—

"Ruth. My darling Ruth. I knew nothing could separate us. I tried so hard to contact you, so many times. And now . . ."

He ran his fingertips along the surface of the water. "You've seen how beautiful it will be. Look again."

And she saw the garden of her dreams; swimming through the undersea beauty with her love at her side, she was young again, and Stephen was a handsome boy-man. All this could be done. All this would continue.

What was there for her, back on the surface? Age, and mourning, and wishing, and regrets. And here, an enchanted existence.

And if she was imagining it all?

Well, if she was?

But it was too real. And she was too much in love.

There was the glass snake, coiled on its pillow. It saw them, and straightened itself. Why, it wasn't a snake at all! It was the champagne bottle from the *Titanic.*

Deftly he uncorked it; the stopper was a precious little sea creature, a crab or a shrimp of some kind, that skittered off to join his fellows among the heavenly cloud of bright orange and yellow sponges. A large bubble the color of the sun at day's end undulated above their heads and she thought of her favorite hymn: "Now the Day Is Over."

Yes. The days were over. Time was over. She would drink the shimmering, silver potion that poured from the bottle. She would drink, and in the twinkling of an eye—

—nearer, my God—

Ruth's hand gripped the sink edge, spasmed, dropped to her side. The last oxygen bubbles of her life flooded out of her mouth.

It did not hurt.

Thank God for that.

King Neptune said, "Very good, Cha-cha. Let her go."

Cha-cha stepped back. The lady's head bobbed in the sink. Her hair was a floating mass of jellyfish tentacles. Her hands slipped down to her sides, she collapsed to her knees, and then she flopped over onto her back, smacking the floor hard. Her eyes were open, staring at him sightlessly.

"She's at peace now." The king clapped Cha-cha on the arm. "You did a good thing. Now, for your reward."

Cha-cha stared down at the dead woman. A good thing? Why was it a good thing?

"Come, Cha-cha."

COME

Cha-cha started at the sound of the *other*. Saw that King Neptune hadn't heard it. Puzzled, he followed his master.

Shut the door after him.

"I can make them jump," the king said offhandedly. "I whisper to them, over and over, and they hear me. They do it. Because I am the power." He shrugged. "Others are not so . . . receptive. They don't hear me." His face hardened, and Cha-cha thought the king was mad at him.

He looked up at the king and said, "Officer Donna? She heard . . . she was down where you found me. She was there, freakin', before you came."

There was a change in the king's face that knocked Cha-cha for a loop. For one sec, he was just nothing, just a heap of puss—

No! Flashback, that was all!

"Cha-cha, come," the king said impatiently.

COME.

"Yessir," Cha-cha said, and for another sec, he wasn't sure which of the two voices he heard was the one he was answering.

Make that three or four secs.

But just two voices, baby.

Just two.

Donna ran—was chased, no of course not—into her stateroom. With a gasp she slammed the door shut and stumbled into the center of the room. God, why come back here, to the place that frightened her the worst? Why come back here, indeed, when she needed to find the others, needed to figure out what the hell had happened. Toxic reaction. Something organic. Like the blindness, something . . . reasonable

'Cuz there had been something down there, don't deny it; some kind of spook-show vision. She had seen something, felt something. Now it was cloudy, but the terror remained. She was heaving with exertion and fear; tears of shock ran down her cheeks. Hyperventilating, and trying to stop as she reeled with dizziness.

Something was very wrong on the *Pandora*.

And someone had her gun.

She turned to go back out.

Something was in the room. A stinging cold hopped onto her back, spread like syrup down her chest. Something was right behind her.

"All right," she said. "All right, freeze."

But it was she who was freezing. She shivered, tried to move her head. And slowly, as if someone were projecting a movie of her into the room, she collapsed forward, slow, slow, chin tilting upward an inch, two, three; her lips parted, slow, slow, slow; her wrist lifted toward the ceiling, fingertips arching—so very slowly; and it all floated

down

down

down, her face against the back of the door, smacking it a cell at a time, a tissue at a time, and her head rocked backward; and her neck slid down the slick latex paint like a cat's languid tongue, and she caved in at the threshold, crumpled in a heap; and her mind said

Heeeellllppppppppppppppp

because the floor was covered with fog, thick gray, and putrescent. There was something in it, colder than ice; it was hot-cold; and it tiptoed up her backbone

on little cat feet

and it whispered past her ear, right into her brain:

Tell me your Desire, you bitch. Tell me.

What potions I have drunk of Siren tears

What do you want? What will open you?

What will make you come aboard?

What potions, fair Donna Pandora, belladonna; why are you so closed, that chambered nautilus of yours, that hard shell of a heart that I CANNOT CRACK! And make you see,

and make you do,

and make you die.

The voice, urging, *Swim to me, Donna, swim down, and*

don't hold it any longer. It will only hurt a moment; it will feel so good to let it out, all in one deep breath. Open, open, and

For all I know, Billie Holiday sang. And this was what was known:

Tahoe. So senseless. Choking like that, on his vomit. She should have run faster. That bastard, that bastard; she should've . . . her fault, her fault, her fault. Never forgive herself. Never.

. . . *This is a dream.* Glenn. Please, Glenn, please. So alone. Other people had lives. Other people. Mom, brothers; where was her dad? Don't cry, don't be a baby . . .

. . . *And I dream* . . . House and kids, p&j in a brown paper sack, don't miss the bus! Mommy ashtray, papers on the fridge.

. . . *to know your heart* . . .

What do you want?
One note, one long, sad, keening note . . .

"Please," Curry moaned, his eyes tightly shut as the sounds came closer.

A hand of bone and ice prodded—and didn't prod—his shoulder. And a voice he recognized whispered, "We want to mutiny. Go to the woman. The one he can't quite get. Tell her."

"Wh-what?" Curry rasped. He started to turn his head, was too terrified to. Lately, everything went away if he looked.

Lately, he saw what they all were: illusions. Ghosts. Rotted things somehow animated. The figureheads that crept in the night. He, Curry, had bargained with the devil. He hadn't known it.

"Tell her. Save us. And yourself. Mutiny."

The clack of bone; a squishy sound. Curry turned his head and saw nothing.

A mutiny? Could it be possible? How could corpses do anything? How could they dare fight against the captain?

Hope sparked inside him. Mutiny! Yes! He *would* find her.

He knew who they meant. And he would tell her everything! He would save himself!

He rose to his feet and began to walk, slowly, numbly, very like a dead man. But his heart pumped fast, and full, and his blood rushed like a river through his veins.

One long, sad note, as she floated on the floor of her stateroom.

The sea has wide arms, Donna, and they are open for you. Jump, you sodding, sodden bitch.

25
Bobbing

*And I am barbing my hooks, and throwing out the net yet again,
for the most delectable of fishies.*
The small boys,
the boys,
the Nathaniels.

It was early morning, and they'd just finished getting
dressed when Matt's dad realized Nemo was having her babies. It was kind of scary: she squalled and yowled, crouching,
shifting, bracing herself. Her body shuddered as if she were
boiling, and then she grunted a couple of times, and rocked
back and forth.

She was in the cardboard box they'd fixed up for her and
pushed into the closet where it was private and dark. His dad
told him when she wanted to have her kittens she would
probably climb into it.

Sure enough, she had. Matt was very impressed with his

father for knowing how to arrange everything. But then, of course, his dad was a doctor. And his dad was also his dad.

Matt's knees ached, but he wouldn't move for anything. His stomach did flip-flops every time the cat cried and shook, but his dad said she had to do it her way, and unless she had an emergency, they could only watch.

"Easy, Nemo," Matt's dad said as Matt hung over the box. Kitties! Four so far, black and white ones, and one all black. They were tiny, and mewing, moving like windup toys. They were so little, and squirmy, and *cute.* It was so weird, and cool, that they came out of her and just started . . . living.

He had already given them names: Leonardo, Donatello, Michelangelo, and John, 'cuz that was his dad's name. His dad wanted to name the other three Paul, George, and Ringo, but Matt didn't get it—he knew his dad was making a joke—and his dad said it was mean, but okay, to name them after a pack of washed-up mutants. Matt got that one, and socked him on the arm for it. He still liked the Turtles, and they weren't washed up.

Nemo made her funny growl and jerked like a puppet. "Here comes another one!" Matty cried, bending over the cardboard box.

"Any second now," his dad said softly. He had told Matt to speak quietly, but Matt kept forgetting.

Another tiny head poked between Nemo's legs.

Nemo struggled. Her eyes rolled. John said, "Okay, kitty, good kitty."

She pushed the kitten from her body. It was ooshy and wet and she began to lick it at once, and to bite at the cord. It didn't make any noise, just sort of shivered hard. Matt's heart thrilled. It was so amazing he was almost afraid of it.

This one was all white. Donna, he decided. He'd call it Donna. Oops, it might be a boy.

"Can we keep them all?" he asked. He wanted very badly to touch them, but his father had warned him that Nemo wouldn't like it. "They're a family, Dad."

His dad smiled. "What if she has a dozen?"

"So?"

"Well, Nemo belongs to the men on the *Morris*. They might want to keep them."

Matt extended his hand to pet one of the tiny kittens, then remembered again and drew his fist back and held it against his chest. Things were too complicated sometimes. They had saved Nemo, so they should get to keep her and her babies.

His dad was just making an excuse, anyway, so they wouldn't keep her. For a second or two, Matt was angry—how come his dad said no so much?—but then Nemo squalled and yowled again and Matt eagerly leaned over the box. *Another* one?

There was a knock on the door. "I'll get it," his father offered. Without taking his eyes off the mother and her litter, Matt nodded.

It was Dr. Hare, and he had a little boy with him. He was small with brown hair, and he had on way too many clothes for indoors—ski stuff and mittens. Matt regarded him curiously, until Nemo's thrashing drew back his attention.

"Oh, excuse me," Dr. Hare said, peering around the door when Matt's dad opened it. "You're in the middle of something."

"Nemo's having her kittens," Matt's dad said in a friendly voice. "Come on in."

"Oh? This will be an experience." He prodded the boy forward. "Matt? This is Dane. I thought you might enjoy meeting a boy your age."

"Hi," Matt said without turning.

"Matt, Dane is deaf. He can't hear you. He can only read your lips," the doctor said. "You'll have to look at him whenever you want to speak to him."

Matt stared at the boy, fascinated. "Can he talk back?"

"Yes, but it sounds a bit different. It takes some getting used to, eh?" He tousled the boy's bangs. The kid had on his ski jacket hood and everything. He must be really sick, Matt thought. Whenever he had to go to the hospital, he had trouble staying warm.

"Dane's from Lake Tahoe," the doctor added, shepherding Dane over to Nemo. "Look," he said precisely. "The cat is giving birth."

The boy knelt beside Matt, who scooted over to give him some room. His skin had a funny bluish tint.

Nemo thrashed around and meowed. Her eyes blinked open, shut, and she growled low in her throat. The kitties mewed and lurched on their stubby legs. Then she backed away, slowly, into a corner of the box, hissing.

"Maybe one's stuck," Matt said.

Then a big yucky glob of goo spewed out of her. "She's expelling the afterbirth," his dad told the boys as he walked over and stood behind them.

Dane wrinkled his nose and Matt made a puking noise. "Gross."

Nemo hissed again. She shifted her weight onto her front legs and arched her back; the hair on her back stood straight up, and so did her tail. The fur bristled as she focused her gaze on Dane, and she shook hard and bared her teeth.

Dr. Hare chuckled. "Protective little creature, isn't she?"

"I think we'd better give her some privacy, boys." Matt's dad gestured for them to move away and he pulled the closet door three-quarters shut. "I think she's finished, and she wants to clean them and nurse them."

"Oh." Matt was disappointed.

To Matt's dad, the doctor said, "Well, if it's over, then. May I speak to you a moment?"

There was one of those funny pauses adults shared sometimes, and then Matt's dad said, "Hon, I'm going to go get some ice and Cokes for you and Dane. Be right back."

That frosted Matt a little. He never got to have Coke this early in the morning. His dad didn't need to make dumbo excuses to talk in private. He understood about that. But he also understood his dad was under a lot of strain. So he nodded carelessly and said, "Hurry back. Nemo might need you."

"I'll be gone just a few minutes." His dad faced Dane and said, "I'm going for Cokes. Be right back." Dane nodded. He hadn't spoken a word, and Matt wasn't sure he wanted him to. Sometimes things like that were awful—hearing people talk funny, looking at people with scars—just really embarrassing. He couldn't explain what he meant, but he kind of wished the doctor hadn't brought Dane by.

"Do you know about the school bus," Dane asked in a flat voice. It wasn't too bad. He didn't make his voice rise the way you do when you're asking a question, but he didn't sound like a retard, either.

Matt shook his head.

"It fell into Lake Tahoe. Sank. All the kids were still in it, and the driver, too. Nobody could find it. The lake is so deep no one's ever found the bottom. We're s'posed to have a monster, too."

"Cool," Matt said. Dane nodded, and Matt was pleased that he'd understood him.

"But every once in a while, the bus comes up. And you can see all the dead kids floating around inside. It's so cold in the lake that the kids didn't rot."

Behind the closet door, Nemo growled low in her throat.

"You know what some people do with new kitties," Dane asked. Still goggle-eyed from the bus story, Matt waited. "Tie 'em in a sack and drown 'em."

Matt made a face. "Uck! That's gross."

"I saw some in the lake," Dane went on, with an odd, satisfied grin on his face, like he'd shoplifted something and gotten away with it. He spoke at the cat as if he were taunting her. "They freeze in there, and they don't rot. Just like the kids."

"Gee, Dane." Matt rocked back on his heels.

Dane lowered his head and giggled, a deep, naughty snigger. Maybe Dane wasn't so cool after all. Maybe he was pretty weird.

Dane reached into his pocket and pulled out a pair of mittens, red with yellow reindeer on them. He moved forward and stuck them through the opening in the closet door, dangling them over Nemo's box. Nemo flattened herself on the bottom of the box and her eyes spun around and around like marbles on a sidewalk. She hissed like a snake, a really pissed-off one. And suddenly Matt had a sense that all was not right in the stateroom; that something was

cold

and

wet; no, make that freezing. That he was in a refrigerator, or some kind of long box filled with ice; that he was *not rotting.*

Down in the water, and not rotting.

He gripped the edge of the box hard. The room spun around and around; he was so cold; he was dizzy and he was going to faint. He was . . .

"Nemo," he said in a bright, unfrightened tone, groping through the vertigo to prove he was okay, "are you having more kittens?"

The cat yowled.

Cold and wet. Matt heard dripping. He heard people singing the way they did in church, slow, all together in a chorus. Something about being near to God. *Nearer, my God, to Thee.* Yes. He cocked his head. Someone must be practicing next door.

A dog. Barking far, far away, as if it were playing inside a tunnel. Calling and woofing: come play. Come play with me. *Woof, woof, aouuu.*

It sounded like his dead dog, Julie. Julie had crawled under the pool cover, his dad had told him. Couldn't get out . . .

He wiped sweat from his upper lip. Although he was freezing, the sweat was dripping off him. His skin was layers of ice and fire. He must be sick. Oh, no. No.

Dane started laughing. He skipped over to the bed and plopped down on it, began bouncing.

"What's the matter?" he asked between bursts of laughter, and he wasn't talking in that flat way anymore. He didn't even sound like himself. His voice was deep and grown-up. "What's wrong with you, Mattman?"

Matt started. No one called him that but his dad.

A few seconds passed. Dane forced himself to stop laughing. But his shoulders moved and his eyes twinkled, and his big, goofy ears turned red. He leaned back on the bed.

"Mattman, Mattman, I know a way you can never be sick again. I know how to freeze the cancer, and it will never rot inside you again."

"Wh-what?" Matt managed, shocked and frightened. His heart thumped hard. "How do you kno—"

Dane swung his legs. "It's easy. It's quick." He clicked his tongue against his teeth. "I was going to talk to her myself but I think it would be better if you told her what I said. And gave her these. More . . . imaginative."

He tossed his mittens to Matt, who automatically reached out and caught them. They were stiff with cold and sopping wet. They were—

—dry as dust. Dry as a bone.

Matt's mouth dropped. He put a hand to his forehead to check for a fever. His skin was cool.

But you could be very, very ill without a fever. You could be dying.

Dane slid off the bed. He hummed to himself as he skipped toward the door, pausing to trail his hand across the closet door. Nemo growled. Then he went to the front door, wrapped his hand around the knob, and looked over his shoulder at Matt.

"Tell her what I said."

"Wh-who?"

"Why, Donna, of course. It's definitely the boy she wants. The angel of forgiveness. A figurehead for the absolution of her monstrous sin. And he is lovely, is he not? He is beautiful."

He laughed, opened the door, and skipped out of the room.

"Dad," Matt whispered. He flung the mittens on the floor and wiped his hand furiously on the carpet. Then he rose and ran to the stateroom door. Tried to open it. It was locked.

"Dad." He knocked loudly. "Daddy, open the door!"

There was no response. He knocked harder. "Daddy!"

Across the room, Nemo poked her head out of the box. She sank back down, showing just her eyes, and watched Matt intently.

"Nemo, help! Dad. Daddy!" He bashed the door with his fist. A bruising stinging shot through the heel of his hand. "Shit!"

Matthew. Mattman. Someone spoke. Someone in his head. Matt looked around.

In the distance, the barking of dogs. The laughter of a child.

Of many children. And the singing. *Nearer, my God, to Thee.*

Matty, you are getting sick again. You know you are. But you can stay here forever. You can keep from becoming ill.

Forever.

"Who's saying that?" Matt shouted, pushing himself from the door, whirling around. "Who's talking to me?"

The stateroom doorbell rang. Matt cried out and stared at it, eyes wide, wider, widest. Some thing was on the other side, some (say it, yes, say it)

some

Some gho—

"Matt? It's me, Ruth. Ruth Hamilton."

Matt cried out again and ran to the door. He threw it open and flung himself into her arms, and they collided.

"Help me!" he shouted. "Help me!"

In the box, Nemo squalled and yowled and hissed. She thrashed wildly, her paws battering the sides of the box. She growled, then shrieked in a feline scream of pure agony, her cat voice hurtling toward the moon. She shrieked again.

And then was silent.

My darling, my precious small love.

My bait.

26
Shattering

Pleased with himself, the captain stood on the bridge with his hands behind his back. Mr. Creutz had the wheel, and the man was *there*, all of a piece, straining at the shackles of control the captain had placed on him; ha, brave Captain Creutz! Went down with his ship, and this was his reward; and his hatred was what made him so interesting, so *alive*, to Captain Reade.

The beautiful little boy in the ski jacket had just returned from his visit to the other beautiful child, Matty. Now the boy put his hands on the captain's thighs and smiled up at him. His baby-fat mouth glistened pink and promising. The captain remembered this one, from the frigid, bottomless lake; and Donna, of course: Grab, grab her! that comely ankle, that meaty calf, grab and *pull*! and how she had eluded him. Once, m'dear, but not twice.

No one gets a second chance on the Sea of Death.

"I shall love you always," Reade said to the child, who

smiled. Blessed was he, Thomas Reade, who made the deaf
to hear, the dead to walk. But though he stroked the boy's
head and reached for him, in his mind's eye he saw little
Matty and sighed with longing. He would love him, too. Not
for always, perhaps, but often, and well. Like his one true
love, Nathaniel.

"Full ahead, to the Sea of Death," he sang out.

"Aye, sir."

Creutz was more agitated than usual today, it seemed. Or
was it his own nerves? Reade was so tired lately. He needed a
rest; the *Pandora* was showing signs of . . . wear. The survivors were straining his reserves; or that damn slut Donna
was, at any rate. Everyone else was climbing aboard Charon's
boat with charming ease. Thus far, her delicate ankles yet
remained on deck, but what about that glorious break-
through when she had seen Mrs. Reinstedt in the finery she
had drowned in? The sweetness of that victory enlarged him,
engorged him; he fed on that moment, and knew her surprise
as a tasty morsel.

And then he had feasted upon her, lain in wait and swallowed her up in her "stateroom," poor Jonah-girl! Forcing
her out and down, so far down. Sweet she was, sweet and
mysterious, his sea-witch, his mer-girl. Though she refused to
see the horrors he prepared for her—to the point of going
blind, that early first attempt!—she'd moved awash in fear,
swimming through her terror like one who sees the ship on
the far, far horizon. And when she dared to believe she could
reach safety, he had keelhauled her mind through the ice
rivers of his power, and now—at last!—he knew the size and
shape of the lure that would catch her: the boy was heaviest
on her mind; he was her Desire.

He knew he had succeeded with her once, when on the
Morris he had made her think she had touched this little boy
in Ruth Hamilton's cabin. Absently he patted the child, who
beamed at him. And later, in the lifeboat, she had dreamed
of little deaf Dane.

But the captain had assumed her truest desire lay else-
where—with the man, Glenn—else, how could she have
fought him off, though he spoke to her and called to her and

ordered her to obey, and yet she did not respond? His siren call of the boy had been false . . . or so he had believed, until now.

"Ah, child," the captain said lovingly, and the boy fell to his knees,

full fathoms deep.

"Soon, soon." And briefly, he reminded himself to tell Cha-cha to murder Captain Curry; and then he let it slide away as the little floater made him feel alive, alive, all, all alive, alive on a wine-dark sea.

The ship flickered.

White walls melted away, and a cold wind shrieked through the ribs of a dead ship; metal flaked and crusted and dead men lay in heaps, rotting. A torso, glowing with mold. A foot of bone and leathered skin; barnacles on the deck and crabs inside a wrist. Such death. Such waste.

Curry stayed where he was, in the shadows, his hand laid over the smashed head of a Tiffany lamp. He had snuck for an hour through the death trap that was currently masquerading as *Pandora,* and had been many other vessels in his years of servitude; and icebergs and kelp beds and whatever else was required to destroy the captain's prey.

For three years he had slaved for that monster, and survived; but now, with the undreamed-of hope of escape before him, he began to lose heart. He would never find Donna Almond; he had no idea where she was. But he knew who she was. The captain was obsessed with her, and with trapping her into dying aboard the ship. It would not do well to stand between the captain and anyone he wanted, mutiny or no.

Maybe he, Curry, didn't need to find her. The flickering was happening more often; the bodies and the tatters and the rotten wood blurring into substance. Perhaps Reade was dying, or the mutiny had already begun. Why take the risk of being discovered? Of dying here?

Because if he didn't take that risk, and try to help, he knew he would be damned in another way. Damned if you do.

Cursed by hell itself if you don't.

The ship blurred back into the lavish newness of the *Pan-*

dora, Oriental cooks chopped vegetables where stinking heaps of bones were truly piled like prehistoric altars. The cooks believed themselves to have been there all along; it was only a few of the crew who had begun to realize they were . . . not real, not what they once had been. That they were dead, and reanimated in some way by that fiend. The mutineers had to be the ones who knew. But what a course to take, for what would happen if they failed?

What would happen if they succeeded?

Curry crawled over the kitchen floor, shielding himself with the maze of meat lockers and what he knew was in them —crewmen, passengers, some from his own ship. They had been feeding them to the survivors of the *Morris* . . . with a little fresh belly timber—their own crewmates—thrown in.

"God help me," he whispered, and inched on.

The corridor stretched endlessly before John and Dr. Hare, bowing in the distance. Disoriented, John turned and walked a few steps backward, trying to pinpoint his stateroom door.

"Doctor?" Dr. Hare queried with a raised eyebrow.

John scratched his chin. "I thought the ice machine was right here." He gestured to the right. "I don't remember going this far before."

"Mmm." The doctor kept walking. "I think it's a ways ahead."

John moved his shoulders. "Ah, well. I never had much of a sense of direction."

"It seems to me you do," Hare replied. He laid a hand on John's arm and said, "Let's talk, Dr. Fielder."

John waited. The doctor cleared his throat, assuming a professional air John recognized: the authority, the somber, almost expressionless face. The seriousness.

"It cannot have escaped you," Hare said, "that in the past few days, your son has gotten much, much worse."

John's ulcer flared. He gasped behind his hand, lowered it to his side. Except for the fire pit in his gut, he went numb.

"I . . . I thought so," he said. Panic ripped through him.

No, no, no. He wanted to scream. He couldn't handle any more.

Jesus, Jesus, get it together. Your kid needs you. Maintain.

"Are you all right, Doctor?" Fielder asked, halting. He cupped John's shoulder.

John nodded mutely. "I . . . I'm sorry. Please go on."

"I don't know how to broach this," Hare said. "It's harder when dealing with a fellow professional. You know about all the processes taking place inside his body. What cancer cells look like, what he looks like inside. You can envision the prognosis, the outcome, step by step."

"Christ," John breathed, wiping his forehead, pressing his fingertips against his eyes.

"I'm sorry. I don't want to cause you pain. No one here wants to hurt you. We want to help you." Hare smiled kindly. "We want what's best for Matt."

John lowered his arm. "I don't understand." The hallway was so damn long, he thought irritably, distractedly. Where was the goddamn ice machine?

"I have to get back. Matt—"

"Doctor. Doctor, listen."

"Look, if this is some bid for funding for your frozen barnacle shit . . ." But John knew it wasn't. He was angry because he was scared. He didn't want to talk about this with this man, with anybody. He wanted it to go away. He wanted it to stop.

"By now you know Australia doesn't matter. Nothing matters."

"What?" John asked shrilly.

"There is nothing on earth that can save Matt. You know that."

John stared at the doctor for a moment. Then he doubled his fist and raised it over his head. "Don't be stupid!" he shouted. "Don't you be so stupid!"

The doctor stood unafraid, with his calm, sad smile, and his certainty. "The new age is so unfair. In the old days, you could put on animal skins and toss colored powders into a fire, and he might get well. Or you could pray to God, and he might get well. I know you have," he added. "Prayed, I mean.

But I doubt you seriously believe God will do anything. Or can do anything. And science has told you that man can't intervene on Matt's behalf. There is nothing you can do to stop him from worsening and dying."

"Stop," John whispered. Tears rolled down his cheeks. The numbness spread. His fists floated above his head, far away, far, like a cork on the surface of a lake. He couldn't tell where he ended and the hallway began. He was dizzy, and sick, and he wasn't sure he was speaking aloud.

"But there is something *we* can do, we of the *Pandora*. He need not die." The doctor grabbed John's arms. "He need not die, if he stays here with us."

John stared at him. The doctor nodded. "Surely you accept that the *Pandora*'s not just a ship. You've felt it. You all have. John, we want you to come aboard. Both of you."

"What—?"

"Look. I'll show you."

"You're fucking crazy!" John shouted, and pushed the doctor aside as he strode down the hall, back toward his stateroom, and crashed against a tall woman as she caught his shoulders. Her face was broad, friendly, big-boned. Her hair was a bubble-helmet and she had on a simple A-line dress of black and white geometric shapes. Rings of white beneath her eyes, and lips of dead-white. Purple and red teardrops dangled from her ears and she smelled of—no!—she smelled of patchouli oil, very big back then—

Back when?

"Easy, man," she said, releasing him, grabbing his hands. She reeked of marijuana.

"What?" He looked past her, beyond. They were on the Sausalito ferry, at night; the stars gleamed over San Francisco Bay, and there dozens of kids sprawled everywhere, with straight hair down to their butts, flared bell-bottom jeans, and shirts with paisley and African prints; a kid in velvet with a Carnaby Street hat.

A radio blasted Jimi Hendrix, and the detonation of an electric riff blew up John's backbone, straight up bashing and crashing;

he staggered backward and knocked into someone, and whirled around like a drunk.

"Easy, easy," said the doctor.

"Where the fuck . . . ?"

"We're on the *Pandora*," Hare assured him. His hand took in the ferry, the kids. "Do you see anyone you recognize?"

He stared. Saw Hare's nurse, who was lounging on some stairs with his orderlies, smoking a joint. A few people from the dining room, dressed in clothes of the time. Donna's steward, Adalberto.

"This ferry went down," Hare said. "Do you remember the big disaster in '67? It was the *Sausalito* itself. You remember it?"

John covered his face. "We've been hallucinating. All of us. We've . . ."

"No, John. It was your happiest time. Your Summer of Love. You can live there. You can live there with Matt. It was your happiest time."

John shook his head.

"Come aboard, John. Of your own free will." The doctor's voice was soft, hypnotic. "Come aboard for Matty's sake. Now. While he's still well."

Shook his head, shook it, hiding his face.

"Because we freeze here, John. However we were when we came aboard is how we remain. And Matty is getting sick, John. Matty's getting deathly ill. We won't be able to help him much longer, John. Dr. Fielder, can you hear me?"

Shook his head, shook, shook, shook.

Screaming.

Curry minced out of the kitchen and stood behind a palm. No one seemed to notice him. He had never been able to tell how far the captain's control extended; how many of the actions of the—what? ghosts? phantoms? zombies?—were independent. Free will, in dead things? In memories and fantasies?

Free will. Could he have done other than he had? If he had refused to obey, if he had let him . . . let the captain kill him . . .

He pushed his hand over his face to keep himself from weeping. He was distraught, barely able to cope. He wanted to puke out his fear, beg someone to help him. The woman had to. She had to believe him, and do something.

Matt had calmed down, and when Ruth told him that his father had sent her to fetch him, he agreed at once to go with her. After a moment's hesitation, he picked up the mittens and stuffed them in his pockets.

"What are those?" she asked pleasantly as they went out into the companionway.

"For Donna," he said.

"Oh." She held out her hand, and he took it.

"Dr. Hare has some medicine for you to take," she said as they strolled along. "Something that will make you feel better."

An alarm sounded in Matt's head. "But I feel okay," he said tentatively. His dad had gone off with the other doctor to talk about him. Because he *wasn't* okay. Because he was dying.

That couldn't be. That just couldn't be. He didn't feel bad at all.

"Maybe we shouldn't leave Nemo alone," he ventured, turning back. Because suddenly he didn't want to go with her, but he couldn't tell her that because she was a grown-up. Besides, she was nice, and he didn't want to hurt her feelings.

Ruth's hand squeezed around his like his dad's when he forgot how skinny Matty was. It hurt, and he flinched. She smiled quickly.

"Nemo will be fine. She needs to be alone with her kittens right now."

"But . . ."

"Matt, come on." She practically dragged him down the hall.

For an old lady, she was really strong.

Donna awoke on the floor. There was a terrible cramp in her neck and she swore under her breath as she rolled over. All the nerve endings in her body shot up. Without moving, she raised her arm and fumbled for the phone. Got the receiver in her hand and yanked it to her ear, pulling the entire phone set onto the floor. The bell jangled once and for a second she was back in Ruth's cabin on the *Morris*—

brrrnnnng

knocking over her alarm clock in the fog.

"He-ehllo," she managed.

Finally realized the phone was still dead.

And that when she'd gone down, she'd been by the door. Now she lay next to the bed; her arm was stretched under it, hidden by the dust ruffle, and her foot, as if something were pulling at her, pulling her under—

God! She dropped the receiver and half jumped, half rolled away from the bed. She pushed herself up on her hands and knees and staggered to a standing position. Ran like hell out of there, stumbling, yanking open the door, and flying into the corridor.

Where, just outside her door, a pair of red snow mittens embroidered with yellow reindeer lay on the carpet.

Cha-cha walked to the doorway of the museum, ringing his hands. The king was waiting for him. He would be angry, so pissed, p.o.'d, for sure.

"Cha-cha!" Neptune cried. "Come! Dance, Cha-cha! Dance the hornpipe!"

"Um, Your Maj," Cha-cha murmured, confused. His master capered at the far end of the room, scraping and bowing to the rows of figureheads. The king straightened and ran up the stairs. Clasping the nearest, a statue of a dark-eyed woman in his arms, he thrust his pelvis forward and ground it against the wooden lady.

"Fuck, Cha-cha! Fuck all my ghosts!" He flung himself away from the figurehead and hung over the railing, waving Cha-cha to draw near.

"Ah, um . . ." Cha-cha scratched his head. "The dude is, like, uh . . ."

Flustered, he trailed off. Oh, no. Those couldn't be figureheads, if the king was talking about ghosts. Cripey, he'd gotten so crazy he thought everybody was a statue! Time to go back to the hospital, Cha-cha, whether the Nammie-ghosts get to come aboard or—

"I couldn't find him," he said. "Sir, Your Majesticness, the man . . ." Had not been in the room His Oceanic Majesty had sent him to. Curry. The man Cha-cha was supposed to kill.

Neptune reached a hand behind him and fondled the breast of the figurehead. "Come, my vassal, don't you fancy any of these ladies?"

Cha-cha sighed low in his throat. He was so *confused.*

"Any of these fair sirens?" the king said in a funny, high voice.

And then His Supreme Oceanic Majesty was surrounded by beautiful, busty mamas with long, flowing hair and—

Cha-cha blinked—

and *tails,* man. They were mermaids! Mermaids!

And they were singing to him, man. With the sweetest voices he'd ever heard. Reaching out their arms, nipples like the big pink gumdrops in the white dish in Dr. Brown's office back at the hospital; shimmering gumdrops and his stomach growled because he was

HUNGRY.

He jerked his head around just as the king shouted, "Don't listen!"

Then Neptune began to dance again. He hoisted himself up on the railing and jigged along it, shouting and laughing; and Cha-cha had an awful moment where it occurred to him that maybe, just maybe, His Majesty needed a little vacation. He was kind of acting . . . scattered.

"Hi, Cha-cha, hi!" said a voice, and suddenly a head poked up from behind the mermaids. It was Captain Esposito's boy, the one Neptune had taken so long ago.

"Hiya, Roberto," Cha-cha said brightly. He waved. "How ya been, lovechild?"

"Groovy, Cha-cha. You should come aboard soon."

"Right on, baby." Cha-cha felt confused again. He thought he was on board already.

"Dance!" Neptune commanded. Cha-cha glanced down at his sneaker-clad feet.

"Oh, oh, hey!" Cha-cha bellowed. They were wet. Water was seeping from beneath the floor, and that meant, that meant—

"The *Pandora*'s filling up with water!"

Neptune laughed and danced. "And when it goes down, it won't be airtight!"

COME!

Neptune danced. Laughed. Launched himself into the line of beautiful mermaids, who caught him, laughing.

The water soaked Cha-cha's shoes. "Oh, hey," he said. "Gotta get help, sir. Gotta—"

"They should have killed me. They were so afraid. I had my occult books. I had my magic wand; I had my chants. Superstitious fools, and now I use them. She was my first victim, the *Royal Grace*! I made her see rocks! I made her heel over and go down! I made her see—" He pointed at Cha-cha. "I make you all see, but you *don't* see!"

COME

Neptune didn't hear *the other*. Or was shining it on, man. And maybe *he* could, but the pull was major strong on Cha-cha. It was hard to stand there, and not go. He thought of the hatch, the psychedelically bitchenitis door to something supergroovy, and his heart danced a jig along the railing of his arteries.

Then the room shimmered, hard, once. They weren't in a museum at all! They were in some horrible, dark place, and it stank like death. Something grabbed him. He screamed, jumped away, landed on the face of a black dude lying on the floor. No, not lying there, chained there.

"Hey," Cha-cha said.

Black dudes chained to the floor everywhere, a mine field of Afro-American brothers, moaning and writhing.

"Oh, brothers," he said, staggering. The water was rising up to his insteps—

—their ears—

—his ankles—

—their cheeks.

They struggled, bellowed, and screamed. Naked, scrawny, sores glistening on them. Rats, cheeping and shrieking, climbing on top of them 'cuz of the water, man, the water that was coming fast—

And Neptune shined it all on. He didn't see it, Cha-cha realized. He didn't see what was happening. There were two other boys with him, one bundled up, one missing . . . missing *everything*—

COME

"Ohmigod, ohmigod," Cha-cha said in one breath.

King Neptune turned his head, with its rays of light like Jesus, his golden karma aura. "What are you going on about?"

"Gotta go," Cha-cha pleaded. Go to the voice, the *other*. Maybe the voice could help. Make it stop. Make everything groovy. Fix the boy with no face.

"Go? Where can you go?" Neptune asked testily.

"Oh, man, gotta go." Cha-cha jabbed his fingers downward at the black men and the water, the boys. "Please, you see? You see?"

"No, Cha-cha. No. You've got to dance first." King Neptune raised both hands over his head. "I am the captain I am I am I am." He interrupted himself with laughter. "I am I am the I am that I am."

Oh, bummer, major bummer, bad trip, the king was wigging out. Bad acid, bad synapses. Oh, no.

COMECOMECOMECOME

"Oh, man, oh, man," Cha-cha groaned.

And then he was back in the museum, and the king had his fishy cock out, and he was feeding it to the nearest of the beautiful brown-eyed—

—women? Cha-cha blinked. No mermaids. No figureheads. Just the three boys, and lots of people, and some of them were moving and some of them were talking, and some of them were crying.

And one of the boys—couldn't tell which—was giving head to King Neptune.

The king smiled at him. "Been a long time since someone gnawed your bone, eh, Cha-cha? Don't worry. Very soon now, someone will. Oh, yes, someone will gnaw all of them."

"Oh, oh," Cha-cha fretted.

COMECOMECOMECOME
Fearfully he glanced in the direction of the museum door.
Hadda go. Hadda go. Hadda go.

COMECOMECOMECOME

COME

COME

The king threw back his mane of golden seaweed hair and
groaned with ecstasy. He pushed the child away and stuck his
cock back in his pants. The faceless boy. There was blood all
over the king's cock, his pants. Blood and . . . clumps.

"Time for the real fun to begin, Cha-cha. Let's go."

"Wh-where?" Cha-cha quailed as the king stepped down
the stairs, one at a time, slow and regal.

COME

"The shipwreck party, of course. You wouldn't want to
miss that, would you?"

Wide-eyed, Cha-cha shuffled his feet. "Oh, no. Of course
not."

"And you have been a good acolyte, and deserve holiness."

Cha-cha cleared his throat. Better confess now. Better tell
him. Je-hesus H. Christ, his king. His king was freaking *out*.

Better confess. If he found out and Cha-cha hadn't told
him . . .

He licked his lips, over and over, cotton-mouthed. "Um,
Your Highness? I couldn't find the guy."

The king stopped, stared at him. Cha-cha said helpfully,
"The one you wanted me to kill? C-Curry?"

For a moment His Majesty turned white. His single eye
spun. Then he laughed and said, "It doesn't matter, Cha-cha.
He's done for, no matter what. He can't do anything."

COME

COME

COMECOMECOMECOMECOME

"Come, Doctor, it's time to make your decision," Hare
said to John as he dragged him down another corridor. John
was no longer moving under his own steam. Most of his energy was consumed in the battle to hold his mind together.

Gone was the *Sausalito*. They were back on the *Pandora*—

at least, he thought they were—but things were happening to it. The walls flickered and disappeared, reappeared. The carpet grew moldy, became tile, metal, reasserted itself. John saw all this, but by then he was so out of it the shock was minor compared to the explosion caused by the first . . . hallucination, that of the ferry. The stars had sparkled, the wind had blown. He had been there.

He had been there.

"Where . . . ?"

"The grand ballroom of the *Titanic,*" the doctor said. "It's the most beautiful room on the *Pandora.*"

"Oh," John replied dully. Inside, his mind was going: *notcrazyMattynotcrazyMattynotcrazyMattynotcrazydon'tdiedon'tdie*

"You lied, you know," the doctor said. "You said you'd do anything."

Matty Matty Matty Matty Matty Matty Matty crazy crazy crazy crazy crazyMatty

"I guess I'll have to tell the captain you're in no shape to act. I hate him, you know," Hare said easily. "But there's no alternative. I hate him. That's the only part that's left of me, and so I cling to it. And I'm grateful that he loves my hatred so well. Because if he didn't I would be . . ." He trailed off.

"Not even belly timber," he said after a time.

"Come on, dear," Ruth said, jerking on Matt's wrist. "Let's get this done and go to the party."

They were in the freezer room. The large, white oblong freezers stood in rows like hospital beds. Overhead, a few light fixtures hummed dully and cast a sheen of blue-gray light on the old lady's face. She looked terrible, all sunken in and . . . dead.

He wasn't prepared when she bent down, gathered him around the waist, and sat him like a toy on top of one of the freezers. It was on; the vibrations needled his butt. He folded his arms across his chest.

"I want my father. Now."

"Drink this first. This is the medicine Dr. Hare prepared for you."

She held out a brown bottle with a prescription label on

the front. Matt had swallowed many things from many such bottles, wondering what they were, knowing only that his dad and the other doctors had their fingers crossed that one of their potions would save his life.

"Drink it, sweetheart," she said gently.

"I ought to check with my dad first."

"Dr. Hare thought that might be what you'd say. In fact, he was hoping your father would administer it himself. But . . ." She scrunched her face in a silly smile and jutted her head forward like a snake. "We have to hurry, Matt. They'll be waiting for us."

Matt eyed the bottle. Why was he arguing? After all, she was his friend. She'd comforted him in the lifeboat, and played with him on the *Morris*. He had no reason to doubt her.

"Don't you want to go to the shipwreck party, dear?"

Maybe he had no reason to doubt her, but he should still check with his father.

"I—" he said, and then the room wobbled. It went blurry, and—

—the bottle was green; it was the captain's special bottle, and the room wobbled again, and—

—he was sitting alone in some kind of shed, and there was a ship's wheel in front of him. Wind and rain whipped his face. He shielded his eyes and focused in on the bow of an immense ship, heading right for him.

"Help!" He grabbed the wheel and turned it left, right, left, remembered his lesson on the bridge with the captain, remembered she responded slowly, and pushed it all the way to the right and held it there.

A klaxon blew, long-long, short-short-short. Fog rolled in, obscuring his vision, but the water in front of him chopped and sloshed and rolled. It was coming closer. It was almost on him—

"Jump!" someone called. Matt looked to his right and saw a hooded figure on a small, curved boat. He'd seen that person before, hadn't he? He'd—

He cried out as something smacked the front of his boat. A face! A woman's face, the statue lady—

"Ruth!" he screamed. "Mrs. Hamilton, where are you?"
Jump overboard.
Jump, jump
for my love.
There was no other choice. Matt let go of the wheel and
ran to the side of the boat. It was a tugboat, he realized
distractedly as he balanced in the doorway. The hooded figure gestured for him to hurry, hurry, and Matt jumped
    into the freezer.
And the heavy lid fell shut from the force of his momentum.

"Ah. Excellent." Dr. Hare smiled. "The choice has been
taken from you, Dr. Fielder."
"Wh-what?" John stammered. "Where's Matty?"
"I believe we'll meet your son at the party. Come this
way." He dragged John after him.

Donna knocked on John's door, heard a plaintive mewing
on the other side. The cat. Maybe she was having her babies.
"John! Open up!" She slammed both fists on the door.
Again. Pushed with her shoulder. Too thick. She was very
aware of the mittens in the small pockets of her dress, bulging like hand grenades. Where had they come from? And
who had left them before her door? The shithead who stole
her gun?
But who cared about that, Donna? Who cared about one
swiped firearm when you heard something in the hatch—yes,
yes you did! You heard something and you felt something
that gave you the screaming meemies, and someone had
brought her yellow reindeer mittens, just like the floater's,
the little Tahoe boy's. Name, name had been Dwayne or
something.
The mom had knitted them herself, that's what one of the
paramedics said. So fucking tragic, all that love, those little
red mittens . . .
    . . . in Donna's pocket.
And someone had moved her across the floor. Ice water,
something being pulled out of her mind, out of her . . .

"John, goddamn it!"

She didn't get this, not any of this. Her mind raced through horrible pictures of what lay beyond the door. Boy and man, shot through the head with her gun. Boy and man, bludgeoned.

Christ, Christ, calm down. A shipboard crime, a vivid imagination, and maybe they'd gone for help with the kittens. Get some towels, milk. Yeah, 'cuz the phones were out and the steward couldn't fetch and carry for them. That made sense. Her guys weren't in danger, 'cuz that made sense.

She shuddered hard. She didn't care if it made sense. Pulled herself away from the door and ran down the companionway, bellowing, "Phil! Elise! John! Captain Reade!"

Shouted, looked, turned corners, went on.

"Matt!"

Marched into the reception area, the foyer with the horse mosaics and the ship mural and—

there was no one there. No one.

No one.

She stopped so abruptly she stumbled. Flew around in a circle.

No one.

Her stomach grabbed. Cautiously, she walked over to the registration counter and dinged the bell. No one came.

"Hello!" she shouted.

No one answered.

Swearing, she left the foyer and headed for the elevator. Punched the button, but when it came, she found she couldn't go inside it. She thought of the fuses in the captain's ready room, just from a blender for God's sake; what if something bigger blew, had already blown?

"Damn it." She unconsciously moved her hands to smooth her dress, felt the fingers of the mittens and yanked them out and tossed them on the floor.

She ran a hand through her hair. Saw the stairway sign, and took it. *Where she lands, nobody knows,* she thought, but suddenly and sharply, she felt herself running as fast as she could,

for the museum.

27

Glass-bottomed Boat

Panting, Curry staggered into the companionway. Beneath the pounding of his heart, he heard a *ping, ping, ping,* almost plaintive, almost a great distance away. But he wasn't fooled; as he wrestled with his claustrophobia, he watched a green glow sicken the walls. The wreckage of the submarine was there, beneath the camouflage of the hurricane lamps and the sturdy, upright walls. He remembered how Reade had maneuvered that one: made the sub crew believe they were diving, and they rammed whatever the *Pandora* had been at the time. Whatever Reade had made them think it was.

Then he salvaged—how?—part of it and added it to the floating graveyard that now paraded as the *Pandora.* That's all the *Pandora* was, a mishmash of the vessels that Captain Reade had destroyed. Bits and pieces of them clung to each other, somehow adhering, the material foundation of a sur-real vision. Was even *that* a delusion? Was there something else beneath the pieces of wreckage? How did Reade make it all change? How did he keep it from sinking?

The captain had laughed at those early questions, never deigning to enlighten him.

Curry heard the *ping* again. But all he saw was the *Pandora* companionway near the museum, and—

—he walked closer to a shape on the floor. Shut his eyes for a moment, forced them open.

"Oh, holy God, I'm so sorry," Curry whispered. He recognized the features, distorted as they swam in a heap of gristle and bone. The face was battened down from a storm of blows; the arms and legs gashed and cut.

It was the man he had tried to warn, the Spanish one.

He looked away. And incredibly, horribly the heap of flesh shifted. He heard the squish, the sigh. His stomach turned and he made himself look back at it. Put both hands over his mouth. Acid flooded his mouth at the sight, though he had seen piles of fresh . . . meat . . . many times. Rendered men, many, many times.

Curry bent down. The eyes in the pile stared at him. He didn't see the mouth.

"Oh, man, are you alive?" Curry asked, revolted. "Is the captain using you? Are you real?"

Pieces gleamed like snake scales as they moved. "Dead," came a voice.

"What?" Curry leaned over it. Steam rose from the entrails and the heavy odor of blood assaulted him. He fought to keep from retching. "What, man?"

Silence. Curry considered looking for a pulse. Couldn't decide where, and what good it would do. Then something went out of the eyes.

With a deep, steadying breath, he stood. He stepped around the pieces, the blood. Was this some trick of the captain's? Or was the man finally, blissfully, forever dead?

And what was that, dead? Curry was almost afraid to know.

Almost. The alternatives that he knew about were too horrible to endure.

* * *

In the freezer, Matt's lids closed and he stirred weakly. How could it be warm when it was so cold? How could it feel good?

"Daddy," he whispered. "Daddy."

He lay on stiff, lumpy things that poked his back and neck. Buffalo steaks, he thought vaguely.

Rest, Mattman. Rest. You are my choicest prize, and I shall save the best for last.

He scowled. Who was that? Who kept talking? Who kept sounding crazy?

Rest.

"Fu-fuck you," Matt said.

Something laughed.

The tears on Matt's cheeks froze.

Unchallenged, Donna rounded a corner and started down the companionway that led to the museum. She had found no one on the ship. No John, no Matt, no steward, no crewman. No other passengers. She was

alone, alone, all, all alone.

And if she didn't figure out why real quick, she was going to lose her fucking mind.

The mittens had taken on additional significance: a pair of gauntlets, a challenge, a dare. Some kind of lure.

Damn it to hell, what was going on?

She kept walking, senses alert, back stiff with nerves, and then she saw it.

The captain's special green bottle, in the middle of the hall.

She touched it with her foot as if it might detonate. It tipped over and described an arc like a needle in a compass. Eeenie, meenie, out goes *you.*

It pointed directly at her. She took a step back and reached automatically for her gun. For where her gun should be.

The yellow light from the hurricane lamps gleamed on the green glass and the chunks of red and green stone. Donna moved toward it and crouched down.

Son of a bitch, it was uncorked. She poked at the cold,

hard glass with her finger. Nothing special. Ah, but there was something inside.

With an unconscious breath, she slid two fingers into the neck and caught the object between her middle and forefingers. It was a very thick, clothlike piece of paper, same stationery as the invitation to the Captain's Table. Folded several times, and then rolled into a scroll. Cautiously, she unrolled and unfolded it.

There was a skull and crossbones—no, an anchor, her mistake—engraved in black at the top. Below it, in shiny, embossed script, were the words:

The Captain, H.M.S. Pandora,
cordially invites you

Nearer, my God, to thee.
Donna glanced up at the sound of the faint music. "Yes?" she called. Waited. There was nothing more. She read on:

to a shipwreck party
in honor of our newest shipmates:

Ruth Hamilton
John and Matthew Fielder
and Our Special Guest of Honor,
Donna Lynn Almond

on the Titanic
now

"Holy shit," she said, examining the paper, turning it over in her hands, What the hell kind of game was this? Had the *captain* knocked her out, taken her gun?

And what was this about the *Titanic*? Her "favorite ship," as Reade had put it. She read the invitation again. No mention of Phil or Elise, and what about Ramón? The people who were missing weren't mentioned.

She held the bottle to the light, examining it. Had they been left all over the ship, like Easter eggs, with invitations

crammed inside? Why was she the guest of honor? 'Cuz he'd
hit on her, or hit her, more like?

Nearer to Thee—

She almost dropped the bottle. Then she realized how enclosed she felt. Claustrophobic. And she heard a strange *ping,
ping, ping.* She considered it, found herself thinking of submarine movies.

She looked to the left, and she had the strangest sense that
something was there, near the wall, but she couldn't see it. A
shadow of a shadow. A smell of a smell,

of a smell that was Death.

And the echo of wind, blowing fierce and far away.
Shhhooooo, a gale, a hurricane, but muffled.

Then gone.

Slowly she rose, cradling the bottle and the note. Holy shit,
holy shit, holy shit. Goose bumps coated her, outside and in.
Holy shit.

Okay, make it work: the captain was nuts. He'd started
picking off the *Morris* survivors—oh, God, let that be wrong
—and he was rounding up the ones who were left. And he
had somehow gotten rid of everyone else. Yeah, right. He just
stashed them somewhere, Donna. Right. That all made
sense.

Nearer, my God, to Thee.

Shhhoooooo.

Make it work: a tape. Someone was rehearsing a play. A
music system, heretofore unused.

With feet like lead weights, she walked toward the museum. Make it work. Jesus. It didn't work. None of it.

Low, nasty laughter jittered down the hall, the kind a boy
made when he snuck-read a dirty magazine or a little girl saw
her big brother with his girlfriend: a sexual, titillated laugh,
kiddie-porn night with the guys.

Her hair stood on end. It was loud, as though amplified
through a sound system; and it was off-center, the laughter of
someone who wants not to laugh, but can't help it.

"Hey. Who's there?" she demanded in a strong cop voice.

It rose half a note, faltered, then trilled hysterically up the
scales, bass to alto to a falsetto high C. Donna scratched her

knuckles and kept walking. Someone was out of control. No shit, Sherlock.

And the Special Guest of Honor was going to bust him. Or her.

Had to be the captain. But why? How?

She turned the corner. The museum door was open. All the lights were off. The place was dark as a cave.

And the laughter flew out of it, like a winged thing, and swooped down on her. Donna ducked as if something were really coming at her, straightened as soon as she realized it was only noise.

"Okay, come out," she called. Waited, chewing the inside of first her left cheek, then right. Her heartbeat revved; the tips of her fingers tingled. Her stomach started to pull into itself. Her senses grew sharp, alert, poised, the old fight or flight response. Blood pressure up, vein in her forehead doing the chimichanga.

The laughter rang forward, ebbed, crashed closer, ebbed, like a tide.

"That's real neat," she said. "I'm impressed. You could get a job in Hollywood. But if you're finished—"

A harsh white light focused on her, flicked off her, beamed at the scores of bottles overhead. They were swinging back and forth, and their surfaces sent out sparks of light. Back and forth, back, forth, rhythmically, out on the open sea. Out on the—

on

the

lake; trying to save that kid, trying to stop everything from happening. The lake was liquid ice, so absolutely draining. It just sucked the will out of you, the strength and the power; you were nothing in that lake, just a fucking corpse in suspended animation, dreaming as you went down

down,

down; moving on in your head to a future you were not going to have. Moving on, as you drifted in the ice, rocked gently as death curled around you and tried to get inside you before all your warmth evaporated; Death is cold and so very alone; Death is lonely for you and what else do you have, anyway? No family, no man, no talent, no life. And you're too dumb, too slow, powerless.

Let him grab your ankle and pull. Let him do it, now, and you'll go

down

down

"Good morning, heartache," Billy sang, *really,* in Donna's ears, and it was that that jerked her out of her stupor.

Shit, was somebody trying to hypnotize her? Was that it? Some kind of Mission Impossible group hypnosis tripping them all out?

Slowly, the light descended, bringing with it the bottles. They lowered en masse, eye level, revealing a flotilla of pitching miniature vessels inside them. Battleships and schooners and subs and sailboats. Luxury liners, tankers, barges, steamboats.

The *Titanic.*

The *Normandie.*

The *Robert E. Lee.*

The *Bismarck.*

The ships in bottles floated around her like bubbles. They rode on seas that seemed to froth and swell: an illusion, she told herself. Caused by the lights.

She grabbed the nearest one, a model of a tug. It vibrated in her grasp, shooting a charge into her forearm. Her hair stood on end as she released it and it hovered, connected to nothing, hanging in the air of its own accord. A magic trick. She passed her hand over the nearest ship, under it. No wires, no transparent filaments.

Cautiously, she drew back her hand and stared at the bottles.

"Cute. Real cute," she said at the light.

The laugh was successfully muffled this time. She took a step forward. Another. Another. Walked halfway into the museum.

The light jerked from her to a case on her right. The case where the green bottle usually lay, cloaked with a velvet cape.

She slid her glance toward it. Inhaled sharply.

The drape had been removed, and a bottle identical to the one she held in her hands rested in the case.

Stay calm, she told herself. That didn't mean anything. So there were two bottles. For all she knew, there were fifty of them. He bought them in Hong Kong.

There was a note inside the second bottle, too. It practically glowed, some Alice in Wonderland magic: *Read Me.* Donna strode to it, deliberately making a lot of noise, because creeping made you look frightened and frightened made you vulnerable to attack, and reached inside.

A tidal wave of maniacal laughter, half screams, half hissing, rose around her, crashing, foaming along her spine. Ignoring it, she stuck her hand in—

—and a low, visceral terror spread across her skin like a layer of gellid paste, contracting, constricting, pulling the hairs on her arms, her legs, her head. Get your hand out of there, she commanded herself. Get it out or you're going to lose it—

—oh, God—

and because of the terror, because of it, goddamn it, she had to pick that fucking bottle up and read the fucking note.

"Shit," she said under her breath. The laughter caromed around the room. When she found that asshole, she was going to cram the damn bottle down his throat.

She hesitated one more second, forcing herself to keep her eyes open. They watered from the strain. Unknowingly, she drew back her lips. God, here goes. Here goes.

She picked it up.

Every time I close my eyes, I jerk awake . . . Donna came by to ask for a sleeping pill . . .
. . . we never did find anything . . .
This fog . . .
Ulcer . . .

John. John Fielder had written this. What the hell was it doing here?

There were more pages:

. . . Everybody thinks Cha-cha's a harmless old guy, but he's scary, man. Only thing in that net were some fish and some damn shark or something, the one who chomped my finger off, practically.

The lady cop is right about one thing: if something does happen, like if King Neptune tells Cha-cha to go for it, I don't think the crew will be any help at all.

That sounded like Kevin. She read the last page, a fragment from a lined, bound book:

15 April 0900

. . . my God, my God, I never believed Cha-cha was dangerous, but he's butchered them! Sweet Jesus, when I came on deck, and saw what he'd done . . . and then I realized they'd taken him into the lifeboat. They're alone out there with that maniac, and there's no way I can warn them.

This is my last entry. We're taking on too much water. I'm amazed we haven't gone down yet.

Wait! What's that? I hear another ship!

Thank God, we're saved!

Cha-cha? Oh, God, not Cha-cha. She thought about the missing people. Before or after he came on board? Think, Donna, missing before or after?

But how come Reade had told them there'd been a false alarm aboard the *Morris*? If it hadn't gone down, would Esposito have warned Reade about Cha-cha?

At a noise, she glanced up from the pages. Captain Reade stepped into the glow from the hallway. He angled the flashlight under his chin; it shot his face with harsh, ghoulish streaks of white. He was dressed in a ship's officer's uniform from another time, dark blue coat and white trousers. His eye stared at her and his mouth was drawn back in a wild, fierce grimace. His skin was shiny with sweat; in the light it looked as if it had been varnished, as if he'd been made of wood. A six-foot-tall nutcracker, the features painted on with a less than steady stroke. His head tremored like an old man's. His teeth clicked together and he blinked rapidly.

"What does this mean?" she asked evenly. Christ, he was totally insane. What the hell was she going to do?

The captain shook his head. "You are so thick. What do you think it means? Or *can* you think, you bitch?" He raised the flashlight above his head, brought it down in an arc and hit his open hand. "Are you capable of thought?"

She breathed through her mouth. She said, "I think these are papers from the lifeboat."

He sneered at her. Took two steps forward, hit his hand with the flashlight again. "Do you? Do you really?" His mouth twitched; he covered it with a gloved hand, and a high-pitched giggle, almost a squeak, erupted from behind his white fingers. The flashlight beam cut a jag through the blackness as he fought for control.

"You know they're from the *Morris*."

"Cha-cha brought them in his lifeboat," she insisted. Did he cut up everybody? Jesus, Jesus.

The flashlight flew upward, down. Up, down. His hand was beginning to swell. He advanced on her, smiling. Cawing noises spurted out of him, sea gull laughter. He lowered his head and peered coyly at her through his lashes.

"Oh, yes? Did you, Cha-cha?"

She watched, stunned, as Cha-cha bobbed into the light. His face and clothes were clotted with blood. He looked featherlight, wan, terrified.

He looked pleadingly at Donna. "Do you hear the voice? The other voice, down there? Do you hear it? I tried to go down there again, but I couldn't find the ladderwa—"

"Cha-cha," she said, taking a step forward. Then she bolted toward him.

"Cha-cha, defend yourself," Reade ordered.

Cha-cha drew her revolver from the waistband of his jeans. He hunched over like an old man and aimed it at the floor.

"It's loaded," he said miserably. "Office D., I put the bullets in it."

"Careful then, Chach," she said, halting. "There's no safety."

"No?" he asked querulously. "No? But he said, but he said
. . . do you hear the voice?"

Reade snapped his fingers. "I repeat: You know they're
from the *Morris,* and you know I took her down. Admit it!
Admit it and I won't hurt you."

"You won't hurt me anyway, you crazy son of a bitch." She
lunged at Cha-cha and wrested the gun from his limp grasp,
ran backward, and took aim. With a cry, Cha-cha pushed her
out of his way and ran out of the room, slamming the door
behind him. The floating bottles swung back and forth, like
so much sea junk on the waves.

"Stop!" the captain shouted. "I order you, Cha-cha! This is
your king!"

"I'm coming!" Cha-cha cried in the distance.

"Let him go. He's hallucinating," Reade said, as if to himself. "There is nothing calling him. There is . . . I . . ."

Reade shook himself. He moved his shoulders in a strange,
agitated way. Then the moment seemed to pass. He gazed at
Donna and saluted her with the flashlight angled smartly
against his tricorne.

"Please, Miss Almond. Say it with me. 'Captain Reade, I
know you sank the *Morris.*' "

She gazed at him. He scowled at her and lowered his arm,
said, "That's why these pages are in the trophy room. All
these things." He gestured left, right. "They're my . . .
scalps." With a smack of the flashlight, he said, "Quickly,
now. No more foreplay. I have invited you to come aboard.
I'm waiting for the pleasure of your reply."

Silently she cleared her throat. She would not freak out;
she would not. "I *am* aboard."

As the flashlight moved across his face, she saw him smile.
Then he burst into gales of laughter.

"You are so foolish, you're such a sodding bitch, you fool,
you loose whore of a fool; you have no idea, none, you don't
know. You haven't figured it out, have you? That things are
not what they seem here? Things on my ship are the way I
want them, and no other way? Haven't you seen, haven't you
heard? Are you so thick, then, that you can't be fully

reached? Are you so damnably thick? Why haven't you been sucked farther down?"

He pawed the air, waving the flashlight. Spittle flew from his mouth. His eye flashed like a green beacon in the light. "It doesn't make sense! You've seen this much. Why don't you see everything?"

She wanted to take a step backward, didn't dare show weakness. She had no liking for killing; there must be a way to stop this, here and now, and no lives lost. But God! How had he done all this? And how had he gotten so fucking crazy? Or rather, how had he acted so normal?

"What are you talking about, Captain Reade?"

"No," he said decisively. "No, I won't hand everything to you on a plate." To her astonishment, he spun slowly in a circle, his hands out at his sides, his head tipped toward the ceiling.

"Charades, my dearest slut bitch Donna Almond. I spend eternity playing charades. What am I now? Am I a spinning boy, or a spinning bottle? The wheel of fortune? Or your lover? The call of loss, the call of love? Which call for you?" He jerked to a stop and shined the light into her eyes. She looked away; the room flashed like a piece of film negative. She almost dropped the gun.

Then the ceiling dropped to within a breath of her height. The stench of human shit and piss and sweat rammed down her nose. The floor squirmed and wiggled. Black fingers pawed her foot.

"God!" she screamed.

"Yes. Now it begins with you. I think it is the boy, after all. My beckoning to you, the thing that finally makes you listen. Makes you see. You can save him here, Donna. You can save him."

"What?" She plowed through the mine field of hands, pulling at her ankles, her calves, down . . .

"How do you know we aren't still there, at the place we first met, oh, my lady of the lake? How do you know I haven't caught you, and now we're beneath the surface, you and I, me beauty, and the shadow of this ship passes above us. And you think, Thank God, thank God, you're saved. But you don't know how wrong you are. You don't know!"

The hands wound around her and pulled, and Donna's finger jerked the trigger. The report was strong; there was no evident effect. The hands still reached, clung. Their nails dug into her ankles, tore.

"I am the Flying Dutchman," Reade said in a sharp, vicious voice. "I am he, and I want you to be my Life–in–Death. Instead of Cha-cha, I choose you. I'll let you see things you can't imagine. I'll let you live, Donna dear. And I'll bring them back for you. I'll bring you the boy. And the man." He smiled slyly.

The hands grew arms, attached to men, shackled to the floor. Black faces, contorted in fear. Arching backs. Naked, filthy bodies. With a shout, she forced one leg free, only to be caught by another.

The captain waved his arms. The hands in the floor, the men, disappeared in a flash. With a grunt, Donna staggered to the left, caught her balance, and ran for the door, knocking bottles left, right. Pushing them away; an armada of them in her way, swinging, pummeling her. She covered her head and hit the wall.

Fumbled for the door. It was shut. Locked. Fuck! She raised her gun and smashed the glass door with it, with her hand. The shards sliced her open, pierced her cat-scratch scabs. She inhaled sharply as she fumbled for the knob. Her ankles streamed blood on the solid floor.

Then he was behind her. She whirled around and smacked against the door frame.

"Ah, you begin to see, now that I've accepted you. In your stateroom, luv. I did it to you. I read you. At last. That's why I made the mittens for you."

"What?"

"Go ahead. Shoot me." With a hoot, he thrust forward his leg, stepped up to it like a boy playing Simon Says, taking a giant step. Another. He stood perhaps three feet from her.

"Shoot me."

Men on the floor, men; gone now, but she'd seen them, seen—

Hallucinations. John and she talked about them. The toxic waste. Or something else.

Steady, Donny. Steady. Don't think. Act.

She cocked her gun. "It's ready to go," she warned him.

"And so am I." Another giant step—he came at it, flying at her, his tricorne flying backward, and she squeezed the trigger and the bullet

shot out and lodged inside his chest and he grunted

and then

he stood there, unhurt, and giggled.

She gaped at him. Her eyes darted toward the gun. He'd messed with it. While she was out, and had foolishly left it tucked in her drawer, he'd disabled it, given her blanks.

He advanced on her, one step at a time. "Seven-league boots," he said. "I have seven-league boots. I stand astride the oceans like a Colossus."

She reached forward, grabbed one of the bottles, and hurtled it at him. He dodged it and it smashed to the floor, shattering.

The wind-sound roared around her, a gale of shrieking blasts permeated with a stench that made her double over. The stink of rotten meat was on her hands, in her mouth. Rotten and pulpy and purple, long-drowned, long

down

down

down, way down deep in the murk, where no amount of dredging could locate the bus, and the kids bobbed around like marionettes, their mouths gaping and fish-eaten, nibbled through their sockets into their brains, where the icy Tahoe water washed away all their memories, their hopes, their nightmares. A Zen peace, a null heaven.

Way

down,

down,

down,

a little boy with reindeer mittens struggled in the water, making no sound; and the shape of a ship made him hold his breath just one more second, and one more, because they would help him, and the bottle, the green bottle drifted down,

waiting.

"Come on. Jump overboard, Donna," he taunted her. "Jump in. The others are." He put his hand to his ear. "Even now, the doctor is framing his RSVP. It is only polite, you know. Only for the sake of form that I've even issued invitations."

He took another step toward her. She shot again. Again. Turned to one of the glass cases—the mermaid—and shot at it, to see what was wrong with her bullets, because blanks just didn't make sense; where did you get blanks in the middle of the goddamn ocean?

The mermaid skull threw back its head and screamed.

And suddenly the captain screamed, too. He made fists in the air, punched; screamed and screamed, "No! NO! Stop!"

Impossibly, he pushed her out of the way, crashed through the door, and fled down the companionway.

Donna prepared to pursue.

And then someone fell out of the shadows behind the door, someone covered with filth and sores, someone screaming, "My God, Reade's dead! *That's* what he meant! He's *always* been dead!"

Donna raised her gun, even though .38 Specials took just five bullets, and said, "Don't move."

28
Shattered

As the captain ran through the ship—through all his ships, war vessels, freighters, submarines, pleasure craft—all of them pleasure craft—his mind looped round and around, like a piece of flotsam on the water, a crate disgorged by the ocean after a particularly wonderful sinking:

Something bad, something wrong . . . an old stanza forgotten. Something forgotten, and I am in danger!

And unaware of the dangers that were charging toward him and lurking close—oh, so close—by, Cha-cha kissed the dirty metal of the hatch and closed his eyes. He was home, sweet home.

All his goodbuddies from the *Morris* were there, his own little crew; oh, yes, 'scuse me for crapping out on you, King Neptune, but you are too much for me, big kahuna, and this *voice* is so much louder than yours. It just led me here, called me and I heard it so good, and this time I knew exactly where I was at.

"Yes," Cha-cha said. "Oh, yes,"

He remembered the gash in the bottom of the door, and he would probably have bent down and called, "Yoo hoo?" to the voice, and seen somebody in there who would answer back, "Chach! Dude!" and unlock the door. Except that now there was a big drum like the ones on the *Morris* in front of the door, like someone was closing it off. Keeping things tidy, like his galley back on the ship.

No prob, he would just move it. He put his hands around the rim and heaved. But the drum wouldn't budge; either it was too heavy or bolted to the floor or something. He squatted and tried again. No luck.

"Bum-nation," he said, wiping his forehead.

COME, said the voice, and his ghostbuddies from Nam whispered, "Hurry, Cha-cha, get her out of there."

So he found him an ax, so easy to do. And when that sucker came down on the top of the drum, it shook his entire body. His bones rubbed together and it hurt, man, but he hefted the ax again and brought it down again. And again.

Then one of his goodbuddies suggested he skip the drum and go for the latch. You broke that open, you maybe could push the hatch inside and wedge past the barrel. Copacetic!

So he switched his attention to the handle. *Wham!* The ax made a scritching sound as the rusty latch started to flake apart like oxidized cheese. Yeah, yeah, cool!

He axed it again. Break, baby, break.

COME COME COME COME COME COME COME

"ASAP, baby," Cha-cha said happily, and his breath condensed like London fog; and he was so excited he ignored the goose bumps on his arms and the fact that his grubby sneakers were freezing to the deck.

Scritch.

Scritch.

Chatter-scrabble.

COME COME COME COME COMECOMECOME COMECOMECOMECOMECOMECOME

and it sounded like *Oooommmm,* like with the Maharishi;

and all the *Morris* ghosts—the little black-and-yellow bumblebee kids, and the carved-up girls, and the dudes without their
ears and gonads—the Khmer dudes, or whatever, the dads
and moms—they had swum aboard and were all grouped
around him
    on the Group W bench, as Arlo Guthrie would say—
    No, no, they grouped around *him* and the *door,* and they
pushed on the bulkhead in a great bumblebee throng, *buzz!*
trying to tear down that wall, baby.
    "Hurry, Cha-cha, hurry!"
    As Cha-cha raised the ax, they helped him lift it, Iwo Jima
style, hands on hands on hands. Cha-cha's eyes filled with
tears. Finally, he could do something to help them.
    What that was, he had no idea, but he knew that was the
case.
    Scritch.
    Chatter-scrabble.
    Scritch.
    Cooooooommmmmmmmmmmmmme.
    Meditatin' on freedom, yessir!
    "Yay, Cha-cha!" They were cheering him on, their hero!
Their war hero! And Cha-cha had a memory of a hammock,
and a mom of his own, and a lullaby, and all these things
were psychedelically, synaptically connected to this room,
and the voice inside it, you betcha.
    A charred little boy put his arms around Cha-cha's legs
and hugged him hard, speaking in Vietnamese as Cha-cha
smacked and whacked that danged old latch. The metal door
was gashed and scratched.
    Scritch.
    Chatter-scrabble.
    Chatter-scrabble. And a low gong noise, as something on
the other side of the hatch hit the drum, real **hard**.
    "Almost there!" Cha-cha announced to his goodbuddies.
    For a flash he remembered about Officer Donna, leaving
her up there with the big dude, whoops.
    And the sound of rushing water came up behind him like a
shark.

                              *   *   *

"C'mon, goddamnit, calm down," Donna growled at the blithering sack of bones and stink, and reflected that if she lowered her weapon it might just do that.

"He's dead, don't you see, dead." The figure staggered forward. Dear God, it was a young man, very young. Handsome, once, by the shape of the features beneath the dried blood and the feces.

"What'd they do to you?" Donna asked in a soft voice. "What's happened to you?"

Staggering, he held one hand up as if to ask her forbearance; then he said, "The captain is some kind of sorcerer." He laughed hollowly. "I know how that sounds. He makes you . . . he makes you see things. This ship . . ." He waved his hand. "It's not here. The people. They're dead."

"And you, are you dead?" Great. She was standing here with a nutcase while Cha-cha was running around loose, and the captain

—she had shot him, hadn't she? The bullets had not missed—

—was probably offing the passengers, and—

Nearer, my God, to Thee.

"How'd you do that?" she demanded sharply. With a quick motion, she pushed her hair from her eyes. Christ, she was sweating like a pig.

"You heard it, didn't you?" the man asked. His eyes shone through the crusty overlayer like beacons. "You heard the singing!"

Fresh fear prickled her scalp. The walls went up around not only her heart but every other organ, including her dinosaur brain and the one Glenn called her coptosaurus cerebullshit.

"You saw the slaves. This section was a slave ship." He began to whoop with fear, sucked on the knuckle of his left hand to stop himself. At the sight, Donna almost barfed right then and there.

"Over there was a ferry. This isn't a museum. It's his trophy room. All those ships . . ." He threw back his head and wailed. "My ship!"

Donna swallowed. Her gun wavered and she steadied it,

making a tripod of herself, legs apart, arms forward, the way they did on cop shows. *He* didn't know how many bullets a .38 Special took.

"C'mon, c'mon, pull yourself together. Talk to me," Donna urged. "C'mon, man. What's your name?"

"He made them sink! He made them see things. Your friends—" He fell backward against the wall and slid to the floor, grabbing his head and keening like an animal.

When he didn't resume speaking, she said, "What about my friends?"

"We've got to get away." He looked at her with mad eyes. "They're mutinying. They're going to take the ship away and then who knows what will happen? Maybe he's the only thing that's keeping it together! It flickers! I've seen it flicker."

"What? Who's mutinying?"

"You saw it flicker!" He reached his hands up pleadingly. "You did!"

Men in the floor, the stench, the stench . . .

She shook her head. Just the facts, ma'am. The facts, not the hallucinations—

—the moving bottles, the music, the men in the floor, the bullets that hadn't killed him.

"What's been happening to the passengers?"

"He makes them come aboard." He wove back and forth, back and forth like a snake. For an instant she thought he was going to spring at her. Instead, he hung his head and mumbled something.

"What?" she practically shouted at him.

"They told me to find you! They said you'd save us! Because you're the one!"

She's the one. Ice water in her brains; ice, and fear, and a knowing—

"What one?"

"The one he can't penetrate," said a voice behind her. Then a footfall behind her. A thunder of them. Right behind her. Inches behind her. She jerked her head over her shoulder and saw nothing.

Ice-water fear; her heart slogging in that awful, slow-motion helplessness where you see not your life, but the end of it. Donna had faced her own death twice, that of others, many times. You shook it, shook that terror and moved on. You took a breath, hitched up your pants—

She couldn't blink. She couldn't breathe. There was nothing behind her.

Nothing.

"Tell her!" the man shrieked.

Then a shadow cast a net high and wide over her. The chill thudded through her heart, spread like a glacier to her groin, her lips, her forehead. Cold, very cold; she shivered hard. Gooseflesh rose on her arms; the hairs stood on end. This was more than the creeps. This was *knowing* something was coming, or happening, or beginning.

There was something in the room with them.

"Wha—wha—" she whispered. Her throat was so tight she couldn't speak. Her hands gripped the revolver until her knuckles turned white.

"Now you see, don't you?" the man demanded, advancing into the room. "You see the ghosts and the pieces he collected! He made them! He caused them!"

"I don't see a fucking thing!" she shouted, looking left, right. Her arms shook as if she were being electrocuted.

"The one he *almost* couldn't penetrate," the phantom voice said again; and a cold, thick fog—

—the sick fog of the *Morris,* of the sea, the heavy blankets, formed about half a foot in front of her, and unfurled toward her, the mist falling in upon itself, heavy, sodden, thicker, thicker still, taking form; walking vapors, walking

men, and women. With dead faces and shiny, dead eyes, in costumes: Victorian sailors, Japanese World War II soldiers, women in satin art deco evening gowns and men in tuxedos. A walking hologram of sodden zombies; and at their head, Lorentz Creutz.

"Late of the *Kronen,* which sank in 1676," he said to her.

"Yeah, right." She leveled the gun at him, at the mob. Not what it looked like, no way, Jose. Okay, José. It's okay, José. Jumpin' Jesus, José. "And you sound real Swedish, pal."

"No, I don't," Creutz said, almost in a whisper. "I should,

and I don't. I don't even think in Swedish." He took a breath. "If I really think at all."

His face was tinged with gray and for a moment, just a moment he was—

—no he wasn't, bullshit, he wasn't—

"I cannot endure this any longer. If oblivion is the consequence, I . . ." He gestured to the people behind him. "If there is something more. If perhaps, a god . . ." He lifted his chin. "I must ask you to believe that the captain has somehow enslaved our souls. He sank our ships through trickery, and captured us."

"He *mutilated* our souls," said a tall black man. "He made us eat, drink . . ." The man turned away. He looked hard at Curry. "We ate. We were starving. But dead men don't starve!"

She swallowed. Didn't understand any of it, and believed less.

Creutz held out his hand. If he touched her, she'd shit. "We need your help. Reade must be stopped."

Donna's other reeking buddy stepped forward. "Reade's not alive! She shot him! Over and over! He's one of you!"

"What?" The crowd drew back as one, looked at each other, began to roar.

"Quiet!" Creutz commanded, facing them. "We must hurry! We must plan!" He turned to Donna. "Is that true? That you shot him and he didn't die?"

Maybe I'll pass out now, Donna thought. Or maybe just go stark raving mad.

"All you assholes stop talking and start explaining," she said, crossing her arms. "Nobody's going anywhere until I get some answers."

Creutz opened his mouth, closed it. Looked at Curry. "We must try to make sense of this."

Curry nodded.

Donna said, "Good luck."

The chandeliers.

John looked up with glazed eyes. The same as in the foyer. The ones the captain picked out personally. They were the same. The room was familiar; he had seen pictures of the vast spaces, the chairs and tables . . .

But he couldn't be on the *Titanic*.

"But you are," Dr. Hare assured him. "See their clothes? See the name above the door?"

John blinked. He could, and couldn't see, the immense gilded room, the jewels, the mirrors. The grand carved stairway he'd seen on TV when that man, Ballard, found the *Titanic*. The photographs they'd shown. Yes.

No.

He could, and couldn't hear, a band playing *Nearer, my God, to Thee.*

"It's Miss Almond's favorite," the doctor said.

"Donna?" She seemed a distant dream. Everything but this room existed in another time, another space, when he had had the energy to affect it. Now he was along for the ride. An onlooker, a passenger. A voyeur, a voyager.

The doctor folded his arms over his chest. "She'll be along."

John saw, and didn't see, Phil and Elise dancing. Phil wore a tuxedo, and Elise a cream satin gown and a net over her hair. Elise outshone the candles and the swaying chandeliers with her radiant happiness. They turned and waved, beckoned.

Come aboard, John. It's all right. It's wonderful. Come and join the party.

And he saw, and didn't see, Ruth Hamilton in the arms of a silver-haired man. Her husband. John knew it without being told. At last, at last; he felt her joy in waves as her husband leaned her back in a dip. She lifted her hands over her head, let them fall back, as her husband held her. Arched her neck, and he kissed it. She wore large white flowers in her hair, and she was dressed in a soft blue evening gown. Her husband wore a tux, like Phil. The glamorous years, and they were all together, forever.

Come aboard. They, too, waved. Dazed, John waved back.

"You see? Everyone is happy." Hare made an expansive gesture. "All these people. They're all aboard. Come, John, come aboard."

"I . . ." He looked around. Everywhere his gaze fell, the people, chairs, and chandeliers blurred and smeared, then snapped into focus. He had to sit down. He was so confused. So very confused.

So tired.

"My son. My baby," he managed as he staggered.

"Don't have the stabilizers yet," Hare said, chuckling. "Invented later."

"Matt."

"On his way."

Donna stared slackjawed. Creutz had been trying to explain it to her so reasonably, as if of course it all made sense. As if you came across the Flying Dutchman every day.

"He came from the 1790s, or so he says."

"Aye," said a man dressed in rags, with a long full beard of gray. "1797. I were on his ship, the *Royal Grace*. We set him adrift. He were a murderous, evil man. He killed the cabin boy, Nathaniel, to do his witchery! So we cast him off, with no food nor drink; and we thought the sea would take 'im . . ." He drifted off, looked at his feet. "The sin be on our heads, that he lived."

"But Curry claims he *didn't* live," Creutz said. "And I can't account for my presence aboard this damnable ship, for I went down in 1676. Either he's lying, or . . ." Creutz glowered. "He isn't bound by time."

"Listen," Donna cut in. "If he was alive in 1797, he couldn't possibly be alive now." She thought about what she was saying—what they'd been saying—Curry some kind of cannibalism pimp, these guys some kind of combination of hallucinations and memories?—and shook her head violently. "Fuck it. You're here and I need help." She thought about that, too. "I'll say," she muttered. "Like, a thousand sessions with the force shrink."

She ran her hand through her hair. "Okay. There's this old guy, Cha-cha? I think he's been murdering the passengers. I—"

"Damn, woman! Don't you understand what we're telling you?" Creutz thundered, then exhaled. He scratched his temple, let his arm drop. "Ah, what does it matter? However we help one another, perhaps we can do something, eh?"

"C'mon, then," Donna said. "We'll straighten this out later. We'll talk about this later."

Creutz held a hand toward her. "We may not make it," he said.

"Yeah, well." She snapped her head at Curry. "Can you walk?"

"I'll look for a means of escape," he ventured.

"You'll come with us," she retorted, and led the way.

The hatch dangled by some threads, man. You could practically blow on it and it would come off.

COMECOMECOMECOMECOMECOME

Cha-cha's buddies were laughing and dancing. Yeah, okay, and saying he was the captain! Saying he should lead them and they would go do stuff and—

sink?

Suddenly the drum rocked forward and rolled sideways.

Chatter-scrabble.

A quick stab sliced Cha-cha's ankle. "Ow!" he cried.

YESYESYESYESYESYESYESYES

"Where's Matt?" John repeated, slumped in a chair in the strange ballroom. So tired.

"I told you. He's on his way," Hare replied.

But . . ." John cupped his forehead. He was going to fall forward,

down

down

down,

and land deep, beneath the surface. He was going to jump, just like—

—Ruth

Elise

Phil

but not like

Kevin or

Ramón.

Then the doctor shouted once, very loud. Everyone in the room froze, echoed his shout.

With a crack, the room blackened, brightened, flashed in a strobe *chop-chop-chop-chu-chu-chu*. A wind rose up, and the rumbling of great machines, and the shrieking of people as if from far away.

"Man the lifeboats!" someone shouted.

The room popped like a burning photograph, *chop-chop-chop*. Around John, the passengers jerked, smeared, ran, floated.

"Captain Reade!" Hare screamed. His face slid off his skull like a piece of rotten fruit thrown against a window. John backed away in horror. Hare's eyes popped, and the vitreous liquid ran down his cheekbones. As he raised his hands, the meat rotted, slid off. The bones cracked apart and thudded on top of the pulp.

John stumbled backward, hitting a chair. It crumbled like a fungus.

A chandelier blew apart, hung at odd angles, became coated with cobwebs, no, with seaweed. The mirrors cracked, tarnished.

Chop-chop-chop-chu-chu-chu

"Reade!" someone shrieked. "Reade!"

The people ran; most fell to nothing, their silks and satins and small, lacy shoes disintegrating.

"Mutiny! Mutiny!" came a cry from the entrance to the room. John turned.

Donna dashed in with a throng of men behind her. They shouted, raising cutlasses and rifles and harpoons and hooked hands. Donna's gun looked like a toy.

"Mutiny! At last, shipmates!" someone called.

"Yes!" The remaining passengers swarmed toward a man beside Donna—Jesus, one of the ship's officers, young, with a handlebar mustache, pushing John roughly out of the way.

"I'm taking over the ship!"

"Mutiny!" a woman cried, standing on a chair. "Mutiny!" Then, slowly, she turned in a circle and began to melt like a candle.

John called, "God!" and held out his hands. "God!"

His ulcer tore at him and he doubled over as the passengers dashed around him. The room shook once, and then it reared up at a forty-five-degree angle, and there was nothing to do with a ballroom or chandeliers or passengers. John was in the deep-freeze room and freezers rushed at him as he slid along the floor with them. Electric cords popped and slithered like snakes in the avalanche of metal and freon. Wind whipped around them, sharp and chill and—

a flood of water poured over them, crashing against the freezers like breakers and pummeling John. It picked him up and carried him away. A freezer slammed past him, hit the wall, and burst open. His son fell out.

John blinked as he shouted, "Matt, Matt!" and the freezers became

icebergs,

became freezers,

became chair legs, tabletops, orange crates, barrels labeled "DANGER. CORROSIVE."

As he darted toward his unconscious son he was surrounded by flotsam and jetsam: headboards, shackles, a net, a jar. A bottle. A light, that moved and beamed.

Matt's fist, clenched as it sank—

His dream. John took a breath and dove into the water. He dodged shoes, gray shapes, black kelp, rotted lace. A flashlight, on, casting through the water. A gray fish swam over the light; and something that slithered away.

And Matt!

He grabbed his sinking boy around the waist and yanked him to the surface. Matt sputtered and choked, cried, "Daddy! Daddy!"

"Baby." His kissed Matt's face, every inch of it, and held him. His child, his child, thank the dear Lord.

"Daddy, the boat's sinking!"

Yes. Yes. John's mind raced. What to do? Find a boat. Something that would stay afloat. Paddles. Food and water and—

No, no. The boat first.

"Grab hold of my neck, baby," he told Matt, sliding him

around onto his back. "Can you do that for me? Not too tight," he cautioned as Matt nearly cut off his air.

He started swimming toward the up end of the room, reached it, and used a locker wedged against an underwater object to drag them out of the water. Used the mirror that had slid against the locker to give them a way to climb up the slope. A barrel rolled onto the mirror, and he used that to take another step. As more things piled against the locker, he was able to walk through them and reach the edge of the room.

He snaked his hand around the open door.

"Put both your hands around my wrist," he said to Matt.

After the boy had done so, he pulled him along and both of them made it out of the refrigerator room and into the kitchen.

Only it wasn't the kitchen anymore.

The walls were a patchwork: one was a towering slab of corroded metal, another, of rotted wood, jutted into it at an angle; another was round and curved and covered with shreds of red-flocked wallpaper.

"It's like a fun house," Matt said in a strong voice, and John filled with pride at his son's courage.

"Yes," he said. "Like a fun house."

They staggered together, bumping into piles of cracked dishes, an overturned bathtub. A mash of tables had gathered to their right, skittered in a jumble toward the doorway.

The floor was dry, but parts of it were missing, and it was the same crazy quilt as the walls—wood here, something like cork farther on, linoleum, metal.

"Daddy," Matt croaked. "I—"

And then it was the kitchen again.

And half of it was underwater.

On the other side, Donna and a man who looked like he had been horribly burned waved at them. John's panicked mind registered a flash of shame: in his terror for Matt, he'd completely forgotten about her.

"Here!" Donna shouted, at the same time the man kept shrieking, "It flickered! It flickered! They're gone!"

Then Donna jumped into the water and started swimming

toward them. He roused himself and gathered Matt in his arms.

The captain froze at the top of the ladderway that led to the hold where . . . where . . . she . . .
. . . where he had found Cha-cha before, crooning to . . .
. . . to *nothing*.

Then everything flashed into blackness. Around him, the night whipped and slashed. Rain thundered down on him with sharp needle mouths. The *Pandora*! Where was she?

He pounded his fists together. "I am. I am the I am that I am. The sea is my mistress. The sea, mine."

COME

And he heard it. He *heard* it. The call, the cry, the promise. The threat.

And he remembered the forgotten stanza of the siren song:

The yacht swam away from the Royal Grace, *and the man inside the canvas raved. Thomas Reade called on Satan, his Dark Master, and he begged Diana, goddess of the moon, and every other deity of his infernal studies, to save him.*

The storm abated, but he was sick inside the bag, fevered and bilious and mad with thirst; and it took hours to work his way out of it. The bird, yes, the bird came.

Nathaniel's head was there, yes.

He found the bottle in the boat and blest the ocean and swallowed the contents; and thought that if he ever met the generous seaman who slipped it aboard, he would deal with him kindly. Yes! That was what he had thought.

And the head of his darling, yes. They were so afrighted, they threw the head in. And though it was old by then, and stinking, he ate of his beloved; he ate everything; coconut crack! the brains, still moist.

But the night descended on him, and with the blackness came new thirst. And he prayed again, and again, and gnawed the skull, picked clean now, and dry.

The day came, and with the light, the thirst.

And he lay in the yacht and cursed all men and all gods.

And the evening and the morning were the second day.

On the sixth day, he tore a piece of the canvas, bit by bit, all day; his fingers bleeding, his teeth ripped out, and he wrote in his own blood for help. He threw the bottle over the side and fell back, marveling that he wasn't yet dead.

And on the seventh day, the reply, the answer, in the green glass; it rose, it rose, it came to him, singing, with fish, and it spewed water into him, and it promised, it promised—

And he promised.

They became One.

"No," he whimpered now. No, as everything flooded back in a deluge of terror, because he had betrayed her. He had promised.

And he had lied.

And *she* was looking for someone else to keep his pact.

Fog, slick and slithery; in it, a hand that snaked through the hold, the door and the nails were a glittery green, kinda cool. And it fanned its fingers to touch him again; and it said HUNGRY, but what Cha-cha heard was:

The steady sway of the hammock, and the scent of summer; and his mother calling, "Charlie? Would you like some lemonade?"

Or maybe he heard that pretty little gal back in Nam, who called herself Betty, and she had those crazy kung-fu fightin' nails and she loved him. Maybe they'd get married, yeah, and take all her little cousins and brothers and her teeny-weeny mom and dad to the States, yeah.

And then the napalm . . .

He leaned against the door with his eyes closed. Something made scratching noises near his feet, which were numb; why were they numb? And he was so cold, even though it was summer—

No, it wasn't! He was on the *Pandora*, with his goodbuddies. He looked down. Oh, hey, that wasn't a hand at all, it was a shimmering thing, no, a beak, no, a tentacle, no, it was a hand, a lady's hand, and it was supercalifragilistically beautiful.

And whoops! the nails sliced him as they caressed his foot.

Bad bummer, man, 'cuz it *hurt!* And the blood froze as it seeped through his sneaker; pop! like snot on a subzero continent, yeah; but it *hurt.*

Okay, though, 'cuz it was so good. Hey, howdy, somethin' behind Door Number One, just for him

COMECOME

HUNGRY

And whatever that groove-thang was, it started pushing on the other side of the cold, cold door.

"Dang," he breathed. "You see that, goodbuddies?"

No one answered.

Cha-cha was alone.

The hand poked from under the door.

And someone started singing:

> *"Bye, baby bunting,*
> *Daddy's gone a-hunting,*
> *Going to find a rabbit skin*
> *to wrap his baby bunting in."*

Cha-cha's eyes filled with tears. "Mom," he murmured, kissing the door. His lips stuck to the frozen metal.

But he sang along anyway.

Matt's head thumped against his father's shoulder as his dad, Donna, and Curry, the monster-man, ran down a corridor that was not a corridor on the *Pandora,* but on some other ship, one that had posters on the walls with army guys in helmets and life jackets, and guys saluting a flag; and one of a ship slipping under the waves and underneath, the words "LOOSE LIPS SINK SHIPS."

Fog rolled in, dry-ice tons of it, a heavy, sodden net unfurling as his dad raced into it. Matt cried out and threw his arms around his father's neck, and when he looked back, he saw the gray raging water of the ocean rushing toward them at a thunderous pace. Within seconds, it washed around his dad's thighs, splashing whitewater into the foggy air. A piece of seaweed whipped around his leg—no, it was an eel!—and shapes spun and danced beneath the surface of the rising waters.

Matt raised his hand and pounded on his father's shoulders, crying "Daddy!" but his father didn't answer him, just kept running and praying and running on. Donna was saying something to him and he was nodding, and the other guy made a funny noise in his throat and Donna smacked him one but good.

The water grew choppy as it built and roared and churned shapes to the surface: the bisque head of a doll, china plates, a piece of net, a bathing cap, a chair leg.

A figurehead, hands clasped over her naked tee-tee's, with brown eyes and flowing dark hair; and in her hands she held one of Dane's mittens. She bobbed past, late, late for an important date; it was the lady he'd seen, the statue lady!

Matt screamed, and screamed, and screamed, but his father plunged on, not hearing him.

Farther on, another set of posters was plastered on the walls, with funny stick writing all over them, and all the men had cat-shaped eyes. They were faded and old, half rotted away; there was a hole in the wall and Matt saw not another part of the ship, but the sky, and it was pitch-dark out, and things were exploding in the air, bombs or something, and airplanes droned and whirred—

—and something shot downward, and the hallways shook. Chunks of the ceiling rained down on them. Matt covered his head and something struck his fingers, cutting into them. He cried out and jerked up.

But the adults kept going, a powdery coating like snow covering their heads and shoulders. The water rushed around their thighs; it lapped up and drenched Matt's bottom.

"Daddy!"

Farther on, wooden signs hung on the walls: "All Steerage Passengers Must Report to Assistant Purser," and Matty's mind reeled, because the ocean was swallowing up the ship, and airplanes were bombing it, and the wall was a patchwork of green paint and gray metal and dark wood, and some of it was streaked with slimy stuff, and some of it was streaked with brown splotches. He didn't know what the hell was going on but steerage had to do with cows and he thought of the freezers and moaned.

They reached the deck of an old sailing ship. It was the playroom Matt had seen on the way to dinner.

But no, it was a ship, a real ship, or part of one. It jutted topsy-turvy, all smashed up, and a mast to Matt's right had cracked in half, and the other end had crashed through the floor, leaving a huge hole less than an inch from Matt's dad's right foot.

And beside the other foot, there was a pile of bloated, purple bodies that stretched to the other side of the deck, maybe ten feet away, and one of them was—

—Matt's mouth dropped open and he threw up.

One of them was a boy with no face. Two eyes peered from an oval that pulsed red gore, but when he smiled, his teeth sparkled and glittered, clean and pearly; and then a crab crawled out of his mouth and dropped into the goo, and flailed in it, its claws and body sinking, sinking into gut quicksand.

The boy sat up and reached a hand toward Matt. He wore old-timey clothes, all rotten and torn: a striped shirt and a pair of black pants that stopped just below his knees.

"Climb, baby. Climb up the mast," his father said. Matt stared at him, at the boy. His father didn't see the boy!

"Daddy . . ."

"The water's coming. We've got to go up."

"But the boy! The boy!" he shrieked.

"C'mon, Matty," Donna said, pulling him out of his father's arms. Matt screamed and clung to his father. Donna pried him off, one piece of him at a time, and the monster-man helped.

Matt reared away from them as the boy stood up.

"Climb, Matt!" his dad pleaded as Donna pushed him against the mast. "The boat is sinking!"

"Daddy, he's coming!" He jabbed wildly at the air. They all looked, but Matt could tell they didn't see him standing there, blood running down his face.

"No! No!"

"Get up there, goddamn you!" Donna slapped Matt's face and pushed on his butt. "Please, baby. Please."

Grinning, the boy slogged toward them, right through the gooey bodies, guts squishing under his bare feet. He was maybe six feet away. Sobbing, Matt shinnied up the mast. It was old and splintery. The wood tore at his hands and pants knees.

"Go up, Donna," his dad said, but she shook her head and moved away.

"I'm going to find the captain. Curry, come with me."

They argued while Matt watched the boy come closer, closer. Matt gave a shout and began to climb. His dad came after him, boosting him with his hand as Matt scrabbled up the mast for all he was worth.

They went high, very high. Ignoring Donna and Curry, who still must not have seen him, the faceless boy put his hands on the mast.

"Oh, no!" Matt shouted. He stopped, frozen.

"Please, sweetheart, please, Mattman." Distantly, his father's voice, from another world. Matt's heart was the loudest thing he had ever heard. "You can do it. Think about James Bond."

The monster-boy started to climb. Matt's heart roared in his ears. If he didn't move, the boy would get his father! Even now, he could see his fingers, just bone, with pointy ends and blood—

Matt scrabbled upward.

"Good boy. That's my Mattman."

Matt tried to go faster. The boy's hands were grabbing for his dad's feet. Faster, and faster, and—

With a cry, he lost his grip and fell
down
down
down, into the rushing water. He heard his father's wail as his head went under.

There was a second splash, and the boy's worm-eaten face cannonballed down on him, and his hands came around his throat. Matt tried to push him away, but he kept coming, kept pushing Matt down, and Matty thought he heard him say, *This is how it feels to drown, Matt. It's not so bad, is it? Just let it happen. Let it go. It's better than dying of cancer. Believe me. Far better. We're doing you a favor.*

29
Drowning

This couldn't be happening, Donna thought distractedly as they pulled Matt from the water and raced to higher ground: the top of a stack of crates marked "SPECIMENS."

"I dreamed this," John husked as they tried to force the water out of Matt's body.

And lived it? Donna tingled with a horrid déjà vu. Not Matt, too. Not another little drowned kid. Not here.

She fell to her knees beside John. His face was white. "There's no pulse."

As they looked at each other, she began to shake. She clenched her muscles tight to make herself stop. It didn't work. Not Matt. Please, God, not again, and not Matt.

"You compress," she said steadily. "I'll breathe."

"No, he has cancer . . ." John blurted.

"Compress," she said evenly, waiting.

Drown, how could he drown? John pushed his bony chest five times, nodded to Donna. She listened for his breath, breathed into him. His lips were cold and soft. She thought of other small lips. The mittens. The failure.

The death.

"Compress," she said. John began to pump.

Oh, God, oh, God, the water was sloshing over the tops of the crates as the level rose. Curry, useless Curry, screamed and moved toward the center. Wouldn't do any good, Donna thought. Reade wanted them, he had them . . . unless they could get him first. Son of a bitch. What the hell was he? Son of a bitch, she shot him and he didn't die. Her cop brain raced ahead to possible scenarios, showdowns, outcomes. Curry was hopping on one foot, the other, screaming how they mustn't drown on board, any of them, or *he* would have them.

Mutilate their souls. Jesus, what a load of crap.

But the bullets. The bottles. The floor.

The air changed, violently. A swirl of fog, the poof! of magic smoke from a lamp . . . and then her world cracked open.

Her little floater crouched at Matt's feet. Same Windbreaker, same soft brown hair. Those jug ears. Those eyes. She hadn't seen his eyes until she'd checked his pupils.

She froze and stared at the ghost. John's glance ticked at her. *I'm so sorry, ma'am,* she'd said to his mother. *I'm . . .* and the lady had fainted, dead away, without a word.

You okay, Osmond? Listen to this, what do you call a dead floater? Bob.

What kinda wood floats?

Natalie Wood.

You lose some, Officer. Now and then, you lose some.

"Breathe," John ordered her sharply. Automatically she complied.

Gonna lose him, the floater said, and didn't say. *Lost him already.*

"John," she whispered.

"Breathe!"

She obeyed. The floater watched with a smile on his face. He held up his hands to show her his reindeer mittens.

You lost me. You could've had me if you hadn't let your boy-

friend hurt me. You were too wimpy to stop him in time. If you weren't such a whore, I'd be alive today.

"No." She breathed for Matt without John's prompting. He couldn't be gone, could he? Not little Matty. Not this one, too.

You're a whore. You know you are. Going after another woman's husband. You know your Desire. You want to be a slut.

She breathed for Matt.

"We're doing good," John said, panting. "We're fine here."

It's your fault, the boy said. *You killed me, and you don't even remember my name.*

"Dane," she murmured. And she'd tried, goddamn it, she'd tried; and she knew that. She knew she did her best. She'd forgiven herself. She had.

She breathed into Matt.

No. It was your remorse pulled you to us, to him. A Desire for relief. You want to pay for losing me.

Wrong. She had wanted to save the boy; and she wanted to save these guys, too. And that was her strongest desire: to protect and to serve. To save. Social worker with a gun.

Breathe, baby. Breathe, sweet baby.

"A pulse!" John cried.

Water spewed out of Matt's throat. John flipped him on his side again and patted his back. The boy vomited, coughed, choked. John held him and rocked him.

Dane faded away without another word, another gesture.

Shaking, Donna got to her feet.

"Now we've got to get a boat," Curry said. "We've got to get out of here."

Donna licked her lips. "You three go ahead." With an unsteady hand she tousled Matt's wet hair. "Can you help your daddy, hon? Can you move okay?"

The water sloshed over the crates, and then everything heeled backward, slamming them against the wall. Matt screamed and fell hard on Donna. His father followed after, and all the breath was knocked out of her.

"We've got to get out of here!" Curry cried.

"It's going down." Donna pointed to a metal ladder that led up to the next deck. It rose from the waterline at a thirty-degree angle. "Get a boat, get off the ship, wait a while for me and the others. If we don't come, get away. The suction . . ." Her heart skipped a beat. Christ, ghosts or no ghosts, she didn't want to die on the *Pandora*.

"Come with us," John urged. He took her hand.

She shook her head. "I've got to find the others. And stop him. If any of it's true . . ." She laughed bitterly. "Christ, just go. I don't know what the hell I'm talking about. But the damn boat is really sinking, and I've got to get the others."

A low, slow moan shuddered through the room, metal against metal. Matt's eyes widened. "Get him out of here," Donna said fiercely.

John gazed at her as Matt climbed around his waist. Kissing the top of his son's head, he murmured, "You won't be able to do anything."

"Yes, I will. I will." To Curry, she said, "You help them. You know where things are. You know what's . . . real. Get them off here."

Curry nodded. He dropped his gaze. "I'm so ashamed. I—"

"Save it," she said, took a breath, and jumped—

—don't let her hit anything big and heavy!—

off the crates.

Keening, the captain started down the ladderway. *He must stop, because I am come to do my penance! I am hurrying to your side, oh, Stella Maris! Forgive me, forgive, and await your slave!*

Cha-cha stood in the doorway, totally overwhelmed as the water rushed back out of the room and flooded around his waist. It sluiced around him like a buffalo stampede and ran off.

COMECOMECOMECOME

He took a step closer. The room was frigid and filled with cold mist. When he breathed, he sent out a stream of breath-smoke that curled into the air. Water ran from the top of the doorway, melting ice, and blankets of fog unrolled as he stepped closer.

COMECOMECOMECOMECOME
He recoiled as the fog billowed left, right, making a path
for him.
COMECOMECOMECOME
The king! No, something glistening. His mom! No, something sharp and shiny, like a kaleidoscope. Something with
tentacles! An octopus! No, something with a little Nessie
head, sea serpent! A mask, all white. A spider face. A skull.
No.
No.
Things that were, and weren't. In the center of the changes
and the movin' and groovin', like in a lap, an old, wooden
boat teetered as the things—the colors! the mists—drooped
over it and seeped along the boat's gunwales. A boat encased
in ice, and a guy sitting upright inside it?
Cha-cha cocked his head. That couldn't be—
A scream of terror behind him. Cha-cha jumped in the air
and turned, ax at the ready.
That couldn't be the King Neptune in the boat, man, because here was His Majesty, standing right in front of him.
But the Big Guy was *freaked.* Cha-cha doubted he had ever
seen a look like that anywhere but on the faces of the sailors
on the old *Morris,* when she was the *Abernathy,* and all her
ammo did its thing to all the Vietnamese who crackled and
grizzled on the delta shore.
His Oceanic Majesty staggered left, right, fell to his knees,
screaming all the time. Over and over.
Cha-cha looked back at the boat. The block of ice obscured his vision, but that thing in the boat was a body,
mostly bone but with some meat still clinging to the ivory;
and lots of a face, and that face was King Neptune's.
Except for where *his* king wore an eye patch, the boat king
had a green bottle stuck in the eye socket, and a—a what?
A pincer,
a ripple of shadow,
a pretty hand with green nails
was, like, pushed through it, or had grown through it, or he
didn't know what. And it wiggled at Cha-cha from a thatch of
dried, bleached hair that sat on top of king's—of this dude's

—head, like the stuffed mom in *Psycho*. He blinked, wondering how anything could move in there. Must not be frozen all the way, he thought; and realized—even he!—that that was the least of the things he was looking at that should totally wig him out.

Then the ice made a wrenching sound—*Titanic* hits the iceberg, they blow up half of Nam!—and slid in big, honkin' chunks to the floor.

"Shee-it," Cha-cha whispered. Then the head made a popping sound—a single gunshot—and it cracked open like a coconut husk. And the thinking stuff was in there, man, fresh and clean and knobby, slick and set and thumpin'. Pieces of the wiggly pincer-shadow-green-nailed-hand were buried down deep in it, like fingers smushed into a piece of watermelon; and everything was . . . pumping, living,

doing.

And King Neptune grabbed his own head and threw it around and around in a circle, Jane Fonda Workout on speed, like he was trying to whip it off his neck and slam-dunk it—

—and Cha-cha stood there, completely befuddled, more than a little amazed; and all of a sudden, *clang-clang-thump, thump!* somebody else joined the party.

Officer D. raced down the stairs.

"Freeze!" she shouted.

He raised his hands, even though hers were empty.

Donna clambered over the railing of the catwalk, ran through the droppings and litter on the deck beside it. She saw the captain, and Cha-cha, and—

My dream of life, all over

Billie Holiday's voice; Donna saw the singing; and feelings, saw them: a black column of pain and tears; something that reached for her, stretched with such pleading. So blue, so lonely; ice-blue, so lonely. A purple-black stream of unbelievable desolation: Oh, baby, baby, I am hurtin', I am friendless, no one to call my own. I am so

down

down

down,
I'm as low as you can go. I hurt so bad I cannot breathe.

Singing, drawing her in; Donna's cheeks were wet with tears and she sang back; yeah, she sang it, she knew it:

Alone, in the ocean depths.

Alone, a hundred thousand fathoms beneath the sea.

Alone, in the cold and the dark, the last, the very last of the race, no hope, no future.

And a man, and a promise. And the risk, and the betrayal.

Alone, alone, all, all alone,
no one to call my mate, my own.

And I am callin' you, oh, please, I'm so awful lonely;

I am so blue,

I am so empty.

I am so hungry,

so hungry,

so HUNGRY

The bruises and colors and the hurt and the endless pain reefed over her; and Donna raised her hand, yes; she understood; yes . . .

Without warning, Reade sprang at her and pushed her over.

"Don't you touch her!" he shrieked. "Don't you dare!" He hit Donna in the face, fire and breakbone, God; he pummeled her, slamming his fists into her. He screamed and shrieked and hit her, over and over; she was all bruises and loose teeth; she was losing consciousness, going black.

Something coming, slithering along the deck like eels, like Medusa serpents—

in the garden—

the snake is a friend—

Donna's head snapped sideways. And she saw Cha-cha waving an ax, and beyond that, she saw fog and mist, and saw that she'd almost walked right into it; she'd fallen beside the hatch. She focused hard—

In the room, chunks of ice, and a boat stuck in them, and inside the boat was, was, a body, and it was, it—

Connections went off, lightning fast, because necessity is the mother of understanding. *That* was Captain Reade, the castaway he'd told about in the museum; yes, *that* was him. That bottle in his eye, that was the bottle he loved so much. The ghosts were right; he made it all up, and somehow this . . . *thing* . . . made it all happen. You make me think I'm still alive, I'll give you something, too.

I'll be your mate. I'll be your friend. I'll make you not lonely.

And she, Donna, had driven him berserk because she never saw—never saw and never heard—

The dreams of the Lorelei.

"Not real." She gaped at the shape that was hitting her. "Cap'n, you're not real either, asshole." One of her teeth spit out with her words.

He raised his hands above his head. "I am! I survived! I was in the lifeboat and they set me adrift! But I opened my bottle, and I prayed to the sea, and she made me the Master of a thousand ships! And I have sailed through time and space, and like a siren, I've made their drowned souls serve me."

A prism of glass sparkled toward her; and then it was, and wasn't, a tentacle. She saw, and didn't see, the end of it, a round mouth filled with teeth, hundreds of them like spines, drooling red that spilled onto the metal deck with a *hisssssss* and ate holes in the thick plate. And then it was a lily-white hand, and then a black one. They called Billie Holiday the Black Lorelei, didn't they? And then it was prisms and sparkling crystals that blinked and wobbled, danced closer, closer. Shadows, rippling. Depths.

"You're nothing," she said to Reade. "That's you, and that thing is using what's left. You're a dead man's dream. That's all you ever were."

The captain's fists arced down. "No! I am hurting you! Ghosts cannot hurt the living!"

"So say you," Donna rasped. "But looks like you were wrong about that, baby. Or did you just invent it, and believe it?"

"No!" And he came down on her with everything he had, centuries of rage and fury.

Cha-cha shouted, "Okay! Okay! I'm doing it!" as if he

were talking to someone. He darted into her range and brought up the ax.

"Stop messing with her!" he shouted, and swung it across the head of the corpse in the boat.

It exploded like a melon; the bottle shattered, and ice flew into the sky and rained down, bone soup and shards of grass; pricking, cutting.

Straddling her, Reade screamed once—

—and then he was gone.

Donna's eyes rolled up in her head and then *she* was gone.

30
The Rime of the Captain, DCLXVI

Officer Donna was passed out. Alone, Cha-cha faced the creature.

BLACKNESS
LONELINESS
THIRST

She was a gray, floating mass, like silvery clouds, like lumpy fog; pieces reached at him like shaking eager hands. Sometimes they were tentacles, and sometimes they were pincers, and sometimes they were fingers; and as they touched him, they severed the muscles and veins and the other shit in his leg, but it was cool. It was cool that she was connecting with him. She was grokking him, like they used to say in the sixties; really getting him, Vulcan mind-thing, hey, Mr. Spock.

BLACKNESS
LONELINESS

"Yeah, I grok *that,* ten-four." Cha-cha knew about loneliness. He let himself be open to it, to the creature. Another *something* slithered toward him and he let it do something to him, too. And he saw:

Eons of searching, and fury, and rage: once beautiful, once adored. Scylla, a name somehow retained in memory.

Catastrophe: the first betrayal. A change: a monster.

Abandonment.

Power, and no object.

He was confused. "Someone turned you into a monster?"

And she was pleased that he understood. She let him know that, but she also let him know that wasn't quite true. It was the only way she had of explaining herself to him, because Captain Reade's . . . influence . . . was still there; she still saw things through his dying essence.

Wow.

Then she let him see some other things. He grokked: Captain Reade was not the first. Other captains had come before, way, way before him. Try the Stone Age, man.

But Reade had been evil. He was nuts. He kept her locked away, fed her just enough to keep her alive—

—something about love-baby Kevin Cha-cha couldn't quite get—

So she looked for a new captain, sent out her fog and traveled in it with her feelers; Ruth had stepped on one on the *Morris*. The bottle was like a symbol, man, that Captain Reade had dreamed of, and she had made happen for him.

Then he heard Dr. John's voice but echoey and far away:

> *"All we see or seem*
> *Is but a dream within a dream."*

"So, it's like the captains dream for you," Cha-cha said, awed. "And they're like filters, man. Like, *your* trip depends on what's in *their* heads. You take head trips."

Again, she was pleased with his cleverness.

And then he grokked again: She wanted *his* head.

Cha-cha stiffened, afraid. But she was already moving in, taking over, and promising: all his buddies, alive again! And him, their war hero! Yeah! Forever.

Forever.

COMECOMECOMECOME

There had to be a captain. He dug it. There had to be a Dreamer.

Okay.

The thing rolled over on herself, and over. Cha-cha sat on the deck beside the gray Jell-O clouds, and put his own hands out.

Something spread around his fingers, washed to his wrists, trickled around him, and wet his knees. The stuff was cold, and fog was whirling so thickly around him he couldn't see what it was. There were hard lumps in it, little pellets that rolled beneath his palms and caught in the indentations around his kneecaps.

It smelled like the stew meat that had fallen out of the fridge back on the *Morris,* and love-baby Kevin had forgotten to put it back, so it had stayed out for a couple days. But that was okay. That was cool.

Serpent feelers, green-nailed tentacles, albatross pincers, swirling in the gray, wrapped around his wrists and knees and the toes of his blood-soaked sneakers, caressed, fondled, embraced. The gooey stuff coated his clothes; made his hands burn like they were scalded.

It crept up to his elbows and thighs, gathered up the front of his rainbow T-shirt and coated his chest; and it swallowed up his ass and coagulated around his neck. The arms, the wanting things, entwined him, and if he could've, he would've hugged back.

He turned and saw Officer Donna lying nearby. Had to help her. Had to—

The stuff reached the juncture of his lips. Something very like a kiss landed softly on them. Tears of happiness—freaked happiness, but happiness nonetheless—rolled down Chacha's cheeks.

"Yeah, baby, no more loneliness. Cool. And my Nam buddies," he said.

A *reaching* touched the top of his head. He closed his eyes. Then it bored into his skull.

With a silent scream he struggled to move away. So cold, yanga, *freezing;* his whole brain was a hunk of ice, psychedeli-

cally frozen, yeah; and thinking that it would be over soon, and thinking that he wished he could know if Officer Donna was okay, and
     suddenly, not thinking.

     And after a while, he started thinking again,
     but he *knew*, he *grokked*, that he wasn't exactly Cha-cha anymore.
     Baby, he was
     Something Else.

31

Descent into the Maelstrom

Wake up, Officer Donna. Wake up.
Or this will be how it is when you drown.

Bitter wind whistled around Donna. A shroud of wet covered her from head to toe, weighty, exhausting. She tried to raise her head; someone was telling her to, begging her, over and over, but it hurt to even think about it. Her face stung and pounded and her body was a hammered side of meat; tenterhooks sliced through the muscles in her shoulders and stretched out the pain in a long, slow-motion burn.

"Wake up, wake up, oh, please, please."

And it was all a dream, she thought. I woke up on the *Morris,* no, I woke up in Long Beach, and I lived happily ever after the end.

"Wake up, ladyfuzz." Someone cracking her phantom limbs with a pair of shovels.

"Ouch," she said, and popped her eyes open.

Cha-cha bent over her. His leather face, his toothless snag-
gle face: good old Chach, saved her life from that—

"Jesus!" she shouted, bolting upright. She grunted with the
pain and gingerly examined her face with her fingers as she
collected herself. Everything was swollen and bloody. That
bastard had beaten the shit out of her.

Her mind whirlpooled. That bastard had vanished into thin
air. And that thing, that creature . . . she looked toward the
room. It was empty.

"Yeah," she said, forcing herself to be calm. "Okay. Okay,
Cha-cha, we've gotta get out of here."

Cha-cha shook his head. He crouched like a monkey on
the metal stairs. He was covered with stinking slurpy stuff
that looked like rotten gravy. His eyes seemed to be spinning,
round and round they go, what they see, God only knew.

"You gotta book, Officer. I gotta stay." He pointed across
the hold, over her shoulder.

As she turned to look, it dawned on her that she was sitting
in the wooden boat she'd seen in the . . . the room. She
recoiled, lifting her hands from the bottom. Swaths of blood
and dirt coated her palms; and streaks of green, purple, and
black sizzled and smoked. There was a chunk of ice in the
boat, and a chunk of . . . something else. She made herself
scrutinize it. God. Desiccated brain.

A chunk of green glass.

Not a hallucination. It had happened.

It had happened. She started to lose it, mouth twitching,
her hands spasming.

"It's cool, it's cool," Cha-cha said, patting her. "I did it.
But I'm new. I'm real new, so I'm not so good."

"What?" she said, barely able to speak. Dead men. Sea
monsters.

Dead men.

The boat wobbled beneath her. It was sitting in water. The
entire compartment had flooded, and even as she registered
that fact, the waterline rose at least four inches. Fog lifted
from the water and wafted around the two of them, traveling
as if of its own accord up the stairway.

"We're goin' down, down, down," Cha-cha chanted in a

Bruce Springsteen voice. "Going on a trip, baby, and you best not come."

"Get in the boat, Cha-cha!" she shouted. Then she realized something he hadn't—there was nowhere for the boat to escape from, once the water reached the top of the space. They would have to swim to the stairs, try to get up to the next level, and up again.

"Officer, look," Cha-cha said impatiently, stabbing his finger in the air for emphasis.

She turned. About a foot and a half above the water, a jagged hole like the aftermath of an explosion had formed in the hull of the *Pandora*. The bright blue day shone beyond it, just too fucking normal for the goings-on inside.

"Starfish did it," Cha-cha told her. "They digest things with their stomach acid. I told the suckers to take care of it. 'Nibbling, nibbling mousie, nibbling at my housie.' " He grinned. "Gross, or what?"

"What?" She half rose, seeing no starfish, now not sure there really was a hole. It was this place, wasn't it? Made you see things that weren't there.

"Cha-cha, talk to me. What . . . where's that thing?"

"You gotta get over to the hole," he said, "and when we fill up enough, you gotta go out. But you gotta do it just right. Or . . ." He grabbed his neck and made choking noises. "Dig?"

She stared at him. He seemed different, more together. Still Cha-cha, and yet not as much Cha-cha.

"Why can't you come?"

He shrugged. "Captain always goes down with his ship."

Donna swallowed. Oh, fuck. "And are you the captain now?"

Their eyes met. He nodded slowly. A chill wrapped around her, squeezed.

"Don't freak," he said kindly.

But she was freaking. Her whole body started to shake again. Christ, that . . . *thing*. Reade. He had simply vanished. And Creutz and the *Pandora* had vanished, and now she was going to fucking vanish into madness. The boy, Dane. The little boy.

"Explain it to me," she managed, forcing down her hysteria. "Tell me why, how." And when it made rational sense, when she could point to toxins or food poisoning or mass delusion, she would put the brakes on her personal Grand Prix toward pure, unadulterated insanity.

Again he shrugged. "It's a word I don't know." He thought a minute. "Like in the Haight. I help you, you help me."

"Symbiosis?" She was surprised she knew a word like that. That freaked her even worse. That was not a word she knew; why was it in her head?

Cha-cha nodded thoughtfully, looking far away. The boat drifted toward the hole. "Yeah. I let her . . . like, mind-meld. You know, like Mr. Spock? We're together now."

"Who? Who, Cha-cha?" She leaned forward, waiting for his answer. The water level was still rising. "Who?" she asked again, shrilly.

He took a breath. "She's old, really old. There've been so many of them—captains—but King Neptu . . . Reade was different. He was really wacko." He wiped his forehead, looked startled at the clump of gray in his hand. "He's still in there. She's having flashbacks. He's like acid for her. All that acid. It's a mega-bad trip for her, total bummer. I gotta help her lose that dude. And all the bad stuff. She's kinda confused right now."

He stretched out a hand. She jerked, even though he was too far away to touch her. Couldn't stop the shaking. Couldn't stop. Couldn't stop. Wild laughter quivered in her throat.

Keep it together. She watched the water reach his shoes, soak them. That was too much to ask. Too much.

"She's welcoming all my Nam buddies. We're all gonna live here now." He rubbed his hands together like a happy little boy.

"Cha-cha, oh, Jesus, you're wacko, too, hon. Don't you know it?"

His gap-toothed grin. His bloodshot eyes like cracked marbles. He gave the boat a strong push backward. "Get to the hole. I'll find the others." He regarded her. "Most of 'em are

dead. Mr. and Mrs. van Buren. The other lifeboat dudes. I
. . . I killed them."

She shook harder. Felt her mind, going, going—

He stood. He flickered in and out of focus. She saw—

—*Reade*—

—a hideous black hole of pain—

—no, she saw nothing but Cha-cha, nothing.

And heard—

Wrong answer! Nothing! She heard nothing.

He flashed her a salute and started up the stairs.

"Reade acid!" he shouted. "Loose it, baby!"

She watched him go as her boat drifted toward the opening. Puffy white clouds greeted her imminent arrival; the sun
gleamed innocently as she passed beneath cobwebs and lines
of stinking seaweed hung out like wash. Crabs scuttled over
the bulkhead and clicked their pincers.

And then she realized the boat wasn't drifting, no siree!
Wrong answer! Someone was swimming under it, and guiding
it along.

Something floated toward her. She recoiled. Then Nemo
mewed and Donna saw it was a big plastic container, and she
and her kittens huddled inside it.

Donna started to laugh. And cry.

There was a moment of sublime temptation, just one, when
the boat hit the water outside. The sun was bright and
golden, the sky clear. A single white bird flew overhead.
Close to land! Paddle like hell and don't look back.

But just one moment, as the fog closed over the sky and
the bird disappeared, and the *Pandora* filled with screams and
bullet shots.

And Donna clenched the sides of the boat and thought,
Protect and serve, goddamn it all to hell.

It wasn't over yet.

It was raining bullets and flowers, and people on fire ran
shrieking through the *Pandora*, which had completely transformed into a naval warship. Absurdly, in the middle of the
screams someone was playing "The Crystal Ship" by the

Doors. A calliope of the sixties, of Viet Nam, of somebody's nightmare memory loops.

"Let's go this way," John said, taking Matt's hand. Curry ran behind them. A ton of fog had crashed down onto the deck with stormlike force and they could see nothing as they prepared to abandon ship.

They ran into some kind of tunnel, or bunker, and there was a black-light poster of a sailing ship on a concrete wall, glowing. Ship of Peace; John remembered it. God, where were they?

"Daddy!" Matt pleaded. "Please, Daddy!" John understood: he wanted to be gone from there; he didn't want to be imagining this.

No. He *wanted* to be imagining this. Because if it was real, it was too awful to handle.

"C'mon!" someone shouted. "John! Matt! Curry! Over here!"

In the distance, John saw a red glow swaying in the fog. Back and forth, very fast, a signal.

"C'mon!" Now he recognized the voice. It was Donna.

"Donna!" John cried. He shifted direction.

"Daddy, Daddy," Matt whimpered.

They headed toward the figure. Wind whipped around them. They were outside, John guessed; and then, as if to confirm his suspicion, the air cleared for a moment, revealing a blue sky. Then the fog rolled over them again. Mortar fire blazed through the air like lightning.

"Jesus!" he cried, ducking.

"Daddy, Daddy," Matt whimpered.

Donna teetered on the edge of the deck, sopping wet. She looked like hell, and she had a flare in her left hand.

"I've got a boat. You have to jump overboard," she said through swollen lips. Her hair was thick with blood. "Right here. Do it. Do it." She jabbed her hand, pointing to the dark water below.

John paused. A trick? Hadn't that been what the captain wanted? *Jump overboard.* Hadn't he heard that somewhere in his mind?

"No, no, please," Curry whimpered, voicing John's fear. He cringed. "It's a trick, no, please."

Without warning, Donna grabbed Matt and pitched him overboard. His scream as he fell was agonized.

"Go, John!" And John dove in after him,
down
down
down

And suddenly bodies leaped from the ship and fell around him, on fire; skeletons turned and saw him with no eyes, and swam through the air with their clawed fingers to catch him; hundreds of skeletons, all around him, a rain of bone. He couldn't stop screaming. He heard Matt shouting in terror; and Donna, shouting, "No, Cha-cha! Stop yourself!" and then he hit the water and went under.

Something grabbed his ankles and yanked him down into the frigid sea. He gulped in water; it rushed into his lungs as he kicked and struggled, thinking, I dreamed this, I dreamed of drowning, where's Matty? He opened his mouth to shout, but there was so much water inside him, outside him, and whatever—

—whoever—

held him fast.

Not like this! No! he thought, making fists and hitting blindly. He would not die like this.

Something plunged into the water beside him, diving beneath him, and the grip around his ankles loosened enough for him to dart away. Someone swam beside him; oh, Lord. He turned his head long enough to register that it was Donna.

"Get in the boat!" Donna shouted, hauling herself in, reaching for Matt. Curry crawled in on the other side.

John looked up. The *Pandora* was no longer a cruise ship, and neither was it a warship. Her hull was a pastiche of metal vessels from which wooden masts and bowsprits extended helter-skelter like spears stuck in a carcass; a propeller at least a story tall; half a steamboat paddlewheel, the wheelhouse of a tug. Near the bow, the bulbous nose of a submarine extended toward the waterline. And the huge, unbelievable mass and weight of it was sinking.

Panting, he dragged himself into the boat and scrabbled to his knees. The skeletons were everywhere, swam everywhere, rotten fabric draped around them; cutaway coats, bustles that flopped around pelvis bones; knuckles poking through gloves. A navy-blue officer's coat and hat, and a slight stick figure beneath it. Khaki, Mexican ponchos, kimonos, the wolf's head of the Nazis. Clacking and snapping. He heard scraping on the hull of the boat; he heard them hissing through their voiceless mouths. He thought he heard the words "belly timber," and he thought he heard his name, in Cha-cha's voice.

No more fell from the ship. The top deck was deserted.

"Don't just sit there, John!" Donna shouted at him. She was punching at the skeletons, throwing things at them, smacking them with her fists and feet. They clattered, bone against bone, and Donna grunted as they came at her again. She was a tornado, and they kept coming, *clack clack clack.*

Her courage snapped him out of it. The skeletons clicked their jaws as they surrounded the boat. In the distance, the screaming, rocket explosions, the Doors. He and the others faced outward in a circle, and finally he made himself push the nearest one away; bone only, nothing else. Bone that moved.

The rock music aboard the ship. The bullets. Screaming. The cat, mewing and growling.

"Ruth!" John cried. Donna turned.

In a sopping nightgown, Ruth Hamilton ran along the top deck, hands outstretched, crying, "He's not my husband! Help me, he's not my husband!" Her hair was dripping wet; water ran from her slightly tanned fingers.

"Jump, Ruth! Jump!" Donna shouted, standing with her legs spread wide apart. "We'll get you!"

Ruth hesitated. "Come on, damn it!" Donna motioned wildly.

Ruth jumped. She fell end over end with a cry. Elise reached with the others to rescue her, as the skeletons converged—

—and when she hit the water, she was nothing but a

bloated corpse floating on the water. Like piranha, a pack of skeletons threw themselves upon her and dragged her beneath the water.

The others renewed their assault on the lifeboat, thrashing in the water, lunging and grasping. One jumped out of the water and threw itself at Matt. He shrieked and Donna grabbed Matt around the waist, batting at the thing.

Its finger sliced her cheek, aimed for her eye—

"Cha-cha, damn you!" Donna bellowed, punching the thing away. "Damn you to hell, you liar! You're worse than he was! You fucking nut! John, did you see anyone else? Is there anyone alive on there?"

"No," he said quickly, ashamed. Even if there were someone, he doubted he would tell her.

"Ramón?" she said.

"Dead!" Curry shouted. "I saw him!"

"Then I want to kill this thing. This fucking thing!" She stood in the boat. For one alarming second, John thought she was going to jump into the water.

She ripped off her shoe and flung it at the *Pandora*. It landed a few feet shy, and sank.

"I'll come back!" she shouted, nearly toppling over. Tears and blood streamed down her face. "I'll come back and get you. I swear I will!"

And then, without warning, the *Pandora* rolled sideways, away from them, and groaned long and low; the sound vibrated through the bottom of the boat. John heard it—

COMEBACKCOMEBACKCOMEBACK

—something insatiable; a horrible, soul-wrenching loneliness in the call. He grabbed his chest as his heart swelled in response;

MOREMOREMOREMOREMOREMORE

The fog roiled up, thick as a forest fire. A skeleton clicked its jaw at John and slid back into the water.

One by one, the others did the same.

COMEBACKCOMEBACKCOMEBACK

White water churned and roiled, and the fog reverberated with keening. Donna sat visibly shaken. The tears rolled down her face.

"If it's not over, I *will* come back."

"It's sinking," John said.

Cha-cha's voice came to them in the tumult: "I'll get better. Come back, come back. Please. I'm so . . . I'm alone." Softer, softer, no more.

A wave rocked them, teeter-totter, teeter-totter, for a few seconds.

The fog clung to the lifeboat.

In the sky, a gull cawed.

And Cha-cha's voice, so faint:

Lonely.

They drifted. It was warm, but the fog didn't lift; it lay over them like a shroud.

Donna tried to talk. She briefly told them about Reade and seeing his corpse in the lifeboat surrounded by ice, fog, and mist. And about Cha-cha, how he was taking over, but hadn't quite yet, or something, because Reade's memories were too strong to simply erase.

She didn't tell them about the singing. About how she had felt so . . . needed.

"Everything was a mirage?" John asked. "None of it happened?"

"No, a lot of it happened," Curry said miserably.

"But what were they?" John held Matty.

"Figments of his imagination. The captain's," Donna murmured.

"Reade?"

"They weren't just his. They were real," Curry cut in.

It was too much for her. Her mind was anesthetized, and she supposed she should be grateful for that.

At the last, she had seen something. As what had once been the *Pandora* sank into the water she had seen the ship slip into a bottle, and a face, an evil, empty face—

No. She had seen nothing. And she would never tell anyone about what she

hadn't

seen.

Her lips grew dry, and her stomach growled, and Donna wondered what the hell would happen next.

They drifted through the purgatory fog like a quartet of damned souls.

Made it.

His baby and him.

John nuzzled Matt, and Matt nuzzled him back. Would his boy be all right, after all he had seen?

And what had he seen? With the passage of the hours, everything was fading. Those things couldn't have happened. They must not have. It was the toxic waste from the *Morris*, as he and Donna had feared. Had to be.

Had to be.

"Donna, what was it?" he asked.

She sat with her head on her knees. She had been silently sobbing for over an hour. He didn't know why. He wanted to tell her not to cry, because she would dehydrate herself. But how on earth do you tell that to someone who'd just been through what they had?

"A lonely woman," she said in a muffled voice, hiding her face.

John wanted to hold her. He wanted to make love to her. She seemed terribly vulnerable. If anyone knew the most there was to know about loneliness, he suspected it was Donna.

"Check it out," Curry said excitedly, and John leaned his head on Matty's head as he stared tiredly out to sea. The fog sliced into his eyelids and—

—he got what the other man was so excited about:

The fog was lifting. Or they were moving beyond it.

"Oh, my God," he murmured, crossing himself. "Oh, thank you, God."

Donna reached over and hugged the three of them. Scratched Nemo's head. "We're gonna be okay," she said. Her nose was stopped up. "We'll get found."

John nodded. "Hear that, Mattman? We're okay."

Matt scooted in his embrace. "You're holding me too tight, Daddy."

"Sorry." It took everything in him to loosen his grip.

They drifted closer to the edge of the bank. It was uncanny the way it simply ceased to be, just as it had simply appeared in front of the *Morris* and they had sailed into it.

He and Donna looked at each other at the same instant. "Maybe it *was* the fog," she said and he nodded. "That made it happen. The fog came first. Like a force field."

He hesitated. He put a hand on her back. "When we get back . . ."

She snaked a hand behind herself and gripped his. "You married?"

"No." He squeezed her hand. "But right now, after everything, it wouldn't matter."

"Don't bet on that."

"Daddy, you're still hurting me," Matt whimpered.

"Gosh, honey, I'm sorry." John frowned and looked down—

—and before he could react, Donna grabbed Matt—

—what used to be Matt, oh, God! Oh, heavenly Jesus! The blackened remains of his child, kicking and snarling like an animal, showing teeth that were dripping with John's own blood as he ripped the flesh from John's forearm. One eye, it had only one eye, and in the other, something wiggled and burrowed—

—and Matt raged, and Donna wrapped her arms around his legs and together, struggling to the side of the boat and—

"Daddy! Daddy, help!"—

—tossed him over, into the fog.

Into the fog, where he became Matty again, his Matty, who splashed in the water, his head going down, fighting to the surface. In the fog, where he was Matty.

And the lifeboat bobbed halfway out of the fog.

"Daddy! Don't leave me!" Matty wailed, holding out his arms. "Daddy!"

And John knew it might not be his boy, but he knew it might. With one last silent prayer, and one last deal with God, he jumped out of the boat.

"No!" Donna and Curry shouted.

"John, it's tricking you!" Donna screamed. "Get back in the boat!"

But all that was behind him now. He knew it as he swam toward Matt, who was going under. He dove under the water and found his child, and held him, even as Matt clasped him hard and laid his soft cheek against his.

All that was behind him, and he let himself sink with Matt, who was heavy as an anchor. The chains of fatherhood are unbreakable, and that was all right. He hadn't lied; he really would do anything. That was okay. Cha-cha had a good heart, and in time, perhaps, he would marshal his forces and make a good captain—

and they sank

down,

down,

down,

John struggling now and then, holding his breath, knowing that soon he must inhale. And though he couldn't see Matt very well, as his glasses had blown off his face; he could feel Matt's love around him. His arms around him, helping him to stay under.

He looked up at the surface, where the fog covered the sun. Panic eddied through him once or twice, but he'd made his choice.

Something bobbed against his hip. Matt reached for it and showed it to his father. The green bottle, with a blur of white inside. Yes. The invitation. Was Reade still in command, then?

They hung suspended like space-walking astronauts while John's lungs fought the good fight; his brain clouded over and fear took hold for a few last moments. What had he done? What was he doing?

Was this Matt? And if so, how—

No more questions, then, as an approaching shadow chilled the water above them. Hull-shaped. The *Pandora*, or whatever the hell it was.

Perhaps someday Cha-cha would rename it the *Good Ship Lollipop*. The old guy thought like that. He thought, he thought . . . John lost track. He swirled into himself. This was it.

He opened his mouth and sucked in the ocean.

"Welcome aboard, Daddy," Matt whispered in his ear.

EPILOGUE:
RSVP

Alone, Donna and Curry alone, drifting endlessly on the hazy, nickel-plated ocean. Donna thought a lot about drowning; imagining how it would feel. First you would tread water, then you'd try to float. You'd tire. You'd start to go under . . .

Curry kept whimpering, "It's a trick. We're still there. He's making us think we're safe. All that stuff about Cha-cha, that didn't really happen. He made you think it."

Donna considered strangling him, just to shut him up. 'Cuz what if he was right?

And who the hell was safe? The boat was starting to leak, and there was nothing to drink.

God, they were all gone, all those people. The van Burens, once so hilarious in their yupster-squabbling. Ramón, the poor asshole—Curry told her all about it—who started it with his goddamn barrels of shit. No, of course he didn't. Curry said in order to encounter the *Pandora* someone had to call to the captain; had to want something bad, and that would draw them to the ship. That had been Ruth. (*Not my husband, not,* and she had bloated in the water like a rotten rubber mannequin, and the others, diving at her . . .)

Little Matty, lost anyway. He must have drowned after all while they were trying to revive him. Within the fog, the illusion of life could be maintained by whatever ruled aboard the *Pandora* now.

John, his long-suffering father. Had she really believed it would ever be okay for them? They had seemed marked, those two. Or was it just that she had never believed in happy endings?

Cha-cha. Dear God, what of Cha-cha? What was he now? Had she dreamed all of it?

"Talk to me, Curry," she said. "Tell me about it. Tell me everything you know. How it—she—he captured you." Make it real, hoss, or she was going to go out of her mind.

"What did you see in there? In the hatch?" he asked her in return. "Tell me again."

"Sea monster," Donna said curtly, again. And she heard that lonely song, that voice: *Oh, baby, I am so lonely. Oh, baby.*

Her throat closed over. "How far away do you have to be from it, that it can't influence you?"

Curry shook his head. "I dunno. I'm so scared. I'm still so scared."

Drifting, drifting; the sky and the sea stretched into endless, heartless gray, bone-bleached and pitiless. If the boat went down, there was nowhere to swim to. And how long can you tread water?

How long can you hold your breath?

"Talk to me, Curry. Tell me how it controlled you," she muttered through cracked, peeling lips.

Curry made no reply. Then he said, "I don't deserve to live. I'm evil."

And she had no answer for that.

* * *

Drifting, drifting; dreaming of water, water, everywhere, in buckets and bowls and in goblets and bottles. Fresh, clear as a mirror, as glass . . .

And being pulled up, up, slowly, dangling in the air . . . oh, no, she must be out of her body, floating, dying . . .

His voice. "Baby, oh, Donna, baby."

Glenn.

She slept for hours, and the doctor stuck her and tested her; for a second she panicked, remembering the blood pressure cuff on the *Pandora,* and the thing that rattled in the cup . . . it had been drugs all along, yes, that was it . . .

No . . .

And you wouldn't think she'd want to, you'd think she'd just lie there in the close, dim cabin and scream; but Glenn came into the cabin and sat beside her. Looking as perfect as ever, the beautiful, conceited bastard; and then he bent over and gently touched her swollen lips with his mouth.

She gasped and he said, "It's okay. Barb left me. It's okay." Which struck her funny, in a tragic way, it being okay. It being that anything in the universe was okay.

But right then she wouldn't have cared if Barb was in the cabin, pulling off his pants for him. The ointment dulled her sunburn and he was as careful as a burning man could be; he went right inside like he belonged there, sliding into home, oh, my God, my God, oh, Jesus; how could you drown in love? But you could, *my man, I love him so;* and it was too much, too happy, too relieving; she wept against his shoulder until she fell asleep.

She didn't wake until the cabin was dark. She started violently. A trick, just like Curry said! They were back! They—

"Shh," Glenn said. And she asked questions, dozens of them. He told her the Coast Guard had been searching the area since first word of the *Morris*'s difficulty. They had found Donna's lifeboat within thirty nautical miles of the freighter's last known position. She had been missing for a week.

"I don't think that's right," she murmured.

She slept a deadened, dreamless sleep.

Then she woke again and said, "I hated you when you said . . . when you told me you were going to get a new partner."

Naked beside her, Glenn gaped at her. "Donny, I haven't talked to you since the day you left Long Beach."

Reade was that good? She shuddered.

Later, they talked, on the small Coast Guard cutter, tiny cabins, gray and white, bunks, everything, and it seemed so amazingly simple, so lifelike, so real: "We had it out that day I dropped you off." His exquisite smile was grim and sad. "At Disneyland. She knew I'd driven you up. She told me it was cruel to her and you both, pretending. She . . . she said she had someone else, too." His face was flushed. "I don't really think that's true, though. I think she's just hurt."

"God, I'm sorry," Donna said. "I shoulda—"

"Donna, if you'd died out there . . ."

They made love again. Not protected, she thought; birth control pills lost at sea, too. Then; who the hell cares? And they slept in the cherishing embrace of the smooth blue waters.

She woke to ravings. Curry was out of it, Glenn told her, and who was he anyway? Not from the *Morris,* so where *was* he from?

She told him, and he didn't believe her.

She didn't know how she was going to handle it, if she'd explain it away eventually, forget about it. But there was Curry, the evidence.

Oh, Matty, John, Ruth. Poor Phil. Elise, how had they died? She never saw them. Tears ran, pooled on the pillow. She drifted.

Her eyes opened in the dark. For all she knew, they could have still been alive when she abandoned ship. And she hadn't gone back for them. She'd let Cha-cha convince her. Or was it Curry who had convinced her? Or was it all a lie?

Had they been alive, the ones she hadn't seen?

Finally, land ho. Hawaii, Don Ho. At the bow of the Coast Guard vessel, she stood on wobbly legs and stared at Diamond Head.

"Do you know you can die from drowning two–three days after you've been revived?" she asked, tracing the landscape with her eyes. Palms. High-rises. The blessed, blazing sun. "It's called hypoxia."

"Yes, hon," he said, careful of her sunburn, of her. "Yes, baby." Like she was crazy.

Across the deck, something moved on
little
cat
feet,
but there was nothing there. Once out of the fog, Nemo had proved to be dead, too, and all her babies. Little kittie-ghosts, nurtured by the milky evil of the fog.

Nevertheless, a few of the crewmen now swore they heard kittens mewing; and Donna had felt the pressure of a small animal between her legs as she dozed.

"How's Curry?" she asked.

"Still sedated," Glenn replied. She wondered if Curry's mind had drifted away to a safer sea; if it would ever drift back.

The Coast Guard vessel moved past Aloha tower. A helicopter buzzed overhead.

They talked about what they'd do back in San Diego. Barb was moving out. Donna said she'd need some time, but she knew that was a load of crap.

He was beside her, really there, in the heart and the flesh; and inside she was cracked and opening for him . . . *hello, my love, please, please, don't hurt me.*

They walked off the ship together, hand in hand. And then a man in a white uniform gestured Glenn aside, and he collapsed.

They had drowned: Barb, and the two little bastards, in a freak accident: facedown in a neighbor's pool, and no reason for it. Their new swimsuits. The girls had been drinking lemonade. Barb was there to get some emotional support—the neighbor was somebody's ex-wife, too.

No reason for it.

* * *

Donna threw back her head and screamed. She ran for Curry, ran and roused him; and on the nightstand beside him, in a pool of wet, a sparkling green glass bottle spun lazily in a circle.

"No! No!" She rattled him hard. "Where are we? Are we there? Curry!"

"No more!" Curry sobbed, half-unconscious. His face was white, his eyes wild. "No more!"

She had faced the Lorelei:

(Oh, baby, I am so lonely.)

I want my man.

(What is your Desire?)

My man.

(What is the thing that will draw you to me?)

To protect. To save.

My man.

"No!" Donna picked up the bottle and smashed it against the nightstand. It didn't break. It glittered in the soft light like a beacon as she brought it down again and again, swearing, weeping, hefting it with both hands. Curry staggered out of bed and fell to his knees, pleading and begging with something, with someone.

They pounded on the other side of the closed hatch as she fell down beside him and shook him, saying, "Are we still there? Damn you, are we on the *Pandora*?"

But it didn't matter. Because either way, she was going back. It wasn't finished. It—*she*—knew Donna would go back. For Glenn—the threat to him was clear. For his wife and babies, to save them from a hellish existence, if that was what it was now. If they needed saving. And she wouldn't know that unless she went. And the . . . thing knew it.

Oh, baby, I am so sad and lonely.

Lonely enough to make Donna—who also understood lonely, who could be a soul mate—a *mate*—come back.

Or was this one of Reade's games? Was she really back on the *Pandora*, right now?

"Cha-cha, don't you have any say?" she whispered. "Are you there at all?" Perhaps he'd been too gentle, too crazy.

Maybe the creature was already looking for another Dreamer.

And reeling her in.

The bottle spun lazily, as if to say, Remember, there are plenty of other ways—and people—to drown. The particulars don't really matter. Someone else's boat might sink, or their plane may go down, and there are, as you know, ponds and lakes and rivers. And bathtubs. Or hot tubs. Dreadful things can happen in Jacuzzis. Have happened.

You will be my Life-in-Death. The woman who brings death . . .

unless you come.

The bottle spun slowly, like a boy on a lake. Is that where it all began? Because she didn't go gentle into that frigid water? No second chances, big girl, on the Sea of Death.

How do you know we aren't still there, at the place we met, oh, my lady of the lake? How do you know I haven't caught you, and now we're beneath the surface, you and I, me beauty. And as the shadow passes above us, you think, Thank God, thank God, you're saved. But you know how wrong you are.

You know.

The bottle twirled, rolled.

To protect and to serve. To rescue. To save. Donna's foremost Desire. *Oh, my man, I love him—*

"All right, you goddamned monster," she whispered. "Okay, I'm coming. *Alone.*"

But she knew that wasn't true.

She knew.

And that is what it will be like. And more or less, how it will happen.

So nice you can join us.

© Scott Nelson

NANCY HOLDER is the author, with Melanie Tem, of the acclaimed Abyss novel *Making Love*. She is also the acclaimed author of various women's fiction titles, as well as short horror fiction. Her short story, "Lady Madonna," won the 1991 Bram Stoker Award for Best Short Story from the Horror Writers of America.